Helensburgh Library

~2 MAR 2012   22 APR 2014

17 NOV 2014
15 JAN 2016

18 APR 2012 - 4 OCT 2016

30 OCT 2016

-6 JUN 2012   CPL transfer

14 JUN 2019

26 JUL 2012

-5 OCT 2012   17 SEP 2019

17 NOV 2012

-8 JAN 2013
-9 DEC 2013

ARGYLL AND BUTE COUNCIL
LIBRARY AND INFORMATION SERVICE

Books should be returned on or before the date above.
Renewals may be made in person, by telephone,
or on-line if not in demand.
Visit www.argyll-bute.gov.uk/libraries

Argyll and Bute

I am Cyrus

I AM CYRUS

THE STORY OF THE REAL PRINCE OF PERSIA

his passion captivated hearts

his courage inspired a nation

the story of the real prince of Persia

Alexander Jovy

cyrusnovel.wordpress.com

Garnet
PUBLISHING

I am Cyrus
The Story of the Real Prince of Persia

Published by
Garnet Publishing Limited
8 Southern Court
South Street
Reading
RG1 4QS
UK

www.garnetpublishing.co.uk
www.twitter.com/Garnetpub
www.facebook.com/Garnetpub
garnetpub.wordpress.com

First Edition

ISBN: 978-1-85964-281-8

British Library Cataloguing-in-Publication Data
A catalogue record for this book is available from the British Library

Typeset by Samantha Barden
Jacket design by Haleh Darabi

Printed and bound in Great Britain by
TJ International Ltd, Padstow, Cornwall

For my princess

ACKNOWLEDGEMENTS

I cannot begin to thank adequately those who helped make this story come alive. I am especially grateful to James Essinger, and also to Nicola Savoretti, Shahrokh Razmjou, and my parents and friends.

I would also like to thank Arash Hejazi and Marie Hanson at Garnet Publishing for their enthusiasm for this project and careful assistance with all stages of production.

They will ask thee concerning Zul-qarnain. Say 'I will rehearse to you something of his story. Verily we established his power on earth, and we gave him the ways and means to all ends.'

Qur'an, verses 18: 83-84

Thus says the Lord to Cyrus His anointed, Whom I have taken by the right hand, to subdue the nations before him, and to loose the loins of kings; To open doors before him so that gates will not be shut: I will go before you and make the rough places smooth;

I will shatter the doors of bronze, and cut through their iron bars. And I will give you the treasures of darkness, and hidden riches of secret places, that you may know that I, the Lord, which call thee by thy name, am the God.

Isaiah 45:1-6

Archaeology has succeeded in identifying ancient cultures which take no account of present-day geographical boundaries. The amazing splendours of ancient civilizations have been revealed through the efforts of archaeologists who have retrieved treasures from the dark, silent places where they have been lying hidden since ancient times.

Mohammed Reza-Kargar, Director of the
National Museum of Iran

The Persian monarchy appears, in fact, even as we look back upon it from this remote distance both of space and of time, as a very vast wave of human power and grandeur. It swelled up among the populations of Asia, between the Persian Gulf and the Caspian Sea, about five hundred years before Christ, and rolled on in undiminished magnitude and glory for many centuries.

Jacob Abbott, *Cyrus the Great* (1878)

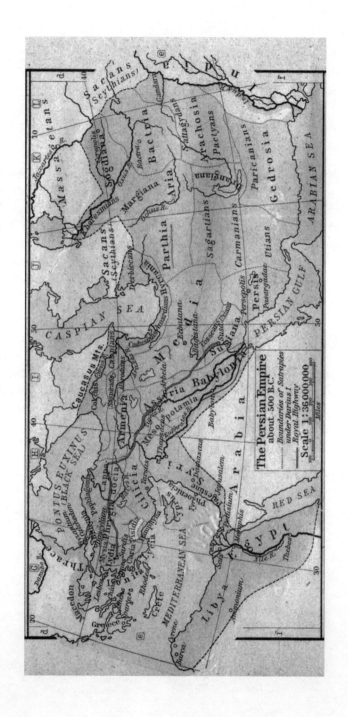

The Persian Empire
about 500 B.C.
Boundaries of Satrapies
under Darius I
Royal Highway
Scale 1:35000000

CONTENTS

Book Three: Undying Love

The lives of most of us are brief flames soon extinguished by the vastness of eternity.

Yet there are some who, thinking no effort too much, no sacrifice too extreme, save their souls from obscurity by their deeds here on earth and are remembered forever.

This is the story of one such man.
His name was Cyrus.
In time, he became known as Cyrus the Great.

BOOK ONE

CHILDHOOD FRIENDS

1. The Black Scorpion

The wind from the east was starting to freshen. The stranger in the dark blue hooded cloak squinted, feeling breeze-blown dust pecking at his face.

Here, in this scrub-land on the edge of the plains, only a few palm-trees and prickly bushes eked out a frugal living. To the north, the land rose sharply toward the summit of a wide sand-dune. Beyond this were the mountains, their peaks covered with snow no matter the season in the lowlands.

The stranger began walking to the south, his hooded cloak concealing his features except for his thoughtful dark brown eyes.

Presently he came to a road that was little more than a dirt track. As he reached it, he noticed a black desert scorpion scuttling across. A few moments later he heard the roar of an approaching car.

The stranger stepped out into the road, stooped and picked up the scorpion, holding it firmly just under its lethal sting.

The car, a patched-up faded green Mercedes, screeched to a halt. An unshaven driver wound down the window and started swearing.

The stranger, his face still obscured, only walked off the road in his own good time. He ignored the driver's shouts.

The car raced past, spewing black smoke and curses whipped by the gathering wind.

When the stranger was some way from the road, he laid the black scorpion onto the sandy ground and watched it dart away. He knew the scorpion was even more poisonous than the desert cobra, but it had held no fear for him.

For a few seconds the stranger stood in complete silence and stillness, trying to remember, as if a moment of the past had caught up with him. Features of the surrounding landscape... how familiar they suddenly were!

Finally he headed toward the nearby town, using for his guides the rough road... and a memory, slowly becoming more substantial within himself, that he couldn't understand... let alone explain.

2. In the Marketplace

Even now, no-one but the stranger appeared aware of the approaching sandstorm. Rusty cars, donkey carts, old bicycles and dilapidated motorbikes competed for the narrow dusty roads leading to the marketplace. There, stalls offered spices, fruits, freshly-cooked kebabs, desserts dusted with icing sugar, bright silks, intricate carpets, exotic costume jewellery, knives, daggers, even firearms.

Children scampered among the crowd. One, a boy of about six or seven, suddenly crashed into the stranger.

The boy fell to the ground. For a few moments he was silenced by shock, then burst into tears.

The stranger kneeled down and helped the boy to his feet. The child's cries redoubled. But the boy's eyes caught the kindness in the stranger's mystical gaze.

For a moment, it was as if the boy and the stranger were held in a brief communion of their own. The boy felt, though he could not have articulated, the stranger's inexplicable power.

The man gently wiped the boy's tears with the fabric of his cloak. A rip in the dark blue cloak had been neatly sewn up some time ago, and the cloak was faintly stained with what might have been blood-marks.

The boy did not move, yet felt no fear, even though the stranger's face was still obscured.

A few moments later, the stranger smiled at the boy, patted him gently on his head, and muttered a blessing in an ancient language.

It was a tongue not even the most polyglot of stall-owners could have understood.

3. The Bell

The instant the stranger stepped inside the shop, the noise and bustle of the marketplace vanished.

It was one of those stores, fragrant with incense, found in almost any Middle Eastern bazaar, that gives the impression of selling anything a heart can desire. Tapestries and carpets hung on every wall. Glass-fronted cabinets boasted bottles of unguents, perfumes, oils and ointments. There were wicker baskets, teak chairs and well-varnished tables. Other cabinets displayed gold and silver jewellery.

The proprietor, a fat man with skin the colour of strong coffee, was sitting in a wicker chair beside a glass counter. He stood up, rubbed his hands, and bowed to the stranger, whose hood still made his face impossible to see.

'*Khosh uomadin, befarmayin!*' the shopkeeper exclaimed. 'My wise and good friend, greetings!'

The stranger made no reply, but just looked calmly and dispassionately at the shopkeeper.

The master of the emporium found it curious that the stranger was keeping his face obscured, but... a customer was a customer. 'Congratulations, my friend, on entering the finest emporium in our beautiful city! Welcome to heaven on Earth! All you could wish for is here. The finest hand-woven silks for one of your beautiful ladies? Persian carpets stitched by our finest craftsmen? Knives of the sharpest and best quality Zanyan steel? What is it you desire?'

The stranger remained still for several moments. He said nothing, then abruptly nodded toward a shelf on the right.

The proprietor's expression at once became a study of excitement and greed. Clambering up a wooden step-ladder with surprising nimbleness for one so stout, he brought down a display of jewellery and other valuable – or at least expensive – objects on a black lacquered tray. He spread the merchandise on the glass counter next to an antiquated manual cash register, then took a step backward.

'Please, sir, come closer!' he exclaimed. 'Note the workmanship of these items! They are worth a king's ransom, but here in my shop, I sell them at a foolishly low price, for I am regarded as a man of ridiculous generosity by my friends and competitors!'

The stranger paid no attention to the shopkeeper's prattle. He peered down at the jewel-encrusted knives, precious rings and coins, seeing at a glance that most of the items were worth little or nothing.

Then something on the lacquered tray caught his attention.

He reached out and picked up a small bronze bell.

The bell was only about two inches high. The stranger held it by a little hooped handle at the top.

As he did, there sprang into the stranger's mind a memory of the agonized face of a man, a great man, the greatest man of his day, dying from a dreadful dagger wound.

The jolt of memory was so sudden, and struck the stranger so deep, that for that moment he could think of nothing else.

Involuntarily, he found himself remembering more.

'Ah, that wondrous old bell!' the shopkeeper exclaimed, cutting into the stranger's thoughts. 'An admirable choice! It is a most rare item, and five hundred years old! The only one of its kind that still survives. My beloved daughter, who has the eyes of a hawk, found it amongst rocks in the desert. Regrettably, it does not ring any more, for its ringer is rusted. But it is most fine and extremely precious!'

The man in the hooded cloak looked toward the proprietor, yet still did not show his face. The stranger knew that the proprietor was lying, or just plain ignorant, for the bell was far older than five hundred years.

The stranger revealed his face for the first time. At once, the proprietor fell silent. A moment passed. All you could hear was the shop door starting to creak gently from the wind of the approaching storm.

The stranger lifted the bell to his ear and gave it a gentle tap. Nothing happened. He tapped a little harder and now, as if from a distant land, a single ringing note hung in the room. The stranger tilted the bell. The ringing sounded again.

He closed his eyes. The ringing grew louder.

4. The Immortals

The bell was still ringing, but now it was hanging from a piece of twine round the neck of a goat, one of a dozen that a great king, in a dream, was watching a young goat-herd round up in the scrub-land on the edge of the desert.

The king was being visited by the dream only a few months after the bell had first been cast.

It was a time when the silent mysteries of the stars were seen as speaking eloquently of the god the Persians called Ahura-Mazda, the great Creator of all things: the god the people of Media knew as Mithra.

It was a time when the notion of hours did not exist, but only the morning, the afternoon, the evening, the night – from when the first star appeared in the sky to midnight – and late night, from midnight to when the stars disappeared.

It was a time when the sun was believed to travel around the Earth.

All the goats had bells about their necks. The king, in his dream, saw the boy who was herding them flick the goats' tails with a stick. The dreaming king heard the boy shout at his charges, until a sudden sound of hooves beating against sand made the boy glance round in alarm.

Now the king saw a horseman riding a black steed that had appeared from above the broad ridge of the sand-dune to the north.

The apparition had materialized so suddenly, it seemed to the dreaming king that the horseman had come out of nowhere.

The warrior on horseback was in full armour. He sported a bronze helmet with a plume of white feathers. The armour and plume showed the horseman to be a Scythian, and a general.

Scores of other Scythian horsemen now appeared over the ridge.

From over the summit of the sand-dune, an entire mounted army started to appear.

The dreaming king watched the boy flee for his life. Suddenly, the ringing of the goats' bells was obliterated by the sound of a rhythmic chorus of thousands of other ringers.

Now, the dreaming king saw a great throng of mounted warriors, all on black steeds, and all with bells ringing in their long hair, heading above the first wave of Scythian cavalry like a raging tide.

The king, still immersed in his dream, saw horsemen he had never seen before, or ever imagined could exist. He knew from their uniforms that they were Persian, yet he saw in his dream something he had never seen in real life: that they were each wearing dozens of small bronze bells woven into their long, matted, uncut hair, every bell representing an enemy they had killed. The armour of the horsemen and the sheen of their spears shimmered like sunlight striking the sea's wavetops.

And then the dreaming king saw that the warriors were being led by a mighty horseman mounted on a magnificent white stallion.

The warrior leading the charge wore a breast-plate of bronze, armoured breeches, boots of leather and a bronze helmet gilded with gold. He rode his horse as if it were part of his own body and he a centaur.

He held an iron spear in his right hand, and the reins of the white charger in his left. His shoulders were bare. The dreaming king now found himself looking at the mighty horseman from close by. The armour on the horseman's arm did not quite reach up to his shoulder, and now the king saw the warrior's right shoulder carried a strange purple birthmark, which seemed to the king's horrified mind to resemble... in his sleep the realization seemed even greater than it would have been had he been awake... *the paw-print of a lion.*

The great host of mounted horsemen swept into the Scythian army. The mighty warrior on the white steed caught up with the Scythian general in a swelter of sweat, clash of swords, stench of horseflesh, and sheen of armour.

The king saw the Scythian try his utmost to fight off the warrior, but the Scythian was hopelessly outmanoeuvred and outwitted. Finally, exhausted, the Scythian made a desperate effort to lunge at the mounted warrior with his sword, but the warrior was too fast for him and dodged the lunge, wheeled his horse with lightning speed, drew back his own sword, and cleaved the Scythian in two from one side of his chest to the other, with just one sweep of his sword.

As the general's torso toppled away from the bloodied stump that was the rest of his body, the Scythian had just enough air left in his shattered lungs for one final, earth-rending scream...

The king heard the scream as if it had been uttered by Mithra himself.

'Cyrus!'

The moment the king heard the scream, he knew that Cyrus was the name of the warrior on the magnificent white horse.

The name echoed again through the king's dream.

'*CYRUS!*'

5. The King's Nightmare

Astyages, who had reigned over the kingdom of Media for thirty years, screamed as he lurched awake in his bedroom in the palace at Ecbatana.

He sat up in bed, panting, and wiped the cooling sweat from his face with a corner of a bed-sheet. He was wearing a thick black cotton sleeping garment: it was early spring, and the Median capital was cold at this time of year.

He glanced with contempt at the woman sleeping by his side. She was Azara, a gorgeous black-haired concubine, one of his favourites from what was known as the Palace of Queens, the community of slave-women who lived in a special part of the palace at Ecbatana. Azara had been granted the privilege of sharing the king's bed that particular night.

Astyages's hawk-like features soured. He shook her awake. She had had the audacity to sleep through his scream, *his* scream. Her cotton sleeping-robe was white, and fragrant with the myrrh she liked to wear in bed. Her lips and teeth were still stained red from the strong Persian wine she and her master had drunk before, during and after their exertions.

Smiling drowsily, she reached for his manhood. 'Sire... do you want me again?'

'Be silent, foolish whore,' Astyages replied, abruptly pushing her hands away from him. 'Fetch Farna-zata. *Fetch him*, if you wish to live to see the dawn.'

Azara roused herself, hastily got out of bed, slipped on a light-blue silk gown and hurried out of the bedchamber.

The kingdom of Media had been created more than two centuries earlier by Deoices, a Median general. Astyages, who had by now ruled Media for three decades, was only fifteen when he was crowned, yet an expert warrior even at that age. As a boy of twelve, armed with a spear, he had killed his first man – a servant who had enraged Astyages's father, King Cyaxeres. Astyages had had his first woman, a beautiful chambermaid, when he was thirteen. On ascending the throne Astyages gained access to the women of the royal harem, and he had not stinted himself.

Inevitably there had been some who thought a boy of fifteen too young to rule Media. Such a view turned out to be fatal to those who held it. The boy-king had spent a pleasant sixteenth birthday afternoon supervising the beheading of his regent and three of his tutors. The young king had come to suspect the regent of incubating kingly ambitions. As for the tutors, Astyages had tired of them, and readily believed rumours that they'd been involved with the regent in his scheming.

Besides, Astyages had found the demise of all four men immense fun to watch. There was something about a suddenly headless neck spurting blood that appealed to the young king's tastes.

Nowadays, six feet tall, blessed with excellent health, a fine head of black hair, a vigorous black beard, and eyes full of intelligence and cruelty, Astyages loved his life. Forty-five was an age few of his poverty-stricken subjects ever attained, but good food, wealth and nights of passion supplied by beautiful slave-women utterly devoted to his pleasure had kept him young. Astyages was still a man of immense physical strength, energy and vigour, as his numerous concubines – and the ghosts of his many victims – could have testified. His scribes and poets wrote sycophantic prose and verse narratives in cuneiform about his exploits. Yet not even the most fawning chronicler of the king's life could have had a higher opinion of Astyages than he did of himself.

He was profoundly superstitious, of course, yet no more so than any of his countrymen. Was not the world, after all, full of terrifying mysteries? Were not human beings only granted by the god Mithra the most limited privileges of understanding the world he had created for them?

Dreams made Astyages even more superstitious than usual. Being king, he regarded his own dreams as especially rich with meaning.

Astyages broke wind loudly, grabbed a black velvet cloak and hurried through a narrow entrance from the royal bedchamber into a sort of reception room whose walls were hung with all types of weapons and elaborate shields. It was here that Astyages met his own loyal advisers. Of these, none was more illustrious than Farna-zata, grand vizier of Media.

Farna-zata arrived a few minutes later, bowing low before his great master. A wavy-haired man in his forties whose wealth was second in Media only to the king's, Farna-zata was wearing his crimson robes of state. He had not been to bed that night. He was breathless from running from a room in the far wing of the palace, where the unclean act of giving birth had taken place.

The grand vizier paused only briefly to catch his breath. 'Your Majesty, I greet you! At your behest mountains cleave themselves asunder, your enemies' armies tremble, and...'

'Be quiet. Is my daughter's child born?'

'A short time ago. I would have woken you, but I know that your Majesty hates being disturbed at night, so I thought...'

'Is it a boy?'

'Yes... yes, sire. But how did you know?'

'I am king. A king knows everything. And there is a purplish birthmark that somehow looks like a lion's paw-print on his right shoulder, is there not?'

'Sire... yes. You... you know that too?'

'I do, Farna-zata, indeed I do.' Astyages nodded meaningfully at the grand vizier. '*Kill him.*'

'Is... your Highness serious?'

'Hear me. I have just woken from the worst dream of my life. But I praise Mithra for the dream, for in it he has told me what I must do to safeguard myself and my kingdom.'

'What did you see, sire?'

'I saw a king in all his splendour and power. Farna-zata, I know that my daughter's boy shall become the king I saw in my dream. I know this king shall win power at the expense of my throne!'

'May Mithra and Varuna prevent that, sire!'

'We cannot rely on Mithra and Varuna to protect us. As the magi are always telling us, the ways of the gods are mysterious. No, we must grasp fate ourselves. The boy cannot be allowed to become a man. Do you understand?'

'Yes... yes, sire,' Farna-zata murmured.

'He must die this very morning.'

'But sire, Cambyses shall hate you. The Persians will bay for blood.'

Astyages gave a contemptuous snort. 'Let them. Much good may it do them. Persia is weak, the Persians are ignorant pigs. Frankly, I am surprised my son-in-law Cambyses, imbecile as he is, managed to impregnate my daughter at all. I had always suspected him of being a eunuch. As for him, my daughter and the Persians, they will believe what they are told.'

'Yes, of course, sire,' Farna-zata said, 'but... still, there is no need for... unnecessary dissent in the southern part of your territory, especially when such dissent can be avoided by a mere...' (the grand vizier paused, then murmured his favourite word) '*stratagem.*'

'Well? What do you suggest?'

Farna-zata went over to Astyages, placed his right arm around the king and paced slowly about the room, now accompanied by Astyages.

'A terrible tragedy, Farna-zata!' the grand vizier exclaimed, as if he had suddenly been transformed into Astyages himself. 'Oh, it is in vain to console me, for my grief is too fresh!'

Astyages gave a faint smile. 'Very good. So... tell me, what fate befell my new-born grandson?'

'Oh, Farna-zata,' returned the grand vizier, 'this very night, this new prince of Persia, a child so precious he might have been my own son, was snatched by traitors from the arms of the midwife while she was taking the boy for his first bath. She, poor woman, was slain by the bandits who stole my prince!'

The smile on Astyages's own face deepened. 'You are as ingenious as ever, you scheming fox.' The king smiled wryly. 'There is treachery everywhere, is there not?'

'Alas, yes, sire,' said Farna-zata, with a pretence of piety. 'But we shall scour the kingdom to return the boy to you and find the traitors. When we do, they shall be executed slowly and painfully.'

Astyages suddenly stopped pacing about the room alongside Farna-zata. Now, his expression was instantly serious.

'The brat must be buried far from the walls of this palace, you understand?'

'Yes, sire.'

'His body must never be found. If ever it is, Farna-zata, it is *you* who shall be executed slowly and painfully.'

'I shall not fail you, sire. I know a soldier, a young man of great height and strength, who shall be sure to carry out the task in... every particular. His name is Harpagus.'

'Very well,' the king said, 'make it happen. By daybreak I must be mourning the tragic loss of my grandson.'

Soon afterwards, as dawn began to purple the east, Harpagus, who was nineteen years old, galloped westward from the royal palace into the side of the world where darkness still reigned.

He secretly detested Farna-zata, but Harpagus knew that a commission from King Astyages and Farna-zata was not something that could be turned down, even when the commission was as dreadful as this.

Harpagus was still unsure whether he could go through with it. Yet he knew that if he did not carry out the command in every particular, he would be executed, and that very likely his family would be as well.

Even before this night, Harpagus had been progressing rapidly through the ranks of the army. He was a phenomenal warrior, a giant who was taller by the length of a fore-arm than the next tallest man in the Median army. Harpagus was skilled with all the weapons of the army, and had killed enemy soldiers with his bare fists. He had been so eager to carry out the king's command, he had not even paused for breakfast.

Harpagus's horse, the giant warrior astride it, galloped out into the darkness of the cold early morning.

In the saddle-bag, a bundle wrapped in a length of fine white cotton bounced gently up and down.

6. Two Bundles

Mithradat collapsed in despair and began to sob.

His poverty was something with which he had to contend every day. But even that seemed nothing compared with this, the death of yet another new-born baby.

He sobbed even more loudly for this death than he had for the others. They had all been girls. This one, this poor new dead one, was a *boy*.

I would have had a son, Mithradat thought.

The boy had breathed a few times, then slumped into sudden lifelessness, just like his sisters from the past. Mithradat held the boy, and the father's tears drenched the baby's cooling forehead.

And Spako, my darling wife? Will she live?

Spako, exhausted by the birth, was slumped on a rough bed of rushes and rags, too sick even to cry out for her baby. 'How is my baby?' she moaned, 'how is my child?'

The elderly village midwife glanced at Mithradat.

'Don't cry. You must be a man. Your baby is gone, but Spako shall get better. I have seen many cases like hers. If they are strong, as your wife is, they recover.'

'If Spako dies I would wish to be dead, like my son,' Mithradat said, through his tears.

'Do not speak folly. Spako shall not die. Dying is easy. There are berries in the forest whose poison kills in a few moments. Living is what is hard for those who are poor and have nothing. Live now for your wife.'

Mithradat made no reply. He wiped the tears from his eyes using the left sleeve of his tunic. Then, in a sudden swift, movement, he stood up, wrapped the dead baby in a grey blanket that smelt of sheep, and took his dead child in his arms.

'Where... where are you going?' demanded the old woman.

Mithradat made no reply. He headed to the door of the gloomy hovel. The old woman instantly got up and held onto him with arms which, while wizened, were surprisingly strong. But Mithradat was stronger, and he shook himself free.

'Come back!' the old woman cried. 'Spako has lost her babe. She shall cry for you when she wakes. She will need you!'

Mithradat said nothing. As he left the gloomy hovel, he grabbed a full and stoppered clay pitcher of wine from a shelf near the door. It was wine Spako had made the previous spring.

'Why are you taking that?' the old woman asked,

Mithradat gave a despairing grunt. 'I cannot do what I need to do with a clear mind.'

And then he was gone into the cruel, cold, early morning.

Harpagus rode like a fleeing ghost on horseback, along a route that even he, who knew this countryside well, had never taken before.

His aim was to find a place dark and dismal enough to be far from the eyes even of Mithra, the Supreme Being, the Infinite Wisdom who created all things. For what forgiveness could there ever be for one who deliberately killed a new-born babe? Such a killing would be dreadful no matter who the baby was, *but this is the son of the king and queen of Persia. This baby would one day be the king of Persia himself!*

Yet what choice do I have? Harpagus thought. He had been there, in the dingy outer room of the palace, with the smell of blood nearby, when Farna-zata handed him the baby and gave him the instruction: *ride until you are far from the palace and the city, then bury the child where it can never be found.* Harpagus, having given the swaddled new-born a quick glance and seeing that its eyes were shut and it made no sound, had assumed that the infant had been born dead. *Well, if my military duties must now include burying dead babies, so be it.*

But then the baby had opened its eyes and began to cry.

'It's alive!' Harpagus had exclaimed, thankful that Mithra had, after all, blessed the baby with life. *Good, now I can go back to bed and get some sleep.*

Farna-zata just glared at him. 'Of course it's alive. Do you think I would waste my time here if the baby was already dead? Listen, the king wants him buried, do you understand?'

'Buried? But the babe lives!'

'He will not live long after you bury him, so don't worry. Harpagus, the king has demanded someone he can rely on for this... delicate matter, so I've chosen you. Regard it as a great privilege.'

'But sire, it would be murder.'

'So? You're a soldier, aren't you? Murder's your calling in life. *Just do it.*'

Even Harpagus, so used as he was to obeying orders, continued to hesitate. Killing an enemy using a weapon or his bare hands was one thing; killing an innocent baby was another...

Suddenly another voice was audible. '*See,*' the harsh, hoarse voice had said, and in the same instant a hand pulled away the blanket from around the crying baby to reveal a birthmark, like a lion's paw-print, on the baby's right shoulder.

Harpagus recognized the voice at once.

'You notice the birthmark, Harpagus?' demanded Astyages.

'Yes... yes, sire.'

'It looks like a lion's paw-print, does it not?'

'Yes... yes, perhaps it does, sir.'

'I saw that birthmark on the shoulder of a mounted warrior in a dream. You can guess what it means. This boy, my daughter's new-born son, bears the birthmark of the lion's paw-print. He will destroy me if he is allowed to grow up.'

The baby just kept on wailing. Farna-zata put his right hand over the baby's mouth. Astyages stared fiercely at Harpagus.

'Do you understand, Harpagus? This baby, whom my foolish daughter has named Cyrus, will rob me of my kingdom when he becomes a man, unless he dies tonight. Do this deed, and you shall have my friendship and gratitude for ever. Fail, and you and your descendants shall feel my wrath.'

Harpagus looked at the king, at Farna-zata, and then at the baby, which was still trying its best to cry through the hand clasped over its tiny mouth.

Harpagus had ridden until daybreak was some way advanced. Already, he could see well enough by the half-light. He found himself approaching an old forest of oak and ash trees. His heart heavy in his boots at the thought of the terrible instruction he had to carry out, he rode toward the edge of the forest.

He slowed his horse to a trot. Soon he and the horse began passing through a glade of young oaks. Presently Harpagus heard a murmur of water. As he proceeded the sound grew louder.

He found himself approaching a clearing, where a swift stream, no wider than two lengths of a spear, ran fast and deep. Harpagus brought the horse to a standstill, dismounted and tied his steed to a tree.

As he did so, he saw a peasant appear on the near side of the stream. The peasant had a pitcher in one hand and a bundle in the other. The peasant hadn't seen him.

Harpagus had been a soldier since the age of ten. He was schooled in all military skills, including concealment. Instantly he blended into his surroundings, edging more closely to the stream to find out what the peasant was doing.

The fellow, Harpagus noticed, was crying.

He watched as the peasant, who was now combining his weeping with singing a lament, put the pitcher down and gently laid the little bundle on the bank. The peasant stood over the bundle for a few moments, gently picked it up with both hands and laid it in the stream. The rushing water carried the bundle away immediately.

A peasant's version of a burial at sea, Harpagus thought.

He drew his sword.

Harpagus, despite his height and size, could move as fast as a desert fox. He had no difficulty approaching the bereaved peasant without the wretch being aware of him. A moment later, the tip of the giant warrior's sword was resting on the peasant's left shoulder.

'It seems this night does not favour the new-born,' Harpagus murmured.

The peasant turned round slowly. He looked utterly terrified. Harpagus was pleased; his great height and enormous muscular development tended to have that effect on people.

Harpagus saw the countenance of a man in his thirties, whose face was lined by poverty and worry. It was the face of a man whose ignorance, Harpagus felt certain, would be as limitless as the sands of the desert.

'Mercy, sir, mercy!' the peasant exclaimed. 'My wife has lost her son this night, may Mithra preserve her from losing her husband, too!'

'She shall certainly lose her husband if he does not give himself to silence,' Harpagus barked.

The peasant said nothing.

Harpagus looked around. The forest, the clearing, an unwilling pair of hands that the threat of a sword-blade between the ribs could certainly render willing... in an instant everything made sense.

'What's in your pitcher?' Harpagus demanded.

'Wine, sire,' the peasant replied. 'My wife's best, made from the wild grapes of forest-vines. I brought it so I could numb my grief, but please, drink it if you wish.'

Harpagus smiled. 'I do wish. Unstopper it for me.' *I need to sink into oblivion before I can complete this duty... or command it to be completed,* he thought.

The peasant, moving slowly and carefully, picked up the pitcher, removed the stopper and handed the pitcher to Harpagus. Holding the pitcher in his free hand, he took a long swig. The coarse, strongly intoxicating liquid hit his empty stomach like a warhammer.

Harpagus prided himself on his ability to tolerate that kind of drink which, for reasons no-one knew, conferred intoxication, but he had eaten nothing since the previous night, when the first star had appeared in the sky.

'Now, dig,' Harpagus commanded. He nodded toward a patch of earth a few feet away. 'Over there.'

'With... with what, sir?'

'What do you think, idiot? With your hands. And hurry. This is a deed that must not see the light of day.'

'Are you going to kill me, sir? Do you wish me to dig my own grave?'

'Not unless you want it to be. Now dig or die.'

With frantic haste, the peasant at once he began to dig. Harpagus, his sword still pointing at him, watched the peasant and took another swig from the pitcher with his left hand. The wine was rough; nasty stuff made, doubtless, by ignorant people, but it was just what he needed at that moment. He felt it flow into his veins like new blood. *This wine will suffice for breakfast,* he thought.

The digging seemed to him to be going painfully slowly. 'Hurry up, fool!' he shouted to the peasant.

'The ground is hard,' the peasant called back.

'I have no time for your excuses,' Harpagus called out, taking another swig of the powerful country wine. 'Dig.'

The peasant went on digging while Harpagus continued drinking. Presently the hole was about two feet deep.

Harpagus knew he was tipsy, and beyond, but he was sure he was still his own master. 'All right... now go over to my horse. You'll see a white bundle in the saddle-bag. Fetch it. And if you're thinking of running off, remember this: I can throw this sword and hit you at thirty paces. *Move.*'

Harpagus gulped more of the wine as he watched the peasant hurry toward the horse, find the bundle and bring it back. As he did, the bundle emitted a loud wail.

'It's a baby, and it's alive!' the peasant exclaimed.

'Of course he is. Now, put the baby at the bottom of the hole, and bury him.'

'*No, sir, I shall not do that.*'

'If you don't obey me, peasant, you shall die, and I... I shall go through this forest and find your wife, and she shall... she shall die too. She cannot be far away; you have come on foot, not mule-back. I am an agent for King Astyages, and am acting on his personal orders. Do you think I wanted these orders? Of course I didn't. I wish the baby had perished as it was being born. *Now, do what I say.* And remember – if you ever breathe a word of this to anyone, I shall find you – and kill you and all your family.'

Harpagus was glad to have got to the end of this speech, for he had a fair idea by now of just how drunk he was. But even through the fog of his drunkenness he was still fiercely proud of his idea of commanding the peasant to do the actual burying. Harpagus knew, even drunk as he was, that this way he would spare himself a lifetime of guilt.

The peasant can live with the guilt. His kind are too primitive to be affected by such emotions.

'Sir, why you are asking me to kill an innocent babe?'

'That is none of your business, fool,' Harpagus retorted.

'At least, sir... if I must do this, tell me... tell me the poor child's name, so I can say a prayer for him and ask Mithra to take good care of him.'

Harpagus belched loudly from the pit of his stomach. 'All right, his name in the sight of Mithra is Cyrus. Now, bury him, say the prayer and we can both go home.'

'Very well, sir,' the peasant murmured.

Harpagus belched again. He felt sick, though he blamed it less on the rough country wine than on the pangs of guilt.

He would rather have been without them, so he drank from the pitcher again and this time drained it.

Possibly that was a mistake, for a few moments later, as he watched the peasant (who had begun to weep again) place the baby at the bottom of the hole and start whispering a prayer, the forest suddenly seemed to dissolve into grey, and into black, and then into nothing.

When Harpagus woke from his stupor, his head felt full of pebbles and his mouth tasted like camel-spit.

The sun was high. There was no sign of the peasant. Nor, for that matter, of the pitcher... or the baby.

The hole had been filled, with grass and leaves sprinkled on top of the disturbed earth.

Harpagus smiled. *So the foolish peasant has done my bidding.*

Harpagus's horse gave a loud neigh.

The giant soldier got to his feet, belched yet again, wondered whether he was going to be sick, decided he wasn't, then walked unsteadily back toward his horse. On the way he was sick, and again on the ride back to the palace at Ecbatana.

Many miles away, Spako was already beginning to regain some of her strength. She was weeping tears of joy as she held a baby in her arms and let it suckle her.

'It's a miracle,' breathed Mithradat. 'I was all ready to cast our poor son, whom I believed to be dead, into the water, when suddenly... he began to cry. I could scarcely believe it. The fresh morning air must have revived him.'

'It is indeed a miracle,' Spako murmured, still weak but full of love for her babe. She smiled at her husband. 'It is as you say: the baby is a miracle from Mithra.' She sat in silence, cuddling her baby, then glancing at her husband, said quietly: 'When I met you and you told me your name is Mithradat, I thought "this man's name means the gift of Mithra: perhaps he shall be the man for me." Oh, my dear husband, your love for me has truly been a gift of Mithra. But today... we have an even greater gift from our god. My love, we must sacrifice a goat.'

'We shall,' Mithradat said. 'It shall cost us dear but we shall. And listen: as I walked back here with our boy, Mithra even whispered to me what we must call him: Cyrus.'

Spako smiled. 'Cyrus,' she murmured. 'Yes. it is a perfect name for a perfect boy, and it shall be so.'

Mithradat was confident that the boy would grow up and live his life far from King Astyages and that terrible drunken warrior. The shepherd would have felt it a blasphemy in the eyes of the all-seeing Mithra to have changed the name that the great Creator had bestowed upon him.

Harpagus, still feeling queasy and dizzy, but fairly confident there was nothing left inside him to throw up, slowly rode back to the royal palace to report to Farna-zata, in complete secrecy, that the baby was now sleeping not in his mother's arms, but in the arms of Mithra.

Farna-zata relayed the news in similar secrecy to Astyages, who rewarded Farna-zata with a five gold bars.

Farna-zata, who well understood the concept of profit, rewarded Harpagus with one gold bar, and a promotion.

7. Orphans

Ten years passed. Moons waxed and waned; the sun rose and fell across the lands of Media and Persia, the mighty Euphrates river to the south flowed with rippling sinews through the prosperous neighbouring state of Babylonia, watering the land and blessing it with richness and fertility. Onward the Euphrates flowed to the sea, through the proud city of Babylon itself, the largest city on earth, whose pious and prosperous people thought their massy walls proof against any risk of foreign dominion.

Astyages still ruled Media with a fist of bronze. Convinced that his grandson Cyrus had been buried alive, Astyages felt himself as safe as the desert scorpion, which is feared by all the creatures of the desert, even the black cobra.

'Cyrus!' Spako called out one morning in the square of a small town called Paritakna, a morning's ride south of the Median capital of Ecbatana. The square was filled with children chasing chickens, engaging in mock-fights with wooden swords, and trying to avoid their mothers, who kept shouting for them to come home and help with the household chores.

Around the square, and along ragged little streets for a few hundred paces behind it, were one-storey buildings, most made of wood, some of dried clay and straw. One of these buildings, larger than the others, was used as a school for the children of the town, where they were taught about the great all-seeing one, Mithra, and about the need to obey the word of Mithra and to speak the truth, and where they also learned how to fight with wooden swords, to shoot with a bow and arrow, and to ride ponies.

One of the children looked very different from the others.

He was taller and stronger than they were. His jet-black hair was ample, long and healthy-looking, nor were there any disfiguring marks about his face, blessed with intelligent brown eyes, from an encounter with smallpox, a disease that, like innumerable other ailments, had ended many young lives in Paritakna well before their time.

'Cyrus!'

The boy stopped running with his friends, skidded to a standstill in the dust and glanced at his mother.

'Come here at once!' Spako called.

The boy shouted out to two other boys, two brothers, who were chasing chickens with him. 'Raiva! Asha! Wait for me! I must speak to my mother!'

Raiva, a rugged boy with handsome, sickle-cut looks and eyes so dark as to be almost black, and who liked nothing so much as hoarding the few trinkets he was given for doing little jobs for other townspeople, slid to a halt. His younger brother Asha, a skinnier boy with a friendly face and bright brown eyes, tiptoed toward a chicken, then suddenly dashed at it. The bird just about managed to escape with nothing but ruffled feathers.

Cyrus didn't bother to call to his other playmate, a dark-haired, pretty, earnest-looking, strangely serious eight-year-old girl called Roshan. She was just a girl, and not worth the effort. All the same, he knew she was clever, perhaps even cleverer than he was, and this troubled him. Cyrus and the other boys in the town mocked Roshan because of the things she often said, the meaning of which they couldn't always understand, and also because she had made herself a little garden in the stony, dry land near her home and struggled to carry buckets of water to it from one of the town wells so she could water the desert flowers she'd planted.

Cyrus had once tried to help her by building a small dam in the town stream and doing his best to divert the flow of the stream to her garden, but the dam burst almost at once.

Roshan could fight as well as any boy in the village could, except Cyrus, who was stronger and taller than his playmates. When the children of the village played games, including a game in which one of them was the king and the rest were his army, it was always Cyrus who was king, or any other kind of leader the game might have required. As for Roshan, she was adept at fighting with the wooden sword, at shooting the bow and arrow and using the sling-shot. She was always willing to fight other girls, and boys too if they angered her. Even Cyrus would have had to admit he enjoyed playing with Roshan, even though she was a girl. Occasionally he would snatch a kiss from her, partly because he liked doing so and partly because it made her cry.

Right now, Cyrus and Roshan were practising with their sling-shots at hitting a broken pot Cyrus had placed upside-down on a thin branch of a tree he had stuck vertically into the sandy earth.

Cyrus watched Roshan pick up a small pebble from the ground, place it into her sling, then whirl the sling round before loosing it from a distance of about twenty feet. The pebble missed the pot, though not by a long way.

Cyrus laughed. 'How can you expect to fire the sling well? You're a girl.'

'Girls are just as good as boys!' Roshan exclaimed.

'Never!' cried Cyrus.

'Cyrus, you idle loafer,' Spako called, 'fetch wood instead of bickering with that sweet girl who is so devoted to you. '

'Mother, I shall fetch wood,' Cyrus said. 'But first...'

And, abruptly casting his sling-shot to the ground, he drew his wooden play-sword and launched himself at Asha, barely giving the other boy a chance to defend himself, though Asha managed to draw his own sword just in time. Raiva, taking his cue from Cyrus as he so often did, drew his sword and began to duel with Roshan.

'Leave me alone!' Roshan shouted.

'No,' said Raiva, 'I'm going to make you promise to marry me some day.'

'I'll never marry *you,*' Roshan said to him, with calm resolve.

'Who else would ever want to marry you if I didn't?' Raiva demanded.

Roshan didn't reply, but began to fight Raiva with her own play-sword. He fought back, but she was strong, quick, and angry. The moment she saw a weak spot she pounced. She whacked Raiva hard on his chest with the flat of her sword. Winded, he dropped his sword and was doubled-up with pain as he struggled to regain his breath. Roshan, Cyrus and Asha roared with laughter.

'You terrible children!' Spako cried. 'Why do we bring you into this world?'

'My father says he doesn't try, but children just happen,' said Asha, still fighting Cyrus.

'Don't speak like that, Asha, or I'll tell your father what you just said,' Spako told him.

Asha glanced at Spako for a moment, as if he were about to apologize. Cyrus, seizing his chance while Asha's attention was momentarily distracted, rushed at him, overpowered him and rubbed his face in the dirt.

'I am Cyrus!' he cried, taunting him. 'I am the greatest warrior in the world!'

'Maybe,' shouted Spako, 'but you'll have a great smacked bottom this evening when your father returns from the fields!' Yet the shout was tinged with affection, for he had always been her miracle.

At that moment Cyrus heard the strangest of sounds, a clanking of what sounded like iron against iron. It was followed a few moments later by the bray of trumpets and horns. Cyrus turned in the direction the sounds had come from. His eyes rested on the sight of dozens of ragged and half-naked people bound together by chains, followed by three horse-drawn carriages, each with two drivers atop them, controlling the horses. To the side of the carriages soldiers walked in single file; heading toward the town square. Cyrus counted about a score of soldiers altogether.

The man at the head of one of the column of soldiers was the tallest soldier Cyrus had ever seen. He wore a purple plume in his helmet. Cyrus knew this meant he had the rank of captain.

The procession emerged fully into the town square, then came to a lumbering standstill.

Spako stared at the extraordinary gathering. Cyrus, Asha, Raiva and Roshan all followed her, with even greater wonder.

Most of the people from the dwellings around the town square had emerged from their houses now, staring in amazement at the caravan and particularly at the half-naked and chained wretches. The slaves begged the townspeople, hands outstretched, for food and water. Some spoke in incomprehensible tongues; others in the language Cyrus knew, but in strange accents.

Roshan, standing next to him, started to cry.

Cyrus turned to Spako. 'Who *are* these people, mother?'

'Slaves,' Spako whispered to him.

'What crimes have they done?' Cyrus asked.

Spako quickly walked closer to her son and put her right arm protectively around him, as if she feared that at any moment the caravan might choose to enslave him, too.

'They have committed no crime,' she whispered, 'except to be born in a different place, or to worship a different god. Come away, children,' she added in a louder voice, including Cyrus, Asha, Raiva and Roshan in the command. 'This is no place for you.'

Raiva, Asha and Roshan went with Spako, and were soon some distance away on the other side of the square. But Cyrus felt drawn to the slaves, as if he knew that watching them might teach him something. Spako called to Cyrus to come with them, but he remained where he was.

One of the slaves, an old man, fell to the ground. Instantly, one of the soldiers began whipping him. The old man cried out with pain. At once another slave, a grown man, with a full black beard and rosy cheeks, burst out of the throng of slaves and pushed himself between the soldier and his victim.

'Out of my way, fool!' the soldier cried. But the man who had pushed in ignored this command and stood his ground. Cyrus, still carrying his wooden play-sword, gazed at the newcomer. Cyrus was fascinated by his bravery. The other slaves looked desperate and afraid, but this man did not.

'Whip me instead,' the man said, calmly, to the guard. 'I am younger and stronger than this old fellow, and better able to stand it.'

The guard stared at the man who had spoken, then spat onto the ground. 'Jew,' he said. 'No, I shall not whip you, Jew. The strength of my right arm is too valuable to be wasted on one of your race.'

The guard turned away, then strode off with a contemptuous wave of his left hand.

Cyrus had no idea what a 'Jew' was. The bearded man smiled at Cyrus. 'That's a fine sword you have there, boy. So, are you going to grow up to be a great warrior?' He glanced around at the other slaves, looked at Cyrus again, then spoke to him in a softer voice.

'Grow into a great and strong warrior, boy,' he told Cyrus. 'Then you can kill the wicked King Astyages who has enslaved us, and who ruins the lives of so many people in Media, including many Jewish people.'

'I would never wish to kill the king, sir,' Cyrus returned.

'You may, boy, when you know him better and also know about the crimes for which he deserves to die,' the bearded man returned, still speaking softly.

Cyrus said nothing.

'Tell me, boy,' the man said, 'is your father a warrior?'

'No, sir. He is just a shepherd.'

'Why do you say, "just a shepherd"? My young friend, true heroes are not only found on the battlefield, but also on farms and in small towns like this one. The men who rise before dawn and do not rest until dark are strong men who will fight to the death to defend their families and houses. They could be the saviours of this land.'

Cyrus stared. Never in his life had he heard anyone speaking like this.

'I am not of your faith,' the man went on. 'My name is Daniel. Look at all us slaves, boy, and see the proof that the king of Media is a wicked man who deserves to lose his throne.'

Cyrus let his eyes sweep among the slaves. He felt sorry for them, but powerless. *What can I do to help them?* he wondered.

Other townspeople, including Roshan's parents, started to approach the slaves and offer them water and food, all the while looking fearfully at the nearby soldiers. Cyrus waited for the fury of the soldiers to show itself. He was sure that at any moment they would intervene and put a stop to the townspeople's generosity, but they didn't.

'The soldiers only allow the people to feed the slaves so that they don't need to feed the slaves themselves,' Roshan observed.

Cyrus hadn't noticed Roshan coming back. He wondered whether she had heard what the man called Daniel had said.

'I shall never, ever, be a slave,' Cyrus said to his mother.

'You wouldn't have any choice, if you were taken prisoner,' Roshan told him.

'If I were taken prisoner I would escape,' said Cyrus. 'I would escape, and enslave him who had enslaved me!'

Too late, Cyrus saw that his loud exclamation had attracted the attention of the giant captain. He turned, saw Cyrus and headed over toward him.

Spako hastily went to stand in front of her son to protect him. The captain continued his relentless strides toward Cyrus.

Cyrus gazed at the bronze plated armour of the captain. The captain was taller than him almost by the length of a man's arm, the captain's powerful arms each as thick as one of Cyrus's thighs.

'So, boy,' the giant captain said, still smiling, 'if you were enslaved you would free yourself and enslave your enslaver?'

'The boy is a fool,' Spako returned, at once, defiantly, but Cyrus could hear the trembling edge of fear in her voice. 'He does not know what he is saying. He is not right in the head.' She glanced at Cyrus. 'Come, foolish boy. Leave this gentleman alone.'

Cyrus, frozen into awe but not fear at seeing the huge captain, just stared up at him.

'Tell me your name, boy,' the captain demanded, pushing Spako out of the way.

'I am Cyrus, sir,' Cyrus replied, fearlessly.

'"Cyrus"? What manner of name is that? It sounds like the name of a desert rat. Well, you know what happens to desert rats, boy. I take my sword and I...'

But the captain suddenly fell silent.

He looked harder at Cyrus. 'Cyrus, you said?'

'Yes, sir,' Cyrus replied.

The captain tore at the fabric of Cyrus's tunic. A moment later, the captain set eyes on the lion's paw-print birthmark. Cyrus had grown so used to it he had all but forgotten its existence.

The giant captain recoiled with surprise and shock, staggering backward a couple of steps before collecting himself. Finally, anger glowering in his face, he turned to Spako. '*Does your husband live?*'

'Yes... yes, sir,' Spako stammered.

'*Where is he?*' the giant demanded.

'In the fields, sir. I expect him home soon.'

The giant grabbed hold of Cyrus's right arm. The grip was so powerful, Cyrus knew he would have no chance of freeing himself.

'Find him, woman,' the giant said. 'Quickly, unless you want to see your son spitted on the end of my sword.'

'Sir, sir, let him go, please,' Spako wailed. 'Kill me, not him.'

'I shall kill both of you, if you do not go and bring me your husband right now,' the captain said.

Weeping, Spako ran off. She kept glancing back at Cyrus who, realizing the futility of struggling, stood in the captain's vice-like grip, while the townspeople and more of the captain's soldiers, who had come to see what was happening, looked on. The people of the town watched the scene in silence, but the soldiers laughed and joked.

It was no more than a few minutes before Cyrus heard his mother's voice calling, though he could not see her. 'Sir, my husband is here! Please don't harm my boy!'

Cyrus saw his mother and father rushing around the side of one of the clay and straw houses. His parents raced toward him. Mithradat took the lead, but to Cyrus's astonishment he saw his father's steps falter, until he stopped still and began backing away into the middle of the square.

His father was staring at the captain, and now Cyrus saw that the giant captain, ignoring Spako, was glaring at his father. Suddenly Cyrus felt the vice-like grip on his arm loosen.

The captain drew an enormous sword.

He stomped toward Mithradat.

Cyrus, terrified, followed him.

When the giant confronted Mithradat close to the middle of the town square, the only people close by were Cyrus and Spako. The other townspeople were hanging back, Cyrus could see, out of terror. As for the other soldiers, they were watching from a distance. *They don't think the giant needs any help to deal with my mother and father* was the jagged thought that stuck in Cyrus's mind.

Cyrus had never seen his father look so afraid. Mithradat, unarmed, was cowering. The eyes of Mithradat and Harpagus remained locked on each other.

'You,' said the giant captain, raising his sword. '*This is your boy. His name is Cyrus. He was the baby I commanded you to bury.*'

'Mithra defend us!' Spako said, collapsing to the ground.

'Sir, this isn't Cyrus,' Mithradat pleaded to the giant captain. 'I had another son... a year later. I named him Cyrus too... out of respect for...'

'Don't lie, wretch!' the captain shouted. 'I saw the baby. He had a birthmark on his right shoulder, a birthmark like a lion's paw-print. Your son has that same birthmark. Why did you not obey me? What did you bury in the grave?'

Mithradat said nothing.

'Well?' Harpagus demanded.

'The cause... the cause of your slumber...' Mithradat mumbled. 'The pitcher.'

Cyrus felt bewildered. *What are my father and the terrible giant talking about?*

A moment later Cyrus saw the captain dash forwards and plunge his sword through his father's unprotected body. The tip of the sword, bathed in what looked like red paint, emerged from his father's back.

Cyrus felt faint. His father gurgled. Transfixed by the sword, his father had still not fallen, but was staggering, the sword still in him.

There was more laughter from the soldiers and screams of anguish from the people of the town. Cyrus wanted to bury his face in his hands so as to rob his eyes of the pain, but he forced himself to keep watching.

Two of the laughing soldiers hurled their wooden iron-tipped spears at Mithradat. One struck clean through his neck, the other in his left thigh. Mithradat screamed in agony, blood now gushing from all three wounds. The man Cyrus knew as his father sank to the ground, and fell face-first into the dusty earth.

'He won't anger you ever again, Harpagus, you can be sure of that!' one of the soldiers called out in a jaunty voice.

The giant captain's name – Harpagus – instantly lodged in Cyrus's memory.

The soldiers laughed.

Harpagus pulled his huge sword out of Mithradat's body, bringing a stream of blood with it. Cyrus, appalled beyond utterance, knew his father must be dead.

The giant captain quickly bent down to wipe his sword on the rough ground, then stood up, glanced at his soldiers and pointed at Cyrus.

'Kill the boy!' Harpagus barked.

'*No!*' yelled Spako, and instantly, suicidally, ran between the soldier and Cyrus, shrieking to other people of the town as she did, 'Save him!'

'Do not harm my mother! Leave her alone!' Cyrus yelled, but his cries were drowned out by Spako's screams, as several of the soldiers hurled spears at her, while others charged at her with their swords.

A few moments later his mother's massacred body, already consisting of little more than ripped and shattered flesh, was a mere blood-soaked plaything for the soldiers.

Cyrus fled faster than the desert wind. The soldiers, still laughing at their easy sport of slaughter, began to run after him, but their armour and weapons slowed them. Cyrus ran towards a house whose door was open and he sprinted through the house and out into the untidy, chaotic warren of houses and paths behind it. He knew those paths and the lay-out of the town intimately. Soon he had fled into the heart of Paritakna, leaving behind little more than a cloud of dust.

The soldiers, soon seeing that they had lost their quarry, returned to the town square in a fury, lashing out at any townspeople they could see. They killed several at once. Other fleeing villagers ran into the passageways of the town, but they were slower than Cyrus, and not as agile. The soldiers, anticipating easy slaughter, raced after them. Yet it was not quite a one-sided contest, for the townspeople, not enjoying the good diet of King Astyages's men, weren't as tall as the soldiers, nor anything like as broad-shouldered; and so they could scurry away into the nooks and crannies of the town much more easily. Also, the soldiers were handicapped by their heavy armour and long spears, whose angles of approach they had to change continually to get the weapons through the narrow doorways and alleys.

Despite this, dozens of townspeople were slaughtered. The furious soldiers, appalled at how these primitive peasants could outwit them, lashed out at anyone within reach. But the killings slowed the soldiers down even more, and so did the task of kicking dead or dying bodies from their path.

That night, with the search for Cyrus abandoned and all the townspeople who had survived the massacre having fled to the semi-desert countryside to the east of Paritakna, Harpagus – dining with his men around a camp-fire – cursed the boy and the boy's parents and swore that any soldier who found and killed the boy on the morrow would receive triple pay for that month.

But early in the morning a messenger from King Astyages reached the caravan – which had purchased the slaves from a sea-port in the south – to deliver an order to proceed at once to Babylon. The message said that King Astyages had heard that the price paid there for slaves had recently risen.

Before leaving, Harpagus addressed his soldiers. None of them knew exactly why their captain had been so angry, for by the time they had arrived on the scene the argument between Harpagus and the peasants was over, and the peasants were dead.

Harpagus, naturally, did not have the slightest inclination to report the discovery of Cyrus to King Astyages. Some of Harpagus's soldiers, including his most loyal comrades, asked him why he had been so angry with the peasants. But he deflected the questions, merely saying that the herdsman and his son had enraged him.

'We shall leave at noon,' Harpagus announced. 'But first, carve this town from the land of Media as you would cut a bastard from the womb of a pregnant whore! Destroy all you have time to destroy! Burn all you have time to burn! Do not waste a moment!'

Cyrus, Roshan, Raiva, Asha and many of their friends and other villagers managed to slip away into the surrounding forest, which they knew so well from when they had been sent into it to gather firewood and berries.

The soldiers slept the sleep of those have tried to drown their guilt in liquor. Cyrus, Roshan, Raiva and Asha and the others spent the night in the forest, huddling together for warmth.

Cyrus hardly slept that night. He had seen the people whom he believed to be his mother and father butchered before his eyes. He had heard the terrible strange and mysterious conversation between Harpagus and his father, though even the dreadful events that had followed had driven the actual words into the deepest recesses of his mind.

That night Cyrus wept, turning his face from Roshan who slept close by him. He did not weep often, for he knew that a boy of ten was a young man. But that night, knowing he now had no protector in the world but himself, he could do nothing but weep. He wondered how he would earn his daily bread. But above all he wept because the mother and father he loved were dead.

In the morning, others came into the forest to tell them that the soldiers were gone, that much of Paritakna had been burned to the ground, and dozens of townspeople murdered or taken as slaves.

The soldiers had departed with the caravan, bound for the royal city of Ecbatana.

Later that day, Cyrus stood in the town square with Roshan, Asha and Raiva, staring at the smouldering embers of their town.

Fires the soldiers had started, and which the terrified townspeople had not been there to put out, had reduced about half the dwellings of the town to ashes. Dozens of people lay slaughtered, many incinerated, in the ruins of their homes.

Cyrus and his three closest friends stood there with the surviving adults and children of Paritakna.

Of the four playmates, Asha was the one who so often made them laugh with silly jokes and ridiculous behaviour, but not now.

Cyrus could not help weeping. Nor could Roshan and Asha. They both knew that their parents were among the dead, but the men of the town would not allow Roshan and Asha to see their bodies.

Raiva did not cry. He was expressionless in his grief.

'Our parents were killed because they were poor and no-one thought them important,' he said, in a tone of voice Cyrus could not remember Raiva having ever used before. 'When I grow up I shall be rich, and everyone shall know how important I am.'

Cyrus said nothing.

Later, Asha found another cause for sorrow.

Frada, his pet billy-goat, whom he had reared since it was a kid and for whose sake he had extracted a promise from his father that it would never be killed for food, was among the dead. The animal had managed to escape being burned, but Asha found it lying dead, shot through the neck by an arrow it could not elude.

After he had stared down sadly at his dead pet for some time, he knelt and took from around its neck the little bell it wore there, attached to a collar of sinew by a piece of twine. Asha stood up, detached the bell from the sinew then, in a moment of sudden impulse, wove the bell into his own hair by tying strands of it through the little brass ring at the top of the bell.

Now, every time he moved, the bell rang.

Raiva laughed at him, but Cyrus and Roshan did not. They understood.

'The ringing of the bell shall always remind me of Frada,' Asha said.

Cyrus had often thought Asha a little crazy. But, as Roshan had pointed out more than once, he had a good heart.

Later that day, the townspeople buried their dead.

Cyrus and the other children were kept from the mass burial site. Standing some distance away, they heard the wails and lamentations from the adults all around them.

Cyrus's thoughts were different to Raiva's. *My beloved mother and brave and good father died because they were not strong enough,* thought Cyrus. *I must be much, much stronger than they were.*

He glanced at his friends, who were now silent.

Cyrus wondered if they were thinking the same thing.

Torrents of emotion, some familiar, some completely new, flowed through his mind.

His eyes scarcely blinked.

8. Destined for Greatness

The dark brown eyes were just as deep, but now they belonged to a handsome, thoughtful man of twenty-five.

The eyes missed little, even in the dusk. In the bright light of day, they missed nothing.

He was looking down at the floor of a valley from the top of a high ridge at the forest that had by now become so familiar to them, indeed their second home after Paritakna had been mostly destroyed. Next to him was a beautiful, tawny-haired woman with a bow slung over her back, two daggers in her belt in front of her, a sword in its sheath, and her favourite sling attached by a bone clip to her leather belt. The sling was made from catgut, and had a soft dark brown leather pouch for pebbles or small iron balls.

The pouch was loaded with a small grey stone.

Cyrus smiled faintly at Roshan. Twenty-three years old, admired by all who knew her, she smiled back with a proud, piercing, look. Her eyes, like his, were dark brown.

Down below, a caravan moved slowly along the floor of the valley. From their position and height the caravan looked like a large, gaudy, slow-moving caterpillar. It was made up of about a dozen wooden coaches painted in gold and mauve – exotic and expensive pigments purchased, Cyrus could guess, from the fabled bazaars of Babylon.

The caravan was protected by a score of heavily armed guards, who rode alongside it. Behind the caravan, in chains, a retinue of wretched slaves followed. With every village the caravan passed, more slaves were captured.

Cyrus smiled at Roshan again. It was the smile of a leader of a desperate, hungry and courageous group of bandits, a leader now expressing the deepest feelings of friendship for one of his number: a fearless, sublimely beautiful woman who, in her heart, had never forgotten he had once told her that women can never be the equal of men.

Cyrus was their leader because... certainly it helped that he was the tallest among them, but in truth he had always somehow been the one to whom they all looked up, in their different ways. His words, his commands, carried the kind of natural authority that is all the more powerful for being implicitly accepted rather than demanded.

Now, he and Roshan took off most of their weapons and laid them on the ground. Roshan, though, retained her sling, which she attached by a small leather hook to her saddle, making the weapon barely visible.

Cyrus and Roshan leaped onto their horses and began to descend the steep path that led to the valley floor. The steepness would have been a fatal challenge for most horses, but their mounts knew the path's every twist, turn and gradient.

Within a few minutes Cyrus and Roshan had reached the floor of the valley. They emerged at a canter and headed for the caravan.

The guards just stared at them, trying to decide whether they represented a threat.

Cyrus cantered up to the front coach of the caravan, which lurched to a halt. Some of the guards took their bows from around their backs, though they did not draw them. After all, these two country bumpkins were unarmed.

Cyrus and Roshan smiled at the guards. They both did their best to look like ignorant yokels, smiling foolishly at each other.

The door of the first coach opened. From it emerged a haughty-looking nobleman dressed in rich silks of many colours, though expensive purple predominated. The black leather belt he wore around his substantial midriff was studded with jewels.

'Why, hello, zur,' said Cyrus, in an affected rustic accent. 'Might me and my sister take a peek at what you be selling? We may wish to buy something, don't you know, zur.'

'Begone, fool,' the nobleman said. 'There is nothing for you here.'

'But that bracelet you be wearing, it looks nice,' said Cyrus, still affecting the same accent. 'How much will you sell it me for, zur?'

'It is not for sale,' the nobleman said.

'The slave traders of the coast may, however, wish to buy *him*,' another richly-dressed merchant in the caravan said suddenly, emerging from a door in the second caravan. 'He looks strong,' this second merchant added. 'He'll fetch a high price.' He nodded in Roshan's direction and gave a smile. 'As shall she, in view of the excellent entertainment she'll no doubt furnish to her owner... once she's been tamed by the fist, the boot and the whip.'

Cyrus just stared at him. 'Zur... friend, be this hospitable?'

'He's not your friend, peasant,' a mounted guard standing nearby said. 'You heard the gentleman. Welcome to your new life as a slave.' The guard glanced at Roshan. 'And you, too, my beauty.'

'Zur, tell me, what wages does a slave get?' Cyrus asked.

The first merchant just smiled. 'Red weals from a whipping on his back if he misbehaves, and a small bowl of rice every day if he's lucky.'

'I don't be thinking my sister and I is wanting to be slaves, then, zur,' said Cyrus, shaking his head slowly, as if he had given the matter serious consideration.

'Then you shall both die,' said the guard. He reached back to his quiver, slotted an arrow against the bow and drew his bow.

The air suddenly filled with arrows. Members of Cyrus's band had concealed themselves behind rocks and trees high up the walls of the valley. The arrows, tipped with needle-sharp iron points, spat into the guard, easily piercing his armour, and penetrated several of his vital organs. He was dead before he'd fallen off his horse.

Other guards grabbed their bows and drew their swords. They, too, were cut down by a torrent of arrows. But the darts missed a mounted guard who was thirty paces or so from Roshan. He drew his sword, and shouted to his horse to charge.

By the time the horse began to move, Roshan had already snatched up her loaded sling and started spinning it with tremendous force, so that the little leather pouch whirred round and round at the end of the sinews as if the pouch were tracing an unbroken circle. The guard's horse broke into a gallop. Roshan released the pouch with the unerring accuracy she had learned from all her years of practice.

Quick as thought, the pebble flashed from her sling, its great speed increased further by the pace of the horse's gallop. The missile embedded itself in the centre of the guard's face, just above his nose and below the helmet, smashing the bone there and sinking two inches into his brain. He toppled forwards off his horse.

Soon the remaining guards were either dead or had surrendered. Cyrus's people, more than a hundred strong, emerged from their various hiding-places.

A roar of triumph echoed round the valley.

Some time later, looking through everything in the coaches, Cyrus found a golden bracelet, made in the shape of two griffins, whose heads were close to touching.

He went to show it to Roshan. 'We shall send this gold bracelet back to Astyages,' he said. 'It shall be our gift, to show him how much we appreciate the riches he bestows on us!'

9. Royal Plans

'*I know what this means*,' King Astyages said, waving the bracelet in Farna-zata's face. 'This bandit thinks he's got the better of us! He is trying to show me who is master, don't you understand?'

'Yes, sire... yes, indeed.'

'Well, I shall show *him* who is master. I promise you, disrupting our trade routes is the very last thing that desert-rat shall regret.'

Both men were now a quarter of a century older than when they had plotted to send a baby boy to his extinction. They were both even more accomplished schemers than ever.

Age had not withered Astyages. Aged seventy, he was nonetheless still strong, nor had the energy of his younger years yet left him. But he was greyer and gaunter than before, his eyes colder, his temper worse. And as he had aged, he had grown to favour ever younger women: something Farna-zata, and the eunuchs who kept the Palace of Queens well-stocked, took care to remember.

'Farna-zata, you scheming fox, how can you let this happen? Bandits damage our valuable trade with the southern ports and what do you – nothing! Where are your stratagems when we most need them? And what manner of men are the guards we send to protect the caravans? They should all be hanged and replaced by men who can *fight*.'

Farna-zata was himself greyer, his hair no less wavy.

'Sire,' he replied, 'we hear many stories about the bandit leader. He seems beyond the ordinary mould of peasant: a heroic warrior with the ability to seduce the hearts of his degenerate followers.'

'*Do not tell me he is a hero!*' the furious king shouted. 'He is a peasant, born only to till the land or be enslaved. It is impossible one man can be the cause of such disruption. Do you know how much revenue my coffers have lost because of him? Are you telling me one man can be the cause of this disruption to our trading?'

'Yes, sire, it seems as if this one man can – for the moment,' Farna-zata replied. 'I am told by our messengers he has built himself a small private army. Many tribes have joined him, sire, including former guards of yours, as well as slaves he has freed.'

Astyages stared hard at the still-grovelling Farna-zata.

'I want this peasant's heart fed to my dogs,' the king said. 'I want his eyes cut out, placed on a tray and brought to me, so that I may crush them underfoot! Farna-zata, have you a scheme that will enable us to capture him? If not, be assured I will find myself another grand vizier, and I will send you to nurse lepers until your own body becomes riddled with sores.'

Farna-zata bowed even lower.

'Stand up straight, imbecile,' Astyages told him. 'Do you think your servility will rob me of this bandit? Well, *do you have you a stratagem?*'

Farna-zata hastily stood up. He was silent for a few moments, then said:

'Sire, I suggest we apply a simple law of nature to this problem.'

'What do you mean?'

'Sire, if a rat is starving, it will chase any food, even if the food lies in the mouth of a lion...'

Astyages suddenly began to smile. He nodded slowly, indulgently.

'Continue.'

10. The Scent of Frankincense

In the forest at the foot of the mountains was a camp made up of a dozen or so large, rough tents of coarse canvas, and numerous smaller tents. The tents were cobbled together from rags and any fabric that these men and women, who were such irritations to the kingly purpose of the great and good King Astyages, could find.

It was some little time after midday. All around the camp, Cyrus's warriors were sharpening their swords and spears, and eating what little food they had.

There had been no caravans from Ecbatana for some time.

People from the villages nearby were flocking to Cyrus, but now he could barely feed them. Yet still they remained loyal to him. They had bled with him, fought with him, and if necessary were ready to starve with him.

In better days, when Cyrus and his followers captured a caravan, he had offered the guards who survived the battle a simple proposition: they could join his band of freedom fighters, or they could return weaponless and find their way back to Media as best they could. Cyrus told them that any sign of treachery they showed, if they stayed with him, would be punished by death, but that if they were loyal he would treat them with respect.

Sometimes he did not adhere to the promise. If the guards had been particularly unpleasant, Cyrus would on occasion bastinado them even if he subsequently allowed them to join his band. He was not always able to control his temper; he knew this to be a failing, but knowing that did not help him to control it. Yet he was aware of his weakness in this respect, and he believed that in time he would become a better master of himself.

In any event, many guards, whether or not bastinadoed by Cyrus, stayed with him rather than return to Astyages. There was something about Cyrus that inspired people to want to follow him.

As for the slaves, they had nothing to lose. Cyrus and his warriors were already forging a reputation throughout Media, Persia and beyond for freeing slaves and giving them new lives.

Cyrus did free them, gave them care from the medically knowledgeable people among his band, offered them food when he had it to give, and reunited the slaves with their families if he could.

Unlike King Astyages, Cyrus never insulted his subordinates. He never threatened them with summary execution for trivial offences, and he did not take advantage of women merely because he was powerful enough to do so. Inevitably, there were women who gave him their affection, for he was young, and they were beautiful, and the times were desperate, and he was not always immune to their advances. When he displayed his lack of immunity, his close friend Roshan either turned a blind eye, or pretended not to care.

He was indeed young then, and could be impetuous. Sometimes, after a particularly rich caravan had been successfully plundered, and in the company of male friends such as Asha, Cyrus would drink more than was good for him, though he always regretted this in this morning. He was not naturally especially fond of intoxicating drink, yet he sometimes enjoyed the temporary sense of self-forgetfulness it could confer, and he was too young to realize yet the great hazards of yearning for a desire for self-forgetfulness to be conferred by drink.

Even in these early days he knew that people were best treated as allies rather than enemies.

Cyrus often thought of the parable of the sun and the wind, who were competing to make a man remove a heavy coat. The wind blew and blew, but the coat's wearer would simply clasp the coat more and more tightly around himself. Yet when the sun shone brightly, the person wearing the coat would gladly remove it.

Cyrus knew that loyalty given with affection was infinitely better than loyalty volunteered out of fear.

That was the philosophy by which he lived even then, in the days before he was known as Cyrus the Great.

Accompanied by one of his people who had medical knowledge, Cyrus was helping a Persian shepherd, a former slave who had been captured by a Median caravan, and who had been injured in the skirmish that freed him.

'Can you walk?' Cyrus asked the man.

'I shall walk if you need me to do so, sir,' the shepherd replied, getting painfully to his feet and taking a few steps.

'Your wound was bad,' Cyrus said, 'but it has healed well. You shall recover.'

'A thousand blessings on you!' the shepherd replied. 'May you live forever and may your sons rule the world!'

Cyrus smiled again. 'Thank you. Well, we shall see.'

'Thousands like me will follow you to the death, master. We have many wrongs to avenge.'

'That I know,' Cyrus said. 'But call me friend, not master. You are your own master now.'

Cyrus wished the man good health, and turned away, intending to go to speak to other wounded. Raiva, now one of his lieutenants, hurried up to him.

'Cyrus, we should move the wounded into the caves. They will be safer there.'

'Yes, do it. How are my men?'

'Weary, but ready to follow you.'

Cyrus gave a nod. 'Good.'

'Cyrus, I have heard there's a village half a day's march from here where caravans are still passing through."

'How do you know of this?'

'From talking to people who have friends in the village.'

'I also talk to people, but have not heard of this.'

Raiva shrugged. 'It may not be true but... I think it is worth a try. After all, what choice do we have?'

Cyrus nodded slowly. 'Very well. Gather a hundred of our best men. I'll form a detachment with you as my second-in-command.'

'What about Roshan?'

'Tell her she can come if she wishes. She'll do what she wants to do anyway.'

'So we leave in the morning, Cyrus?'

'Yes, indeed. Before dawn. Let's hope your information is right, Raiva.'

Raiva looked at Cyrus and Cyrus looked back at him. Cyrus had always trusted his friend and there were no secrets he did not share with the man he had known since he was a boy.

'I hope so too,' Raiva said.

A few moments later Asha bustled into the tent. He had more than a score of tiny bells in his hair now, all at present with his hair wound into the ringers so that they did not ring. When he was fighting, he and the men he led, who also wore bells, unwound the hair from the ringers to ensure the bells made the greatest noise.

Asha had never much cared for power; he preferred devoting what spare time he had to whoever was his current lady-friend.

'Cyrus! Raiva!' Asha exclaimed. 'Have you seen that new girl Farna-dukta, the one from the last caravan we freed? The Babylonian with the fair hair? She's so beautiful, and she smells just wonderful; the women love the frankincense we got from the last caravan. I'm teaching her our language. Will she be the first Mrs Asha one day? I'd say it's certainly....'

'Be quiet, Asha,' his brother said. 'We're not interested in your latest conquest. This is Cyrus's tent. We make big decisions here. Why don't you run away and play, little brother?'

Asha stood his ground. 'I can fight just as well as you, Raiva, and I can lead men when I have to. Just because I'm in love doesn't mean I'm bad at my job.'

'Good,' Cyrus said, 'because I need you both tomorrow. But now, please leave me. I have to be alone.'

While the two brothers were leaving, Asha turned to Cyrus.

'Are we going to be bandits forever, Cyrus?'

Cyrus shook his head. 'No, nor are we bandits now. We take what has been stolen from those who stole it, and we return it to the ordinary people who follow us. We are not bandits, Asha, and we never shall be.'

Cyrus began poring over the best map he and his followers had. Drawn by a skilled draughtsman from Cyrus's retinue who had used coloured inks that came from the bazaars of Babylon, the map even had cuneiform writing giving directions and detailing potential hazards in certain regions.

Roshan, he knew, loved maps.

Thinking of her, Cyrus found it strange that he could suddenly smell the scent she had worn for some weeks past. She, like many of the women in the camp, was at that moment often scented with frankincense, like the girl Farna-dukta to whom Asha had taken such a liking. Roshan's scent gave her the fragrance of a lady of Ecbatana, but Cyrus knew she was still as wild and lawless as she had been when they were growing up.

Cyrus heard the sudden padding of footsteps behind him.

'Thanks for knocking,' Cyrus said, making a pretence of sternness, as he turned to look at her.

'One can't knock on the door of a tent,' Roshan replied with an ironic curl of her lips.

Cyrus smiled. 'Even if one day I lived in a palace I think you would still not knock on the door when you came to see me.'

'You know me well,' Roshan conceded. 'So, how is our great one?'

He glanced at her, then he turned back to the map.

'I think I'm lost,' he said.

'All those without love are lost,' she said.

Their eyes met, but Cyrus was the first to break the gaze. 'No,' he replied. 'I am lost because I am not sure which direction I should take us in, once we are in a fit condition to move.'

Roshan nodded slowly. 'I would make my own suggestion, except that I know, from bitter experience, that you don't think my views remotely equal to those of a man.'

'You speak false,' Cyrus said. 'I think you my equal in every respect.'

'I only wish you did. Cyrus, I know you so well. Deep down, or perhaps not even very deep down, you still believe what you said to me when I was a girl: that a girl can never be as good as a boy.'

He looked at her. She moved closer to him. She was tall for a woman, only a hand's breadth shorter than Cyrus himself. He could see her white, even teeth and the mysteries that lurked in her dark brown eyes. Her hair was tawny: long, straight, abundant, the scent of her frankincense sweet and beguiling. He remembered songs he had heard around the campfire of glorious Lydian women who smelled of frankincense and whose lips tasted of myrrh, women who could make a man forget himself completely.

And yet he had never tried to kiss Roshan, or at least had not since when they were children. Somehow, they had become bantering and often bickering friends; friends who laughed together, teased each other, and were never quite prepared to admit how much the other meant to them.

'If you're not sure which direction to go in,' Roshan murmured, 'I suggest you let yourself by guided by me.'

Her eyes fixed his, and this time he had no desire to look away.

'Guided where?' Cyrus asked.

Roshan broke the gaze briefly to glance at Cyrus's narrow single bed in a far corner of the war-room. It was a bed on which

Cyrus often slept after meetings that had gone on late into the night, but he always slept alone.

'I don't know,' Roshan said, her voice low. 'You would have to decide.'

'There are places you could guide me to, yes,' Cyrus said, 'but after I had spent time with you there, I fear I would not be fit for battle.'

Roshan suddenly moved forwards until her lips were only inches from his. With a flash of bewildered excitement, Cyrus wondered if she was going to kiss him. But as quickly as she had moved forwards she backed away again.

'Are you fit for fighting *now*?' she asked, unsheathing her sword and pointing it at him.

Cyrus shook his head slowly, leaving in its sheath his own mighty sword that had ended the lives of so many of those guards of King Astyages's caravans who had preferred to fight, rather than having the good sense to surrender.

'Be careful,' Cyrus said. 'Our tally of wounded is high enough.'

As if to show his contempt of her fighting stance, he reached for a cup of wine on the table nearby and began to drink from it with a pretence of calm indolence. Roshan used its tip like the end of a whip to whisk the cup out of Cyrus's hand. The sword-tip passed so close to Cyrus's face he could feel the rush of air it made. The cup, made of glazed white clay, fell to the ground and shattered.

Instantly, in a movement even faster than Roshan's, Cyrus grabbed hold of her sword with both hands on either side of its flat blade. He held the sword firm. Much stronger than Roshan, he kept the sword rigid, though she tried to snatch it away from him. In a slow, enormously powerful movement, Cyrus tugged the sword towards him, but Roshan still didn't let go. The next instant, their faces were only inches apart.

Cyrus stared into her eyes. 'Don't fight me, fight our enemies.'

Roshan suddenly let go of her sword so that the blade was in Cyrus's hands. For a moment, he stumbled backwards, but regained his balance almost instantly.

'The only real enemies we have are poverty, obscurity and ignorance,' she said. 'The only real enemy *you* have is your refusal to want love in your life.'

He grabbed her sword by its handle and laid the weapon on a nearby table. He glanced at her. 'And who would give me such love?'

She looked at him with scorn in her eyes, then shook her head. 'I don't know. Some foolish woman who is prepared to be a martyr to your folly and stubbornness. Some woman who might even be foolish enough to become your wife.'

Cyrus nodded slowly, understanding her perfectly. But he wanted her to understand him perfectly too.

'Marriage is not on my mind. I want to bring justice into the world. I want Astyages to tremble at the mention of my name. I want to avenge myself on Harpagus, who slaughtered the loving people who nurtured me and whom I called mother and father. I want revenge on those who killed *your* mother and father.'

She just looked at him.

'You understand?' he asked her.

She nodded. 'Yes, Cyrus. Yes, I understand only too well.'

She stared at him hard for a few moments, then turned and walked out of his tent without saying another word.

11. The Village

When Cyrus reached the hilltop overlooking the village through which Raiva had said caravans were still passing, he lay flat and crept up to the summit, waiting for the others to reach him.

Down below he saw a small village, much smaller than his former home town of Paritakna. There were numerous date palms to the north, clustering thickly around a small oasis.

Much more interesting to Cyrus was the sight of about twenty carriages in the centre of the village. They looked more colourful and luxurious than any caravan Cyrus and his band had taken before.

Roshan, Asha and Raiva came to the hilltop to join him. The four friends all kept low, their heads only just above the level of the summit. Cyrus was aware that an observer at ground level would have only seen four black specks, and would most likely think them crows or ravens.

'I didn't know there was an oasis here,' Cyrus said to Raiva. 'It's not on our maps.'

'The map-makers don't know everything,' Raiva replied.

They all went on looking down at the village below them. The caravan seemed deserted.

'The guards will most likely have forced the villagers to provide them with shelter from the sun,' said Roshan.

'Rich pickings,' said Asha quietly. 'Jewels for Farna-dukta, maybe.'

'That girl has gone to your brain, brother,' Raiva said to him.

'And I think you're forgetting, Asha,' Roshan told him, 'that we are not thieves. Or rather, we *are*, but we steal to survive, not to become rich. That's what makes us better than Astyages.'

'Yes, of course,' said Asha.

Cyrus was barely listening. He was forging a plan.

Some time later, in the blistering heat of the day, the four friends, their weapons carefully concealed, walked into the heart of the village. They appeared for all the world like four travellers who just happened to have come to the village seeking food, drink and rest, for which they would expect to pay.

The village still appeared deserted, yet none of them saw anything unusual in this: villages usually were quiet at around this time of day. There were rough dwellings close by, and stables in the distance.

Cyrus, and the three people he had known since his childhood, sidled up to the carriages of the caravan. There were no signs of any horses; Cyrus assumed the beasts were all resting in the stables.

'This is going to be the easiest robbery we've ever pulled off,' Asha quietly murmured, to Cyrus.

'Let's hope so,' Cyrus said, in reply. 'Our people are hungry and thirsty.'

He turned, and gave significant glances to two of his men who were following some distance behind. Almost at once, the rest of the detachment, all former slaves Cyrus had freed and trained in the arts of war and concealment, rose from their prone positions on the outskirts of the village and headed toward Cyrus, Roshan, Raiva and Asha.

Within five minutes the band had completed its takeover of the village square. Yet because there were no enemies in sight, Cyrus could not help feeling uneasy.

'Go with twenty men to the oasis,' Cyrus said to Raiva. 'There are bound to be villagers there. The soldiers must be asleep in the houses: you know how ready Astyages's soldiers are to billet themselves forcibly in village houses. There are probably soldiers sleeping in the caravans, too.'

Cyrus half-smiled, 'By the time they wake, we'll be ready to give them the opportunity to choose loyalty to us.'

He turned to Asha. 'Check the stables. Take a dozen men. All the horses are surely there. With all these carriages to pull, there must be plenty of them. We marched here: we shall ride home.'

Cyrus smiled. He was still smiling when, apparently from nowhere, dozens of black arrows streamed through the air like flying cobras and cut into his men, several of whom immediately collapsed in agony.

More arrows filled the air, and as they did Cyrus heard the war-cries of hundreds of soldiers, who erupted from the village dwellings that until a moment before had been basking in silence in the heat of the day.

'It's a trap!' Cyrus shouted.

He and his band had taken many caravans, but this was something else completely. Outnumbered by four or even five to one, he and his army fought like rats in a cage. He tried to find Roshan in the dust and thick of the battle, but couldn't.

The battle also made it impossible to see what was happening to Raiva and Asha. All around Cyrus was a hellish chaos of swords, knives, arrows, and shrieks of agony. A thought stabbed him: *Raiva led us into this – this was his idea*, yet at once the thought was followed by another: *but I'm commander and I am responsible that we weren't on our guard.*

He thought something else: *why aren't they trying harder to kill me?* for he could tell that the enemy soldiers all around, the ones *he* was trying so hard to kill, were deliberately holding back from attacking him. Enemy archers were nearby, too, and he knew they could have fired their arrows from their powerful war-bows into him at point-blank range. But though they saw him in their midst, and must have known who he was, they didn't turn and fire at him.

Cyrus soon stopped trying to work that out, for close to a dozen enemy soldiers managed to wrest his sword from him, leaving him defenceless. Then they threw ropes around him, and were binding him in the heat and dust of the battle.

The battle became a legend as soon as it was fought.

The royal scribes of Media, literate in the wedge-writing of cuneiform, who would have called King Astyages anything beyond the realms of truth if he'd ordered them on pain of death to do so, wrote enthusiastically of how the great caravan cunningly sent southward as bait had drawn the bandits into the peaceful village.

Cunning Astyages! Foolish bandits! Even more foolish bandit leader!

The same scribes, gloating over the ingenious stratagems they ascribed to their king (but which had in fact been spun from the devious mind of Farna-zata) related how at the very moment when the 'bandits thought their victory and spoils were safe, brave soldiers of the Median army fell upon the bandits like tigers.'

Of course, being royal scribes who were paid a salary, there was much they did not write about.

They did not record how close even Cyrus's band of exhausted, hungry warriors, so greatly outnumbered, came to defeating the host sent down from Media. The scribes did not write of how many brave freed slaves, loyal to Cyrus, fell that day fighting for their freedom, nor how many former guards of the caravans fought so valiantly for Cyrus, whom they had come to respect and love. Nor did the scribes relate how many of the proud king's bloodthirsty soldiers were killed by the furious swordsmanship and archery of Cyrus's half-starved followers.

Still less did the hired wielders of the wedge-shaped writing implements tell how many of the king's warriors were killed with sword, spear or sling by a beautiful and mysterious tawny-haired female warrior before she was allegedly 'cut to pieces by the brave men of the army of our great and all-wise king, Mithra's chosen servant on the Earth.'

But yes, the scribes did write of how the bandits of Cyrus were finally beaten and how their leader was captured alive by a captain of the King's army.

Cyrus, in his desperation and despair, pinned what few hopes he had on having heard the sound of galloping horses, and on not having seen the bodies of Roshan, Raiva and Asha lying nearby. Finally, Cyrus indeed found himself pitted against the captain of the soldiers who had ambushed him and his warriors.

The Median soldiers surrounded Cyrus, as if he were on show. The soldiers close by him now removed his bonds, and handed him a short, blunt wooden dagger: the only weapon he was permitted. He was already wounded.

Now, Cyrus had nothing but the blunt wooden dagger, a mere play-weapon, against the razor-sharp sword of the captain.

The captain sneered at the bloodied and weakened bandit leader. 'Fight! Fight, you wretch! Where is the might I have heard some speak of, that made the desert tremble?'

Cyrus launched a final, hopeless attack. But the man easily dodged his assault, and punched him in the face, knocking him to the ground. When Cyrus was prostrate, the captain whipped the dagger out of his hand, leaving him defenceless.

The armed soldiers standing around laughed their approval. The captain sneered again.

'The king's general, Harpagus, killed my parents,' Cyrus shouted at him from the dust. 'Take me to Ecbatana and I will kill *him*.'

Cyrus had never understood exactly *why* Harpagus had killed Mithradat and Spako. His memory of the words he had heard as a ten-year-old boy had always been vague, for the horror of what he had seen happen a few moments afterwards had made it impossible for him to recall the words clearly. He remembered the giant having shouted something about a baby, and about something being buried, but that was all.

The captain laughed. 'A great general of the king's army does not fight with a mere bandit. Harpagus killed your parents? I doubt it. But if he did, doubtless they richly deserved their fate. They must, after all, have been swine, for they brought you to birth. As for taking you to Ecbatana, where else did you think you are going?'

Cyrus, hearing this dire insult, would have launched himself upon the captain and tried to kill him with his bare hands, but he knew such an act would have been suicidal.

No, I shall not die at the hands of Astyages's men, and in obscurity and nothingness, like my parents did.

The captain walked closer to his captive and kicked dust into his face.

'You shall be beheaded once we return you to Ecbatana. And do you want to know something else? It is this: the king does not wish to waste a skilled executioner on filth such as you. I have heard that you are destined to end your days in agony, your executioner a mere concubine, who will doubtless need a dozen blows or more to take your head off. Indeed,' he laughed briefly, 'the worse job she does of your execution, the more she will please the king. And I am sure that later, after she has despatched you, he will use *her* in his own royal way, to convey his gratitude.'

The captain glanced at his soldiers more purposefully than before. 'Some of you asked me before we came here why we have brought a stout wooden cage.'

He pointed to Cyrus but kept his eyes on the soldiers under his command. 'Now you know why. Throw him into the cage. On the journey north to Ecbatana he is to be given nothing but bread and water. It is time this villain's high spirits were starved out of him.'

12. The Will of Ahura-Mazda

Eleven days later, Cyrus, wearing only a grey woollen loin cloth and a filthy ragged cotton shirt – cast-offs tossed to him by his captors, was dragged barefoot into the king's throne room with ropes around his arms and his legs bound together at the ankles.

It was by far the largest room Cyrus had ever seen, with at least a hundred people in it, grouped mostly around the sides, chiefly people of nobility, he thought, judging from their dress, though some were also clearly servants and others guards. There were lavish, many-coloured carpets underfoot and elaborate tapestries on the splendid walls that were of a stone Cyrus had only heard about in fables: a stone he believed was called marble.

He felt the chill of the tyrant's cold-hearted authority as heavy in the room as if it were a frost on a winter morning.

The king himself was sitting on a great marble throne whose base had arms carved like the paws of a lion.

Cyrus, feeling the cold white floor below him, noticed a beautiful but stony-faced woman standing close to the throne. She was past youth, but she wore her years well and Cyrus saw a clarity and definition about her beauty.

Cyrus was sure the woman must be royal, judging by the splendour of her gold-braided silk gown and her necklace, which was set with emeralds and diamonds. He was struck by the loveliness of her features and by the sadness in her expression.

She doesn't belong here was the thought that stabbed him. *She doesn't belong here any more than I do.*

He wondered who she was and what she was doing there.

The two guards holding the ropes that bound Cyrus's arms dragged him before the king, hurled Cyrus to the ground, laughed scornfully, and retreated to the side of the room.

Cyrus was aware of how badly beaten he was. He had bruises everywhere. Even now, there was scarcely any part of his body that didn't feel painful. He could feel caked blood around some of his wounds, but he had had the wounds for long enough to know that if any of them were fatal, he'd be dead already.

One of the aristocrats standing near the king, a wavy-haired man wearing a garment that seemed to have been spun from pure gold, took a couple of steps forwards and stared at Cyrus with a look of undisguised contempt.

'Lift up your head. I am Farna-zata, grand vizier, and I command you to look your royal master in the face, or die!'

Cyrus unwillingly looked up at Farna-zata. He had heard of the legendary devious, rapacious and merciless grand vizier, for who had not?

Cyrus shook his head slowly, 'I have no king. My only master is the will of my people.'

'You have no people, fool!' Farna-zata shrieked at him. 'The bandits you brought with you to the village were killed in our ambush, and we paid a visit to those left behind in your camp and massacred them. Now be silent, pig.'

Astyages stood up and stepped down from his throne. As he did, the entire court bowed before him. Astyages walked slowly toward Cyrus, paused only a few feet away from him and sniffed the air.

'He smells worse than all the rats in Babylon!' the king observed. 'But he cannot be a rat, for he wears clothes, and I have never seen a rat wearing clothes!'

There was more laughter from the courtiers. Astyages silenced it with a wave of his hand.

He laughed scornfully. 'My friends, I present to you the desert hero who has harried and robbed our wagons! The same villain who sent me this bracelet.' Astyages took the golden bracelet of the griffins from a pocket in his royal cloak and held the bracelet aloft for all to see. 'Yes, he gave me this, to mock me. Well, we can see now who is being mocked! Here is the hero, in all his glory. Look now on a criminal who so richly deserves the humiliating end I have reserved for him first thing tomorrow morning!'

Cyrus, hearing these words, and knowing that this day would most likely be his last on earth, closed his eyes briefly and let his spirit fill with a quick but fervent and heartfelt prayer to Mithra, the great, all-seeing spirit of goodness who had created the world, the light and the day.

Oh, Mithra, Lord! I am contrite for all my sins and I desist from them, from all bad thoughts, bad words and bad acts which I have thought, spoken or done in the world, or which have happened through me. I resign myself to death. May my immortal soul have its place in heaven!

An instant later, Cyrus, who had been oblivious of everything while communing with the maker of the world and the sky and the stars, heard Farna-zata shout a command to one of the guards nearby.

'Rip off this scoundrel's shirt,' Farna-zata commanded. 'It is not fit that this rat be clothed in a shirt before his king.'

At once, the guard hurried forwards. A few moments later Cyrus was on the floor wearing nothing but his loin cloth. Astyages was staring at him with complete contempt.

A moment later, a great change came over the king of Media.

He seemed almost to freeze where he stood, and went deathly pale. He began to breathe with slow, measured astonishment. He turned to look round behind him. *'Bring me Harpagus!'* he screamed.

Astyages kept his own eyes on the birthmark on Cyrus's right shoulder.

A chill passed through Cyrus's body. Even after the shout had died down, Cyrus's ears continued to ring with the name of the man who had slaughtered his father and led the soldiers who killed his mother.

The king stood in silent fury.

For a few minutes there was a heavy, appalling silence in the great throne room. Then the main door of the room opened, and the large form of Harpagus, the man Cyrus hated more than anyone else in the world, hove into view and trod with heavy steps over the limestone floor.

Astyages turned and stared wordlessly at Harpagus, then looked down at Cyrus again. *'What is your name?'*

Cyrus said nothing. He could tell from the blank stare Harpagus gave him that the giant general did not recognize him. But *he* certainly recognized Harpagus, and revulsion consumed him.

Astyages's head suddenly snapped round so he could gaze intently at Harpagus. *'Look at that,'* the king commanded his general, pointing to the lion's paw-print birthmark.

'There must... be some mistake,' Harpagus began. The voice's arrogance was now reduced to servility, but Cyrus remembered that voice only too well.

Astyages looked hard at Harpagus. *'There is no mistake.'*

'Your Majesty, I...'

'Be quiet,' the king said. 'Return to your quarters. We shall talk again later.'

Harpagus obeyed, his military boots sounding like thunderclaps on the white floor as he walked away with a heavy, sullen pace.

Cyrus wondered what the king could mean. Why did he think Harpagus should explain himself? What could there be to explain?

The king's eyes followed every step the general took to the door. The man Cyrus most hated opened the door, and a moment later was gone.

Astyages turned to Cyrus. As he did so, Cyrus saw the woman who had stood close by the throne taking faltering steps forwards.

'Father,' she said, addressing the king, 'what birthmark is this?'

So that is Mandane, the queen of Persia, Cyrus thought. He knew that Astyages had been briefly married to a noblewoman of Media, who, some months after giving birth to Mandane, had died in mysterious circumstances. Some said that Astyages had killed his wife himself, because she objected to him regularly continuing to visit the Palace of Queens even after his marriage.

Astyages turned (almost angrily, Cyrus noticed) to glance at his daughter. 'It is the birthmark of... of your son,' Astyages said, in a deep, faltering voice.

'*Can this be true?*' Mandane replied.

'Look for yourself,' Astyages replied, and Cyrus heard the clearest undercurrent of anger, though suppressed, in the king's voice.

The woman walked over to Cyrus, who did not move. Her expression was no longer stony; now it seemed to Cyrus to be infused with joy. She ran her fingers over the birthmark that looked like a lion's paw-print.

'*It is a miracle,*' Mandane whispered. 'Ahura-Mazda has brought my son back to me.'

'Daughter,' barked Astyages, 'you are a Median. The god of the Medians is Mithra.'

'Father, I was born a Median, it is true,' Mandane replied, with no sign of servility in *her* voice, 'but my husband Cambyses is king of Persia, and I am queen, so my god is now Ahura-Mazda.'

'Very well, very well,' Astyages said, impatiently. 'If you think your husband's religion more important than your father's... your father who could invade Persia and conquer it with a mere flick of his fingers,' Astyages loudly clicked his fingers together, 'so be it. But do not mention the name of the Persian god in my presence again.'

He turned sharply to Cyrus. 'Get to your feet,' the king commanded him. The absence of an insult at the end of the coldly blurted command was extremely noticeable.

Cyrus got up.

'What is your name?' Astyages demanded, in a cold mono-tone, a statement more than a question.

'I am Cyrus,' Cyrus replied.

The king stared at him, but said nothing.

'*Can it be possible?*' Mandane murmured.

The king stared at him. 'Where are you from?'

'I was born in the town of Paritakna,' Cyrus replied. 'Fifteen years ago, when I was but ten years old, my father was murdered in front of my eyes by that general I have just seen, Harpagus. Soldiers under his command then murdered my mother. I have sworn my vengeance on Harpagus.'

'You have, have you?'

Cyrus nodded.

'I see,' said Astyages. He turned to Mandane. 'Daughter, this is your long-lost son,' he said, in a voice that seemed to Cyrus completely devoid of emotion.

Mandane again gazed at the birthmark and then at Cyrus's face, at the birthmark and finally at the king.

'It... it cannot be,' she said. '*It cannot be.*'

'Apparently, daughter, it is,' said Astyages, coldly.

'But... how?' Mandane said.

'I do not know,' Astyages said quietly to her, his voice not carrying much beyond her ears and those of Cyrus. 'I only know that, as I told you then, your babe was stolen by bandits the night you were delivered of him, bandits who first slaughtered the palace midwife. Evidently they showed enough respect for Mithra to retain the babe's name. I suppose they sold him to the people he calls his parents.'

Now raising his voice, apparently so that everyone in the room could hear, Astyages went on:

'Despite all my efforts, and the enormous amount of gold I spent on the search, the men I commanded to track the bandits down and find the boy were unable to do so. Now, it seems a... a miracle has brought Cyrus back to you... to us.'

Astyages glanced at the two guards who had brought Cyrus into the throne room.

'Untie him at once,' he commanded them. He glanced at Mandane. 'Take your son to your personal quarters. Let him be bathed by female servants. When he is hungry, order the finest food for him.' He glanced at Farna-zata. 'If he cares for a woman later, let him have the pick of my Palace of Queens.'

Astyages smiled. 'Perhaps even Farnah, daughter of Azara.' Astyages glanced around at the court. He raised his voice. 'I told Farnah, before I knew who he was, that I would require her to dispatch him tomorrow. Perhaps he may now, later, care to show her *his* sword.'

There was lewd laughter among the assembled court.

'Who is my father?' Cyrus whispered, with a glance at the king.

'Are you so ignorant of the history of Media, the country that gave you birth?' Astyages asked. Yet there was little of the anger and contempt in his voice there had been earlier. 'Your father is Cambyses, king of Persia. You are the prince of Persia. I, Astyages of Media, am your grandfather. The peasants of whom you spoke were not your mother and father at all, so you need not grieve for them a moment longer. Your mother has been visiting my court for some weeks, or she would be as ignorant of your return to court as Cambyses himself is, at present. Now, spend time with my daughter. I must deliberate alone with Farna-zata. By the greatest good fortune a man could ever hope for, you have won mercy here today. Perhaps, Prince Cyrus, you may wish to consider revising your opinion of me.'

Cyrus didn't feel in the least inclined to do that, but he knew that Astyages was expecting a reply.

Mandane suddenly darted forwards. 'Dear father,' she said to Astyages. 'My son is weary from his captivity and tribulations. Let me take him to be bathed by servants. I am sure, on the morrow, after he has slept well, he shall be all you wish him to be.'

Astyages nodded slowly. 'Very well, daughter. Very well.'

He glanced at Cyrus. 'Go with your mother.'

A short time later, Farna-zata was in his own quarters, semi-conscious with pain. There were deep red weals on his back and buttocks.

Astyages, having told everyone to leave the throne room, had summoned Farna-zata and beaten the grand vizier to within a short distance of his life.

Afterwards, Astyages yelled at Farna-zata that he should consider himself lucky he was not going to being executed by Farnah the following morning in Cyrus's place.

'I would very gladly watch your wavy-haired head roll, you villain, but you are too useful to me,' Astyages shouted at his grand vizier.

Farna-zata just moaned.

Later, when he had recovered his senses a little, he called for his own servants to fetch cold poultices to put on his injuries.

After Astyages finished beating Farna-zata and had yelled at the grand vizier to leave the room, Astyages summoned Harpagus.

Seeing his giant general appear hesitantly on the threshold of the room, Astyages beckoned him forwards with two or three contemptuous curls of his index finger. Harpagus, his face grey, slowly approached the king.

Using all his strength, Astyages reached up and punched Harpagus full in the face. A spurt of blood shot from the giant general's nose.

'Tell me what you did with the boy!' Astyages shouted. 'If you speak anything but the complete truth, you will be supper for my lions.'

Harpagus was at least a foot taller than Astyages and much stronger, but made no effort to defend himself.

Harpagus wiped his nose with his right hand, which at once became crimson with blood.

Then, finally, a quarter of a century after the events in the forest, Harpagus told King Astyages the truth of what happened on that cold morning.

When Harpagus had finished, Astyages stared at him in disgust, then punched the giant soldier on the chin with one sweeping blow of his right fist, knocking Harpagus to the ground.

'What am I to do with you?' Astyages demanded, staring down at Harpagus.

'Your... your Majesty,' stammered Harpagus, slowly getting back to his feet. 'If you... if you can find it in your royal heart to forgive me, I shall give you anything, and do anything, to earn your forgiveness.'

'Very well,' Astyages said, his voice now cold and remote and sounding scarcely human. 'Perhaps I shall soon take you up on your offer. *Now, go.* On pain of death do not leave Ecbatana. Understand?'

'Yes, your Majesty.'

'Get out!' Astyages shouted.

13. Waiting

Slowly, Cyrus woke up. He lifted his head from the most comfortable pillow he had felt under his head in his life.

There was an open window in the room. It was still dark outside.

He had no idea how long he had been asleep.

In a faint light, he saw the woman he had seen in the royal court, the woman Astyages had called Mandane, bending over him. Her face was illuminated fitfully by a nearby oil-lamp. The stony harshness he had seen earlier had vanished from her features.

An expensive scent wafted about Mandane. It was not the brazen frankincense Roshan used when she could get it, but a scent that seemed to Cyrus to combine exotic oils and the fragrance of voluptuous flowers.

Mandane's eyes were dark brown, limpid, beautiful.

'So... it is true,' Mandane said. 'My precious son, it is true.'

'What do you mean?' Cyrus muttered. Despite all that had happened, she was still only a stranger to him.

'Some years ago... I heard rumours. I believe they came from Azara, my father's concubine who shared his bed the night you were born. I have heard it said that on that very night, the king woke having had a terrible dream. He seemed convinced a warrior he had seen in his dream would destroy him and take over his kingdom. It was said that the warrior he had dreamed of was my little baby boy. I heard these rumours, but I never allowed myself to believe them. I... I could not believe them.'

'Nor can I,' Cyrus retorted. 'Why would Astyages kill your son on account of a dream? A dream is just that... a dream.' He stared hard her. 'You cannot be my mother. I *had* a mother. When I was a boy of ten, the king's general Harpagus killed my father Mithradat, and Harpagus's soldiers killed my mother Spako!'

'Yes, Cyrus, I know that all too well. I am very, very sorry that such a dreadful thing happened. I cannot understand it, for if my father, who is a wicked, irrational and superstitious man, had indeed commanded Harpagus to kill you, why would Harpagus have let you live? And even if Harpagus did so, why would he have killed the people you thought were your mother and father?'

'No, they were indeed my mother and father!'

'Cyrus, you are my son.'

'I am not your son. It is not possible.'

'But... you are. Ahura-Mazda, the god of the Persians and my own adopted deity following my marriage, has willed it.'

'No, I had a mother. I had a father too. They are both dead... my father was slaughtered by Harpagus, my mother by the villains Harpagus commanded. Harpagus works for *your* father!'

'Cyrus, Cyrus... how can I help my father's wickedness? He has been wicked all his life. But Ahura-Mazda has brought you, my son, back to me, and tells me in every way I am your mother.'

'Then Ahura-Mazda is a fool!'

'Do not... do not ever speak ill of our god. He is wiser and greater than Mithra ever was. And Cyrus... *I have seen the birthmark.*'

'So? Many people have birthmarks.'

Mandane began to weep. 'Cyrus, yours looks like no other I have ever seen. How many people do you think Ahura-Mazda sees fit to bless with a birthmark that looks like a lion's paw-print? Yet it is not only the birthmark that tells me you are my boy. I see it in your eyes, also. They are the same eyes as those of the baby I lost that dreadful night.'

Cyrus made no reply.

'You think... you think a mother does not remember her baby's eyes?' Mandane said, through her tears. 'I know your eyes, and I know *you.*'

'What do you mean?'

'I mean that I see the same face I saw that night. I see even the same manner: the quietness, the thoughtfulness. That night, the night you were born, you did not cry. You just looked as if you were thinking about the world and everything in it. The midwife – poor murdered woman! – believed you were mute. But I told her you were just surveying the world you would one day call your own.'

Cyrus sat in silence, looking away from Mandane. Suddenly he turned to her:

'What am I supposed to think about this? What am I supposed to feel? What do you think it is like to have a woman, who until yesterday was a complete stranger, tell me she is my mother, and that the people I thought were my own mother and father were only kind strangers who brought me up from my babyhood?' Cyrus was weeping too now. 'What... what am I supposed to do with the knowledge? What does it mean for me, as a man?'

'It means you must... you must love me as your mother,' Mandane said though her weeping. 'Can you do that, my boy?'

Cyrus just looked at her. 'I don't know, I don't know.'

'You must try. Please.'

'I shall. But nor can I ever forget the vile cruelty visited on Mithradat and Spako, the good man and good woman who I thought were my parents. I shall always love their memory.'

'Cyrus, love their memory, love it. Without them you would not exist.'

Cyrus nodded slowly. 'No, I would not.'

He wiped his eyes with a sleeve, then looked more intently at Mandane. 'If what you say is true... I am the grandson of an abominably wicked king. But we still do not know how I came to be brought up in a village in the countryside. We still do not know what really happened on the night I was taken from you.'

'But Cyrus, we do. Astyages must have indeed commanded Harpagus to take you away and bury you.'

'But then I ask the question you asked before: why did Harpagus not carry out his mission? And why was he angry with Mithradat? Why, for that matter, is Astyages so angry with Harpagus?'

'Harpagus doubtless knows the truth of the matter,' Mandane said.

Cyrus nodded. 'Yes, but he is hardly ever likely to tell *me*, even if I ever get an opportunity to ask him.'

Cyrus fell silent for a few moments, then fixed Mandane with his intent eyes. 'Tell me, why has no group of people loyal to Media and in love with decency and goodness risen to dethrone Astyages? Surely the people here in Ecbatana hate your father as much as those in the countryside do?'

'Some do,' Mandane replied. 'But many do not. All wickedness benefits some people. There are noblemen, Farna-zata for example, who have made great fortunes under my father's reign. But the dungeons of Ecbatana are full of those who have found only despair in the face of my father's power. As for the graveyards throughout Media, they are littered with the corpses of those he has killed – or, in far more cases, commanded to be killed. And I am sure that my wicked father intends you soon to be lying in one of those graveyards.'

'So you think he still wants to kill me now?'

'Of course Astyages will not want to have you killed openly, for he thrives on secret misdeeds and that grand vizier of his is even worse than my wicked father when it comes to duplicity. Of course he will not have you killed where others would see it, he will prefer to arrange an accident of some kind. But be assured, he will want you dead.'

'You are certain of that?'

'As sure as I am that you are indeed my son. You might have died anyway within a few weeks – as so many new babies do – but now you are a man, and what a man you have become! Ahura-Mazda has, I am certain, spared you for greatness. As for my father... if, twenty-five years ago, when you were new-born, he imagined that his nightmare might come true, think of how much more he must believe that now!'

Mandane insisted Cyrus remain with her, in her quarters. 'If Astyages comes for you, or sends his men to fetch you, he or they will have to contend with me. They will have to kill me if they want to take you away. Even Astyages would flinch from killing me, his own daughter.'

'But when you came here,' Cyrus said, 'you must have come with your own soldiers? Can't we summon them to help us?'

'I travelled here with ten Persian soldiers under the command of their captain, yes, but if I bring them here, Astyages shall find out and know for certain I do not trust him. It may provoke him to an action that, unprovoked, he may prefer not to take, or at least not yet.'

'What do you mean? He wants me dead. You said so just now!'

'Yes, but he may for the time being be willing to let you return with me unharmed to Anshan, the Persian capital. He knows Persia is always at his mercy, and that he can order your death at any time. He is a very difficult man to predict. However, I have some means of defence of my *own*.'

Saying this, Mandane took out from a nearby drawer a dagger whose handle was encrusted with emeralds.

'Are you going to give that to me, so I can defend us?' Cyrus asked.

'No, I will keep it, and if they come for us *I* will defend us, to the death if necessary.'

Cyrus shook his head. 'Perhaps you are indeed my real mother, as you say. I don't know. But what I do know is that you are the queen of Persia, not a warrior.'

And gently, but firmly, he prised the weapon from Mandane's long, smooth, well-manicured but surprisingly strong fingers, then held it in his own expert and much stronger grasp.

They waited, and talked together. Cyrus told Mandane something about his past life, of its joys as well as its sorrows.

Slowly, slowly, despite himself, he really did begin to wonder if it might truly be possible that this woman, the daughter of that monster Astyages, this woman who was the queen of Persia, truly was his mother.

He told her about his friends, Roshan, Raiva and Asha, and how he feared they were dead.

'Raiva was foolish to believe rumours he had heard about a caravan passing through the village where your father's men ambushed us,' Cyrus said. 'But I was even more foolish in agreeing with his plan. I had often thought he brought his ideas and suggestions to my attention with an insistence that made me think *he* wanted to be leader. I should have followed my instincts and not bowed to his suggestion. But as his friend, I loved him, so I did.'

'And do you love Roshan, too?' Mandane asked.

Cyrus, noticing that she had asked the question in the present tense, felt his face glowing. 'Roshan and I were friends ever since childhood,' he said, quietly.

'"Were friends"? What do you mean?'

'I mean that, as I said, I am sure she is dead.'

'She may not be. She may be waiting for you.'

Cyrus shook his head. 'I cannot believe that.'

Telling Mandane about his life, Cyrus realized how hard it had been and how difficult the constant struggle for survival was. Slowly, he found himself daring to hope that a new life, perhaps indeed a completely new one, might be coming into view.

And now... if what Mandane said was true, he had in truth been born a Persian. He had been born a Persian, for all that he did not speak the particular tongue of the Persians. But yes, he was a Persian, and the Persian god Ahura-Mazda – who must become henceforth *his* god – had conferred on him the greatest, indeed so great as to be almost beyond imagining, of blessings...

Well, perhaps it *was* true? Cyrus was prepared to consider that it might be, for all that it was so difficult to believe that his true parents were not, after all, Mithradat and Spako, but the king of Persia whom he had yet to meet, and the beautiful woman sitting here, next to him, her eyes moist with maternal love.

And so if it *was* true?

Then henceforth life would be very different from what it had been... he might even have a chance to make a mark on the world.

They went on waiting. Sometime in the late morning, there was an urgent double knock on the door of Mandane's suite of rooms.

Mandane glanced quickly at Cyrus, then at the door. 'Who is it?' she called in a low tone through the door. Her voice was at once hoarse with worry.

'It is I, Astyages.'

'Father!' exclaimed Mandane, in a voice Cyrus could tell she obviously meant to be friendly, but he heard the tension and fear in it. Cyrus wondered whether Astyages was alone.

'How are you, father?' Mandane asked, still without opening the door.

'I am well, daughter, thank you. I came only to say that you and your new-found son are to be guests of honour at a celebratory luncheon I am giving later, to hail my grandson's return.'

'Thank you... thank you, father,' Mandane replied.

She waited, still not opening the door, as if to see whether Astyages wanted to come in. Cyrus waited too. His eyes glanced at the dagger in his hands.

But Astyages did not ask to be admitted, nor in fact did he say anything else, except a quick, barked farewell. Mandane stayed by the door, listening, until the sound of the king's footsteps had died down in the corridor.

'Why do you think he came in person to tell us of the luncheon instead of sending a servant?' Cyrus asked.

'I suppose to show us the sincerity of his desire to entertain us,' Mandane said. 'I think it's a good sign.'

'Unless he plans to poison me,' Cyrus said.

'In front of me? He would never do that. No, Cyrus, I think... yes, I do dare to think... that we will soon be able to leave safely for Anshan.'

Astyages had evidently spared no expense or effort for the luncheon. He ordered the serving of a lavish feast, attended by the courtiers in all their finery.

Farna-zata and Harpagus, however, were noticeable by their absence.

Mandane had told Cyrus before the banquet only to eat what she ate; Astyages gave no sign of noticing that Cyrus was scrupulously obeying this instruction.

But there are other ways for him to kill me, Cyrus thought.

When the luncheon was well advanced, Farna-zata clapped his hands loudly for silence. 'The king shall speak!' the grand vizier exclaimed.

Astyages waited until complete silence reigned in the large banqueting-hall, then intoned:

'Yesterday a miracle from the wisdom and mercy of Mithra, brought my beloved grandson back into my arms!' Astyages exclaimed to everyone, once most of the elaborate and abundant dishes on the table had been eaten. 'Please join with me in this toast to my daughter and my grandson.'

The king toasted Mandane and Cyrus several times, and the courtiers joined in enthusiastically.

The king questioned him courteously about his life. As Cyrus hesitatingly related the main events, carefully omitting anything about the murder of the people he had until the previous day regarded as his parents, Astyages looked on in what really did seem like a kindly way.

After luncheon, while a strong Median wine was passed round in small metal cups, Astyages suddenly stood up and, addressing his guests, said:

'After such a long and much-grieved absence, I would like my grandson to spend many weeks here in my company. However, a king cannot be so selfish. I have therefore decided that this afternoon, I shall bid a sad farewell to my daughter and new-found grandson, in order that they may journey in the royal caravan to Persia and Cyrus may meet his long-lost father, my dear daughter's husband Cambyses, whom I regard as a son. Of course, they will be accompanied by the brave Persian soldiers who brought them here.'

Astyages smiled at Cyrus, and then at Mandane, as if he were the kindest and most benevolent king in the world.

That afternoon, Farna-zata waited too, cowering in his suite of expensively-furnished rooms, his back and buttocks still red from the vicious beating the utterly furious Astyages had given him. The grand vizier existed in a terrible fear that at any moment the king might change his mind about not ordering his execution.

Farna-zata's servants tiptoed around him, fearing that if they annoyed him, even by accident, he might whip *them*.

In private, Farna-zata cursed Harpagus for having failed in his mission. Harpagus cursed Mandane for having been delivered of a baby boy at all a quarter of a century since, and of course both men cursed Cyrus. As for Astyages, right now *he* cursed just about everyone... but not Cyrus or Mandane, or at least not to their faces.

And so the whole court trembled. And because the court was the centre of life in Ecbatana, the city trembled, too.

Harpagus waited.

Finally, later in the afternoon – by which time the royal carriage had already left for Persia – a messenger from the king arrived at Harpagus's home in Ecbatana to tell Harpagus that he had been summoned to see the king.

'The king also wants to see your son Artabaz,' the messenger informed him.

Artabaz was a strong, good-looking boy of thirteen who was already in training to be a soldier of Media and had shown promising skill with a sword and the spear. Harpagus's wife, whom he had greatly loved, had died some years ago in childbirth and their other children had died young, as was so often the case even with children of the wealthiest and most distinguished Median citizens. Artabaz was the sole child remaining to Harpagus, and now the only family Harpagus had.

The boy was much admired by the girls of the town. He was rather prone to boasting about his father, and the fact that his father knew and was much favoured by the king. But that particular morning Artabaz, who had divined that his father was in some sort of disgrace, had been careful not to boast to anyone about anything.

Harpagus, trembling inwardly but doing his utmost to give the appearance of being calm and noble, though contrite, led his beloved son into the royal presence. Harpagus, who had heard about Farna-zata's beating, was braced for the king to fall into another great fury.

Astyages was sitting at a table in the principal royal dining-room, whose walls were hung with shields and swords. The curtains and carpets were of sumptuous silks and satins.

Harpagus, to his astonishment, saw that Astyages was smiling. The king stood up and walked in stately fashion towards him and Artabaz. The general and his son bowed in the royal presence.

'My greetings to you, Harpagus,' the king said, 'and also to your excellent boy. I have heard, Artabaz, that you are progressing well in your military training?'

'Yes... yes, sire,' Artabaz replied, though in a nervous-sounding voice.

'And why do you train so hard, Artabaz?' Astyages asked.

'So that... so that I may become a skilled warrior, sire,' said Artabaz, now with more confidence, 'and one day serve you, great king, by fighting in your army against your enemies.'

Harpagus saw Astyages smile, reach out his left arm and put it around his son's shoulders.

'Your son is a fine young man,' Astyages said to the general. 'Harpagus, I will not deny that you disappointed me immensely yesterday, but a wise and good king must always be prepared to forgive and forget.'

Astyages smiled again. Harpagus could hardly believe what he was hearing. He thought: *surely Mithra is blessing me. I shall sacrifice two of my fattest sheep.*

'Yes,' Astyages murmured, 'only the totally powerful can be truly merciful. Harpagus, I have decided that as a mark of my mercy, I will hold a banquet this evening for you and a few of your fellow generals. One of my farmers in the west has reared a particularly large and delicious boar that I shall have the royal kitchen serve. Please return here when the light of day begins to fade.'

Harpagus bowed to his monarch. 'Thank you, your Majesty,' he said.

'As for Artabaz,' Astyages said, 'I would like to become better acquainted with him. I wish him to stay here with me this afternoon. It will be a pleasure for me to spend time with such an excellent young man.'

Your Majesty,' Harpagus replied. 'I am greatly delighted at the prospect of Artabaz being privileged to spend time with you.'

A few moments later Harpagus, having bowed yet again to his king, left the room, backing away from Astyages without turning his back, as was always essential when leaving the presence of the man who ruled Media.

Only when Harpagus was out of the room and walking down the stone corridor that led to the military barracks, where he had his own large and luxurious apartment, did he start to breathe normally again.

Thanks be to Mithra, Astyages has forgiven me.

Harpagus prepared for the evening banquet carefully, bathing in the afternoon and ordering one of his female slaves to trim his beard.

Finally, the giant general, who had thought himself an outcast from royal favour forever, dressed himself in his finest robes and best sandals.

By the time Harpagus left his apartment to walk the short distance to the royal palace, he was convinced the king had forgiven him.

His Majesty has doubtless reflected that the charge he entrusted to me a quarter of a century ago was too cruel to entrust to any man. He has surely also realized that his instruction, conveyed to me through that scheming scoundrel Farna-zata, was one his Majesty is glad I did not carry out. After all, Astyages now has a grandson, and a fine man the grandson is!

When Harpagus reached the banqueting room, he was intrigued to see that there was no one else there apart from the king, and that Astyages was already seated.

It was a beautiful polished wooden table. Harpagus knew it had been made in Babylon. Lengthy enough to accommodate at least a score of guests on either side, the table was laid for only two people; the king, who was already sitting about half-way up one side of the table, and the guest's place-setting directly opposite.

The cutlery was gold-plated and the goblets made of silver. Harpagus noticed that there were even some goblets fashioned from the wondrous, fantastically expensive, magical substance that looked like water but was as hard as iron; the strange material known as *glass*. Harpagus had heard that Astyages had some glass goblets used on special occasions.

Astyages rose from his place-setting on seeing Harpagus arrive. 'Welcome, my friend,' the king said. 'Please be seated. As you see, I decided after all not to invite any of your colleagues. I wished to enjoy the pleasure of your company only.'

'Thank you sire,' Harpagus said, tentatively sitting down at the place-setting before him.

The thoughts *is he going to poison me? Will this be my last supper?* rushed through his mind, but Harpagus managed to dismiss them and replace them with the thought *surely, if he wanted to kill me, I would be dead already.*

Harpagus cleared his throat. 'How is Artabaz, your Majesty?'

'Oh, he shall be joining us soon,' replied Astyages cheerfully. He smiled. 'It is good to have a son, is it not?'

'Yes, indeed, sire,' replied Harpagus, allowing himself to relax a little.

'I, alas, have never had a son,' Astyages said, 'for I believed that I would best serve the interests of my people, for whom I sacrifice my own inclinations daily, if I did not marry. You see, Harpagus, I wish to devote all my energies to the welfare of my country.'

Harpagus smiled. 'Indeed, sire, all Media knows the immense sacrifices you make for your people.'

'I should hope they do, Harpagus. Still,' the king smiled faintly, 'at least I have a grandson now.'

Harpagus said nothing.

'Come, my Harpagus,' said Astyages, 'surely you wish to ask me about him? After all, without you I would not have him, would I?'

Harpagus felt extremely awkward. But he knew he had to say something, so he cleared his throat and said, 'Is your new-found grandson Cyrus staying in Ecbatana for a while, so that you may enjoy being with him and Queen Mandane?'

'No, Harpagus, for much as I wish to spend time with him, I thought it only fair that my daughter Mandane should take her long-lost son to meet his father. They have already left for Persia.'

Harpagus felt more confident about his own safety than ever. He was certain now that Astyages had finally come to be happy about Cyrus's survival and even grateful for it. *Yes, surely that's what's happened. After all, why else would Astyages have allowed Cyrus and Mandane to travel to Persia?*

'May Mithra speed them on their journey,' Harpagus volunteered.

'May he indeed,' said Astyages. 'Let us drink a toast to that.'

Harpagus willingly did so, drinking with Astyages a toast of a delicious jet-black wine from a glass goblet, the first time Harpagus had drunk from glass in his entire life. The sensation of the glass on his lips felt so much cooler and more pleasurable than the feel of tin or glazed pottery.

He thought the dinner with the king was proving a surprising success.

It was true that it did seem strange to Harpagus that there was no place-setting for Artabaz, as the king had said he planned for the boy to join them later, but Harpagus assumed that a place would be laid for Artabaz when the lad arrived.

Astyages clapped his hand three times. Immediately a servant, who had been waiting behind one of the silk screens at the back of the dining-room, stepped from behind the screen. On a tray he was carrying a large silver dish covered in a capacious lid. The servant set the dish on the table, then bowed to the king and went back behind the screen.

Astyages got up and walked over to the large serving-dish. 'It gives me so much pleasure to serve you this pig,' he said, with a glance and a smile at Harpagus, 'that I will carve it for you myself.'

Astyages removed the lid, revealing a large roast joint. The meat was evidently very well cooked. Harpagus thought it smelt wonderful.

There was a sharp-looking serving knife and fork next to the roast. The king wielded these, Harpagus thought, with considerable dexterity, carving several slices of the meat and placing them onto a plate for Harpagus. Harpagus, feeling supremely honoured at the king carving for him, wondered whether he now dared finally trust Astyages and believe that the king had forgiven him. Surely this extraordinary royal gesture meant he could?

As Harpagus was considering this, another servant brought a dish containing vegetables and rice. Finally, Harpagus found set before him a large plate of the succulent meat. He served himself vegetables and rice. The king personally poured Harpagus, and then himself, another glass of red wine, smiling as he did so and saying 'I know how much you enjoy wine, Harpagus, and this banquet is in your honour. Please feel free to finish the content of the wine-skin, with my blessing.'

Harpagus drank more of the wine from the glass goblet. Astyages drank, too, and smiled at Harpagus.

'You are not eating anything yourself, sire?' Harpagus asked good-naturedly, allowing an enormous sense of relief to wash over him, and finally beginning to relax a little.

'No, my Harpagus, I am not especially hungry. But it will be my pleasure to watch you dine.'

The king returned to his own place. Astyages smiled as he looked across the table towards Harpagus, who at once began his supper, fully aware that hospitality of this degree was hardly a commonplace offering by Astyages and that it would unthinkable not to accept it.

The meat possessed a succulence and strong flavour that Harpagus had never tasted before.

Harpagus soon finished his plate of meat and vegetables. As soon as he had, the king carved more meat for his general, whilst the servant reappeared and heaped more vegetables on Harpagus's plate.

Again Astyages retreated to his own place-setting and made polite conversation while Harpagus ate. Harpagus was beginning to feel rather full, but he finished every scrap of his second helping.

The king, having seen that Harpagus had finished his meal, stood up and, still smiling, said: 'the meat was delightful, was it not?'

'Yes, your Majesty.'

Astyages nodded. 'Of course, I have the finest chefs in the land. They know exactly how to joint a creature to yield the largest amount of the most delicious meat.' Astyages paused for a moment, then added: 'Of course, when one does joint an animal, there are inevitably some parts that must be discarded because they are inedible.'

'Yes, sire, I can well imagine that.'

Astyages smiled at Harpagus, got to his feet and clapped his hands again. Two more servants arrived carrying a large serving-dish, with a lid, identical to the one from which the delicious meat had been served.

The two servants placed the second dish on the table. Astyages clapped his hands again. The servants left the table and vanished behind the screen.

Astyages walked toward the second serving-dish, put his hand on the lid, and stared at Harpagus.

The king's stare no longer bore even the faintest hint of a smile.

'*You betrayed me*,' the king said, his voice sounding to Harpagus as full of menace as the hiss of a desert cobra. '*You betrayed me. You failed to carry out the instructions Farna-zata ordered you to carry out on my behalf. You let my grandson live. Learn, now, what happens to those who defy the most powerful king in our world.*'

Saying this, Astyages raised the lid of the second serving-dish.

Harpagus, terror striking within his soul, wanted to avert his gaze, but felt absolutely certain that if he did the king would instantly command his execution. And so Harpagus kept looking at the king as Astyages raised the lid.

On the serving-dish, obviously well-roasted but nonetheless clearly recognizable, were the head, hands, and feet of Artabaz.

There was an expression of terror on the boy's roasted face. His cooked eyes were white and opaque.

Harpagus just stared at the sight, simply unable, at least for the moment, to believe that what he was seeing could be real.

'I do hope you enjoyed your supper, Harpagus,' Astyages said. 'Oh, by the way, I have some of your boy's blood here, now.'

Taking hold of a small white porcelain Chinese jug in one hand, and a glass goblet in the other, Astyages poured himself a measure of what was very obviously blood. Astyages raised the goblet to his lips, drank a little, then set the glass down. His lips were stained bright red.

'This toast is to the safe journey of Mandane and Cyrus,' Astyages said, in a gloating voice.

Harpagus just stared at his king's bloody mouth, and then, again, at the roasted remains of Artabaz in the serving-dish.

Only now did the reality of the unspeakable, appalling vileness of the sight overwhelm him.

As it did, Harpagus's stomach spontaneously ejected its contents over the table, and the cold-blooded slayer of Mithradat and the commander of the men who had killed Spako, saw nothing but black fog, then collapsed onto the cold limestone floor.

14. Trust

'Relax on your journey and be comfortable,' Astyages had urged Cyrus and Mandane just before Mandane's caravan – which consisted of two carriages, each pulled by six strong black stallions – left the royal palace.

'My thanks to you, father,' Mandane replied, before kissing Astyages on each cheek. Astyages embraced her, holding her close to him for some time, then released her. Cyrus could tell how relieved she looked at the prospect of journeying home.

But Cyrus didn't feel comfortable.

He knew that now it was possible he was being excessively acute in his sensitivity to danger and in his anxiety, but he also knew he hadn't managed to survive to the age of twenty-five in an arid and violent land without being acutely sensitive in that respect, and lucky too.

Queen Mandane said Astyages wants me dead. If he does, and wants to absolve himself of any responsibility for killing me, just as he did when I was a baby – he only has to bribe my mother's soldiers.

Cyrus thought of this as he looked out at the landscape around them. It was wild, beautiful and raw in the way only the desert can be. Rugged hills in the distance, the same light brown colour as the ground, undulated unevenly alongside the valley through which the caravan was now passing. Farther away, strangely ghostly in the haze, a ridge of snow-capped mountains to the north and the south spoke, Cyrus thought, with silent eloquence of the vastness of the desert and the insignificance of man's troubles and aspirations against the splendour of the natural world Ahura-Mazda had forged in his might and wisdom. And as Cyrus thought of this, he recalled every word of the silent prayer he had made to Ahura-Mazda in the king's throne room, while anticipating death on the morrow.

I might still die today, Cyrus thought.

Cyrus cast a sidelong glance at the Persian captain whom, Cyrus understood, Astyages had personally charged with responsibility for ensuring that Cyrus reached the Persian capital of Anshan safely. All the other soldiers accompanying the caravan were the Persian soldiers who had come to Ecbatana with Mandane.

They had now been travelling all morning. Cyrus had tried a few conversational sorties on the captain without much success.

Mandane was not there to smooth Cyrus's social path, for at the moment she was inside her own caravan, resting or asleep.

It was not that the captain was discourteous; on the contrary, he always called Cyrus 'your highness' and bowed his head to him when they spoke in the Persian language that Cyrus had no problem understanding, and whose dialect he found appealing even on the lips of the gruff captain. But the captain was evidently was more interested in scouring the countryside with his dark, intense eyes than talking of trivialities. Cyrus had felt compelled to speak of such mundane matters, for he did not think it would have been advisable to have asked the captain the question that most preyed on his mind: *has my grandfather paid you and the nine other soldiers under your command to kill me?*

Cyrus wondered whether, if Astyages had bribed the Persian soldiers, he would have instructed them to kill Mandane too.

But *had* Astyages bribed them? Barring asking the captain the question, the only way to try to find the answer seemed to Cyrus to take sidelong glances at the captain from time to time, and at the other Persian soldiers, to try to detect whether their eyes or expressions betrayed how they really felt.

Cyrus had not seen anything that gave him a clue.

And so the caravan rode on through the valley.

Cyrus noticed that now the ridges of hills on either side were growing narrower, the path steeper, and that the mountains, while still remote, were closer than they had been before. Cyrus had never travelled from Ecbatana to Anshan, but he had no problem recognizing the approach of a mountain pass.

He felt even more tense than he had at any stage of the journey, and he knew why. He and his band had often used mountain passes as their ambush points.

The path became yet steeper as the caravan drew closer to the pass. Cyrus could tell that their direction through the pass was easterly, for on the far side, through the narrowing gap, he saw the first signs of dusk in the sky. *No doubt we'll be making camp for the night soon after we get through the pass*, Cyrus thought, then realized, with a sudden stab of unaccustomed fear, that he had deliberately stopped himself wondering how he was going to protect his mother and himself at night if the soldiers turned traitor. But now he did think about this, and the thought filled his mind, for he knew that he could hardly stay awake all night...

Still the caravan continued to approach the pass.

The captain suddenly barked out an order, '*Prepare!*' An instant later, Cyrus heard the swift clink and rattle of iron swords being drawn from bronze scabbards. Cyrus felt his muscles flex as he prepared himself for battle. He wondered, if it came to a fight, how many soldiers he could kill. *Three? Four? Perhaps five if I'm lucky. I'll go for the captain first. If I can manage to kill him, the others will be more afraid than if I start with any of them.*

Cyrus's greatly muscled body was already tense with anticipation. *The captain is right-handed, and I'm on his left, so he's likely to wheel to the left. The instant he does, I'll close in on him. My dagger will have an advantage over his sword at close range.*

Cyrus, prepared for sudden combat with the taciturn captain, was not prepared for what did happen, which was, in fact...

... nothing.

Nothing other than that the caravan simply continued toward the pass, though now the soldiers who guarded its precious royal human cargo had drawn their swords.

Cyrus breathed again. *I'm a suspicious, untrusting fool. These soldiers are here at the command of my second mother. They're Persian, like my second father whom I shall soon be seeing. They're loyal to my second mother... if that is indeed truly who Mandane is.*

Cyrus looked up to the high ridges of the pass ahead, though inwardly he hardly noticed what he was seeing. And it was there, on the high ridge on the left, perhaps a hundred paces away, that he saw some of the sparse grass move in a way that could not have been caused by the wind.

His heart began beating fast.

An instant later he averted his gaze.

He wondered whether the captain or any of the other soldiers had seen the grass move too. Cyrus didn't think so, for if they had, they had no reason to keep quiet about it.

When he looked again, the grass was no longer moving.

But Cyrus had seen it.

15. Eagle Eyes

A pair of piercing eyes had just that moment turned away from peering down at the passing caravan – and especially at Cyrus – from the summit of the ridge.

The owner of the eyes wiped a tear from them so that she could again see with perfect clarity.

What the eyes saw, now, was not Cyrus but that a soldier, riding at the back of the rear caravan, had fitted an arrow into his bow and was bending the bow to fire...

The bowman's horse was, for a moment, unsteady on an uneven stretch of path. The bowman waited to get a steady aim, confident that the man he had to kill would remain the easiest of targets.

That was true enough. Cyrus, riding at the front of the caravan, had not seen the bowman.

Barely ten seconds later, the bowman's horse was walking on even terrain again. Now, however, the bowman was in no position to fire his arrow, for another, loosed a few moments ago from the hillside, had drilled a neat hole through his head, having entered via one ear-hole and exited through the other. The spongy mass of the bowman's brain had slowed the arrow to a standstill, with the result that the arrow-tip was peeking out of the bowman's left ear like the head of a shy turtle.

The captain saw the bowman fall. The captain was sure the arrow from the hillside had merely been a lucky shot. He had no fear himself; no-one, surely, could be that lucky a second time. He shouted out to the other soldiers to look out for bandits on the hillside, yet even as the captain shouted this he thought *I shall finish the prince myself.* The captain's sword was already drawn, but he was right-handed, so – just as Cyrus had anticipated – he began to wheel his horse to the left.

Cyrus stared at the captain for an instant, then propelled his horse towards the captain's.

'*Traitor!*' Cyrus hissed, cursing himself now for being so trusting. He already had the dagger in his right hand, and his muscles were contracting as he propelled himself toward the captain's horse.

The captain, astonished by the speed of Cyrus's reaction, gave a curse, and a stream of insults spewed from his mouth. Then there followed a frantic and alarming *whoosh* sound in the air.

A moment later, the captain stopped hurling insults, unable to speak. Cyrus saw that a second arrow, fired with extraordinary accuracy, had struck three inches deep into the captain's neck.

Blood was jetting from the hole the arrow had made. The captain dropped his sword, groaned, and grasped desperately at the dart, as if he somehow imagined he could remove it and cure himself. But even as he clutched at his neck the wound drained strength from his arms. Cyrus watched as the captain's head sagged. The blood continued to spurt from the captain's neck. He fell from his horse, landing heavily on the ground, dead before he reached it.

As the captain hit the hard earth a gold bracelet rolled out of a pocket in his tunic and came to rest in the hot sand.

Cyrus glanced at the bracelet. He recognized it immediately.

It was the bracelet of the griffins.

The instant Cyrus saw the bracelet, he realized that Astyages could never be trusted.

There was another *whoosh*, and now a third soldier fell, this time the arrow piercing his heart. Cyrus needed no more prompting. Wheeling with all his might, he launched a vicious simultaneous attack on two of the soldiers closest by him. They did their best, but he was Cyrus, for all that he was not yet Cyrus the Great. A few moments later, and the two soldiers' treachery was permanently over.

As for the other five soldiers, seeing Cyrus in deadly action, and then also seeing about thirty men and women rushing down the hard slope of the hill, all armed with swords and some with bows too, the soldiers had the good sense to throw down their weapons and surrender. There were children too, among the band of stragglers, but they stayed behind the ridge of the hill, out of sight for the moment.

Cyrus watched the soldiers drop their weapons. His sword in his hand, he made them back away, calling them traitors. The soldiers fell on their knees and begged for mercy. Cyrus was about to behead them all personally, so angry was he, yet something new in his soul, some new dignity, some new sense of his destiny... checked his impetuousness. He had also suddenly reflected that it was his impetuousness that had impelled him to lead his followers into the village where the trap had been sprung and that that had led to so many of his followers being killed, and would have led to his own death, too, had it not been for the astonishing events that had followed.

Only now did Cyrus permit himself the privilege of a glance up at the slope, whereupon he saw... leading the charge, her bow in her hand and arrows in her quiver...

Roshan.

He gasped. At once he knew that it was she who had fired all three arrows, she who had saved his life.

He dismounted in an instant and ran toward her. They met on the hillside in a passionate embrace, as if, for a moment, they had forgotten that they were only friends.

16. The Queen of Persia

'I knew that you would be taken to Ecbatana and forced to face that vile dragon of a king,' Roshan said.

She was riding next to Cyrus on the captain's stallion. They had left the treacherous Persian captain's body to the falcons of the desert. This was an ambush almost beyond crediting. The other two riderless and ownerless horses had been commandeered by Raiva and Asha.

Speaking the Persian language, the five remaining treacherous soldiers began hastily blaming everything that had happened on the dead captain, who had, they explained, indeed been paid by Astyages to kill Cyrus. Cyrus, threatening the five soldiers on pain of death to tell the truth, soon extracted from them the information that they had accepted money to help the captain, and had been promised a high rank in the Median army when they returned to Ecbatana after completing the assassination. The plan had been to murder Cyrus on the mountain path, when the queen was asleep in her caravan, and blame his death on marauding bandits.

Cyrus, having heard their abject attempts to shift the blame from themselves, told the soldiers that he would indeed spare them, but that if their plot had involved killing Mandane, he would not have done so. Privately, he was glad he had not killed them in his impetuous anger, for he realized that it was only because he had let them live that he had heard the truth about the plot.

'When we reach Persia you shall all be ejected from the army and set to work on menial tasks,' Cyrus told them. 'You should all thank Ahura-Mazda that I am a more merciful man than he who bribed you to kill me.'

Mandane told the guards that if she had been their judge, not her 'merciful son', they would all be dead by now.

She glanced at Cyrus. 'We must proceed to Persia with all haste. Only when we are there do we have a chance of being safe.'

At once the caravan began moving again. The soldiers were now all unarmed and on foot, their shamefaced expressions telling a world of humiliation, embarrassment, and profound gratitude to Cyrus for his mercy. The remainder of the small band of bandits whom Roshan, Raiva and Asha had gathered together rode with the caravan.

'This scented noblewoman here is right, Cyrus,' Roshan said. 'Any Persian soldier who accepted a bribe to kill you deserves nothing less than instant execution. Astyages and his family are all the same. Greedy and murderous butchers!'

She glanced at Mandane, then at Cyrus. 'You still haven't told us who this woman is, with her soft hands and expensive perfume.'

'Greetings from a greedy and murderous butcher,' Mandane said, with a faint smile, looking at Roshan.

Roshan glanced back at her, and then at Cyrus. 'I don't understand.'

'My dear friend and saviour of my life,' Cyrus said to her, giving her an affectionate smile, 'even I, who am at the centre of the extraordinary events of the past few days, can hardly understand them, so how could you be expected to do so? It seems that the Persian god, Ahura-Mazda, has blessed me, for I was born a prince of Persia, but did not know that. Now, I do. There is much more to tell you, and as we proceed to Anshan you will hear it all. But let me, for the moment, introduce to you Mandane, the queen of Persia, my second mother.'

Roshan just stared at Mandane. 'Astyages is your father?'

Mandane gave a nod. 'Yes. But no-one can choose their father, can they? Ever since I was a girl I have known how desperately wicked Cyrus's grandfather truly is.'

For the first time Cyrus could ever remember, Roshan seemed lost for words.

And indeed some time passed before Roshan turned again to Mandane, to speak to her.

'Your son is the rarest and best of men,' Roshan said. 'I don't believe there is a farmer or peasant in Media who would not risk his life to follow him against the tyrant in Ecbatana, if only they knew of Cyrus and what manner of man he is.'

Cyrus glanced at Roshan. He had never heard her speak so openly about him before to anyone. He did not know what to say.

Mandane smiled. 'My dear Roshan, I hardly know my beloved son, but I don't doubt that what you are saying is true. And you, Roshan, you saved my son's life. When we reach Anshan I shall ennoble you. You shall become a lady of Persia.'

Roshan shook her head. 'I thank you for your kindness, but I think you are planning to ennoble the wrong person. I am a poor orphaned peasant-girl from the small town of Paritakna, nothing more.'

'To me, Roshan, you are the closest I have ever had to a daughter,' Mandane replied, 'for without you, and your eyes of an eagle, I would have lost my son today. Yes, you are my daughter, and a lady in rank already, if not yet in name.'

Cyrus saw tears welling in Roshan's eyes. 'Thank you... thank you.'

Roshan sat in silence for a few moments, looking sad and thoughtful, then glanced at Cyrus. 'So... we are going to Anshan, where you shall be the prince of Persia?'

'So it seems,' Cyrus said. 'And I believe that there, in the realm of Persia, we shall all have a new life. A new life, and a new destiny.'

'I myself believe,' Mandane said, 'that Ahura-Mazda has a particularly great destiny in store for you, my son.'

She fell silent. Roshan glanced at Mandane, then said quietly, with mischief in her voice:

'And what destiny do you think Ahura-Mazda has in store for your son in the realm of love?'

'My dear Roshan,' Mandane replied, 'I am sure that the great and all-wise Ahura-Mazda, being a man, is content to leave that decision to the right woman.'

'And who might that woman be, do you think?' Roshan asked.

The queen of Persia looked at Cyrus, then back at Roshan, but gave no indication of what thoughts might have been playing through her mind.

BOOK TWO

THE EMPIRE

17. At Anshan

Anshan's stone towers and the porticoes of its temples rose high above the surrounding city wall.

As Cyrus and his party reached the northern gate of the Persian capital, the guards stationed there bowed to their queen and sent word to the royal palace that the queen had returned; with, inexplicably, a ragged band of people who appeared to be her protectors.

The queen, and the newcomers, including the man she was calling her son, passed through the gateway and into the city of Anshan itself.

Cyrus already knew that Anshan was much smaller than Ecbatana. But he could see, in the bustling bazaars, busy streets and bright faces of the people, that the city was full of life. Almost as soon as he arrived he felt that the Persian capital had a friendliness about it that he had never detected in Ecbatana during his short stay there, even after the prospect of being beheaded by one of Astyages's concubines had receded.

As the caravan began journeying through a main street of the city, in the direction of the royal palace, the people of the city saw their queen at the head of the procession and bowed as the party passed. The people had fresh faces that seemed to Cyrus full of life and hope.

They must know about Astyages, what he is and what he does, Cyrus thought. *But here in Anshan the tyrant is far away.*

'The women here are amazing,' Raiva murmured. 'I could certainly grow to like this place.'

They passed a particularly gorgeous creature, dressed in plain clothes but with the face of an angel, selling oranges in the street from a wicker basket.

'If she's married,' Raiva said, quietly, 'I hope her husband falls out of an orange-tree head-first before the sun sets. Or, if he's in the army, I hope he's fighting some campaign against a tribe that never takes prisoners.'

Asha laughed, and Farna-dukta laughed because Asha laughed; as she still spoke little more than a few words of Persian, Cyrus didn't imagine she would have understood what her brother-in-law had said.

Cyrus smiled, but gave Raiva a brief sidelong glance and thought *he's saying this as a joke, but he means it. He would be that ruthless to get a woman he really wants.*

The royal palace at Anshan, a building of white clay and stone, was of only modest size compared with Astyages's palace at Ecbatana. Still, Cyrus somehow felt there was something comforting and warm-hearted about its appearance, and not only because Astyages didn't reside there.

The guards standing outside instantly recognised Mandane and bowed to her. The royal carriage was left in a courtyard, the horses taken to the stables to be fed and watered, and the surviving treacherous soldiers placed under arrest under Mandane's orders. The guards admitted Mandane, Cyrus, and the others who were the remnants of Cyrus's band, about two score including the children, across a foot-bridge over the moat that encircled the palace.

Mandane told them all to follow her into the main part of the palace. There, she said, they would take Cyrus and his three closest friends to meet the king, once they'd bathed and put on the clean clothes she had given them.

Mandane placed the children in the care of one of her maidservants, asking her to take the children to be bathed and given new clothes in the palace nursery. This, she explained to Cyrus, was for the use of the children of the courtiers. She also told Cyrus she would personally arrange for everyone who had come with him to be given accommodation in Anshan. Once she had done so, she asked Cyrus, Roshan, Raiva, Asha and Farna-dukta to follow her.

'Where are we going?' Cyrus asked.

Mandane smiled at him. 'You shall see.'

She led them down a long, winding corridor whose walls were of polished wood. Finally, they reached a plain wooden door. Mandane knocked on it and opened it without waiting for an invitation to enter.

Cyrus followed her into a room that was about the same size as the tyrant Astyages's throne room, but whose walls had wooden panels on them, not the limestone of the throne room of the royal palace at Ecbatana.

In the middle of the room was a shallow pool of water whose diameter was about four times the height of an average man. There was a flat rock in the middle that rose to perhaps half a man's height above the surface.

On this rock, a man wearing a white gown of cotton or linen was sitting perfectly still, facing the direction in which Mandane, Cyrus and his party had entered. The man's eyes were closed. Moreover, he gave no sign of having noticed the visitors.

The water was still, and as calm as one of the winter ponds that Cyrus had so often seen; shallow ponds dug beside a shaded wall of a town or village so that ice could be gathered from the top when the breeze of the winter evening froze the surface.

'That is your father,' whispered Mandane to Cyrus.

Cyrus nodded slowly, then murmured a question to his second mother:

'What is he doing?'

Mandane glanced at him. 'Meditating.'

'What's that?' asked Cyrus.

'You shall see.'

The king sat in silence, apparently oblivious to anybody else. The others all watched just as Cyrus did. No-one said a word.

The king suddenly started to rise slowly to his feet. As he did, he lifted into the air a sword that his body had concealed from view: an elaborate scimitar with a characteristic curved blade that was much wider at the end than near the handle. As the king raised the sword, a mysterious voice that seemed to come from behind the room suddenly spoke in a deep, measured intonation, and with a slight accent.

'*The mountain,*' the voice said.

The king lifted the sword high above his head, holding its handle with both hands. The king remained motionless in this curious position.

The voice sounded again.

'*The river,*' the voice said.

Now, the king began waving the sword slowly in an undulating fashion as if the sword were indeed a flowing river.

Again Cyrus heard the dark intonation of the voice.

'*The scorpion,*' the voice murmured.

This time, the king manipulated his scimitar with extraordinary speed and accuracy, as if the weapon might indeed have been the darting sting of a scorpion confronted by an enemy or prey looking for the best opportunity to strike.

The sword became a blur. Finally, the king brought the weapon to rest, holding it horizontally in the direction of Cyrus and his party.

Mandane gave a half-smile. Cyrus, glancing at her, presumed this was not the first time she had witnessed this demonstration.

But for Cyrus it was a revelation and an astonishing display, not only of swordsmanship but also of dexterity and yet, in a strange way, stillness. Throughout the display, the king's eyes had remained closed. Cyrus imagined this was because the exercise and the king's concentration were so intense that the king felt that to have opened his eyes would have simply distracted him and made his gestures less precise.

Pride swirled within Cyrus. *So this must be my real father; my second father, the father Astyages tried to steal from me.*

Only now did the king slowly open his eyes and look over to where Mandane, Cyrus and the others stood. The king put his scimitar down onto the flat rock, stepped gracefully off the rock, took a few steps in the water of the shallow pool and lifted himself up onto the margin of smooth brown stone that surrounded the pool.

The king at once came over toward Mandane.

He smiled at her, admiring her. 'My love, you are more beautiful and radiant than ever. Your stay at Ecbatana has made my queen more beautiful than the finest pearl of the Orient. I must thank Astyages, my father-in-law, the next time I see him, for the hospitality he extended to you.'

Cambyses, being Persian by birth, spoke the language of the Persians, which was similar to that of the Medians, though not the same. Medians and Persians could readily understand each other. Yet, to an ear attuned to the Median language, Persian seemed like a dialect, and the wealthiest and most powerful Medians were only too willing to regard Persian as a dialect of lower-born rustics. But to Cyrus, who was of course a native speaker of the Median language, having grown up in that country, Persian sounded more melodious than Median. The Persian tongue had always seemed to him to have an enchantment and mystery that evoked in his imagination an impression of the more remote, little-known land of Persia, and of the art and the beauty of its people, for which Persia was known to the more astute Medians.

Cambyses leaned forwards and kissed Mandane on the lips. She returned the kiss with fervour.

So this is love, Cyrus thought. *This is the love that unites or separates kingdoms. This is the love that lasts a lifetime.*

He glanced at Roshan. She didn't seem to notice him looking at her.

The king and queen broke their kiss. A few moments later a strange figure appeared from behind a wooden screen at the back of the throne room.

He was a bald African with massively developed and well-defined muscles, and with a skin so black it seemed to Cyrus to draw light from all around into it. Cyrus had occasionally seen Africans before, but none with a skin as dark as this man's or with such a splendid figure.

The African wore a simple white gown similar to the king's. His proud bearing itself seemed to Cyrus something majestic, as if there were two kings in the room. He advanced toward them. Seeing Mandane, he bowed slightly. 'Welcome home, my queen.' The man's voice was the same one Cyrus had heard before. The African's Persian was flawless, and only a faint trace of an accent revealed to Cyrus that Persian was not his mother tongue.

'Thank you, Akinlana,' Mandane replied. She glanced briefly at Cyrus. 'Akinlana, who was brought to Anshan when he was a boy and has lived here ever since, is my husband's principal adviser. A great man of intelligence and wisdom, he is very far from being a mere evil schemer like that fellow Farna-zata.'

Akinlana inclined his head in Mandane's direction. As he did so, the king, with a glance at Mandane, said, 'I have already heard rumours that our son we thought lost has returned to us. But can it be true?'

Mandane began to laugh, then almost at once started to weep tears of joy. 'My dearest love, it is so. I would vouch for its truth against the wisest oracle in all of Persia. Yes... this fine and heroic young man... he...' but Mandane's voice faltered with the emotion of the moment. She began to weep, but in a dignified way, that kept her weeping self-contained. She almost seemed to resent her own tears.

Cyrus took a step toward Cambyses. 'I am Cyrus. The queen of Persia says I am your son.'

King Cambyses looked bewildered, then glanced at his wife. 'My love, who is this person? What is he saying?'

Mandane nodded, then, speaking through her tears, murmured: 'It is true. The baby we thought was lost forever has grown up, and is now this fine man you behold in front of you.'

Cambyses stared. 'Can this really be true? Can this truly be our son?'

'See for yourself, my love,' Mandane whispered. 'Witness the birthmark. It is the one you showed to me on the night he was born. It is, of course, bigger now than it was, but it still looks like a lion's paw-print.'

The king inspected it, then nodded slowly.

He glanced at Mandane. 'How is this possible?'

'The tale of what happened is most wondrous and strange,' Mandane replied. 'It is like a tale we might have heard when we were children, the kind of story that no-one would expect to happen in this rough world. But it has happened. My dear husband, I shall tell you all of it, but now all of us who have come from Anshan need to rest.'

'Yes, of course,' Cambyses said. 'You must all rest, and then, my love, tell me this strange story of which you speak.'

He looked at Cyrus again. 'Ahura-Mazda be praised.' 'Ahura-Mazda indeed be praised. His ways are truly mysterious.'

Cambyses took a couple of steps forward and embraced Cyrus.

'My son,' Cambyses murmured. 'My son. Welcome home.'

The Persian king's voice was hoarse with emotion.

Cyrus hardly knew what to say. Neither, it appeared did Cambyses.

Later, when they were all rested and had eaten, Mandane and Cambyses invited Cyrus and Roshan into a private room of the palace. There, Mandane proceeded to relate to her husband how she believed that Astyages had been behind the whole vile business of the baby Cyrus being snatched from the castle, and about the strange rumour of Astyages's dream.

'But there are still many gaps in our knowledge of what happened,' Mandane explained to Cambyses. 'We do not know in what way Harpagus was involved, let alone why, if he was, he did not complete the terrible deed.'

Cambyses slowly shook his head. 'This is a most terrible tale, if it is true. I have always known that your father is wicked; indeed, when I met you I loved you so much from the very outset that I was proud to be able to offer you a new home so far from your wicked father. But I would have thought that not even Astyages – helped, no doubt, by that abominable grand vizier of his – would have stooped to...' he spoke the words in a hoarse, pained voice, as if bewildered that such wickedness was possible, '*planning to kill a new-born baby.*'

Cambyses fell silent. No-one else spoke.

An expression of great pain and anger came over Cambyses. He seemed too much in distress to speak. But when he finally did speak, all he said was:

'I must have words with my father-in-law.'

Mandane nodded slowly. 'You may find that you have those words sooner than you imagine, my love,' she replied. 'Astyages bribed my soldiers to kill Cyrus on our journey here. He may still think Cyrus has been killed. I was not to be killed myself; the deed was to be done when I was asleep and the murder blamed on bandits. This girl, Roshan, a friend of our son since they were children, shot with her bow the Persian captain who was accompanying us and who had turned traitor. This brave and loyal girl also shot two of our own treacherous men. Cyrus has spared the lives of the surviving treacherous soldiers, though they will suffer the fate of obscurity and drudgery which they may well think worse than death.'

Cambyses went and embraced Roshan. 'You saved my son's life. Anything in my kingdom that I can give you is yours.'

'Oh, I need nothing, your Majesty, except perhaps a humble room somewhere that I might call home, and perhaps a little garden in which I can grow things. I am very happy to be here in Persia. After my life in Media, this city feels like an earthly paradise.'

'You are a very good woman,' said Cambyses. 'I am privileged to meet you.'

He glanced again at his wife. 'I *will* indeed have words with my father-in-law,' he said slowly, his voice still heavy with anger.

18. Ushtana

The moment the scouts Astyages had sent to find evidence of Cyrus's assassination reported that they had instead found the buzzard-ravaged bodies of the captain and the four other Persian soldiers, Astyages summoned Farna-zata for another beating. But on seeing how weak Farna-zata still was from the first, and knowing he'd be unlikely to survive a second one (Astyages did not care about Farna-zata but knew that finding an equally devious grand vizier would not be easy), the king contented himself with describing Farna-zata's (long-dead) mother as a whore, a pig, and the daughter of a stinking donkey.

After having delivered himself of these insults, Astyages hurled a clay writing tablet at Farna-zata, which the disgraced grand vizier just managed to dodge. Astyages cursed him and told him to get out, then screamed at his servants to fetch Ushtana, his newest favourite from the Palace of Queens.

Ushtana was Lydian. She had been living in Ecbatana for more than a year. One morning when she was shopping in the bazaars, she caught the eye of Farna-zata, who promptly arranged for her to be captured and brought into the Palace of Queens.

Ushtana had not seemed to mind very much. Her hair was as red as a summer dawn and her perfectly-proportioned face one of immense beauty. In her eyes there was a permanent look of mischief and ingenuity.

Shrewd and cunning like so many Lydian women, Ushtana saw her sudden change in circumstances not as a shameful descent but as a great opportunity. She was twenty-two but looked several years younger. She had been married in Lydia, but a few weeks after the marriage her husband was unfaithful to her, so she left him. She told Farna-zata she was sixteen, and he believed her.

The beautiful newcomer was spotted by Astyages on her second day in the Palace of Queens and later that same day was summoned to see him in private. Astyages was pleased with her. Not only was Ushtana an expert in the amorous arts, but he soon discovered that she had something of a knack for soothing his temper. She even spoke reasonable Median.

That evening, after Ushtana had sported with the furious Astyages for some time and had calmed him in the way that a woman can best calm a man, she asked him what was wrong.

So many times in the past, women from the Palace of Queens had asked the king to confide in them but had received insults and screams for their pains. But somehow Astyages saw Ushtana differently. He told her what was gnawing at his heart, and she listened carefully and thoughtfully.

'What are you going to do?' she asked, once he had fallen silent.

'What shall I do?' barked the calmed but still vindictive king. 'I shall send an armed force to Anshan tomorrow, and give them instructions to bring back my grandson's head!'

Ushtana nodded slowly, drank purple wine from a metal goblet, laid down the goblet, then glanced at Astyages.

'Why do that?' she murmured. 'Your army is much stronger than that of the Persians, you told me so yourself.'

'Yes, yes, of course it is.'

'Very well, then why not wait?'

'*Wait?*'

'Yes.' Ushtana cleared her throat. 'Yes. Why not wait. Why not let the Persians... and your grandson... and the weak king who married your daughter... *wonder* what you will be likely to do?'

'Why... why should I not do what I wish to do now?'

'Because by waiting... by doing nothing... you shall give yourself the upper hand. Let *them* wonder what you might do. Let *them* worry. And there is something else...'

'What's that?'

'Your grandson... this Cyrus... he sounds to me like the type of man who can bear anything... except waiting. If you do nothing I think he will soon want to do something... and I believe that when he does, he will play into your hands.'

'And why... why do you believe that?'

Ushtana smiled. 'Female intuition.'

'And what if your female intuition is wrong?'

'It never is,' Ushtana replied confidently. 'For example...'

'Yes?'

'Well, before I came to live in Ecbatana, I somehow *knew* that if I came here my life would take an interesting change. And you see... I was right.'

'But what if this time you are wrong? What if, by doing nothing, I merely allow my grandson to build up new strength?'

'I am not wrong,' said Ushtana confidently. 'Trust me.'

Astyages just stared at her. 'If I follow your advice... and it turns out to be bad advice... I shall have you beheaded.'

Ushtana nodded slowly. 'All right, I shall take that risk.'

Astyages lay there, breathing heavily. 'This talk of my grandson has made me angry again,' he muttered.

'Well,' said Ushtana, 'you are with someone who can calm you down.'

She smiled, and set to work once more.

19. The Meal on the Terrace

Cyrus, King Cambyses, and Mandane spent every day of the first weeks after Cyrus's arrival at Anshan expecting an attack from the Medians.

Why is Astyages doing nothing? Cyrus wondered.

But Astyages went on doing nothing, and no attack came.

'Perhaps my father has accepted the inevitable,' Mandane said.

It was now about four weeks after Cyrus had arrived in Anshan, and a mere few days after Cyrus had been proclaimed Crown Prince of Persia by Ashavan, the chief magus of Persia, in a ceremony in the principal temple in the city.

King Cambyses, Mandane and Cyrus were having lunch in the rooftop garden of the royal palace. They were sitting under a shade of raw silk on teak chairs at a table made of the same wood, imported from far-off India.

'I can only suppose he knows that invading us in order to capture you, Cyrus,' Mandane added, 'would mean war between our two nations. True, we are weaker than Media and would very likely lose, but war is war. War costs lives, and treasure. Astyages would probably prefer to avoid risking either.'

Cambyses nodded slowly. 'I agree, my dear. It is one thing to allow a dream to lead one to try to murder a helpless new-born baby, but quite another to allow it to lead one into a war. Moreover, why should he do that, when you and I are so deferential to him anyway?'

Cambyses was silent for a moment. Cyrus said nothing; he was too intent upon listening. Mandane made no reply.

'And besides,' Cambyses went on with a glance at Mandane, 'he must know that you would physically put yourself between any of his soldiers and our son. He does not want you to die. And he knows his power is unchallenged. I would not want to be in the shoes of Farna-zata or Harpagus, but they deserve no better. I know my father-in-law only too well. There is a method in the minds even of the truly wicked. I do not believe he will send an army against us as long as he knows he *could* invade us and beat us, at will. He would rather have me in his thrall as a weaker king that he knows he can take over at any time, than as his prisoner.'

Cyrus, who had had only a breakfast of barley porridge followed by a long morning of meditation with Akinlana and sword-fighting with wooden swords against some of the best fencers in Persia, was nonetheless eating little. He was learning much from Akinlana of the art of meditation, widely practised in Anshan and indeed (Cyrus gleaned) throughout all of Persia. It was an art to which Cyrus applied himself as thoroughly as he applied himself to anything he wished to learn. Cyrus had already got into the habit of meditating with Akinlana in the mornings in the palace, before breakfast.

'You know my father well, my love,' Mandane murmured to her husband.

'I should hope I do,' Cambyses said. 'Ultimately I suspect Astyages is not sending an army against us because... because in his pride and wickedness, there is a curious sense in which he enjoys relishing my anxiety that he might do so. We have all seen a cat playing with a mouse. The difference between the strengths of the cat and the mouse is so great that the mouse has one hope and one hope only: that the cat will wish to delay the final execution out of sheer pleasure at the game. And often, during the game, if the cat's concentration slips for only a moment, the mouse manages to dash down the mouse-hole.'

The king gave a hopeless kind of shrug. 'I am content to be the mouse to my father-in-law Astyages's cat, so long as he leaves us in peace here in our comfortable little mouse-hole. No, we are not as strong as Media, but at least we have never been conquered by Astyages. And, if Ahura-Mazda wills it and I continue to be sufficiently ingenious, we will *never* be conquered by him.'

Cyrus struck the table with his right fist. 'Persia shall never be a mouse to the cat that is Astyages! Persia a mouse-hole! How can you say that, father, of your own country?'

Cambyses suddenly looked distinctly uncomfortable. 'I only say it, my son, because I was speaking of my strategy, which is to be...'

'*Weak?*' Cyrus demanded.

'Cyrus!' exclaimed Mandane.

'No, to *survive*,' said Cambyses.

'Cyrus, still your impetuous tongue,' Mandane said. 'You are still young and have much to learn. Your father knows infinitely more of the realities of power than you possibly could.'

'Yes,' Cyrus said, thoughtfully, and after a moment's consideration, 'I am sure that is true, for I have never been a king. But I am not impetuous. No, I have never ruled a country, so I have not had that experience of power. But I have been an outcast.'

His parents were just looking at him, as if they suspected they might not have known him until that moment.

'Yes,' Cyrus said. 'I have seen the good people, whom I thought were my parents, slaughtered in cold blood in front of me. For fifteen years, I thought I was an orphan. I have starved with my friends. I have seen most of my brave people scattered and killed by armed thugs sent south by Astyages. I have been taken prisoner. I have been sent to Ecbatana in a cage to be beheaded for Astyages' entertainment by one of his favoured courtesans. I was saved from that fate by only one thing: a birthmark to which I had scarcely given a moment's thought until that day.'

Cyrus looked hard at Mandane. 'So tell me, do I not know something of the uses and abuses of power?'

Mandane made no reply.

Cyrus this time glanced at Cambyses, who merely looked back at him, but said nothing.

'*Astyages is a tyrant,*' Cyrus said to Cambyses and Mandane in turn. 'He is a murderer, too, and even worse, commands others to murder for him. Because of a dream, he tried to have me killed on the very night I was born. Does Astyages really think Ahura-Mazda is so afraid of us mortals that he would only ever reveal his purposes to us in our dreams? Apparently Astyages did. I tell you, he was a fool then and he is a fool now.'

Neither Mandane nor Cambyses made any reply to this, either. They just stared, in apparent wonder, at their son.

Cyrus nodded soberly. 'I assure you, Astyages's dream may yet come true.'

'But Cyrus, what would you achieve by killing him?' asked Mandane. 'Even if Astyages were to die, another king would succeed him in Media, perhaps someone even worse.'

'I doubt that is possible,' Cyrus replied. 'As for killing him, Astyages is not Media, but merely a man, and no man is immortal.'

'True,' said Cambyses. 'But Media is a nation. A powerful nation; richer and more populous than Persia. Alone, Persia can never defeat it.'

Cyrus put a single green olive into his mouth, chewed it slowly and thoughtfully, then discreetly removed the stone and placed it in a saucer in front of him. He took a sip of his wine, before laying down his cup. He glanced at Mandane, then slowly changed the direction of his gaze so that it rested on the king.

'I know that we can never defeat Media,' Cyrus said. His voice as he said this was quiet, scarcely more than a murmur, but as he continued to speak it began to rise in volume. 'I have seen the future of our people – and of the Medians, who are all also in truth our people in kinship and almost too by language. I have not seen this future in some foolish dream fuelled by drunken lust with a concubine, but in my imagination, in my soul, and in my prayers.'

Cyrus paused. He refilled his parents' cups, and bid them drink. They did so, at that moment perfectly obedient to him. Cyrus then drank from his own cup, as if he were slowly beginning some kind of ritual.

'My dream is this,' Cyrus said. 'It is that Persia and Media shall fight, not against each other, but in unison. Yes, Astyages shall pay the ultimate price for his crimes – I shall see to that – but not yet. Astyages is not the only one who is prepared to wait.'

Cyrus paused, gratified to see the astonishment on his parents' faces.

'But Cyrus, why would Astyages want to unite with us when he could invade us if he wished?' Cambyses asked.

'Is the answer not staring you in the face?' Cyrus demanded, astonished at his father's lack of understanding. The sudden thought *being a mouse too long to Astyages's cat has made my father Cambyses timid* sprang into Cyrus's mind.

'Alone,' Cyrus went on, 'Persia is at heart a solitary tribe. Alone, Media is also a solitary tribe, if stronger than we are. Alone, neither, for all Astyages's boasting, can ever be truly strong. But if we unite on the battlefield, if we unite as it is said the tribes of India in the east unite, and as I have heard the tribes of the great and mysterious land of Cathay even farther east unite, then... then we shall be strong.'

Cambyses shook his head. 'There has been talk of unity before. It has never come to anything. Media is too proud.'

Cyrus shook his head. 'A king who is so afraid of a dream that he attempts to kill his new-born grandson is more afraid than you might imagine. I believe I can persuade him of the wisdom of unity.'

'But my darling boy, how?' Mandane asked him. 'If you return to Ecbatana, Astyages will certainly kill you.'

'I have no intention of returning to Ecbatana,' said Cyrus. He glanced at Cambyses, and then at Mandane. He paused, then added: 'I have a better plan.'

20. The Prince and the Lady

'Are you *serious?*' Roshan demanded.

'Believe me,' Cyrus replied. 'I am in earnest. I am as earnest as the sands of the desert.'

'Please,' said Roshan, 'spare me your similes. They were never your strong point. Sit down,' she indicated a wicker chair, 'over there, under the bow that saved your life... and tell me why you want to do this.'

Cyrus walked over to the chair which was close by her narrow, single bed that was covered by a dark blue silk bedspread. He knew that Mandane had given Roshan some gifts for her room to show her gratitude to Roshan and fondness for her; Cyrus presumed that the bedspread was among those gifts. Mandane had also by now carried out her promise to ennoble Roshan: who was 'Lady Roshan' now, though she wore the title lightly and did not ask her friends to use it when they addressed her.

The war-bow, which Cyrus recognized as the one Roshan had used to kill the treacherous captain and the other two soldiers who would have killed him, was hanging on the wall. Cyrus sat down gingerly, thinking of the war-bow above him and realizing that owing one's life to someone is as likely to make one feel uncomfortable as grateful.

The room, perhaps twenty paces square, had grey clay walls. Roshan had already made the room attractive, hanging it with greenery that Cyrus presumed she had found in the gardens of the palace at Anshan, gardens which, he knew, had been long-neglected, and which Roshan had already begun to improve. Roshan had also decorated the room with inexpensive but beautiful ornaments she had bought, Cyrus imagined, in the bazaars of Anshan. Yet there were a few more expensive ornaments among them, of gold and silver: Cyrus presumed they were also gifts from Mandane.

'I suppose,' said Roshan, 'now that your new mother has made me "Lady Roshan", you think I should find myself a nice big house, like Raiva's. But I have no desire to do so, even if I could afford such a house. I am a warrior and a gardener, and this room is fine for me.'

'You've made it beautiful,' Cyrus said. 'You're beautiful, too. You're a garden flower.'

He checked himself. 'But then I realize similes aren't my strong point.'

'That's not a simile,' said Roshan, 'it's a metaphor.'

Cyrus smiled thoughtfully. He remembered what his new father Cambyses had said about the cat and the mouse. *Roshan and I are like a cat and a mouse, too*, Cyrus thought, *except that I never really know which of us is which.*

The room smelled of frankincense. Cyrus remembered how only about a month or so earlier – amazing that so much had happened in that time! – Roshan had loved to wear frankincense after they had taken the caravan that had been carrying so much of it.

Roshan rose from her chair. She had left a papyrus on the table close by her.

'Interesting?' Cyrus asked pointing to the papyrus.

Roshan shook her head. 'No. It was written in Ecbatana, by one of Astyages's scribes. It contains the usual stories about how wise and brave their great, glorious and all-powerful master is. Now that people speaking our tongue have learned how to write, I wish someone would write something worth reading. Oh, and how I would love to travel, and see this world of ours!

For example, so many wondrous things are said about Babylon. Would it not be fine to visit that city some day?'

'What's so wonderful about Babylon?' Cyrus retorted. 'All the Babylonians do is hide behind their city walls, live on the food grown on the fertile plains watered by the Euphrates, and force slaves to do most of the work. The Babylonians are scarcely better than Astyages, with whom the sinister Babylonian king Nabonidus has a bond of friendship, as wicked people often ally themselves with others like themselves.'

'I don't know about Nabonidus,' Roshan said, 'but truly I doubt he can be as bad as that monster Astyages. After all, the Babylonians are not like him; they value civilization.' She looked at Cyrus wistfully for a moment. 'How I would love to see their fabled Hanging Gardens! I love gardens, as you know. I remember how once you tried to dam our village stream so its flow would be diverted and it would water my garden! Do you remember that?'

Cyrus smiled. 'Yes, very well.'

'Your dam didn't last,' Roshan said, 'but I loved you for trying... I mean, I liked you very much that you tried.' Roshan gave a smile. 'Cyrus, I can think of few things better than to spend all my day in a beautiful garden. Surely you've heard of The Hanging Gardens of Babylon and how wondrous they are?'

'Of course I have. And yes, I know that many Persians – and Medians too – regard gardening as a sacred duty. So at least the magi say, though I must admit I have never myself noticed any magi get *their* hands dirty. But I myself have no time for gardening, for I am a soldier.'

'You don't care about the beauty of a well-tended and flourishing garden?'

'Since you ask me, I must say that I don't especially, no.'

'You don't care about the recreation of the human soul and yet you aspire to lead men? Even soldiers need to find ways of enjoying life in times of calm and peace.'

Roshan suddenly looked very thoughtful, and Cyrus couldn't help thinking, very beautiful.

'Truly, I would love to see the Hanging Gardens of Babylon,' Roshan said. 'Our lives are so full of hardship and so often devoid of beauty.'

'Wherever you go, Roshan, there is always beauty,' said Cyrus.

Roshan drew a scornful breath. 'Yes... well, answer my question. Why do you want to meet with one of Astyages's generals in Aspandana, that village half-way between Ecbatana and Anshan? Have you gone mad, or is it just sunstroke?'

After Cyrus had finished telling her of his plan, Roshan got up from her seat and walked around the room for a few moments in silence. Then she went to stand close by him, looking down at him.

'So,' she said, 'you want to ally your newly adopted homeland with Media. You are mad.'

'No,' said Cyrus. 'I believe I am the only voice of sanity in Persia.'

'Mad people always think they are the only voice of sanity. It is a sure sign of their madness.'

Cyrus gave a shrug.

Roshan just gazed at him in silence, then said:

'Did you have a dream about this?'

'No. I act because of what I think and what I feel, not because of what I see in my dreams. Almost ever since we arrived here in Anshan I have been meditating every morning, but even without that meditation I have had much time to think.'

He stood up. She was so close to him he could easily have reached out and stroked her face, or even kissed her.

'What is the point of a life,' he said, 'where one is born, enjoys a few pleasant times as a child, is then lashed to ignoble labour, lives in obscurity and failure, grows old and frail and dies? What kind of life is that? Yes, by a strange twist of fate I am now prince of Persia. But I will not use my new role merely to indulge my fantasies. I shall use it to fulfil my destiny: the destiny of Persia. And even, yes, the destiny of Media. This is only the beginning.'

Roshan walked over to her bed, sat down on it, then looked hard at him. 'Why do you want me to come with you to the village of Aspandana? There are many warriors here who can accompany you and who would help guard you against danger. Why me?'

'Because,' said Cyrus, 'you are the person I trust the most, and you fight as well as almost any man.'

Roshan gave a scornful laugh. 'There you go again. "As almost any man". I saved your life by shooting *three* men from close to a hundred paces, yet still you say that. You will never think a woman can truly be as good as a man.'

'I am sorry. Let me say, then, that you do fight as well as any man.'

'I know you do not mean that.'

Roshan smiled hesitantly. 'Are there any other reasons why you would want me to come with you?'

'Yes, many,' Cyrus admitted. 'Your knowledge of the country-side around Aspandana is as great as mine. And besides, you have great cunning and resourcefulness.'

Roshan looked levelly at him. 'You want me to come with you, yet you don't even have the courage to tell me you would enjoy my company...'

'I would also enjoy your company,' Cyrus said.

Roshan shook her head slowly. 'Why do I have to prise every compliment out of you, as if I were dragging a rusty sword from an even rustier scabbard?'

'Because I am a warrior, not a flatterer,' said Cyrus.

'Oh,' said Roshan, with a short, bitter laugh, 'no-one could possibly doubt that.'

Later that same day, King Cambyses, at Cyrus's urging, sent an emissary to Astyages proposing the meeting Cyrus wanted to hold at Aspandana. The emissary would take about two weeks to get to Ecbatana and another two weeks to return.

They would have their answer from Astyages in a month.

21. Victims of Astyages

Cyrus saw Roshan several times during that month. They were as they had always been, close friends, but somehow... Cyrus felt that they were closer now than they had ever been before. He had a feeling that Roshan was aware of this too, for all that neither of them said a word about it.

Instead of talking of such matters, they went out, just the two of them, on several horseback expeditions, to hunt leopards with bow and arrow. These expeditions had always met with failure, but Cyrus didn't mind, for Roshan's company, he readily conceded to himself, was always a great pleasure for him.

As for Raiva, Cyrus visited him once or twice but was increasingly conscious that their friendship had changed. There was not the same warmth about it. Cyrus was only too aware that this distance between them derived from Raiva's increasing wealth and from his obsession with the world of business. He assured Cyrus that when his military skills were again needed he would immediately spring to Cyrus's service, but Cyrus couldn't believe that things would ever be the same again between them.

Then, one morning about five weeks after the emissary had been sent to Ecbatana, he returned with the news that Astyages had agreed to the meeting, and would send an emissary of his own to meet with Cyrus at Aspandana.

Cyrus had never been to Aspandana before. He had some idea, though, of what to expect: it would be a small, impoverished settlement of goat-herders, sheep-farmers and even poorer people who could not even afford to buy a sheep or goat but who tilled a frugal living out of the harsh and unyielding land.

Aspandana lay at the foot of a tall hill, almost a mountain really, located on the southern, Persian side of the village. Cyrus had chosen Aspandana not only because it was equidistant from Ecbatana and Anshan but also because he had heard of this hill and knew that if Astyages tried to betray him by sending a detachment of soldiers to meet him and Roshan, the soldiers would be visible from far away once he and Roshan were at the summit. And besides, Cyrus as prince of Persia had already sent word out into the neighbouring countryside that large movements of soldiers were to be notified to him. He had heard no word that any had been spotted.

Cyrus and Roshan left their horses some way down the hill, then proceeded to the summit of the hill on foot. When they reached the crest of the hill and looked down, they saw no sign of any army, only a few humble villagers going about their daily business. Even at this distance, the baa-ing of the sheep and goats was faintly audible. It was a peaceful scene, older almost than time.

'Perhaps Astyages is afraid of you,' Roshan said to Cyrus.

Cyrus was about to reply, but another voice did so for him.

'Astyages is afraid of everything, which is why he has sent me, his only subject who is afraid of nothing, to meet you.'

It was a voice instantly familiar to Cyrus. He span round.

Alone on horseback, about thirty feet behind them, was Harpagus.

In the few months since Cyrus had last set eyes on the man he most hated after Astyages, Harpagus seemed to have aged five years. His beard was white now, not grey, though his body looked to Cyrus as massive and strong as ever.

As for the giant general's expression, formerly always so haughty and proud, it was now deep-riven with some terrible pain and anguish.

Cyrus looked up at the imposing sight of the giant Harpagus on a sweating black stallion. The stomach-wrenching memory rose within Cyrus of the slaughter of Mithradat and Spako in Paritakna fifteen years earlier. Cyrus could still see in his mind's eye the vicious sneer on the face of Harpagus as he ran his sword through the unarmed Mithradat.

Instinctively, Cyrus felt for his own sword. Yes, Harpagus was a giant of a warrior, but Cyrus had little doubt he himself could kill Harpagus, for the giant warrior was close to two decades older, and Cyrus had the strength of his youth.

A moment later Cyrus might have drawn his sword... and a fight would have ensued that would certainly have led to the death of one of them, and the future history of Persia and Media would have been very different. Perhaps the Persian Empire might not even have come into being, and if it had not, the history of so much of the rest of the world would also have changed.

For a moment, truly, history hung in the balance.

But Cyrus checked himself.

He checked himself, partly because Harpagus had not drawn his own sword, but mainly because Cyrus knew that if this was really to be the start of his march towards destiny, the time to begin the march was... *now*.

Yet nothing stopped Cyrus from being breathless with anger. His hand still on scabbard, he saw that Roshan had also turned and was staring at Harpagus in appalled horror.

'*You*,' Roshan said, so angry she could hardly speak at all, '*Astyages sent you.*'

'Evidently so,' Harpagus barked.

Roshan was staring at Harpagus with a look of complete detestation. 'Where's your army?'

'I have come alone,' Harpagus said. 'Unlike the prince of Persia, I do not have a travelling companion, still less one as beautiful as you are.'

Roshan ignored the compliment. 'Why would Astyages send his chief assassin to meet us?'

Cyrus looked at Roshan, reached out his left hand and briefly touched the top of her right arm, 'Please,' he said to her, 'I have not proposed this meeting to embark on hostilities. We have a greater purpose.'

'That may be so, young prince,' Harpagus said. 'However, I will answer the question posed by this beautiful woman.'

'*Do not call me beautiful*,' hissed Roshan, 'when the parents who gave me my beauty were slaughtered under your command by your soldiers and very likely even by you personally. You are nothing but... a vile, cold-blooded murdering monster.'

'No, I am a *soldier*,' Harpagus replied, 'one who was acting on instructions from my king. I acted as I did because when I did so, I believed I was serving my country. But I was also afraid of what the king would do to my wife and my baby boy Artabaz if the king found out that Cyrus was still alive. Destroying your town seemed the only way to conceal the fact. You think I do not know that I sinned? Of course I do. I know that Mithra has already reserved a place in hell for me, which is why I am not in any haste to meet him.'

Harpagus dismounted from his horse. He was taller than Cyrus by half the length of a man's forearm, yet Cyrus was not remotely afraid of him. Cyrus, no longer a boy, was utterly confident that if it came to a fight, Harpagus would be the one who would perish.

Cyrus still felt the strongest of yearnings to draw his sword, but he did not yield to it.

Harpagus took a few steps towards them both.

'Who is this travelling-companion of yours, young prince?' he said. Cyrus expected to hear arrogance in the question, but there was none; Harpagus seemed genuinely curious.

'I am Roshan, daughter of a murdered father and mother,' Roshan replied at once. 'I was born and grew up in Paritakna and lived there until your soldiers killed my parents and destroyed the town. I was then a member of the band your soldiers scattered and mostly slaughtered only a few weeks ago. Now I fight alongside the prince of Persia.'

Roshan fell silent. Cyrus just stared at Harpagus. 'So... Astyages sent you to meet with us to show his contempt for me, and my plans,' Cyrus murmured, in halting fashion.

'No doubt,' replied Harpagus, at once. 'And he also sent me here because, of all his subjects, I am the only one with nothing to fear.'

Cyrus was silent, then his curiosity got the better of him. 'Why should that be?'

'After you and your mother fled Ecbatana,' said Harpagus, 'Astyages gave Farna-zata a ferocious beating. But for me... for me, who as an inexperienced young man, knowing next to nothing about the world, was given the charge of taking away his new-born grandson and extinguishing the baby's life but did not perform that charge, Astyages reserved an infinitely worse punishment.'

Cyrus and Roshan stared at the battle-scarred, anguish-riven face of the general.

'What punishment was that?' Cyrus asked.

Harpagus made no reply for several moments. The giant general was evidently struggling with himself to find words.

Finally, speaking in a hoarse, dry voice laden with pain, Harpagus said:

'*He roasted my son.*'

Cyrus and Roshan fell silent. Cyrus thought Harpagus's voice dripped with pain as if the pain were blood. The general went on:

'When I came to supper with the king, he served me a meal of meat that he said was from a freshly-slaughtered boar. But it was my son.'

'Oh, by Ahura-Mazda, no,' Roshan murmured.

'By Mithra, yes,' said Harpagus. 'It is true.'

None of them said anything for a while. Even Cyrus, who had thought he knew everything there was to know about the depths of depravity to which Astyages would sink, was stunned into silence by the vengeance the king had inflicted on Harpagus.

'And so I have nothing to fear,' Harpagus went on, 'for the worst thing that could possibly have happened to me – something infinitely worse than my own death – has... has already happened. My wife died several years ago, when the plague struck Ecbatana. My boy was my only solace. *Astyages killed him and fed him to me.*'

Cyrus and Roshan just stared at the giant general.

Harpagus looked hard at Cyrus. 'I was young, and foolish, and mad, when I killed the man I had ordered to bury you, young prince, and when I allowed my soldiers to kill his wife. It is no use for me to ask your forgiveness, for I do not deserve it and you would not give it to me anyway. When I did what I did in the town of Paritakna I feared Astyages and what he would do to my own wife and child if he knew you were not dead. But if it is of any use to say to you both that I am sorry, I say it now. I am indeed sorry. There, it is said and I mean it. You both now know, at least, that I, too, have suffered. And now Astyages has sent me to meet you because he knows of my fearlessness.'

'But Astyages must know you hate him,' Cyrus said, finally finding words. 'How will he know you will do his bidding?'

'Because he knows that my career in the army is all I have left in my life, and that I have no wish to lose it. Of course he will know how I really feel about him. But as I have no power over Astyages, my hate causes *him* no fear. Indeed, he told me some weeks ago that I am more important and useful to him than ever.'

Cyrus shivered inside at the limitless wickedness of Astyages.

'We are all victims of Astyages,' Harpagus said. 'Prince of Persia, I was but nineteen years old when I was given the vilest order I could have been given: the command to take a new-born baby far from Ecbatana and bury the babe alive. Imagine you had been given that order... how would you have responded? I could not have disobeyed the instruction, for if I had I would have been executed, and my wife too, and Astyages would have compelled someone else to carry it out: someone who might indeed have done so. I thought I did obey the command, but in truth I committed another crime that was almost as bad: I tried to make a peasant bear the burden of my guilt. All those ten years I believed I had been responsible for the death of a new-born baby, even though I was able to persuade myself that I had not done the actual burying!'

'But why did you think I had been buried?' Cyrus asked.

'I drank the peasant's wine to reduce the pain of the deed I commanded him to carry out. I fell into a stupor. When I woke, I saw a low mound that I thought was the baby's grave. Only those ten years later did I discover that the babe was never buried and that you were alive.'

There was a very long silence.

'Ahura-Mazda gives us all the opportunity to choose between good and evil,' Cyrus said quietly, speaking at last. 'I can imagine what a burden the wicked order felt on your shoulders when as a young man, you received it. But nothing can alter the fact that, as you say, you have sinned, Harpagus. You chose the path of evil. You have been a murderer, a savage, and a barbarian. You killed the man I thought of as my father, who toiled to earn bread for me and who deserved to live out his life until old age. You also brutally and abominably commanded the death of... my mother. By any reckoning of Mithra or Ahura-Mazda, you deserve to die. And soldiers under your command killed many innocent people, and destroyed a town. But... I shall not hate you, Harpagus, even though I have every right to do so. No, I shall not hate you, for we are all brothers and sisters in the sight of Ahura-Mazda or Mithra, and what is certain is that hatred achieves nothing except the breeding of more hatred.'

Cyrus paused. He glanced at Roshan and then back at Harpagus. 'Moreover, I shall show Astyages that he was wrong to imagine he knew how I would react when I saw you here. I shall show Astyages that I can break the cycle of hate. There is far more at stake here than my own feelings and the feelings of my travelling-companion. What is at stake here is the happiness and prosperity of the people of Media and Persia and their children and descendants.'

Cyrus drew a heavy breath. 'Our nations, the lands of Media and Persia, are festering sores spewing poverty, distrust and disunity. Hatred is not... it cannot be, all there is in the world. And if it is, then so be it, I shall remake that world.'

Roshan and Harpagus were looking hard at him.

'I propose a new order,' Cyrus said. 'A new order, in which Media and Persia are united. A new order, in which we put aside all our differences and work together, as one. A world which,' he added, with a glance at Harpagus, 'even the evil demon who is your king shall understand is a world that can be achieved; a world in which Media, like Persia, shall draw strength and wealth from the alliance. My dream is to do this, and create one of the most powerful united nations on earth.'

Cyrus fell silent. Neither Harpagus nor Roshan said a word.

'If we unite our armies it will be like uniting our peoples,' Cyrus added. 'And we shall create a new, united nation in which men and women can be free.'

Cyrus fell silent. Neither Roshan nor Harpagus made any reply.

A rare, heavy cloud passed high across the path of the sun. The crest of the hill grew dark. Then the cloud cleared, and the renewed sunlight seemed to Cyrus all the more magnificent for having been just that moment blotted out.

Cyrus never entirely ceased to wonder whether Ahura-Mazda had heard what he had been saying, and somehow, in sending the cloud to emphasize for a moment the splendour of the sunshine, wished to indicate his divine approval.

22. Unity

Many men, and women too, have the potential for greatness, but few achieve it. Sloth, compromise, and the self-forgetfulness bred by indulgence in the distractions and pleasures of life, bring a growing indifference to the destiny that might otherwise have been waiting for us, like a beautiful bride or handsome husband, ardent for our love. For to be exceptional is painful, and brings a solitude of spirit, and most of us fear that solitude infinitely more than the anguish of obscurity.

Cyrus was only human. He, too, feared the pain of the solitude of spirit that comes from striving to be wedded to a great destiny. The difference was that he was willing to suffer that pain because he knew what he had to become.

After the meeting on the crest of the high hill above Aspandana, Cyrus was sure he had finally found his own destiny. He knew, instinctively, that he would pursue that destiny relentlessly until the day when life fled from his mortal frame.

He now knew just how low Astyages could stoop in bestial depravity. Cyrus also knew that men, their senses addled by wine, often lost all sense of fear. But until Cyrus met Harpagus again after Harpagus had suffered Astyages's wrath, Cyrus had never known a sober man who was afraid of nothing. Yet Harpagus seemed to be such a man.

'Anyone but someone who had nothing left to fear would be committing suicide in telling Astyages what you are proposing,' Harpagus said. 'Yet I shall relish the moment I tell him. For the tyrant knows now that after he roasted my boy I do not care, not in the least, what he does to *me.*'

And indeed it seemed Harpagus was as good as his word, for within a month of the meeting on the high hill above Aspandana, word came from Median emissaries that Astyages had agreed to what Cyrus proposed.

This extraordinary time was the beginning of Cyrus assuming his true destiny. He was entirely aware how momentous his life had become.

This was the start of the new history of the kingdoms of Media and Persia. For, after decades of hate, bitterness and rivalry between the two countries, they were united.

Not yet politically, for the two capitals of Ecbatana and Anshan were still two capitals of two different countries. But the two countries were united in the most important way of all, in their force of arms.

In making his proposal, Cyrus had begun to display the flair for understanding human nature that was so much the reason why he rose to greatness. Aware that Astyages would wish to feel himself in control of the entire new army of the two countries, Cyrus had merely proposed that he himself be appointed a general of the united Median and Persian army, of equal rank with Harpagus. Astyages would still maintain overall command.

But Cyrus was cunning, too. He was aware that the tyrant was now more than seventy years old.

Cyrus was certain that as long as Astyages felt himself to be in overall command of the army, the king of Media would be happy to remain safely and securely in his palace at Ecbatana.

And indeed why would a man voluntarily wish for the privations of life under canvas, with irregular meals, sand in the food, incessant drilling and parading, and the constant risk of a violent and agonizing death, when he could be at home in his luxurious palace, drinking the finest wines, eating delicious meals, and spending evenings and nights sporting with one or other of his concubines whose own lives were devoted solely to his pleasure?

And so the united military force came into being, under the generalships of Cyrus and Harpagus and the overall, if nominal, leadership of Astyages.

Privately Cyrus and Harpagus had, of course, every reason to hate each other, to mistrust each other, indeed to try to kill each other at the earliest opportunity. But neither were fools. Despite their private feelings, they adopted a pragmatic and sensible approach to politics. They were far from being the first men in history, nor would they be the last, to discover that it was in their professional interests to cast aside their personal hatreds in order to advance a greater purpose.

Cyrus presumed that a large part of the reason why Harpagus collaborated so willingly with him was because of the prospect of greatness which the uniting of the two countries' military forces was bringing him. Yet Cyrus suspected there was probably another reason for Harpagus's willingness to participate so readily in the new dispensation.

Cyrus thought it certainly possible Harpagus believed that he might, at some point, have the opportunity to avenge himself on the king of Media.

One bright morning almost a year after the meeting on the hill above Aspandana, Cyrus and Harpagus were reviewing the army they had created. This – though they could not have known it – was the largest military force between the archipelago nation of the Greeks to the west and the great mysterious land of India in the distant east.

The army, tens of thousands of soldiers parading beneath the double flag of Media and Persia (though the Median flag was at the top), was going about its military manoeuvres under the gaze of Cyrus and Harpagus.

Astyages, predictably, was nowhere to be seen, having remained in Ecbatana for almost the entire year during which the unity was formalized and the army created.

Cyrus himself had taken command of a group of warriors he personally named the 'Immortals'; men chosen from the ranks for their military prowess and devotion to him. It was Asha who had suggested the formation of this elite unit and that they might wear bells in battle as Asha himself did, practising a custom that had begun as a reminder to himself of the sad death of his beloved childhood pet, Frada. The Immortals let their hair grow to accommodate the bells, the ringing of which was usually stopped by strands of hair, and also to give them a distinctive appearance that would help with the aim of terrifying their enemies even before the battle began.

When the Immortals rode into battle, they always wore their bells with the ringers unstopped by hair. The resulting sound of untold thousands of bells, and the sight of the superbly-trained mounted warriors in full charge, was terrifying.

In an order that also showed his knowledge of human nature, Cyrus limited the number of Immortals to ten thousand men. An ordinary soldier could, through relentless hard work and devoted skill, have a chance to become an Immortal, but only when an Immortal fell in battle or died of some other cause. Immortals were exalted in that elevated rank until death; only when they died were they replaced.

As for Asha, the leader of the Immortals, he was blissfully happy with his beautiful wife, his son, and the knowledge that his friend was now one of the two principal generals of the Median and Persian armies. Asha, who had long ceased to be the somewhat directionless young man he had once been, now worked harder than he had ever worked and played a vital role in building up the strength of the two previously opposed forces who were now working so closely together.

At first, the new united army merely paraded and trained. But within a few months, a hill-tribe in the east, the bloodthirsty and savage Massagetae, as if perhaps seeking to convince itself that the new united army was not as fearsome as they thought it might be, mounted an unprovoked attack into Persia.

They raided Persian villages to the east, slaughtered the men and boys, ravished the women and girls and took them off to be slaves.

Cyrus, wishing if possible to avoid a full-scale war with the hill-tribes and hearing from his scouts that the attacks had been made by a rogue tribe, sent a relatively small force into the east to capture the leaders of the rebels. But unfortunately, between sending the punitive force and them reaching the border, other hill-tribes entered into a temporary alliance with the Massagetae.

The small Persian force was ambushed and annihilated.

Cyrus had not been not commanding it, and he learnt now of the importance of personally commanding his forces. Hearing of the slaughter of his force, Cyrus gathered his entire army to meet the threat from the east.

When the battle finally broke out, Cyrus used his ten thousand Immortals as the first line of attack, believing the time had come for them to show their skill and ferocity on the battlefield. The hillside tribes' army was far from trivial in size, for the hills were broad and went many miles to the east, and it seemed that thousands of men had been yielded by the hills to try the might of the Medians and Persians. Some observers might have wondered who was going to prevail on the battlefield that day, but Cyrus never had the slightest doubt.

The battle was a great victory for the united army of the Medians and Persians. Thousands of men from the hillside tribes' army met their maker that day at the hands of Cyrus's elite army, with the loss of barely a hundred Immortals. The remainder of the Massagetae and their allies fled back into the hills, and Cyrus had no further trouble from those tribes for many years. For they had become aware of the might of Cyrus, and they trembled in fear at the thought that if he wished he might have sent his united force into the hills to slaughter all of them.

But Cyrus had no intention of doing so, for he had other destinations and objectives on his mind.

He had taken to communing in silence and reverence, and in private, with Ahura-Mazda, often going into the mountains alone to pray to the great being who had brought humankind into existence and who watched over the affairs of men. Cyrus always returned from these solitary forays with a sense of renewed strength, capability and power.

Yet despite his own reverence for Ahura-Mazda, Cyrus did not believe that he, the joint leader of the new united army, had any right to interfere with the beliefs of any Median or Persian. He respected the religious beliefs of others, and made no effort to use his growing influence and power to compel others to follow his own beliefs.

This was Cyrus's creed.

And so he built up his army and, with the assistance of Harpagus – who still felt much more like an enemy than a friend but with whom Cyrus found himself able to work – turned it into a fearsome fighting force. The nations of Media and Persia, gaining tribute from the tribes around them, were more prosperous and powerful than they had ever been.

Yet Cyrus was still biding his time. He had dreams of expanding west, but he was determined to wait until his army was strong enough for these dreams to become a reality.

To Cyrus's great displeasure, Astyages still captured peasants in Media and sold them as slaves in the ports in the south. Cyrus did all he could to reduce what he regarded as a vile trade, but he did not yet have the power to stamp it out completely.

About a year after Cyrus had united the two nations' armies, his father Cambyses – who had been happy to stand back while his son undertook the work that had to be done – died peacefully in his sleep. Cambyses was much mourned, not least by Mandane, who wore white – in Persia the colour of mourning – for the rest of her life. Even Astyages sent a terse message of condolence.

With the death of Cambyses, Cyrus became the new king of Persia. Yet he did not throw his new kingly role around in camp or on the parade-ground. He insisted that his soldiers, and Harpagus too, referred to him only as 'Cyrus.' His modesty as king won him even more admirers in both nations. Astyages was too conceited and self-indulgent to realize it, but more and more people even in Media quietly regarded Cyrus, not Astyages, as their true leader.

Many thought it was now time for Cyrus to marry, but he regarded himself as far too busy even to consider taking a bride. He had his numerous military duties, and was also engaged with building up the wealth of his country through improving the conditions of trade in Persia and by carrying out improvements in agriculture that Cyrus had learned from his advisers. As for the slave trade, his own father Cambyses had banned it, and Cyrus publicly reinforced the ban and stated his wish that the kingdom of Media should also cease a trade that Cyrus regarded as completely repugnant.

Roshan had many duties herself, for she was by now in charge not only of the gardens of the royal palace but also gardens in other parts of Anshan that gave the Persian capital a beauty that Cyrus had never before seen anywhere. As well as this, Roshan worked with the wives and families of the armies' soldiers, to help them with their problems and make life easier for them in so many respects. She no more took a husband than Cyrus took a wife. If she had lovers, Cyrus knew nothing of them.

Cyrus felt he was moving ever closer to his destiny. If he was sometimes lonely, he told himself that was the price we must pay for being true to the fate Ahura-Mazda has in store for us.

When he was younger he had often succumbed to the temptations of women and intoxicating drink, but now... now his life was different, and his concept of himself was different.

For the moment, he pledged himself to chastity, and loneliness, so that he might carry out the great destiny that he sensed had been planted within himself by Ahura-Mazda, the god of his adopted land, the land he now loved. Ahura-Mazda, a god whom Cyrus already thought of as more merciful, more forgiving, and more understanding of the frailties of humanity, than Mithra, the god of the Medians, ever was.

23. Business as Usual

When a nation or empire is growing, politics has a higher profile than business, but business is what really matters, for without it the politicians are little more than talk.

This, at least, was how Raiva saw things.

Ever since he had passed from childhood into being a young man, he had taken the greatest care to look after himself.

He had taken such great care, indeed, that he had not needed Mandane's help to find suitable accommodation in Anshan.

Raiva soon found himself a house in Anshan. He told Cyrus he had won the money to buy it in a gambling game. Raiva went into business almost at once as a spice merchant. Cyrus soon heard that Raiva had befriended a merchant called Farnaspes, one of the richest men in Anshan.

Cyrus never really understood how Raiva managed to set up an establishment so quickly. Occasionally, in his bleaker moods, Cyrus allowed himself to wonder whether Raiva might have betrayed them into entering the apparently deserted, ambushed village and been paid for doing so.

But Cyrus did not dwell on these thoughts, for at heart he could not believe that his childhood friend Raiva would have committed such a monstrous act of betrayal. He had heard that Raiva had taken to gambling and was lucky; Cyrus preferred to believe this was the reason for Raiva's sudden rise to prosperity. Cyrus did not, in any case, imagine how Raiva might have collected a reward from Astyages, or kept this secret from his brother, or why, so enriched, Raiva would have wished to continue to be part of the remnants of the band. But... despite all that, something about the whole betrayal still tugged at Cyrus's mind.

What was not understood was that from the moment Raiva arrived in Anshan he became richer and richer, and better and better acquainted with an ever increasing number of influential people.

It seemed to Cyrus that Ahura-Mazda – or something not unlike Ahura-Mazda, anyway – had blessed Raiva, too.

24. Death Sentence

When Cyrus became king of Persia, he was still careful to discipline his emotions and defer to Astyages as the ruler of the united armies. But in truth Astyages had become nothing more than a figurehead. The real work was done by Cyrus and Harpagus and the captains they had appointed.

By now the united army had a permanent base a few days' ride to the east of Ecbatana, in a wide and fertile plain near two small towns that had been largely converted into barracks. The plain had ample fertile land for growing crops, an abundance of grazing land, too, and was close by mines that supplied iron, copper and tin to make the iron and bronze the army needed for their weapons.

People spoke of the united army of Media and Persia, but increasingly talked of 'Cyrus's army', even though he was still careful to ensure that he never gave himself more power than that accorded to Harpagus, Astyages's representative.

The question was, what would be the army's next conquest?

Cyrus and Harpagus were speaking more and more of Cyrus's plans for the creation of an empire, especially now that the armies were so well-drilled, well-disciplined and thirsty for action, and with the Immortals hungry for battle. Astyages, too, was keen on expansion, but his views of what expansion should mean were very different from Cyrus's.

'Astyages plans soon to use the united armies to move westwards and enslave the nations of Lydia and Babylon,' Harpagus told Cyrus one evening, after visiting Cyrus's tent in the barracks.

Harpagus had had a large stone house built for himself a few hundred paces from Cyrus's tent. The soldiers referred to the house as 'Harpagus's palace'. Cyrus preferred to dwell in a simple though spacious tent.

'Your master Astyages knows my feelings on that matter,' Cyrus replied. 'We have not created the greatest army our world has ever known in order to form an army of slave-hunters that would even put the pharaohs of Ancient Egypt to shame. Only those we conquer who are foolishly stubborn and do not see reason need fear a loss of their freedom. I want our empire to be benevolent, to allow all peoples we may bring into it to continue to worship the gods they have worshipped and to continue to live as they have lived. All we will require is their loyalty, and for them to devote their warriors to our cause.'

Harpagus shook his head slowly. 'Cyrus, Astyages is a primitive man. You know this, and... you know only too well

that I know it. Already he says your plans are those of a...
well, he said they are the plans of a fool; that you know nothing
of the world. He says that every nation we defeat could yield
thousands upon thousands of slaves for Media and Persia.'

'He also knows that I shall never lead armies that seek only
to gather slaves.'

'Yes,' Harpagus replied. 'But Astyages is convinced you can
be persuaded otherwise.'

Cyrus shook his head. 'He is wrong.'

'I shall return to Ecbatana tomorrow for further talks with
Astyages.'

'Do so, and let me know the outcome.'

'I shall.'

That conversation had taken place some weeks earlier. Cyrus
had been expecting Harpagus's return for several days. But there
had been no sign of the general.

One night, while Cyrus was still waiting for Harpagus to return,
he had a dream so vivid that, even after he had woken in the
morning, it seemed even more real than reality.

He dreamed he was sitting at a banqueting-table in one of the
rooms of the palace of Ecbatana. The great table was groaning
under the weight of a sumptuous array of dishes – roast fowl,
roast animals of all kinds, fresh fruit and other vegetables.

The table was presided over by Astyages, wearing his crown
and his royal garb, and with a concubine on either side of him.

In front of Astyages was a great dome-shaped circular serving-
dish, its lid closed.

Cyrus, in his dream, looked all around the table. Harpagus
was there. So were a host of kings, and some queens too,
wearing foreign-looking clothes. The dreaming Cyrus supposed
that these were the kings and queens of other nations in the
region: the nations Astyages wanted to subjugate and enslave.

Roshan was there too. She was sitting immediately to the left of Harpagus. What was strange was that she was naked, her splendid body exposed for all to see; yet nobody except Cyrus appeared surprised about this.

In his dream, Cyrus found himself standing up and telling Roshan to cover herself. But everyone at the table at once burst out laughing, pointed their fingers at Cyrus and started proclaiming him foolish.

What is wrong with a beautiful woman being naked? they asked.

Astyages clapped his hands twice, at which everyone around the table abruptly fell silent.

All eyes, including Cyrus's, were on the king, who leaned forwards and lifted the large dome-shaped lid of the serving-dish.

Underneath the lid, roasted, and as small as children, were the squatting cooked corpses of Mithradat and Spako, their faces, with white, opaque cooked eyes, wearing expressions of sheer horror...

A moment later, Cyrus felt warm breath on his face and a strange, cold sensation at his throat. He felt himself surge into consciousness. He opened his eyes, and in the scanty moonlight that shone through an opening in his tent he saw the bearded face of Harpagus.

The cold sensation intensified. Cyrus knew he must not move, for he felt a dagger at his throat.

'What are you doing?' Cyrus demanded, his courage not deserting him, for all that he was aware it would be a fatal mistake to move a muscle.

'I have just arrived back from Ecbatana,' Harpagus said, in a hoarse whisper. 'Astyages has wearied of your unwillingness to comply with his plans. He has ordered me to kill you, and to assume total control of the armies.'

'And are you going to obey his order?' Cyrus asked.

'If I were,' Harpagus said, 'I would already be on the way back to Ecbatana with your dead body.'

The two leaders of the united army of Media and Persia stared at each other.

'Cyrus, I woke you with a dagger at your throat in order to make you realize just how much Astyages wants you dead.'

The king of Persia just looked at Harpagus in the faint moonlight. 'And you? Do you want me dead too?'

Harpagus made no reply for a moment, then finally said, 'Tell me, are we friends or enemies?'

'Harpagus, we are whatever we need to be in order for us to work together. We work for Persia and Media, you know that.'

'Yes. But I have sinned against you, have I not?'

'Yes, you have.'

'Indeed, and so you should hate me. Why do you not? I deserve it.'

'Hatred breeds hatred,' Cyrus said. 'It creates nothing.'

'Yes, you have often said that. But any other man would think only of his own hate.'

'I am not any other man,' said Cyrus.

Harpagus fell silent again. At last, speaking quietly, he said:

'Cyrus, I have a new life because of you. I believe in what you are trying to do, in what... if you will permit me to say this... *we* are trying to do. Even with the agony the loss of Artabaz brings me every day... my life... my life, Cyrus... has never been as good or as full of purpose as it is today.'

'I am pleased,' Cyrus said. He was deeply moved. All the same, he was still careful not to move.

'But if Astyages thinks you are alive,' Harpagus added, in a sudden and abrupt change of tone, 'he will never reveal the full extent of his plans.'

The sharp leading edge of the dagger against Cyrus's throat felt colder than ever.

'Yes,' said Cyrus. 'I agree.' He paused. 'And so... I need to die.'

'We all die,' Harpagus replied, promptly, as if death were indeed constantly on his mind. 'It is only a question of when.'

25. Grape Juice

Once a woman was sent into the Palace of Queens, she stayed there until her death, or until she became too old to interest Astyages, whichever was the sooner.

The lives of the women in the Palace of Queens were devoted to one purpose: Astyages's pleasure. Newcomers lived in one of the shabby shared dormitories until they were fortunate enough to be chosen by the king to spend a night with him. When that much hoped-for event happened, they graduated to having their own room or – if they had particularly impressed the king – a small apartment.

Once a concubine had been bedded, her fate and fortune were entirely dependent on how often the king demanded her services, and how well she pleased him when he did.

Some unfortunate concubines, known as the 'once-bedded', who had only ever been invited by Astyages to spend one night with him, led a miserable life. They were relegated to the smallest rooms and often ordered by the eunuchs to do the most menial tasks, including cleaning the lavatories. It was common for a once-bedded to make an end of herself (drinking a draught of hemlock was the usual method) after a year or so had passed and Astyages had never again asked for her company.

In practice, few once-bedded concubines ever had the chance to become old: if they didn't swallow hemlock voluntarily the eunuchs generally found some other way of getting rid of them. It was said that the large vegetable garden in the grounds of the palace at Ecbatana owed its great fertility to the former concubines who had met untimely ends and were buried beneath it. The Palace of Queens, like the larger palace upon which it depended and of which it was a part, was rife with strategies, scheming and plotting, with Farna-zata ultimately overseeing all the deviousness, a wavy-haired Prince of Misrule.

Concubines who regularly won the king's favour became the celebrities of the Palace of Queens, giving themselves all the airs and graces that went with celebrity. They were accommodated in the largest and most luxurious suites, had servants of their own, and received extra rations in addition to their board and lodging.

A few fortunate concubines might, on reaching the end of their useful lives in the Palace of Queens, be found some job or other in one of the outlying areas of the palace where the king rarely trod. Occasionally an ex-concubine released from duty received an offer of marriage from a courtier, some of whom found it gratifying, and flattering to their status, to marry a former royal concubine who might still have some shadow of her former beauty.

The competitive nature of career progression in the Palace of Queens created a catty and spiteful atmosphere which made life there little fun for anyone except the eunuchs who ran the place and – being unable to obtain more earthy satisfactions – greatly enjoyed their power. They were presided over by Farna-zata, who while not (of course) a eunuch himself, relished power even more than they did. Farna-zata even sometimes indulged himself, with Astyages's tacit approval, by selecting a bedpartner from the morose community of the once-bedded.

The past few weeks had been even less fun than usual for anyone save Ushtana. Apart from one evening when he and Ushtana had quarrelled, Astyages had forsaken the company of any other of the women from the Palace of Queens. Ushtana had become the king's favourite, and Astyages doted on her as much as he was capable of doting on anyone except himself.

One particular evening, about a fortnight after Harpagus had surprised Cyrus in the middle of the night, Astyages was sitting up in his large bed, naked except for a flimsy red silk dressing-gown, and indulgently eating from a bowl of luscious, full-bodied purple grapes.

Ushtana, also naked, was next to him on his bed. That in itself was not remarkable. What was remarkable was that she was eating grapes from the same bowl, and at the same leisurely pace, as the king himself was.

Astyages's concubines *fed* him grapes; they did not eat grapes *with* him. But Ushtana had by now attained a status far beyond that of any ordinary concubine.

Astyages was feeling even more pleased with himself that evening than he usually did. Ushtana had become a companion to him in every sense of the word. As for that pig of a grandson of his in Persia: well, plans were afoot to deal with that particular problem...

That evening, eating grapes with Ushtana and looking forward to another night of passion, the king felt that life was about as perfect as it could ever be. He sat there, enjoying the grapes and the sight of Ushtana's splendid breasts, and thinking desultorily of all the people he had killed during his reign, or had commanded to be executed or assassinated, and how it was fitting that their inferior lives had been quenched in order to advance his own greatness.

Suddenly three quick knocks sounded on the door of his bedchamber.

Astyages glanced at Ushtana, who smiled indulgently back at him. Sometimes during the past weeks, Astyages had gained the impression that Ushtana thought *she* was the queen, and he, the all-powerful Astyages, her male concubine. Astyages found the idea strangely exciting.

'If it's you, Farna-zata, you villain,' Astyages called amiably through the door, 'you're early. Come back later... I still have much pleasure to enjoy.'

'Sire, it is I, Harpagus.'

Astyages gave a knowing nod, thinking at once: *so that upstart grandson of mine is finally dead, thanks be to Mithra. Now I can use the united armies to do my entire bidding.*

Astyages did not yet command Harpagus to come in, but glanced at Ushtana, supposing that she would want to leave the royal bedchamber for the confines of the Palace of Queens until the meeting with Harpagus was over. But Ushtana shook her head, and drew the bedclothes up to cover herself, though they did not cover her swirling fiery hair.

Astyages glanced at this infinitely exciting heroine of his bedroom who had transformed his life over the past few weeks. He had already noticed, on the two or three occasions when Harpagus had seen Ushtana (though never in quite such an intimate situation as this) that the general obviously admired her greatly. *Well, you may look as much as you wish*, Astyages thought. *She is mine, and while you can only dream about having her splendid body wrapped around you, I need not dream, for it is my nightly delight.*

Astyages pulled up a sheet around him and hid the bowl of grapes under the bedclothes. *No need to make our recent pleasure too obvious*, he reflected in a brief moment of consideration for someone else.

'Come in, Harpagus,' Astyages called out.

The door opened and Harpagus entered, his boots treading heavily on the white limestone floor, his armour clanking. He was wearing his full military uniform and had his sword in its sheath. He saw Ushtana, his eyes meeting hers very briefly. Astyages enjoyed the look of scarcely concealed admiration he saw on his general's face. *Admire her as much as you want, Harpagus*, Astyages reflected, *she is mine, and mine only.*

Harpagus kneeled before the king.

'Forgive me, sire, that I have not yet bathed after my journey. I thought you would wish to hear my news at once.'

Astyages smiled. He glanced at Ushtana, who smiled back at him. Of course he knew what the news was, but all the same he wanted to hear it from the lips of his general.

'You were right to come to me at once, my Harpagus,' Astyages replied, indulgently. 'Well, what news do you have for me... for us?' he added, with a glance of complicity at Ushtana.

'The prince of Persia is dead, sire,' Harpagus said, still not rising from his kneeling position. 'Your royal wish is fulfilled.'

Astyages gave a gratified nod. 'Well done, my Harpagus. You may rise now. Tell me what happened.'

Harpagus got to his feet. 'I woke your grandson, sire, from where he was sleeping like a drunken fool in his tent. I told him there was no king of Media and Persia but Astyages, and then I slit his throat. He died in agony, bleeding to death like a pig. One of my servants shall bring you my saddlebag with Cyrus's head in it later. It is not a fit sight for a lady.'

Astyages smiled even more broadly. He glanced at Ushtana. 'Well, my beauty, it seems you were right in this as in so much else. There will be no need for me to kill you after all.'

He turned to Harpagus and reached out his right hand from beneath the bedsheet, beckoning the general to him. When Harpagus was close enough, Astyages grasped his general's right hand in his own right hand, looking up at Harpagus as he did so.

'Harpagus,' Astyages said, 'you are a good man, and now that you have been properly punished for the one time you failed me, I very willingly name you one of my most trusted servants. With my grandson, the fool of Persia, dead, and with the king of Persia also with that foolish Persian god Ahura-Mazda, and my daughter now having no protector except me... you shall become the general of the united army.'

'Thank you, sire,' said Harpagus.

'It is a fitting reward for you, Harpagus,' Astyages replied, with the nod of an autocrat and despot who perfectly knew his own power and was prepared to condescend to acknowledge the assistance of a mere minion.

'Of course,' Astyages said, getting out of bed in his dressing-gown, 'you did displease me much when it turned out that you had lied about being certain my baby grandson was dead. I suspected you of being weak and foolish, and even sentimental. A baby is a mere mass of flesh: how can it possibly have any feelings or awareness of its own existence? A baby is a mere animal that cannot even control its own defecation!'

Astyages fell silent, his hand still grasping Harpagus's.

'Indeed, you were sentimental,' the king went on. 'But I am a merciful man and instead of having you painfully executed for your disloyalty I decided to punish you instead.'

Harpagus made no reply. Astyages felt convinced there was a contrite and even grateful look on the general's face.

'And to your credit, Harpagus, you took your punishment like a man, when a lesser man might have caused trouble, and obliged me to have him executed after all. You've shown your loyalty to me, my Harpagus.'

'I have always endeavoured to serve you, sire,' Harpagus said.

'And you have done so particularly well now, in lancing the boil that has been irritating my arse for much too long,' Astyages replied, then glanced at Ushtana as if to elicit approval for his superb wit. Ushtana smiled faintly. 'Now, Harpagus, go and sit in that chair over there and listen to my plans for how I shall manage matters, now that the boil is no longer stuck to my arse.'

Harpagus strode over to the chair and sat down in it. Astyages immediately began to speak of his plans for the future of Media and Persia.

'I agreed to my foolish grandson Cyrus's scheme to unite our army with that of Media because I knew that if I said yes he would toil hard to fulfil his dream, and then he could be removed at the right moment,' Astyages gloatingly said, glancing at Harpagus, then at Ushtana, as if generously confiding in them the inner workings of his great mind. 'The moment has come, and thanks to you, Harpagus, the rat is dead.'

Astyages rubbed his hands together. 'Now that my daughter's idiot son has met his end, just as her husband has, I shall truly be the master of our world. The two armies have, I know, forged links of friendship and loyalty with each other. They will follow only my orders. With Cyrus sharing the command of the armies with you, Harpagus, I felt the need to restrict my slave-hunting somewhat. But now Cyrus has handed me the two armies,' Astyages smiled at Harpagus and at Ushtana, 'I shall embark, with you, Harpagus, as my chief commander, and you, most beauteous wench, as my most desired companion, on a mission to find slaves far beyond our borders. I do not believe any army of our neighbours, not even the Lydians, can possibly resist us. I shall become an enslaver of a scale and calibre that will make the pharaohs of Egypt look like novices! We shall...'

But Astyages suddenly fell silent, for he had heard footsteps behind him.

The footsteps came from the direction of the door that led to the Palace of Queens. Astyages, imagining that the intruder was a foolish concubine who had lost her way, was about to deliver an insult, but as he turned round and saw who the intruder really was, his words froze in his throat.

It was Cyrus, in full battle armour.

Astyages's mouth fell open.

He stared at Cyrus, and then at Harpagus. 'You... you accursed traitor and liar!' Astyages snarled. 'Your corpse shall burn before nightfall.'

The king swung back to point his right forefinger at Cyrus. '*As shall yours.* You would not have even breathed air beyond your first night had it not been for the weakness of this giant fool.'

'Perhaps not,' said Cyrus, shaking his head. 'But then I believe Ahura-Mazda, not Harpagus, spared me. As for your plans, tyrant, they shall never happen. The united armies of Media and Persia, under the command of Harpagus and myself, surround Ecbatana and await our instructions. They are no longer loyal to you, but to us, for they know you ordered my murder. I was intrigued about what you planned to do with the armies. Now, from your own coarse lips, I know.'

Astyages was speechless.

'It shall not happen your way,' Cyrus said, 'for the greatest empire the world has ever known shall not be founded on slavery, but on winning the hearts of men – and women.'

Harpagus glared at Astyages. 'It shall be a great empire, but you shall watch it *from hell*.'

'You cannot kill me,' Astyages snarled, seeing, out of the corner of his eye, Ushtana watching what was happening not with fear but rather with curiosity. 'I am king of Media,' Astyages barked at Harpagus.

'No, you are merely a tyrant who is going to perish,' Harpagus snarled back. 'I am loyal now to the king of Persia, who will be the king of Media, too. We have both suffered at your hands.'

Astyages began screaming for the palace guards. But Harpagus, speaking calmly, said: 'The palace is surrounded. Your own guards are no match for ours.'

Harpagus reached inside his military clothes and brandished a small wooden sword, about a foot long. It was a toy sword, for fighting between children, but the weapon looked strong, and the wooden tip had been carefully sharpened.

Astyages stared at the sword as if mesmerized by it.

'This belonged to my boy Artabaz,' Harpagus explained to Astyages. 'I have worn it secretly about my person ever since that day when you conspired to have Artabaz killed, roasted, and set before me at your table. I have used the fearlessness that your roasting of my son had burned within *me* to my advantage. But I knew the day would come when I would avenge myself on you. That day has come now.'

'You are merely a fool and a traitor,' Astyages yelled at him, then, his courage obviously deserting him, began screaming out to his guards, but none came to help.

Harpagus, holding the wooden sword pointing toward Astyages, glanced at Ushtana. 'Lady, you should leave. This will not be a fit sight for any woman.'

But Ushtana shook her head. 'There is nothing I have not seen in my life. Besides, I do not desert my man if he is good to me.'

'Very well,' Harpagus said, his detestation of Astyages being given a fresh impetus by the image that suddenly swept into his mind of the hellish fiend sporting night after night with this wondrously beautiful woman.

'I shall... I shall give you one-half of my kingdom, Harpagus,' Astyages gasped. 'I shall make you a gift of ten thousand gold bars, and...'

But Harpagus slowly shook his head. 'You cannot buy me. But nor shall I kill you in cold blood. Indeed, I shall give you the advantage.'

Saying this, Harpagus went to fetch a sword – a real sword, not a wooden one – that was hanging from a hook on a wall. He drew the sword out of its scabbard and flung the sword handle-first, towards Astyages, who however made no move to pick it up, but just stared at it, and then at Harpagus.

The giant soldier began to remove his own armour. 'I do not wish for any unfair advantage,' he said, unfastening his armour and dropping it to the ground. 'But pick up your sword, and fight like a man.'

Finally, Astyages stumbled over to where the sword lay, and picked it up.

'I am your king!' he shouted, waving the sword erratically in the air, 'you should tremble before me!'

But Harpagus did not tremble. Instead, he launched his attack.

The fight did not last long. Astyages's old skills as a warrior had not entirely deserted him, and once the fight was underway, the strikes he made with his sword would have defeated a lesser man than Harpagus. Cyrus would doubtless have proved more than a match for Harpagus, but Astyages did not. The skirmish grew wild, as Astyages – feeling the demon death winging its black way towards him – became desperate. Finally, he swung his sword with such frantic power that had Harpagus not anticipated the blow it might have killed him. But as Astyages was recovering his balance from the great sword-swipe he had made, Harpagus, crying out *it is Artabaz killing you, vilest monster, it is Artabaz – my son you roasted – who stabs you now* plunged the sharp wooden dagger deep into Astyages's throat.

Astyages shrieked in agony. His sword fell from his right hand and onto the marble floor with a great clatter, as the life-blood Astyages had always enjoyed watching stream from the beheaded necks of mostly innocent people spurted in a frothy fountain from his own throat. Harpagus, no longer seeing any need for restraint, went on stabbing Astyages, filling him with puncture holes that ran with blood. Astyages screamed for as long as he was able to and even with his final breaths gurgled desperate pleas for mercy.

A few minutes later it was over.

Cyrus, was not bloodthirsty by nature. He had only watched the scene because he wanted to be absolutely sure of Harpagus's loyalty. Cyrus saw violence as a distasteful, unpleasant necessity. Yet he knew, if ever a death was deserved, it was that of Astyages.

What astonished Cyrus even more than Harpagus's ferocity was the equally cold look on the face of the concubine who, throughout all this, had watched the scene with perfect calmness.

The tyrant's body was now slumped on the cold floor in a pool of his own blood that mingled with the juice of the ripe, purple grapes the dying king and Harpagus had trodden on as Harpagus completed his ferocious assault.

The door on the far side of the room, the door opposite the one that led to the Palace of Queens, suddenly burst open. Farna-zata rushed into the room. He looked at Cyrus, then at Ushtana, and then at Harpagus. The wavy-haired grand vizier's mouth opened wide with astonishment.

Quick as thought, Harpagus drew another dagger: this time a real one of bronze, and hurled it at the grand vizier. The dagger sped point-first at Farna-zata, striking him in the very centre of his forehead. The needle-sharp tip splintered his skull and sank deeply into his even now scheming brain.

Farna-zata collapsed face forwards onto the floor, with the dagger still in his forehead. As he fell, the handle of the dagger smashed against the hard limestone floor, pressing the blade yet deeper into his dying mind. Dark blood gushed from the wound.

Harpagus smiled. 'Now fashion one of your devious stratagems from *that*,' he said to the grand vizier.

Farna-zata groaned, desperately tried to utter something, but merely exhaled and died.

Harpagus looked down at the blood-soaked body of Astyages and that of Farna-zata.

'I have taken revenge on the men I most detest in the world,' Harpagus said, in full sight of Cyrus and also of Ushtana, who had not moved.

Harpagus kneeled before Cyrus. 'I deserve to die, too, for my own unspeakable crimes toward you and for my evil murder, when I was a young man, of your first father and my wickedness in letting my soldiers kill your first mother. Behead me now, king of kings, and you, too, will have your revenge.'

Cyrus looked at Harpagus. He knew how earnest Harpagus was in all he said and did. He knew Harpagus was ready to die, now that he had avenged himself on Astyages and Farna-zata.

The image of Harpagus slaughtering Mithradat on the outskirts of Cyrus's home town of Paritakna flashed into Cyrus's mind. *Mithradat brought me up and took care of me,* Cyrus thought. *I once thought Mithradat and Spako were my mother and father. Should I take my revenge now, on their behalf?*

But Cyrus reflected it was the poison of Astyages and Farna-zata and their vile scheme to exterminate him that had brought Harpagus, a loyal young soldier, into an appallingly wicked scheme, forcing him to follow a terrible order he could only have disobeyed on pain of death.

'Arise, Harpagus,' Cyrus said. 'There shall be no more bloodshed today. You have sinned, but you are earning your redemption, and if I did not believe in the possibility of redemption, I do not think I could go on living.'

Cyrus fell silent for a moment, then added:

'We have both suffered at the hands of Astyages, and your suffering was even worse than mine, for you lost your only son.'

The giant general, his own hands still bloody from his killing of Astyages, rose slowly and heavily to his feet.

Cyrus reached out his right hand. Harpagus just looked at Cyrus, as if he could hardly believe that Cyrus had not killed him.

'I offer you my hand in friendship,' Cyrus said to him. 'You have sinned against me, Harpagus, but I forgive you, and ask you to be my friend.'

Harpagus was briefly silent, then began to weep in the way a real man does, stubbornly, grudgingly.

Finally he wiped his eyes with his left hand. Reaching out with his right, he clasped Cyrus's hand.

'The days of Astyages are over,' Cyrus said. 'Tyranny is dead. The lands of Persia and Media shall now be governed with wisdom and justice.'

'The days of Cyrus have begun,' Harpagus said, his voice hoarse with emotion. 'Hail Cyrus, king of kings.'

Cyrus smiled, 'Harpagus, I thank you.'

Both men turned to Ushtana, whose beautiful large brown eyes looked back at them fearlessly.

'It seems, lady, you will need to find another man to take care of you,' Harpagus murmured.

Ushtana cleared her throat. She did not feel sick at the sight of the two dead and greatly bloodied men on the floor, for faintness was not part of her character. Opportunism, however, was.

'I was thinking the same thing,' Ushtana murmured, with a smile.

She knew perfectly well how attractive her smiles were. She found herself wondering what the giant general was like in bed.

Harpagus looked hard at her. She met his glance levelly.

'Our world is changing,' Harpagus said. 'We have a new king, the greatest king who has ever lived, and it has been your privilege to see him at the moment when the old world ended, and the new world began. My life has changed too. So may ours. Tell me... would you like a new occupation?'

'A new occupation?' repeated Ushtana.

'Yes,' said Harpagus.

'And what is that?' Ushtana asked.

Their eyes met.

'To be my wife,' Harpagus replied at once.

'Your wife?' Ushtana repeated.

'Yes,' said Harpagus. 'Not my concubine, or my slave, or my mistress, but my wife.'

He just looked at Ushtana, and she looked back at him.

'You will love me?' she asked him.

'I have loved you from the moment I first saw you,' Harpagus replied.

'That is merely lust,' said Ushtana. 'I have seen it in the eyes of many men. I asked if you would love me?'

'Yes,' Harpagus said. 'I shall. But... will you love me? Will you be faithful to me?'

Ushtana gave a nod. 'I do not desert my man if he is good to me.'

Harpagus turned to Cyrus. 'Will you give us your blessing, king of kings?'

'With all my heart,' Cyrus replied. 'You make a proposal of marriage amid blood and slaughter, Harpagus. But you are a warrior, and I would not have expected anything else. Yes, you both have my blessing. Love her, Harpagus. And you... my dear... what is your name?'

'Ushtana, your Majesty,' she said.

'It is a beautiful name,' Cyrus said. 'You are Lydian?'

'Yes, sire.'

'It is a beautiful country, too.' Cyrus smiled. 'Who knows, before long you might see it again...'

26. King of Kings

More than a month had passed since the evil soul of King Astyages, the tyrant of Media, had been banished to the dark underworld ruled – so the Persians believed – by the destructive spirit Angra Mainyu, Ahura-Mazda's most virulent adversary. There, in that underworld, the souls of the damned were believed to suffer eternal torment.

The great united army of Media and Persia was assembled in disciplined formation close by the foot of Mount Alvand, one of the highest mountains in Persia.

For this ceremony, the army was joined by many of the most eminent citizens of Media and Persia. Under the new leadership of Cyrus, Media and Persia were now united not only militarily but also politically.

Night had fallen. Torches and candles burned by the thousands. Anyone who had looked down at the scene from the top of Mount Alvand might have believed themselves gazing at an entire galaxy of stars.

The warm night air was full of the sound of a choir of children from the united nations, singing praises of Cyrus in the tuneful trebles and sopranos of children's unbroken voices.

An opening as tall as a man had been laboriously hollowed out of the rock. The opening led into the side of the mountain, to a tomb where lay a much-loved though never powerful or great king: the mortal remains of Cambyses, Cyrus's father, the last king to rule only over Persia.

Cyrus stood in complete stillness, listening to the sweet singing that filled the air, his soul at peace.

He was a warrior, but he saw violence only as a last resort, when all reason had failed.

Cyrus, having witnessed the slaughter of Astyages, had been surprised at how little relish he himself had for the slaying, though it was true that he would very willingly have fought Astyages himself.

Standing there by his father's tomb, Cyrus reflected that perhaps we can never truly take revenge, because by the time we are in a position to exact it, the comparative impotence of the person on whom we are taking revenge makes our bid for it seem futile. This reflection was further confirmation of Cyrus's conviction that his own destiny lay not in enforcing retribution but rather in inspiring his people to be all they could possibly be, and if necessary even putting aside personal enmity.

Cyrus glanced at his mother Mandane, the widowed queen of Persia, who was on his left. To his right were Roshan, Asha and the ever-wealthier Raiva, who no longer played any role in military life. Harpagus was also there, though out of respect for Mandane, he had told Cyrus he would not stand in her vicinity.

Harpagus, and his new wife Ushtana (they had been married a mere week ago) were next to each other some rows behind the royal party, holding hands. Cyrus had managed to find it in his deep and boundless heart to forgive Harpagus, but Cyrus did not expect his mother to do the same. He knew there are things a mother can never forgive.

The wondrously beautiful singing reached a glorious crescendo, then the youthful singers fell silent.

A dark, sombre figure stepped out of the opening in the side of the mountain and into the pool of light created by the great torch Cyrus was holding and the torches held by Mandane, Roshan, Raiva and Asha.

The figure slowly approached Cyrus. It was Akinlana, the muscular African who had been the sword-master of King Cambyses and who had taught Cyrus the art of meditation.

He was carrying a mighty sword with an ornate handle made of bronze, and inlaid with gold, diamonds, rubies and emeralds.

Akinlana bowed to Cyrus. The bow was courteous, but not abject. The new king had made it clear he wanted respect from his subjects, but not grovelling humility or sycophancy. Cyrus knew that such emotions were never genuine anyway, and he wished his people to conduct themselves toward him, and each other, with respect and true feelings. As for the Palace of Queens at Ecbatana, Cyrus had arranged schooling for the younger women and was seeking good and decent husbands for the older ones among the merchants of Ecbatana. The eunuchs he had pensioned off.

Cyrus had already promised his people, by means of messengers sent to all the corners of Media and Persia, that change would come and that their lives would improve.

'Sire, the ancestral sword of your father Cambyses is now engraved with the legend *Cyrus, king of kings,*' Akinlana intoned. 'The reverse of the sword bears, at your request, not only the name of your father Cambyses but also the name of the man you had regarded as your father and the man who raised you: Mithradat.'

Cyrus remembered, as he had remembered so often, how Mithradat had died. Cyrus knew the memory would always break his heart, and that his willingness to forgive Harpagus his sins would be a daily test of his own creed of forgiveness and tolerance.

Cyrus drew a breath, thanked Akinlana and accepted the sword. The moment Cyrus held it in his hands, he raised the sword high above his head. A huge roar erupted from the crowd.

Once the cheering had died down, Akinlana, in his deep, powerful voice, intoned:

'Long live Cyrus, lawful successor not only of King Cambyses of Persia but also of the tyrant Astyages of Media. Long live Cyrus, king of Persia and Media! Hail Cyrus, king of kings!'

27. The Bracelet

Asha and Farna-dukta's three-year-old son Ariya, was standing on the lap of the king of the Persian Empire, chuckling.

Farna-dukta smiled. Cyrus held the boy's small hands carefully in his own large ones that were gnarled with work, struggle, combat and weapon practice. Cyrus had little knowledge of small children; he imagined they were frail and flimsy and their bones easily broken.

The king was visiting Asha and his wife at their modest, comfortable home in Anshan.

'He's stronger than he looks, Cyrus,' she said. Her Persian was by now fluent, though she still spoke it with a Babylonian accent.

'I rarely have children on my lap,' Cyrus said.

'And it is such a shame,' said Farna-dukta. 'For I believe you would be an excellent father.'

'I agree,' Asha added.

Ariya laughed and began bounding about on Cyrus's lap. Cyrus's pleasure was obvious.

'Cyrus,' Asha said, 'the greatest happiness in the whole world is not money, as my brother believes, nor power. It is family life.'

Cyrus smiled. 'What is my good friend trying to tell me?'

'That he thinks our great emperor and protector would indeed make as excellent a father as he does a king and warrior,' Farna-dukta said.

Ariya chuckled again.

Nowadays, Harpagus was Cyrus's second-in-command of the great united army. The two men worked well together, perhaps because they never took the other's willingness to co-operate for granted.

It was known throughout his empire that Cyrus practised the forgiveness, reconciliation and tolerance he preached, for who did not know that the army commander Harpagus, whose only son the murderous tyrant had roasted alive, had killed the man Cyrus had once thought of as his father and the woman Cyrus had regarded as his mother? Many could not understand how such magnanimity and willingness for reconciliation could be possible; surely their king had a great heart that was second only to that of Ahura-Mazda himself?

Many of the smaller nations that lay close by to the empire of Persia and Media had seen the united army riding toward them during the past three years. Maka, Gandara, Cilicia, Margiana, Bactria and Arachosia, to name just a few, were countries of unhappy, bitter, impoverished peoples who had formerly lived solely for war, but who had now succumbed to Cyrus's army and taken their first steps toward becoming civilized. All the tribes whose territories bordered that of Media and Persia were by now living productively and in peace within the Persian Empire.

The army was commanded by Harpagus, whom Ushtana nowadays always accompanied when he was in the field on manoeuvres. She made homely wherever he might be staying, and she knew how best to welcome him home. Cyrus was certain that Harpagus's happiness had made the giant warrior even more accomplished in his professional duties than ever. The magnificent Immortals, bells in their hair and death dripping from their weapons, easily overwhelmed any force so unwise as to confront them rather than enter into negotiations.

Yet despite his successes, Cyrus did not indulge himself in appreciations of his own skill as a warrior and leader. He sought to create no cult of personality, as Astyages had done. He was content with remaining celibate too, for – so far from keeping a Palace of Queens of his own – Cyrus remained unmarried.

Many of the aristocratic mothers of his empire, whose comely and virginal daughters were of marriageable age, would despair of ever interesting their great king in meeting their daughters.

'Our king is too wedded to our destiny to be interested in women,' they would say when they met in one another's homes over a cup of wine and a sweet pastry.

'You obviously haven't heard that the king thinks most highly of Lady Roshan, whom he grew up with in the countryside,' another friend told her. 'He cares for her a great deal.'

'If this is true why does he not marry her?' one newly-enriched lady asked.

They all considered this, for it had already caused them much puzzlement.

'Perhaps he is too busy with cares of state,' said one.

'Yes, perhaps he considers himself married to the empire he is creating,' said another.

They were right on two counts. Cyrus did feel wedded to the destiny of his growing empire. Yet it was also true that Roshan was always running through Cyrus's mind. They saw each other often, and on the relatively rare occasions Cyrus was not exercising with the army or discussing affairs of state with his officials and lieutenants, he and Roshan might be seen strolling around Anshan's bazaars in the evening... as friends.

Cyrus lived the way he had always lived, devoting himself completely to his empire. The gratifications of power and fame were enough for him and made him feel he did not need satisfactions in his personal life, too.

But the evening with Asha and Farna-dukta, when Cyrus had dangled Ariya on his lap, and heard what Asha and Farna-dukta had said about the delights of family life, had made Cyrus think...

... and dream.

Some of the dreams were of the most pleasant nature, but... one hot night, Cyrus had a dream that appalled him.

He was walking, alone, by the banks of a curious red lake that he and Roshan had visited sometimes on one of their invariably fruitless leopard-hunting expeditions. The lake gleamed in his dream like the polished surface of a crimson shield. In his dream, he had felt an inexplicable sense of loss, and had wandered forlornly along the gravel on the level shelving shore of the lake.

Suddenly, in his dream, his eye had been caught by something in the water, perhaps twenty or thirty paces away. A moment later, he knew he was looking at a body. Right away, he dived into the lake and swam strongly out to the body. He could see, now, by the clothes the body wore that it was the body of a woman, her head floating downwards in the water. He grasped her wet hair, to turn her over and see who she was, but... as her face swung round, he woke up...

He often went to sleep hoping he might have the dream again and see whose face it was, but the dream did not revisit him.

One summer evening, some weeks later, Cyrus and Roshan were mingling with the crowds in the bazaars of Anshan, examining the latest batch of coloured silk garments that had arrived that same day from Babylon. No-one, not even the religious sages of Anshan and Ecbatana, knew the mystery of the origins of silk. This mystery made the beautiful, costly, evanescent fabric, which held bright dyes so well, seem all the more miraculous to those who loved it.

After wandering around the bazaars with Roshan for some time (it was a measure of the love and esteem in which his people held him that Cyrus never felt the need for a bodyguard, though of course many of the people he passed by stared at him), he invited her, as he often did, to dine with him in a private room at his palace.

'I have something of great importance to ask you,' he said, when they were seated.

The table was spread with a variety of delicious warm and cold dishes, a skin of strong red Persian wine, and various freshly-pressed fruit juices. Cyrus rarely drank wine nowadays.

Roshan poured herself a cup of the wine. 'What's on your mind?'

They sat down together at the table, though remaining some distance apart.

'It is the most important question I have ever asked you,' Cyrus added.

Roshan finished pouring herself wine. Cyrus noticed her right hand was unsteady.

She set down the wine-skin, and looked at him intently.

'Before I ask you,' Cyrus said, 'I want to give you this.'

He drew out from a pocket within his cloak the gold bracelet, with the design of the two griffins.

'You remember it, of course?' Cyrus asked.

Roshan nodded. 'How could I forget? You acquired it from that slave-merchant, whose career we ended. You sent this bracelet to Astyages, and he contemptuously used it to try to buy your life.'

'Yes,' Cyrus murmured.

They looked at each other.

'I want you to have it,' Cyrus said.

'Why?'

'Because it is rightfully yours. I owe you my life.'

'So?' replied Roshan. 'We are friends. If wicked and treacherous men try to kill my friends, I try to save them.'

'You saved the man who became the king of Persia and Media.'

Roshan shrugged. 'When I saved him, I did so simply because he *was* my friend.'

'Yes,' Cyrus said, giving a nod. 'And now, your friend gives it to you. And bids you to remember that by making a gift of this to you, I am giving you a part of me.'

Roshan smiled faintly. 'You've become very thoughtful this evening. You ought to relax a little. A cup of wine?'

'No, thank you, prune juice is fine.'

'Very well,' said Roshan. She glanced at the bracelet, which he was still holding. He handed it to her and she took it. She rubbed her fingers over it, feeling the delicacy of its artistry, and the intricacy of the gold filigree.

'Cyrus, what am I supposed to do with this? I could never wear it: people would think me boastful and showy.'

'Then sell it. It is, after all, yours.' He smiled. 'Become as rich as King Croesus of Lydia.'

'I shall never sell this. How can you say such a thing? Besides, not even this would make me a rich as him.'

'Become as rich as Raiva then...'

'Do not talk to me of Raiva,' Roshan said. 'He is different now from the boy we grew up with in Paritakna. He thinks of little else but money, and business. I am sure he regrets that you have banned slavery, for I can easily imagine he often thinks of the money that could be made from slavery if you permitted it.'

She was silent for a moment. 'Cyrus, do you know he has asked me to marry him?'

Cyrus stared at her. '*He has?*'

'Yes,' Roshan said. 'He told me he loved me, and wanted me to be his wife.'

'And what did you say?' Cyrus said, impulsively asking the question before he had any idea what he would do, or think, if she'd said *yes* to Raiva.

'I told him it was out of the question.'

Relief coursed through Cyrus's veins like fresh blood.

'He asked me for my reasons, of course,' Roshan added, 'so I simply replied that I was not in love with him, nor ever could be.'

Cyrus sat back in his chair. He did not know what to make of Roshan's revelation.

She put the bracelet around her left wrist. Cyrus thought it looked as natural there as if it had always been there.

'I think I could only wear this here in the palace or in my room,' said Roshan. 'Cyrus, I should not say this, for you know I am not a vain woman whose soul can be purchased with trinkets, but I adore it.' She stroked the beautiful bracelet, her long, strong, tanned, fingers running over the ornament again. She looked up at him. 'Thank you.'

'I am glad you like it,' Cyrus said.

'I do. Now, please, tell me your reason for asking me here.' But before he had a chance to reply, she added: 'As for your question, you need to know that I intend to say yes to whatever you ask of me.'

Cyrus smiled. 'I know. I have never questioned your loyalty, but as one of my closest friends I implore you to listen before making any decision.'

'I think I can guess what you want to ask of me,' said Roshan, with a smile.

'You can?'

'I believe so.'

'Yes, of course,' said Cyrus. 'After all, we know each other very well.'

Roshan smiled a little. 'Tell me... tell me what you want to ask me. I so much want to hear the words from your lips.'

Cyrus poured himself a cup of prune-juice, drank most of it, then said:

'I do not care for the trappings of power. You know that, and I hope my subjects do too. But I shall not win the respect I wish to win, and need to win, throughout our region – and especially further west, where money and status mean so much to people – unless I have a new palace of my own. My palace here in Anshan is too far south, and more importantly Anshan shall forever be associated with the... well, with the weaknesses of my beloved late father Cambyses, may Ahura-Mazda guard him in peace.'

Cyrus fell silent for a moment, then added:

'I do not want to use Astyages's palace in Ecbatana, because that is too heavily associated with him. I need a new palace further north. To the north-west of Anshan, a day's ride away, lies a plain of great beauty, close by the valley of the river Polvar, a plain as verdant as any in all of Persia or Media. I intend to build a new palace on that plain, and to establish a town there to serve it. The palace shall not merely be a home for me, but a place where all my subjects can come and enjoy the most lavish gardens the world has ever seen.'

He paused. Roshan was just staring at him, but she said nothing.

'I already have a name for the palace and its gardens: Pasargadae,' said Cyrus. 'I understand from Akinlana, who suggested the name, that it is a word from the oldest known form of our language, a form we no longer use. The word means "the place of heroes." All our heroes shall be honoured there in cuneiform inscriptions. In decades and centuries to come the greatest heroes of the empire shall be laid to rest there. And when my own time comes to pass out of this mortal world, if my people will it, I too shall be buried there. Yet Pasargadae shall not be a shrine to death. No, it shall be a place where life, too, is celebrated.'

He paused again. Roshan's expression seemed to Cyrus one of pure astonishment at the vision of Pasargadae that he was presenting to her. He felt encouraged by this. His whole speech so far had been enthusiastic, but now he continued with even greater enthusiasm.

'The Hanging Gardens of Babylon,' said Cyrus, 'are, as you told me not long ago, one of the wonders of the world. I intend that in time to come, people shall hail Pasargadae as another of the world's wonders. Even the eternal paradise we are promised after death, if our good works in life warrant a life in heaven with Ahura-Mazda, shall not rival Pasargadae. I know that some would consider what I have just said blasphemous, but I have no shame in Ahura-Mazda hearing what I have just said. And why not? I shall tell you. The reason is that I am sure he will bless me... and you, and what you will create. For you have done such wonderful work in the palace gardens and the gardens of our public parks, that I wish to appoint you mistress and chief designer of my new gardens at Pasargadae.'

Cyrus fell silent, smiling as he anticipated her pleasure at being offered this great commission.

Roshan, the bracelet around her wrist, was just staring at him in a kind of blank amazement. 'Was this what you wanted to ask me?'

'Yes,' said Cyrus, eagerly. 'I know how much you love gardens. I mean that I want you to devote yourself to creating, in Pasargadae, a garden to rival even those in Babylon.'

He fell silent again.

'Was this what you wanted to ask me?' she hissed at him.

He shrugged. 'Yes. You see, I am hoping that...'

But he fell silent, in astonishment, and just watched as Roshan, having quickly taken off the bracelet and slipped it into a pocket of her dress, stood up, turned from him without saying a word and ran out of the room, slamming the door behind her.

28. The Lake of Blood

'Cyrus, what did you expect?' said Asha.

The king was visiting late. He had arrived after Farna-dukta and their little son Ariya were asleep. There, in the small dining-room of Asha's house, the great leader of the ever-growing Persian Empire quietly related to his friend, comrade, and leader of the Immortals what had happened when Roshan visited.

Cyrus nodded slowly after Asha had asked his question. 'Yes, you speak wisely, Asha. I have been foolish.'

Asha smiled gently. 'I think our great king can see everything in the world except what stares him in the face.'

'You may be right,' Cyrus said, taking a sip of the wine Asha had offered him.

'There is one thing, though, that I believe gives you reason for optimism.'

'What could that possibly be?'

'This. Lady Roshan kept the bracelet, did she not?'

Cyrus shrugged. 'Yes, she did.'

'Well, that's a good sign. After all, if she was truly furious with you she would had left the bracelet on the table, or... more likely, have thrown it at you.'

'I suppose she knows how valuable the bracelet is.'

'Cyrus, that remark is not worthy of you. You know Lady Roshan does not care for trinkets.'

'Then why did she keep it?'

'Truly, you know the answer to that, too. I am sure she kept the bracelet because, even as angry as she was, she knew it was a part of you no-one could ever take from her, and she did not want to lose it. She loves you, Cyrus.'

Silence fell again.

'What am I to do?' Cyrus asked.

Asha shrugged. 'I cannot tell you; that is for you to decide. All I can say is you are a lucky man. Many men love Lady Roshan – including my brother...'

'Yes, I know. She told me of his proposal.'

'He has proposed to her several times.' said Asha. 'But you know what Lady Roshan is like: she only wants what she wants, and if she can not have it she would rather have nothing.'

Cyrus made no reply for a while, but sat quietly sipping his wine.

'I must go to see her,' he said, finally.

Asha looked doubtful. 'Best to sleep on it. Best to wait. Women do not always like impulsive actions from men as much as we men sometimes hope they might.'

'That may be so,' said Cyrus. 'But I am going nonetheless.'

Roshan still lived in the suite of rooms in the outlying wing of the palace where she had been living ever since she arrived at Anshan with Cyrus and the others. She received a generous salary for overseeing the gardens of the royal palace and those in the public parks. Cyrus knew Roshan could by now have afforded to buy a house of her own, but she stayed where she was, dwelling in the same palace as he did, though in a outlying part some distance from the main building where Cyrus himself lived.

He had always imagined that Roshan's unwillingness to move away from the palace grounds reflected her devotion to, and love of, the palace gardens. But now, as Cyrus, carrying a lit torch to light his way, walked quickly to the palace from the house where Asha and Farna-dukta lived with their little boy (they had by now purchased a house in Anshan), he wondered, for the first time ever, whether there might be another reason why Roshan had not left her suite of rooms in the palace.

The long, cool corridor with grey flagstones underfoot that led to where Roshan lived was silent and deserted. When Cyrus reached Roshan's door he paused outside it for a while, wondering whether he should knock, or whether it might be much better, after all, to hasten away, back to the main palace building.

The reason why, finally, he knocked on the door was that he knew that if he did not, he would spend the rest of his life wishing he had.

For some time there was no answer. Only then did it occur to him that she might have gone to see friends, to seek consolation, and was very possibly staying with them.

Just as he'd reached his conclusion, the door opened a few inches, and he saw Roshan's piercing brown eyes staring at him through the gap between the clay wall and the door itself.

'What is it? What is it you want? Why are you here?'

Her expression was blank, and so was her voice.

She was wearing a pink silk night-dress. The bracelet was around her left wrist, the golden griffins glimmering strangely in the half-darkness.

'May I... can I come in?' he asked.

'No.'

'But I want to talk to you.'

'Well,' Roshan replied, 'we can talk... at a proper time and in a proper place. Not here. After all, we're *friends*, aren't we? Or at least,' she added scornfully, 'we're as much friends as a man and woman can be, since because I am a woman I can never hope to be your equal. That's what you think, isn't it?'

'You know I don't...'

'Actually you do,' Roshan said. 'You never truly think I can be your equal.' She paused. 'I will grant you a meeting to discuss your precious gardens at Pasargadae, but not now, when it is so late.'

'I... I love you, Roshan,' Cyrus murmured.

She gave a scornful sneer. 'No, you *do not*. You love only Persia, and the dream of your destiny.'

He said nothing.

'I am right, aren't I?' she said.

'No,' said Cyrus. 'You are wrong.'

They just looked at each other.

A moment later the door of her room opened inward and she beckoned him inside into her warm and fragrant room. There were a few candles lit, creating, along with the light of the torch, vague and ghostly shadows against the wall.

She closed the door behind them. Cyrus put the torch into an inverted cone, made from strands of coarse flat iron, that served as a torch-holder on the wall.

A moment later he and Roshan were in each other's arms, kissing so fiercely and breathlessly that they panted.

'I love you beyond all dreams,' Cyrus whispered, when, after some time, they finally snatched a brief break from their kissing.

'Even if that is true,' said Roshan, breathlessly, 'I know you will marry before long, for sooner or later you will want an heir. I will kill myself if you marry another woman. Or kill her first.'

Cyrus saw how a shadow had fallen across her beautiful face. She began to weep, bitterly, painfully, silently, her whole body racked by suffering. He still looked at her, but now she averted his gaze. And so she did not see him approach her and again take her in his arms.

This time, she felt hard and unyielding, and Cyrus feared she was going to push him away or even strike him again. He felt a spasm pulse through her body, as if she herself was unsure how to respond to his touch. Yet he felt her all womanly, strong and wondrous in his arms, and then she seemed to grow relaxed and even yielding as he held her, and he brought his mouth to hers, and once more kissed her.

His grip grew tighter, and he felt her holding him more tightly. He felt the sense of absorbing her, or being absorbed by her, he could hardly tell which.

Finally, he whispered, '*Leave with me.*'

'What?' she said, 'now?'

'Yes, now. The moon is almost full; it will show us the way. Let's get on our horses and ride off into the night as if we were hunting leopards.'

Her eyes, which he could see were heavy with affection and fear of losing him, met his.

'Let us be together,' added Cyrus, 'far from the palace, far from the cares of state, far from everything we have to think about. Let us be alone, far from all this.'

'What... what will your servants say? They may think you have been kidnapped, or murdered.'

'No, they know that no-one here in Anshan, or anywhere else, would dare to do that, even if anyone had such desires. My servants will simply be told I have gone out into the countryside by myself, as I sometimes do. They know I like to meditate far from human habitation. Come, dearest Roshan, for believe me, I have spent too many years blinded to my love for you. Now I do not want to waste another precious second.'

'Follow me,' said Roshan.

They stole out silently from the palace and headed to the stables to saddle their horses. The stablemen were all asleep. Cyrus and Roshan packed food and drink in their saddle-bags, and tied their hunting-bows and quivers of finely-fletched hunting-arrows to their saddles. They took some blankets with them and Cyrus picked up an old blue cloak. Tigra, Cyrus's powerful black stallion was not well, so Cyrus chose another stallion from his stable.

Talking quietly of where exactly they intended to head for in the surrounding countryside they both knew so well, they cantered their horses quietly out through the palace grounds.

Only once did Cyrus stop, at Asha's house, asking Roshan to remain on her horse out of sight.

When Asha came to the door, Cyrus murmured briefly that he would be away for some days, and that he would appoint Asha responsible for state business in his absence.

'Where are you going, Cyrus?' Asha asked.

'In truth I do not exactly know. I charge you to tell the Court not to grow anxious, for I shall return. In my absence, be me.'

Asha slowly shook his head. 'That is... impossible, Cyrus.'

Cyrus smiled at him. 'Then you must do your best.'

He was gone.

Once he and Roshan were free of the palace grounds, they galloped away into freedom.

There were many forests and valleys in the surrounding country-side around Anshan; they knew that countryside well. Cyrus saw that she was heading to... *surely not there*, he thought.

But that was where Roshan was heading.

Their destination lay about ten miles to the north-west of the Persian capital, and so approximately in the direction of Pasargadae, the new capital Cyrus was planning, whose gardens were the subject of his 'proposal' to Roshan, which had so angered her.

Soon it was clear to Cyrus where she was heading.

It was the place they had both visited before on one of their many fruitless but delightful leopard-hunts. They had loved the place, and had not been concerned that there seemed little likelihood of coming across any leopards.

They arrived after riding for most of the morning.

The place was a small glade of ash-trees that sloped slowly down to the broad, approximately circular lake, about five hundred paces in diameter, and known for being extremely deep in the middle. But the water of the lake, while fresh, had a red colour to it, which came from the reddish soil hereabouts, and no fish were found in the lake, so no village community of fishermen and their families had sprung up here.

As for the reddish soil, apart from the small ash-tree glade that had somehow managed to thrive there, it was too unyielding for even the most optimistic shepherd or farmer (and Media and Persia alike were full of shepherds or farmers blessed by unflagging optimism) to make any attempt to scratch a living.

Not that the reddish colour of the water was visible now, under the moon. The very lack of human habitation, though, made this place, Cyrus had always thought, all the more beautiful. But now, because of his dream, he felt the strongest sense of foreboding, which competed vigorously with his feelings of affection for Roshan.

He and Roshan dismounted from their horses, tied their steeds to a tree and walked together, not holding hands, not touching, in silent thoughtfulness until they reached the deserted border of the lake. Once there, they stood side-by-side, looking out over the dark water.

'In the light of day it always looks as if lovers had spilt their blood in the lake and died in it together,' Roshan murmured.

'Yes,' Cyrus said quietly.

They turned to each other. To Cyrus, the moment felt so full of emotion and tension he could hardly breathe.

At last, slowly, he leaned toward Roshan and kissed her. For a few moments she seemed hesitant, then she responded hungrily, and soon feverishly.

They threw off their clothes and lay together on the sandy shore in the moonlight. The sand felt harsh against their skin, so Cyrus spread the dark blue cloak on the sand and they lay down together upon it.

'Do you still think men and women unequal *now*?' Roshan asked.

She was sitting astride him, her hands grasping his and pushing them back. The long tawny mane of her hair was falling over his face. She had been kissing him long and lingeringly, bending her head down to do so, but had just that moment lifted her head away from his so she could ask him her question.

Cyrus was deep inside her.

'Of course... I do,' he said, breathing slowly and trying to keep calm so as to avoid reaching his climax.

She clasped him more firmly within her in order both to delay him and to show him, and herself, her control of him. 'You don't,' she whispered, teasingly.

'You know... you know I do,' he murmured.

Shaking her head slowly and even sorrowfully, Roshan went on pressing down on his hands with her own, entwining her strong, long fingers among his own strong, stubbier ones, and holding him firmly inside her, as if, far from being his equal, she was at that moment his master.

Cyrus and Roshan stayed by the shore of the strange deserted red lake for three days and nights.

They became as one in their souls, yet Roshan often teased him for what he had said to her when she was a girl: that girls can never be the equal of boys. Her teasing was frivolous, but Cyrus detected an undercurrent of seriousness in what she said. This distressed him, for he realized she meant what she said. He suspected that no matter how often she denied it, Roshan would always believe that he did not esteem women as highly as men.

But they spoke of many other things, too, and they loved each other profoundly.

Cyrus came to see that time as one when he felt he had walked hand-in-hand with Ahura-Mazda himself, who had temporarily come to earth in the person of a woman whom Cyrus had known – and, in truth, loved – since his childhood.

Yet he never forgot the dream he had had about the lake.

As for the dark blue cloak, when the time came for them to leave their haven together and return to the world, Cyrus washed the cloak in the blood-red waters of the lake and let it dry in the sun.

'I shall treasure this cloak always,' he told her.

29. News from Lydia

'So, what did King Croesus reply?' Cyrus asked the three Persian emissaries.

Some weeks had passed. Cyrus was sitting in his throne room at the royal palace in Anshan. Cyrus only called his own room the throne room out of irony; it was in truth the room of a practical man who had worked tirelessly to forge an empire. There was not even a throne in it, just several chairs around a large, rough-hewn mahogany table. On the table was a large map almost as big as the table itself.

The map, whose extremities were secured to the hard mahogany by iron nails, showed what was, for most Persians, the known world: the lands of Persia and Media and the countries, including Lydia and Babylonia and the minor states, that were now part of the Persian Empire. Scattered over the map in various strategic places were small wooden models of chariots, footsoldiers, bowmen and sling-warriors that represented the deployment of the united forces of the empire.

Cyrus was there with Asha, his minister of war. Harpagus, the army's commander, would usually have attended, but he was exercising the army out on the new encampment to the west of Anshan, now that Cyrus had wanted the army to be based closer to the city he loved. He was meticulous about detail. He insisted that the army be kept in a permanent state of readiness.

The emissaries' clothes were still spattered with the mud and dust of their journey.

'Well?' Cyrus asked, in a firm but kindly voice.

One of the emissaries, evidently selected by the others as their spokesman, took a step forwards. He cleared his throat.

'Sire, after we had been kept waiting for some time, in a corridor of the Lydian king's great palace at Sardis, we were finally granted an audience with Croesus. He received us sitting on a throne of what looked like pure gold.'

'That must be good sign, Cyrus,' Asha put in. 'Croesus is known for the contempt he shows to any emissaries or diplomats. I have heard that he rarely receives them in person, but instead that his grand vizier sees them in a room where there is a painting of Croesus, as if that were somehow a substitute for the king himself.'

Cyrus nodded. 'Yes, I have heard that's how Croesus usually treats his guests.' He smiled. 'Well, we must show Croesus what the demands of hospitality truly require, if he is ever *our* guest.'

Asha laughed in a knowing way. The emissaries, who appeared unsure whether it would be courteous of them to laugh in the presence of their great king, merely smiled awkwardly.

Cyrus glanced at the emissary who had spoken. 'And what did Croesus tell you, when he was so good as to allow you into his presence?'

'Sire, despite keeping us waiting, King Croesus was at first courteous. He had an interpreter by his side who knew our Persian language and also the tongue of the Lydians. Through his interpreter, the king bade us sit down. After we had done so, he offered us date wine, and a strange confection similar to jelly, which tasted of the scent of roses, and was sweet and delicious.'

The emissary paused, as if (it seemed to Cyrus) in brief affectionate memory of this treat, then went on, 'While we were sampling his hospitality, sire, King Croesus asked us what message we had from you. Your Majesty, I told him what you had instructed us to say: that the attacks Lydia has made against three of our westernmost towns close by the Lydian border are completely unacceptable and that it is only because you are a merciful man that you are not exacting severe retribution on Lydia for those attacks.'

The emissary drew a quick breath, then went on:

'We also told King Croesus that you wish for a friendly alliance with Lydia, in order that both our nations may ensure mutual friendship and security. We then handed to Croesus the sealed tablet you had given us for him. The interpreter was clearly a scholar, for he could read it. He did so, and translated its contents into the Lydian language for the benefit of the king.'

The emissary fell silent. The tension in the war room seemed to Cyrus as heavy as the mist that often hung in the air early on a winter morning, making the canvas of a tent so damp that if you touched the canvas, droplets of water dripped through it.

'And... what was the king's response?' Asha asked.

'Sire, the king told us, through his interpreter, that he had much respect for you, but he said you were... he said you were impetuous, sire... not to have executed Harpagus for slaying Astyages, who Croesus said had been a good king and an ally of Lydia for many years. Croesus also said that the attacks on our towns were in retribution for the killing of Astyages, and that Lydia was still considering its response to the murder and what it means for Lydia's own security.'

The emissary fell silent.

Cyrus, nodding slowly, as if he had half-expected this response from Croesus, glanced at Asha and then at the emissaries. He thanked them for their courage and fortitude, before instructing Asha they were each to be given an extra month's pay. Cyrus told the emissaries to bathe and to seek quarters for the night in rooms in one of the outbuildings of the royal palace.

'I shall tell the cooks that under my authority they must prepare for you whatever meal you wish this evening,' Cyrus added, 'and that they shall serve it to you with skins of the finest royal wine.'

The emissaries thanked him and retreated backward out of the war room.

Once they had gone, Cyrus glanced at Asha. 'It is as I thought. Our united nations can never be secure while Lydia is our enemy.'

Cyrus shrugged, as if to indicate that he had done his best to reason with Croesus.

'What exactly do we know of the extent of the Lydian forces?' Cyrus asked Asha, the leader of the Immortals.

'They number about ten thousand horsemen,' Asha replied, 'plus about forty thousand foot-soldiers, each armed with javelins, which is the preferred weapon of the men on foot. We know that Croesus has formed a loose alliance with Artacamas the king of Greater Phrygia, with Aribaeus king of Cappodocia, and even, reputedly, with the Assyrians. We do not know how many additional soldiers these allies will add to the Lydian army.'

Cyrus shrugged. 'I thought the Assyrians have vowed that they will never be part of any alliance.'

'Perhaps Croesus has bought them,' Asha said. 'From what I know of the Assyrians, they will do anything for gold and silver.'

Cyrus nodded. 'Perhaps so, but in the field of battle, allegiances bought with gold and silver may readily prove to be less substantial than air.'

'I agree,' Asha murmured. 'I only wish my brother felt the same. To me he seems obsessed by money.'

'Yes, he is,' said Cyrus, 'but when the time comes for a man to pass from this world, and when his friends speak of him at his funeral and the gathering that follows, no-one ever says "he was a most excellent gentleman, for he was rich". Instead, they speak of what good he did in his life, and they speak of his children, and of those who loved him. We enter Ahura-Mazda's kingdom empty-handed, Asha, and Ahura-Mazda greets us – if we are worthy – and looks only at our souls.'

'Yes, Cyrus,' said Asha, 'but I think my brother means to enjoy life now, and postpone for as long as he possibly can the day when he meets Ahura-Mazda.'

The two men were momentarily silent.

'Cyrus?'

'Well?'

'On another matter... you know the wealthy Persian merchant Farnaspes, of course...?'

'Indeed,' said Cyrus. 'I also know that Raiva and he have become allies who are as close as wax... I suppose he and your brother spend their time comparing their treasure chests.'

'No, Cyrus. Farnaspes is not like the man my brother has become. Farnaspes is a good man, who has worked hard to amass his fortune. And... he has a daughter, his youngest, and it is of her I wish to speak to you. Cyrus, her beauty would make a summer dawn... after Ahura-Mazda has tossed the golden orb that chases away the stars... seem plain by comparison. Her name is Cassadane. Quite aside from her beauty, she is a good, sweet person. Do you remember what I once mentioned to you about the source of true happiness? I think Cassadane would make you an excellent wife.'

Cyrus took a few paces around the room. He knew – or at least he felt as sure as he could be – that Asha had no idea of how things had recently been between him and Roshan.

Cyrus stopped pacing, and stared at Asha.

'This is your brother's suggestion, I suppose?'

Asha went red. 'Well... yes, it is. He thinks Cassadane would be a perfect wife for you.'

'And of course it would be perfect for him, too, would it not, for him to be the one who effected the introduction?'

'Yes, Cyrus, that's true, but... I think you judge Raiva too harshly. He is much concerned with acquiring gold and silver, yes, but he also cares about your happiness.'

'And his own, I imagine, even more. He would also doubtless want me to marry Cassadane so that I am less likely to marry Lady Roshan.'

Asha did not reply at once. Then, speaking to his friend, the great king who had once been a mere poor shepherd's child, he said:

'Cyrus, not even you, so blessed by Ahura-Mazda as you are, can live forever. Persia needs an heir. If this need is not fulfilled, when you do finally go to join Ahura-Mazda, and become one of the great souls of his kingdom, your legacy will not be the stability of a dynasty but mayhem and confusion.'

Asha opened his hands wide as he looked at Cyrus, a gesture of calm reasoning and a courteous appeal to commonsense. 'Besides, why would you not like to be a husband and a father? Cassadane would love you, Cyrus. I have met her, and I have seen how her eyes and face light up at the mention of your name. She is a good woman. Her father may be rich, but she values things of the soul more than money. And her beauty...

her beauty is endless and unfathomable. Truly, a man could lose himself – or find himself – in her embraces and kisses.'

Cyrus made no reply.

'I count Lady Roshan as my precious friend,' Asha went on. 'She is the little girl who fought as well as any of us in the old days, and who can still fight well now. I know she loves you. Anybody who sees her when she is in the same room as you can see it. But she is almost as old as you, perhaps too old to be your wife. And say truly, Cyrus: if you loved Lady Roshan as she loves you, and if you thought she could make you happy, would she not already be your wife?'

Asha paused, as if he expected Cyrus to reply. But Cyrus said nothing.

'Cyrus, it is not human to be alone for as many years as you have been. You can bear it because you are a special person, greatly blessed by Ahura-Mazda, and there are some rare people who... I suppose whose stars mark them for solitude.'

'Say loneliness if you wish.'

'No, I shall not say that. I shall say solitude. A man as beloved of his people as you are cannot be lonely. But Roshan is... she is not marked by that same star. You cannot expect her to be alone forever, for if you were to expect that, you yourself would be inhuman. And even you, Cyrus, should not be alone all your life. At least... take the time to meet Cassadane.'

Asha fell silent.

'Very well,' Cyrus replied. 'I have never spoken to Farnaspes, though of course I have seen him at events and ceremonies. I know he is a much respected man in Anshan. I shall think about the circumstances under which I can best meet him and his daughter. What I say to them shall be my own business, but I will tell you now, Asha, that I do not have the slightest intention of marrying Cassadane, however much your brother wishes it.'

Asha nodded slowly. 'I understand.'

'As for your brother,' said Cyrus, 'I think it is time I again spoke to him, so please ask him to come to see me tomorrow morning, after my meditation session. And, Asha, I have an important favour to ask you.'

'I shall do whatever you wish me to do.'

Cyrus went over to the map-table and opened a drawer. He took out an inscribed clay tablet that he had wrapped carefully in soft, tanned leather tied with sinew, strode over to Asha and gave it to him.

'This is for Lady Roshan,' Cyrus said. 'She is in Pasargadae, planning the gardens that will surround the new palace. I should deliver this tablet myself, and I was planning to do so, but the reply from Croesus to our emissaries gives me no alternative but to prepare for war with Lydia, and I must begin preparations immediately. In truth I need you here, too, of course, but someone I completely trust must deliver this tablet, and so I ask you to be its bearer.'

'Am I... am I to know what the tablet says?'

'No, Asha,' said Cyrus, with quiet but firm emphasis. 'I would like you to set off for Pasargadae tomorrow, with a guard of course. You are much too valuable for me to run the risk of you being taken hostage by bandits. So, deliver the tablet, spend one night in Pasargadae to rest, and then return... with Lady Roshan, if she chooses to accompany you.'

'Do you think she might?'

'I think it is possible. I shall see your brother on the morrow. Also, please arrange for a messenger to summon Harpagus.'

'I shall do all this,' Asha said.

'Good. And by the way, I have made my decision.'

'About... about Cassadane?' Asha murmured.

'No,' said Cyrus, 'about Lydia. We shall begin to march on Lydia, under my command, fifty days from now.'

30. The Meeting with Raiva

Next morning, some time after daybreak, Raiva, answering the summon Cyrus had made to him through his brother Asha, came to visit Cyrus at the royal palace.

It was the first time Cyrus had seen Raiva for several months. He looked extremely prosperous. He was wearing fine coloured silks and satins, garments Cyrus knew were only available in Anshan at exorbitant prices from travelling Babylonian merchants. Raiva had, Cyrus noticed, also grown plump and distinctly sleek.

Cyrus took all this in quickly. He had been meditating with Akinlana, and felt calm and full of inner peace, which he knew was exactly the frame of mind he must be in for the crucial thinking he had to do over Lydia. Cyrus had been trying to put the meeting with Raiva out of mind, as it was not something to which he was looking forward.

Seeing Raiva there in his prosperous clothes made Cyrus feel even less that the meeting was likely to be enjoyable.

He can listen to what I have to say, and then he can be on his way, Cyrus thought.

Cyrus greeted Raiva in the main reception room of the palace at Anshan. The palace in the Persian capital was destined to be superseded by the new royal residence being built at Pasargadae, but it was still not finished, so Cyrus continued to make his palace at Anshan his main residence.

'I gather you proposed marriage to Roshan?' Cyrus said to Raiva, the moment the servant had left, Raiva having been served with a cup of wine and a sweet cake.

Raiva, Cyrus was pleased to see, looked taken aback. 'Who told you? My brother?'

'It does not matter who told me. I suppose you may propose marriage to whoever you wish, Raiva. But it is only fair for me to tell you that if you were to propose to Lady Roshan again, you would be putting her in a most embarrassing position.'

'What do you mean?'

'I mean,' said Cyrus, 'that this afternoon your brother is travelling to Pasargadae, where Lady Roshan is currently working on the designs for the new palace's gardens. Your brother will have a tablet, from me to Lady Roshan, containing a proposal of marriage from me to her, inviting her to be queen of Persia.'

Cyrus fell silent.

Raiva just stared at him. 'You wish to marry Roshan? But you *can't* marry her.'

'Why not?'

'Because... well, why would you want to marry her?'

'That, too, is my own business,' said Cyrus.

'Cyrus, if you love her why haven't you married her already?'

Cyrus was silent for a moment. He didn't think this was any of Raiva's business either, but he decided to answer the question anyway, mainly – he suddenly realized – because he wanted to articulate the answer to himself.

'I was not ready before,' he murmured, as if confessing something. 'Now I am.'

'But... but you *can't* marry her, Cyrus,' Raiva repeated. 'You are king of Persia and Media, and if our empire continues to grow, which Ahura-Mazda willing it shall, you will become one of the greatest leaders in the world. But who is Roshan? She comes from nowhere. She has no breeding. She does not come from a good family. She is no-one, *nothing.*'

'What are you talking about? Roshan is better than any of us, do you not understand that? And she saved my life when I was first coming to Anshan, or have you forgotten that? Have you also forgotten that my new mother ennobled her? Roshan is one of the most eminent women of the united kingdoms.'

'Cyrus, I know this. But nothing can alter the fact that she comes from nowhere. You are a king. You should marry a young woman of royal blood, or at least of blood far nobler than that coursing through Roshan's veins.'

'How can you speak like this, Raiva? How can you say this about our friend? And besides... obviously you thought Lady Roshan good enough for *you*.'

Cyrus was expecting Raiva to be ruffled by this, but Raiva gave no indication that he was.

'That's different,' he returned, calmly.

'Why?'

'I am not the king of Persia.'

Cyrus just stared at him. 'What has made you become like this, Raiva? You used to be someone I could trust. Why are you suddenly so fascinated by status, wealth and power?'

'Because they *are* fascinating. How can you deny that, being king? You are the most powerful of all of us.'

'It was a path chosen for me, not by me,' said Cyrus. 'Such is usually the lot of kings. Inside,' he thumped his chest hard, 'I am still a man, indeed I believe I am more of a man than ever before. As for power, I suggest you spend a few days, or rather sleepless nights, as king and then think again about whether you would like to have royal power.'

'I would very willingly be king,' said Raiva at once.

Cyrus could not help noticing the promptness of the reply.

'You might not like being king as much as you imagine you might,' Cyrus said. 'Now, I have something else to tell you. Your brother Asha says that you think I should marry Cassadane, your friend Farnaspes's youngest daughter. I have never met this girl, but as you now know, my choice has been made and my decision is final. You should banish any thoughts of my marrying Cassadane from your mind, just as you must dismiss any thoughts of marrying Lady Roshan yourself.'

Raiva nodded. 'Very well, you are my king, so I must obey. But Cyrus... Cassadane is truly special.'

'Asha has already waxed lyrical on Cassadane's charms. I don't want to listen to all that again. But I respect Farnaspes, for he is one of Anshan's most eminent citizens.'

'And one of the richest,' Raiva interrupted.

'One of the most eminent, yes,' said Cyrus. 'I respect his daughter Cassadane, too. I know you well enough, Raiva, to be sure that you will have filled their heads with notions that you are acquainted with my inclinations, and that I might well indeed marry Cassadane.'

Raiva did not deny it.

'That being so,' Cyrus added, 'I ask you to arrange that within, let us say seven days, Farnaspes and Cassadane come here for supper with me at the royal palace. Be assured I shall treat them in a respectful and friendly fashion. But I shall also make clear that I have no intention of marrying Cassadane.'

Raiva nodded slowly. 'Do you want me to be present?'

'No. I shall meet them alone.'

'Very well.'

The two men looked at each other.

'Thank you for coming,' Cyrus said.

'We must see more of each other,' Raiva said.

Cyrus nodded. 'Yes.'

He didn't suggest when that might be, though.

Raiva cleared his throat. 'Cyrus?'

'Yes?'

'There is something else I should like to say.'

'Well?'

'The doctrine you preach and to which you are so attached... this doctrine of tolerance of all religious beliefs and tribes... I suppose it makes sense in Persia and Media. I mean, we and the Medians are almost of the same blood... and speak almost the same speech. But Cyrus, all these other tribes you're bringing into the empire, some by force, some because they have more sense than to fight you... many of them are savages, scarcely more than animals.'

'Not any more. They are now members of the Persian Empire.'

'So you choose to say, but that doesn't stop them being animals. Cyrus, the Empire could sell some of them... for a handsome profit. The proceeds could be used to make Persia and Media richer...' Raiva smiled faintly. 'Richer even than Lydia, the fiefdom of Croesus. We could...'

'*No*, Raiva,' Cyrus said. 'I am amazed you can even suggest this. Do you think I want to be like Astyages, that tyrant, murderer and slave-driver?'

'No, but I thought that the money...'

'Is that all you can talk about... or think about? Are you not rich enough already?'

'No man is ever rich enough,' said Raiva.

'Evidently.' Cyrus looked hard at Raiva for a few moments. 'Tell me, if I did agree to this scheme of selling some of our citizens as slaves, you would wish to be the slave-broker, I presume?'

'Well, Cyrus, I do have many contacts in the southern ports who...'

'I guessed as much. Listen to me, Raiva. My answer is no, now and forever. My answer is *never*.'

Raiva said nothing.

'Arrange for me to meet Farnaspes and Cassadane as I requested,' Cyrus said. 'And now go. We shall be friends again when you have put out of your mind this vile notion of selling some of our people as slaves.'

Raiva, his face expressionless, bowed courteously to Cyrus and then retreated from the royal presence, walking backward so as not to show his back to Cyrus.

And a man who would be the Empire's most notorious slave-trader has proposed marriage to Roshan, the woman I love, Cyrus reflected, with a bitterness verging, as Cyrus was fully aware, on jealousy.

31. Cassadane

For Cyrus, the prospect of Roshan returning as a woman engaged to be married to him was the most exciting anticipation of his life.

The plain where Pasargadae was being built was about a day's ride to the west of Anshan. It was reasonable to expect that Asha would be back with Roshan on the evening following the day on which he set out. Meanwhile, Cyrus, using all his powers of self-discipline to try to put his thoughts about Roshan to the back of his mind, did his utmost to think only about details of the campaign that would bring Lydia within the fold of the Persian Empire.

But Asha did not return with Roshan on the evening following the day when Asha had set out.

That first evening, Cyrus managed to overcome a strong temptation to visit Farna-dukta and enquire whether her husband was there. Yet Cyrus did not believe Asha would even have considered going to see Farna-dukta before coming to the palace.

And so Cyrus waited, and withstood the temptation, and plunged himself into work. He was aware, after all, that the history of his empire for more than the next century, or even longer to come, might easily depend on the decisions he was making now. Even so, the sense that Roshan, his beloved betrothed, might appear in the room at any time was an enormous distraction.

But there was no sign of Asha, or Roshan, by the evening of the second day either.

By the evening of the third day Cyrus could not stand waiting any longer.

The instant his work was finished for that day, Cyrus left the royal palace to see Farna-dukta. As he hurried to Asha's home, Cyrus was half-expecting that Asha and Roshan might just have returned and could be having a cup of wine at Asha's house after their long journey before coming to see him, Cyrus. In fact, Cyrus was so convinced they would be there that he found himself looking forward to what he would say to Roshan.

'No, Cyrus, he isn't here,' Farna-dukta said as soon as Cyrus, at the threshold of their home, had asked the question. 'Asha hasn't returned yet.'

'Thank you. No doubt he will return soon. This evening, I hope.'

'So do I. I miss him. Would you like to come in for some wine?'

'No, thank you,' Cyrus said. 'I'm sorry, but I have much important work at the palace. I must return there.'

And he went back to work, feeling bewildered and deeply unhappy that there was no sign of Roshan. He toiled alone in his throne room, still expecting Roshan to arrive at any moment.

She didn't.

Nor did she come back on the fourth day.

Cyrus went into the small room where he kept his clothes. He looked intently at the dark blue cloak, the sight of which made him think even more about his blissful days by the red lake with Roshan than he so often did anyway. He reached out and touched the cloak, as if he were aware at that moment that touching it was the closest he could come to touching Roshan.

On the evening of that fourth day, Cyrus again went to see Farna-dukta, who said the same thing: Asha hadn't yet returned from Pasargadae.

Cyrus nodded, behaving with forced casualness about the matter. He did not want to worry Farna-dukta. Besides, he knew perfectly well that, while Pasargadae was only forty miles away, the journey could be unpredictable, as indeed any journey could be. Cyrus was only too aware that if there had been some rainfall on the higher mountain passes, causing sudden floods that could be deadly dangerous, Roshan, Asha and the guards accompanying them would have had to delay their return by making a camp in the mountains until the path was clear again.

But by the evening of the fifth day, Cyrus, who somehow had managed to go on working, resolved that in the morning he himself, despite the demands that his work placed upon him, would head for Pasargadae with a detachment of guards. He knew he simply could not bear a moment longer the tension and worry of wondering where Roshan was and what might have happened to her... and for that matter to Asha.

He worked that evening, too, this time in the company of Harpagus. The two men worked but drank only juice, not the wine it was customary for Persians to drink in the evening. Cyrus did not much like wine, and wine did not have good associations for Harpagus when he was with Cyrus.

Late that evening a messenger, a boy, bought a tablet for Cyrus: a short scroll of goat-skin wrapped in leather and wound round tightly with grass tied with the tightest of knots, so that the grass could only be removed by cutting it.

Cyrus's heart beat fast as the messenger handed him the package. This, surely, must be from Roshan! Surely she had arrived back now, and was full of love for the man who had asked her to be his wife... and queen?

'Who... who is the tablet from?' Cyrus asked the messenger.

'Sire, it is from Raiva.'

'Raiva?'

'Yes, sire,' the boy said.

Cyrus dismissed the boy with none of the usual courtesy he applied to subordinates. The instant the boy was gone, he tore open the scroll.

Hail Cyrus, most high, greatly blessed by Ahura-Mazda, most victorious conqueror of the enemies of Persia, and liberator of our nations!

Cyrus's eyes quickly ran over these words, which he regarded as empty flattery (though the irony of Raiva's reference to liberation was not lost on him), then scanned the message itself.

Cyrus, I have obeyed your royal command. Farnaspes and Cassadane shall pay their respectful visit to you tomorrow evening at the royal palace at Anshan. Farnaspes has asked me to convey to you his humble thanks for the opportunity to be permitted to come into the royal presence with his youngest daughter.
   Yours in affectionate friendship
   Raiva

The instant Cyrus read this tablet, he knew that going to Pasargadae in the morning was impossible.

Yes, it was true he could postpone the visit of Farnaspes and Cassadane, but his intention had been to travel to Pasargadae in secret, to avoid any information about his proposal to Roshan leaking out before his marriage plans could be made official. He knew, only too well, that if he postponed the dinner with Farnaspes and Cassadane he would be obliged to give some reason for doing so, and as it was not his nature to lie, and as revealing the truth at that moment was not an option (especially in view of the hopes he knew Farnaspes had had that he might marry Cassadane), the postponement itself was impossible.

He stared at the scroll again.

'Cyrus, what is it?' Harpagus asked. 'Not bad news?'

'Yes,' said Cyrus, nodding, 'it is bad news. But nothing that will change the destiny of Persia. Come, let us return to work.'

And so it was that the following evening, Cyrus – who had heard nothing whatsoever about Roshan returning from Pasargadae – did his best to focus his mind on the task of entertaining Farnaspes and Cassadane in the royal dining-room at the palace at Anshan.

Farnaspes was a distinguished-looking white-haired gentleman. Cassadane was a girl of, Cyrus supposed, eighteen or nineteen.

Cyrus felt he had to admit that Cassadane's beauty was truly exquisite. For once, Asha and Raiva had not been exaggerating. Indeed, Cyrus could not help thinking that if the Queen of Sheba had looked anything like this girl, it was no wonder she had led wise King Solomon such a dance and had beguiled him so completely.

Cassadane was tall for a woman, almost as tall as Roshan, and dressed as befitted a rich merchant's daughter. She was wearing a glorious silk gown of a brilliant pure white: a gown that, Cyrus knew, betokened not only her father's wealth, but also her virginity. She wore a fragrance that gave her a delicate scent of vanilla. Her jet-black hair was tied up and wound with gold thread, beads, and jewels, including emeralds and sapphires. Yet Cyrus thought of the beautiful bracelet he had given Roshan and the profundity of what it meant to them both compared with these trinkets Cassadane was wearing.

Cassadane's skin, Cyrus also noticed, was the wheaten, healthy-looking skin of a girl whose father is so wealthy she does not need to labour with her hands or indeed perform any tedious tasks about the house or in the fields.

Her countenance and figure, though, were so beautiful that Cyrus was astonished to find that, despite Roshan filling his mind and soul so completely, he was genuinely taken aback.

Cassadane's incredibly lovely, almond-shaped face was perfectly proportioned in a way that was quite rare in Persia, where even the most beautiful women might have noses, mouths or even eyes that were slightly too large.

Yet, all this said, Cassadane did not have the fierce, free, independent, wild beauty of Roshan, whose own face, and thoughts of whose naked body, were endlessly threading through Cyrus's mind. There was, Cyrus saw, a distinct virginal modesty about Cassadane's beauty; yet also Cyrus could not help noticing a fire in her eyes that reminded him of the banked fire that continues to glow from red-hot logs all night after sand is scattered over them, and which an experienced fire-maker knows how to bring to life again in the morning, to cook barley-porridge in the pot and flat bread on the griddle.

Suddenly, and almost involuntarily, Cyrus murmured:

'You are very beautiful, Cassadane.'

'Thank you, your Majesty,' the girl murmured, modestly.

Cyrus glanced at Farnaspes. 'You must be proud of your daughter, sir.'

'I am prouder of her than anything in the whole world, your Majesty,' Farnaspes replied. 'She is the joy of my old age. My dear wife died almost twelve years ago.'

'I am sorry to hear that,' Cyrus said.

'Sire, after a life of being a good and loving wife to me and a fine mother to my children, my beloved wife is now with Ahura-Mazda. Meanwhile, all my daughters, sire, are married but Cassadane, who is my youngest... and the most beautiful.'

The tone in Farnaspes's voice, as he finished this short but obviously – at least to him – very significant speech, made it clear to Cyrus that Raiva had not broken the confidence Cyrus had bestowed on him about his intentions to marry Roshan. Of course, Cyrus would not have expected Raiva to have broken the confidence, but... Cyrus never knew exactly, nowadays, how much he could trust Raiva.

The old man certainly doesn't waste time getting down to business, Cyrus thought, as he beckoned Farnaspes and Cassadane to their places at the table, on either side of him.

Cyrus glanced again at Cassadane. He knew that the best and most sensible thing to do would be to confide in Farnaspes and his splendid daughter that he had already made a decision to marry another woman.

After all, there would be no need for either of them to have any idea who that person was. Farnaspes and Cassadane would doubtless be greatly disappointed, but at least they would know the truth and they could all then enjoy supper, become acquainted with each other and even perhaps become friends. Cyrus did not imagine Cassadane would be short of subsequent marriage proposals from the noblemen of Anshan or Ecbatana.

Yet, to Cyrus's surprise, he found himself disinclined to confide his decision to Cassadane, and instead found that he enjoyed talking to her. Roshan, though, remained at the forefront of his mind, and sometimes, as he spoke to Cassadane... Cyrus was alarmed to realize that he could hear Roshan's voice in his head, adding an ironic commentary to what Cassadane was saying, almost as if Roshan was there with them.

'What pastimes do you most enjoy, Cassadane?' Cyrus asked her, as the servants began to lay out the various courses, hot and cold dishes together, as was the custom, on the table.

'You mean, apart from my studies, your Majesty?' Cassadane replied, demurely. Cyrus noted the beautiful sound of her voice, with its rather deep and modest tone yet somehow also a confident melodiousness.

'Yes, indeed,' said Cyrus.

'Sire,' said Cassadane, 'I like to make visits to the poor families of Anshan and help them with my purse or my advice. Also, I love to travel.'

'Yes, in a comfortable carriage and waited upon by servants, no doubt', Roshan's voice intoned within Cyrus's head. 'The king of the united kingdoms of Persia and Media, does not travel in such a fashion. He is a warrior, and would expect his queen to forgo such luxuries.'

'I see,' said Cyrus. So,' he paused again, somewhat nervously wondering what on earth Roshan's voice inside his head would be likely to say next, 'where do you like to travel?'

'Oh, anywhere I can when my father takes me when he travels on business,' Cassadane replied. 'My favourite destination is Babylon. I have been there once, and I loved the city very much.'

'*Yes, not surprisingly, for you stink like a Babylonian bazaar!*' Roshan's voice inside Cyrus exclaimed. '*Do you enjoy the smell of sweat? Of blood? Of army latrines? If not, don't marry the king of Persia, or your sensitive nose will be incessantly offended and you will run back to daddy.*'

Cyrus cleared his throat. 'I see.'

Roshan's voice inside his head was making him feel truly confused, and he was also uncomfortably conscious of not really knowing what to say to the girl. But he knew only too well that, as king, it was his responsibility to lead the conversation. 'And do you also know how to... sew and embroider?' He did not feel this a very inspiring question, but he felt it was the best he could manage at that particular moment.

Cassadane smiled. 'Yes, of course, your Majesty. But I must say, I do not only wish to pursue such traditional female tasks.'

'No?' said Cyrus, suddenly genuinely intrigued.

'No, sire, for I have also tried my utmost to be diligent in my studies.'

'My daughter can speak Babylonian, your Majesty, almost as well as she speaks her native Persian,' Farnaspes put in.

'I am glad you speak Babylonian, Cassadane,' said Cyrus, as they all began to eat. He still had Roshan at the forefront of his mind, but he was enjoying the presence of Cassadane, despite himself.

'Why is that, your Majesty?' Cassadane asked politely.

Cyrus found himself smiling. 'Because, Cassadane, perhaps you can be my interpreter if ever we bring Babylon into the fold of the Persian Empire!'

Both father and daughter laughed at this; a laugh Cyrus knew was as much an indication that his joke had broken the ice as that they found his remark especially funny.

'My daughter is able to speak some Lydian, too, your Majesty,' said Farnaspes.

'That too, may soon be an accomplishment with much practical usefulness,' Cyrus said. The servants poured wine for Farnaspes and Cassadane, and juice for Cyrus.

'Tell me of some of your other educational accomplishments, Cassadane,' Cyrus asked.

'Your Majesty,' said Cassadane, 'I can read maps, and I have studied the celestial globes.'

'*No doubt*,' said Roshan's lewd voice inside Cyrus's head, '*and I am sure your future husband will spend much of his time studying your own celestial globes, the two at the front and the two at the back.*'

Cyrus drew a breath. He liked Cassadane, and he even liked Farnaspes, but this evening was proving even more difficult than he had expected.

When, finally, the time came for Farnaspes and Cassadane to bid farewell, Cyrus gave Cassadane a strong yet gentle embrace. And, as he embraced her, Cyrus impulsively did something he had not for one moment expected to do until he actually did it.

What he did was kiss Cassadane gently on the forehead, and fix her with his smile after he drew his head away from her and bade farewell to her and her father.

Cyrus shook Farnaspes's hand warmly enough. *He is a more agreeable fellow than I expected him to be*, Cyrus thought. All the same, he had no plans whatsoever to make Farnaspes his father-in-law.

32. A tablet from Roshan

Cyrus slept fitfully that night, drifting in and out of sleep.

He woke in the early morning, when the dawn had not yet fully broken. For a while he wasn't sure whether he was still asleep or awake. He looked to either side of him, somehow expecting to see Roshan there. But he was alone.

He slipped back into a deep, dreamless sleep from which he was woken, some time shortly after sunrise, by a vigorous knocking on the door of his bedchamber.

At once he was fully alert. The knocking persisted. He shouted out through the door to whoever was knocking that he would be with them in a moment, at which the knocking ceased abruptly. Cyrus never received servants or visitors in his bedchamber unless he was dressed. He dressed very quickly, then went to the door and flung it open.

It was Asha.

'Well?' said Cyrus. His throat was dry, his voice hoarse.

'Can I come in?' Asha asked.

Cyrus nodded, standing back to let Asha enter. There was a tray containing a jug of pomegranate juice on a table near the bed: Asha asked for a drink, so Cyrus poured some of the juice into a cup. Asha thirstily drank the cup dry; Cyrus re-filled it. Asha drank about half of the second cup, then set it down and began to tell Cyrus his story.

Asha said that he had ridden to Pasargadae, with the guards Cyrus had provided.

'We had a good journey to Pasargadae, hiring fresh horses in the larger villages we passed. At once we headed for your new palace, which is becoming splendid, Cyrus and...'

'*What about Roshan?*'

'Cyrus, she wasn't there. The gardeners who work for her said that she had headed into the valley of the river Polvar, alone on her horse, as she liked to, with a large saddle-bag. They said she loved to go looking for new plants and then taking cuttings from them and...'

'Did you find her?'

'Only when she got back.'

'Why didn't you go looking for her?'

'Cyrus, there would have been no point. The plain where Pasagardae is being built is vast. She could have been anywhere. The gardeners said she would be back within a day or so, so I... I waited. And finally, after three days, Lady Roshan did return, and as soon as I saw her I gave her the tablet.'

'And?'

'The following evening she came back with me.'

'The following evening? But... why did she not return immediately?'

'Cyrus, she was exhausted from travelling. Also, she said she needed to plant the cuttings she'd gathered and...'

'Stop talking about the cuttings! Asha, how was she... you know, when she read the tablet?'

'I did not see her read it, Cyrus, for she took it away to read it in private. But afterwards... I would say she looked very thoughtful...'

'"Thoughtful?" Nothing else?'

Asha seemed to have a good think about this, then slowly shook his head. 'No.'

'All right, all right, so yesterday evening you and Roshan headed back here?'

'Yes. There is the kind of full moon that outshines the stars, so we could ride all night. The guards escorted us to the town of Zarqan, but their horses were tired, and this road from Zarqan to Anshan is known, after all, for being safe, so Roshan and I rode on to Anshan alone.'

'And where is she now?'

'Cyrus... Cyrus, listen. Let me explain. We arrived back on the outskirts of Anshan earlier this morning and...'

'Why didn't you come and see me right away?'

'Because ...' Asha said, 'on the outskirts of Anshan, when we could see the lights of the city glowing faintly in the distance beneath the moon, Roshan gave me a tablet... a tablet for you, and then... Roshan made me promise, Cyrus, on Farna-dukta's and Ariya's lives, that I would deliver the tablet to you personally, but... not until the sun had moved a hand's length across the sky.'

'Why... why did she ask that?'

'I don't know. Roshan wouldn't say. I told her *you* would want to know, but she still refused to tell me. You know what Lady Roshan is like, Cyrus, how stubborn and..'

'Yes, yes,' said Cyrus. 'But... did you not think of disobeying her?'

'Cyrus, I could not do that. Yes, if it had been a day's delay she asked for, most likely I would have felt that my duty as your subject and friend were greater than my obligations of friendship to Roshan. But she only asked me to delay while the sun moved a hand's length... I simply presumed she wanted time to bathe and make herself more presentable to you after our long journey.'

Cyrus nodded slowly. 'Very well. I understand.'

'Here is the tablet.' And Asha drew it from within his dusty hooded cloak and handed it to Cyrus. The tablet consisted of a rectangular tablet as wide as a man's hand and twice as long, tightly wrapped round with tanned leather and tied with sinews.

'Have you read it?' Cyrus asked, looking hard at Asha.

'Of course not.'

'Forgive me,' said Cyrus, 'I should not have asked that. Where is Roshan now?'

'I don't know.'

Cyrus stared at him. 'What do you mean, you don't know?'

'Cyrus, after she gave me the tablet, she galloped away into the darkness.'

Cyrus shook his head in astonishment. 'Why? Where was she going?'

'I don't know.'

'Why didn't you gallop after her?'

Asha shook his head. 'If she had wanted me to follow her she would have asked me to do so. She would have hated me if I'd just ridden after her, and besides, she's such a good rider that if I'd done so, she'd have shaken me off anyway.'

Cyrus nodded slowly. 'Yes. Yes, of course.' He drew a breath. 'Thank you, Asha. Now return to your wife and son. I suppose you have seen them already?'

'No, I knew that if I did go to see them, Farna-dukta would insist I came to see you right away, without waiting for the time Roshan had requested, and that if I refused to come to see you right away, Farna-dukta would have come to you herself to tell you I had returned. I did not wish to implicate her. So, after Roshan left, I dismounted and rested with my horse in a nearby gully, until the sun had moved that hand's length across the sky that she had asked me to wait. Then I came here.'

Cyrus nodded. 'I see. Well, thank you again, Asha. Please leave me now. I must read the tablet.'

Asha bade Cyrus farewell with a salute. When Asha was gone, Cyrus closed the door of the bedchamber after him and instantly began to untie the tightly-tied sinews from around the leather wrapper of what, he knew, would be a clay tablet inscribed in cuneiform.

And so it was. There, on the tablet, Cyrus saw five lines of cuneiform, which he knew Roshan could write as well as he himself did.

I have read your tablet proposing marriage. Why you would send me this I do not understand. Cyrus, I have always known in my heart you do not really want me. You will never think of me as your equal, for you think a woman can never be equal to a man. In your eyes I will only ever be second to you. I cannot live any longer in a world where I will never truly have your love in the way I hoped I would have it. Ride this morning to the lake, beside which we loved, and bid farewell to me.

Cyrus stared at the tablet in utter astonishment.

His first frantic thought was that Roshan had lost her mind.

His second thought was more rational. It had occurred to him that perhaps... perhaps the tablet was not written by Roshan. Perhaps there had been some mistake.

Because cuneiform writing was made by a wooden wedge-shaped writing implement dipped in lampblack, the individual marks themselves looked much the same whoever had written them. And so, to authenticate tablets, a cursive form of cuneiform, written with a point such as the sharpened end of a stick, had been developed that was used by tablet-writers to write their names. Sometimes the cursive cuneiform was even used to write tablets to friends; Cyrus had employed it to write his tablet to Roshan in which he had proposed marriage to her.

She had written her name at the end of the tablet in the cursive hand, and Cyrus, looking hard at her name, found himself forced to accept that this was unquestionably Roshan's handwriting.

His third thought, which he had now, was the terrible memory of his dream.

He thought of running after Asha and interrogating him more about Roshan's mood and behaviour on the journey from Pasargadae back to Anshan. And he might indeed have done that, but the sentence in Roshan's tablet *I cannot live any longer in a world where I will never truly have your love in the way I hoped I would have it* stood out in the tablet like a festering wound.

Surely Roshan, *Roshan*, did not intend to...?

A moment later Cyrus tore off his gown and hurriedly put on his riding-clothes, dressing himself so quickly he almost tripped over himself. He hurried to the palace's kitchens and wolfed down a large piece of bread with a fresh slice of goat's milk cheese on it, and washed down with a cup of goat's milk. With his bow and quiver on his back and his sword in its scabbard, Cyrus hurried to his stables and asked his stable-boy whether Tigra, Cyrus's strongest stallion, had been fed and watered that morning. The stable-boy said yes, he had.

A few minutes later Cyrus, full of dread, was on the back of Tigra, his great black stallion, galloping away to the north-west, to the borders of the strange red lake.

33. Shrine

The heat of the morning was already on the land, but Tigra was strong and fast and Cyrus used every fibre of the stallion's strength to reach the red lake much sooner than when he had come here with Roshan.

His heart pounding with dread of what he might find, and his dream at the very forefront of his mind, he slowed Tigra to a canter as the lake, with its small glade of ash-trees, came into view.

The strange eeriness of the remote, solitary, silent place struck Cyrus with a force that had been completely absent those few weeks ago.

He realized ruefully that it hadn't seemed lonely then.

But now it did. And, in the hot sun of the day, the red lake, the colour of blood, seemed to Cyrus the colour of death. The tops of the ash-trees did not sway, for there was scarcely any breeze; nor was the unrelenting calmness of the surface of the lake disturbed by even the faintest flicker of a wave.

Cyrus, his eyes straining for any sight of Roshan, and telling himself *a dream is just a dream, it isn't real*, led Tigra down to the level border of the lake and let the great horse drink from a leather water-bag he had brought with him. Cyrus kept hoping he would see Roshan approach him, but there was no sign of her.

Once Tigra was watered, Cyrus tied the mighty beast to an ash-tree. Cyrus had a strange feeling, though he could not be certain, that it was the very tree to which he and Roshan had tied their horses when they had come here together.

He was more confident in the certainty of his memory that he and Roshan had walked beside each other, not holding hands, not touching, and in silent thoughtfulness until they reached the lakeside. He recalled, too, how, once they were there, they had stood side-by-side, looking out over the water and how, presently, they had turned to each other and kissed each other with complete and absolute passion.

He choked back his tears.

He was desperate to know where Roshan was.

He thought, *perhaps she will appear from behind a tree where she's been hiding, and we'll fall into each other's arms.*

But she did not appear.

He was alone.

Presently, Cyrus walked down to the water. His eyes were wet with tears, and his soul scorched with fear at what might have happened to Roshan.

He looked out over the red lake. His eyes scanned its margins. He wondered exactly what Roshan had meant when she said that he should ride to the lake so that he could 'bid farewell' to her. And he was still wondering this when, in the bright sunlight, his eyes caught a glint of what looked like a miniature fallen star lying on the shore of the lake, close by the water, about a hundred paces away.

Puzzled, he at once started walking toward the star. As he did, it glinted more and more, and now he saw, very clearly, that close by the star there were... *women's clothes*. The instant Cyrus saw this, his walk turned into a run, and then into a sprint. He cursed himself for not noticing the clothes and... the star before.

But even as he ran he could see what the star really was.

A few moments later he reached it, and the clothes nearby.

The star was the gold bracelet with the griffin design.

The gold bracelet. The very bracelet Cyrus had sent to Astyages to taunt him, and that the vile and unlamented Astyages had used to try to buy Cyrus's life.

The bracelet which Cyrus had given to Roshan because she had saved his life. And because he loved her.

Cyrus collapsed on the bank of the blood-red lake and wept.

He wept for a long time. When he finally glanced at the clothes his glance only confirmed what he already knew: the clothes were Roshan's.

Her leaving her clothes there made clear to him her intentions. The leaving of the bracelet, though, confirmed it to Cyrus beyond even the faintest glimmer of a doubt.

He was certain she would never have left the bracelet by the lakeside unless she was set on destroying herself.

Why has she done this? he wondered.

His lips tasted salty with his own weeping.

But he knew the reason even as he asked himself the question.

She had said in the tablet that she thought he would never see her as his equal. He could only suppose she could not bear the thought of entering a marriage with a man who did not see her in that light.

He had always known Roshan had a sensitive disposition, but even he was surprised to find she was as sensitive as this.

He looked out over the red lake.

There and then, by the shore of the lake, in weeping, tortured prayer, Cyrus begged forgiveness to Ahura-Mazda for his own crime of never truly understanding how much Roshan loved him. He also begged forgiveness for Roshan's suicide, which he knew that Ahura-Mazda saw as a great crime.

Even in his weeping, Cyrus resolved to issue an order that the lake must always be kept sacred, and must never be sailed upon, and that its name must ever afterward be 'The Lake of Lady Roshan.'

Cyrus sobbed again after he had finished.

He picked up the bracelet and clothes and walked back to where Tigra, with an animal's obliviousness, gave Cyrus a welcoming cheerful whinny.

Cyrus returned to Anshan at a desultory trot. His soul was sunk deep in despair. The journey back took three or four times longer than the journey there had taken. Cyrus could not, not for a moment, understand why, why *on earth*, Roshan would choose to end her own life rather than marry him.

He interrogated Asha again and again on exactly what had happened when he, Asha, had given Roshan the tablet in Pasargadae. But Asha stuck to what he had said.

'What message was in the tablet you sent Roshan that might have distressed her?' Asha asked.

'*Nothing!*' Cyrus exclaimed, in a moment of complete anguish. 'Surely your brother told you what the tablet was, didn't he?'

'No, Cyrus, he didn't.'

'Then... then I'll tell you. My tablet was a marriage proposal!'

Asha just stared at Cyrus. 'Then... why would she kill herself?'

Cyrus just shook his head. 'I don't know. *I don't know.* She seems ... she seems to have despaired that I would ever think her the equal of me. But she knows I did. *I told her I did.* She must have had... a moment of madness.'

'Yes, it must have been madness. She... she loved you, Cyrus. But we all... well, we knew how sensitive she was. When Roshan got an idea in her head... it was impossible to dislodge it unless she cast it away voluntarily.' Asha drew a breath. 'Even so, to kill herself for such a reason... it is seems insane.'

Cyrus nodded slowly. He could hardly speak. 'It... it may seem so to us,' his throat agonizingly dry. 'But Roshan... she was not like us. She was wiser, more sensitive. I think none of us ever really knew her at all. We grew up with her, we were friends with her, but deep down... she was a mystery... as profound as the soul of Ahura-Mazda.'

Cyrus wiped his eyes. Despite being plunged fathoms deep into the darkest mire of sadness, he did his best to find within himself some semblance of kingly composure. He summoned the guards who had accompanied Asha and Roshan on the homeward journey as far as Zarqan. He asked them what impressions *they* had of Lady Roshan during the return journey. But their stories essentially matched Asha's: she had looked intensely thoughtful and had hardly spoken.

Cyrus immediately gave his instructions that the red lake was to be known henceforth under the name he had already chosen. The lake was to be a holy lake, nor was any attempt ever to be made to recover Roshan's body.

Cyrus knew Roshan well enough to know that whenever she did anything, she always made a good job of it. He felt certain that she must have swum, naked and probably carrying some stones, and reached the water above the deepest part of the strange red lake before letting herself submerge...

Cyrus did his best not to think of her slowly sinking in the middle of the lake, but he thought about it, many, many times.

Meanwhile, he sought solace for his agony of spirit not in the juice of narcotic plants, nor raw wine, sumptuous food, or sporting with courtesans.

Instead, he sought the solace of the two great allies that had so often come to his aid in the past. Work and action.

As for the dark blue cloak, from that day it had a place in his heart, and in his soul. It became his most precious possession.

'I shall always wear it henceforth when I go into battle,' Cyrus muttered to himself. 'When I am wearing it, Roshan shall be with me.'

Cyrus knew that an emperor's plans must never be delayed or diluted, for the very life and well-being of his empire depend on them. During the month between his agonized second visit to the red lake and the army's departure for Lydia, Cyrus did little except work. He frequently met with Asha to discuss military matters. Asha and Harpagus would be his two principal generals for the campaign.

Cyrus had by now confided to Harpagus, too, that he had proposed marriage to Roshan and that some moment of inexplicable madness had led her to take her own life rather than agree to become his wife. Both men knew by now the terrible pain Cyrus was suffering over her. Otherwise, if any of Cyrus's subjects guessed the true state of his feelings for Roshan, they kept the knowledge to themselves.

Asha was careful not to mention Cassadane to Cyrus. Yet it would not be true to say that Cyrus never thought about the beautiful, thoughtful, young woman.

That Roshan had drowned in the lake Cyrus had named after her naturally became public knowledge, though no-one but Cyrus himself, Asha and Harpagus knew the circumstances of her drowning. Cassadane sent Cyrus a sweet tablet of condolence about Roshan's death, a tablet that Cyrus could not help finding deeply moving. The tablet didn't contain a single word that might have been interpreted as evidence Cassadane felt anything but unalloyed sorrow about what she described as 'the passing into Ahura-Mazda's kingdom of Lady Roshan, the wisest and most beautiful woman in our Empire.' Cyrus naturally wondered whether Raiva had told Farnaspes or Cassadane anything about the marriage proposal that he, Cyrus, had made to Roshan. But if Raiva had, there was certainly no evidence of that in Cassadane's tablet.

Cyrus liked Cassadane's tablet and had kept it, but he had not replied.

As for Harpagus, the giant warrior told Cyrus, in private, that if he could have 'brought Lady Roshan back to life' by means of giving up his own life, he would have made that sacrifice in a heartbeat.

A little more than a month after Cyrus's solitary visit to the borders of the red lake that had once, for three days and nights, been an earthly paradise for him and Roshan, the king of kings led the army of the united kingdoms of Persia and Media toward the fabulously wealthy western kingdom of Lydia.

The united army of Persia and Media – the army that was now increasingly being known as the army of the Persian Empire – journeyed on horseback, mule-back and camel-back to present its compliments to Croesus, who was renowned – even by those who had travelled to the remote eastern kingdoms of India and China – as being the richest king in the world.

Cyrus, at the head of the great army, was clad in the dark blue cloak. Wearing it, he felt that Roshan was with him.

34. The march on Lydia

Croesus, king of Lydia, was a pampered, intelligent man who was fond of his riches, his wife and good food, in that order.

A large part of his wealth stemmed from the great fertility of much of his land. This allowed his farmers to practise agriculture and animal husbandry with great success, producing more than enough for Lydia's own needs, and also plenty of surplus to sell to neighbouring lands that were less fertile, or whose population was too large to be supported solely by home-grown produce.

Babylon, for example, by far the largest community in the kingdom of Babylonia, had long been friendly to Lydia, mainly because it needed Lydia's fruit, vegetables and meat to feed its population. Babylon's great success as a trading and manufacturing city gave it the money to pay for this.

Yet Croesus's wealth derived not only from agriculture. Lydia's location close by the very meeting-point of the European and Asian continents, and the legendary prowess of Lydian sailors coupled with the strength of the Lydian navy, brought great prosperity to Lydia, which taxed the maritime and land-bound trade that passed through its waters and across its borders. The silk trade alone, involving the transport of silk fabrics both dyed and undyed from China along the Silk Road to Europe and also of course to Lydia itself, was fabulously lucrative for Lydia.

It was true that, to the west, the borders of Lydia did not generally extend all the way to the coast, which was mostly owned by the Greeks, but this made little difference to Lydia's importance as a trading nation.

Croesus, who was a great lover of money and property, did not especially like war and battle, for they disrupted trade. Military conflict also necessitated his farmers and merchants wasting their time, as he saw it, in military exercises, training and battle rather than devoting themselves to the farming and trading work they did best.

On the other hand, Croesus did not object to fighting a war – or, at least, commanding his soldiers to fight one – if he was sure it could be easily won. He liked to indulge his love of money and property, and he knew that war could be a highly effective shortcut to obtaining both these much-desired things.

On a personal level, however, Croesus found the thought of battle both frightening and stupid. He always preferred to watch battles from the safe and agreeable vantage point of the summit of a nearby hill.

The idea of personally leading his men into battle did not appeal to him in the slightest. Was not the king of Lydia, he would insist to his generals, far too important to the Lydian nation, and much too beloved by his people, to risk the terrible blow that his death would be to them? Was not the head of the king too necessary to the continued wealth and happiness of Lydia, the greatest kingdom on earth, for him to be committing the grave folly of risking it in this way? It would be anything but selfless to offer it to a foreign invader's mace or, worse still, expose it to ignominious attack from a pebble hurled by the common foot-soldier's sling.

That, at least, was Croesus's view of matters.

Croesus's generals always nodded sagely as he assailed them with these, surely, indisputable arguments. The advisers were all well-paid and lived comfortably in large houses in the vast grounds of the royal palace in the Lydian capital of Sardis.

Yet it was ironic, considering the great affection King Croesus had for his comfortable life and his abhorrence for acts of violence, that it was such an act, two centuries earlier, that had brought into being the royal Mermnadae dynasty, of which Croesus was the most recent descendant. Every Lydian adult, and even most Lydian children younger than the age at which such a bloody and sensual act should be related to them, knew the story of that act of violence, and its cause.

The Mermnadae dynasty had been founded by a handsome young Lydian called Gyges, who was twenty-one years old at the time of his ascent to kingly power.

Gyges was not a king by birth, but had been a household servant in the court of a Lydian king known as Candaules, a man in his sixties who had married an extraordinarily beautiful young woman called Nyssia and made her his queen. Nyssia was only seventeen years old when she and Candaules were wed.

The beauty of Lydian women was renowned even far from the country's borders. Yet the women were not only famed for their charms; their deviousness and ingenuity had also justly won them widespread notoriety. Lydian women did not have any power in the politics of their country, but this only made them all the more ready to use their best weapons – their good looks, cunning and ruthlessness – to bend the world to their advantage.

King Candaules was a kindly, rather foolish man, who had been a widower for many years after the death of his first wife. Fantastically wealthy like all the Lydian kings, Candaules adored Nyssia and gave her everything she wanted: jewels, fine clothes, and even a great estate of her own in the south of Lydia, near her parents' home.

When Candaules married Nyssia he knew she wasn't in love with him, but he hoped she might one day grow to love him. It never seemed to occur to the doting Candaules that girls of Nyssia's age don't usually fall in love with men as old as him, even when the older man is a king. In spite of this, Candaules, whose personality was pleasant but whose mind was not of high quality, remained optimistic that he would win Nyssia's affection in due course.

Candaules was a friendly man, and counted several of his household servants among his close friends, including Gyges. One day, during one of their private conversations, Candaules asked Gyges whether he did not surely agree that Queen Nyssia was the most beautiful woman in the whole world.

Gyges replied that while he did not think it seemly to comment on the queen's beauty, he certainly agreed, as the king had been so good as to ask his opinion, that Queen Nyssia was a truly enchanting woman.

'Well, yes, Gyges,' the king replied, 'of course everyone in the court can see how beautiful Nyssia is when she sits in state in her regal clothes. But I tell you, my friend, only I, who am infinitely privileged to see Nyssia when she is naked, can appreciate how beautiful she truly is.'

Gyges, a deeply respectful young man, politely told the king he could well believe it.

But Candaules was not even content with this. Being a proud and stubborn old man, he could see no reason why Gyges should not witness the truth for himself. And so Candaules commanded Gyges to hide that evening inside a large wardrobe in the queen's dressing-room and to peek through a little slit in the wardrobe and watch her getting undressed. 'Then, when my wife is naked,' said Candaules, 'you shall be able to see her in her full majesty.'

Confronted with little choice in the face of the royal order, Gyges agreed to go along with the king's preposterous plan. Candaules retired to his own dressing-room, which was a short distance away from Nyssia's, though out of earshot.

Presently Nyssia came into her room and took all her daytime clothes off to change into her night attire and go to bed.

Gyges, in his hiding-place, was struck so totally, absolutely and completely by the wondrous beauty of her naked person that, trembling with excitement at seeing the queen thus, he accidentally knocked against the wooden wall of the wardrobe and revealed his presence.

Nyssia, horrified, was about to shout for her guards, who would certainly have killed Gyges. Terrified of losing his life, Gyges stammered out an account of what had happened.

Nyssia, knowing her elderly husband only too well, listened attentively. She had in any case long been struck at court by the handsome face, figure and manly demeanour of Gyges. Now, she saw her chance.

As for Gyges, the instant he had seen Nyssia naked, he had at once conceived a passion for her no less considerable than Candaules' own love for his queen. The difference was that Nyssia was perfectly ready to return Gyges's feelings.

'No man but my husband should set eyes on my naked form,' Nyssia said, still completely unclothed, fabulously beautiful, brazen and shameless as she spoke to Gyges, who was actually making a feeble and ridiculous effort to use his left hand to shield his eyes from the sight of the heavenly creature before him. 'You have seen me unclothed, Gyges, due to my husband King Candaules' foolish and wicked insistence. Because of this, it is only fitting that *you* now become my husband.'

'But... but how?' Gyges stammered. 'You are married already... *to the king!*'

'Not for much longer,' replied the young queen, going over to a drawer in her dressing-table and taking out a sharp dagger. 'You must now go and kill Candaules with this,' she instructed, handing the dagger to Gyges. 'I have always admired your handsome face and figure, Gyges, as well as your loyal and good nature. You shall make a wonderful new husband, and when that day comes I shall greatly look forward to going to bed, rather than dreading it, as I do now. Moreover, because I am queen of Lydia, when you become my husband, you shall become king.'

Gyges stared at her in astonishment. 'But King Candaules is my friend,' he pleaded. 'I can't just *kill* the poor old man. Besides... once the palace guards find out he has been murdered they'll search the palace for the perpetrator. When they catch me they'll hang me.'

'No they won't, Gyges,' replied Nyssia. 'The guards all dote on me. There's not a man among them who wouldn't give everything he has to be in your fortunate position. I'll simply tell them that the king was playing with his dagger to impress me with his martial skills and that he suddenly slipped, fell on his dagger, and tragically died. Don't worry about Candaules. He's very old,' Nyssia added, blithely, 'and most likely would not have been much longer for this world anyway.'

Gyges still looked unsure, so Nyssia walked up to him, embraced him with her naked body and kissed him passionately and lingeringly on the lips. After a while she teasingly broke the kiss, leaving Gyges red-faced with excitement, and she held the dagger out to him again.

'Do this necessary deed,' she instructed Gyges, 'and then come back here, to me, and we can sport ourselves in every way you wish, for certainly...' here she gave him a wicked smile, 'I just felt that an important part of you, Gyges, is definitely in favour of my plan. Come on, *hurry up*. It is a cold night, and it will be much warmer in bed with you. My husband shall be in his dressing-room, at the end of the corridor. Make sure you leave the dagger in him.'

Gyges, almost out of his mind with passion and excitement, and reflecting that, after all, Candaules was an old man who probably did not have much time left to live, suddenly made his decision. Taking the dagger, he held it behind his back, crept softly down the corridor, hurried into the king's dressing-room and stabbed the king in the heart even as Candaules was smiling and asking him what he thought of Nyssia's beauty. The king perished at once, without saying another word. Gyges was careful to obey Nyssia's instruction and leave the dagger in the king's dead body.

Gyges returned to Nyssia's dressing-room and told her what had happened. She kissed him many times, thanking him profusely for relieving her of the company of 'my boring husband, who was wizened in every respect'. She then led Gyges to her bed, where she rewarded him abundantly for the service he had performed for her. She continued to reward him, thus, for much of the night.

In the morning, when Gyges was lying, exhausted, in Nyssia's bed, hardly able to believe that a night of such passion could be possible, Nyssia went to see the palace guards and informed them that King Candaules had met with a terrible accident.

Candaules was duly buried with full honours, Nyssia wearing a black mourning gown and weeping profusely as the king's coffin was laid to rest. A few weeks later Nyssia married Gyges, appointing him king. And so the Mermnadae dynasty was created.

Cyrus, with Asha riding on one side of him and Harpagus on the other, led the great Persian army that numbered the ten thousand Immortals and close to forty thousand other soldiers, all skilled in the sword, spear and sling. As they rode, Harpagus told Cyrus this story of the unfortunate King Candaules, who had come to such an unpleasant end due to the scheming of his beautiful young queen.

Alongside Harpagus rode his beautiful flame-haired wife, Ushtana. It had not escaped Cyrus that the story of Candaules, Gyges and Nyssia bore some resemblance to the circumstances under which Harpagus had married Ushtana, nor did Cyrus imagine that Harpagus had failed to notice this himself.

'I told you, Ushtana, that before long you might see Lydia again,' Cyrus said. 'As you see, I am a king who keeps his promises.'

'Ushtana has kept her promise too,' Harpagus said. 'She is all I could have dreamed of in a wife.'

'Well, not all Lydian women are like Nyssia,' Ushtana said. 'Perhaps I was once, but not any more.'

Cyrus had hardly been in the mood for hearing the story of Gyges and Nyssia, and he was sure Harpagus was aware of this. But he knew the giant warrior well enough – or at least, the man Harpagus was nowadays – to be aware that Harpagus was absolutely devoted to him, and was recounting the story to make a clumsy, yet well-meant, attempt to lift his spirits.

Cyrus smiled half unwillingly as Harpagus told the story, and could not deny that Harpagus had, probably unintentionally, made the story of Nyssia and Gyges both compelling (Harpagus had told it in great earnest) and comic, especially when the giant warrior made his voice high-pitched in order to attempt to sound like Nyssia when she was speaking. He could not help feeling grateful to Harpagus for the story.

Story-telling, Cyrus knew, was an important way for the soldiers to entertain each another on long marches and round the camp-fires at night. The best story-tellers were always regarded as the ones who kept themselves out of the story but simply recounted what the characters in the story said, did or thought. Some soldiers in the army were so prized as story-tellers that they received extra pay because of how Cyrus considered their contribution improved the morale of their fellow warriors.

Until the evening when the great army of Persia finally reached the borders of Lydia in the west, their entire journey took place through friendly territory, so successful had Cyrus been in his quest, to build an empire.

But Cyrus's was not the kind of empire of which the late and unlamented King Astyages (and Raiva) had dreamed of; an empire founded on hatred or subjugation, and worked by slaves who had been bought and sold with cold indifference to their humanity. It was an empire founded on tolerance: tolerance of the rights of individuals to seek happiness and a good life; tolerance of different cultures, languages, and different religious beliefs; tolerance of how people might choose to live their lives, as long as those choices did not interfere with the smooth running of the Persian Empire.

Cyrus practised tolerance of all kinds because he had seen, only too well, to what intolerance led. He also practised religious tolerance because, at a practical level, he genuinely did not care what religion his subjects practised as long as they were loyal to him.

Cyrus was immensely proud of his empire. His grief and despair over Roshan were as great as ever, but somehow he had found within himself the ability to transmute these desperate feelings into a spearhead of action. As he led his armies to Lydia he believed that his destiny as a founder of a great empire was his only destiny.

Because the army had indeed been marching through friendly territory until it reached the border with Lydia, and as Cyrus was universally loved by his subjects, when the army passed by towns and villages, townspeople and villagers streamed out to offer gifts to their king. The giving and receiving of gifts was only brief, for the enormous army was too large to stop in its progress, but Cyrus thanked every gift-bringer personally, and treasured the most humble gift from a poor old lady – a small, fragrant goat's cheese or a plate of dates, for example – far more than expensive gifts, such as a golden dagger or a silk tapestry, offered by a wealthy inhabitant of a town.

Cyrus arranged for all the food brought out to him to be given to the unit responsible for providing food and drink for the gigantic army. The army marched on a healthy but frugal diet of barley porridge improved every few days by mutton or goat's meat from animals the army paid for along the way, sold willingly by farmers.

As for drink, the army consumed considerable quantities of fruit juice diluted by water to make it last longer. In the evenings, when the soldiers and beasts of burden were resting after their day's journey, date wine was served, and Cyrus enjoyed spending some time with his soldiers and drinking with them. He rarely drank intoxicating drinks, but he did not deprive himself of them completely.

The mighty army of the Persian Empire soon passed across the borders of Lydia and for the first time into hostile territory.

Not that there was much hostility visible to Cyrus, for the inhabitants of the villages and other settlements of the eastern-most regions of Lydia merely trembled inside their barricaded houses, praying to their gods that their king would soon make peace with the Persians, or buy them off, and that soon the Persians would be heading back home. Cyrus, for his part, commanded his army to behave properly toward the Lydians, only to take what sheep and goats they needed for survival, and always to pay in silver for the animals they took.

'*We are liberators, not thieves,*' he said to Asha and Harpagus, and this order was passed down through the entire army.

And besides, Cyrus's advance scouts had already told him that the entire force of the Lydians and their purchased, mercenary allies was waiting for them on a plain about six days' march from the border. Cyrus had no desire to let his men tire themselves or lose the discipline of the march through wild and cruel forays into Lydian villages.

Cyrus, as always, had his eye on the real prize. For all his despair about losing Roshan, the woman he loved, Cyrus did not for, one moment, lose sight of it.

The prize was Lydia.

35. Kings

Croesus was as rich as Croesus, but right now he was anything but happy. Ever since turning down the proposal to be allied with

Persia, he had been busy forging alliances with smaller, weaker neighbouring countries and organizing his army, or rather letting his generals do the organizing for him while he gave instructions to them from the safety of his palace at Sardis.

At this particular moment, Croesus's six generals were now all standing before him in the royal tent on the battlefield in which Croesus was waiting to hear from his scouts that the Persians were close to arriving, at which point he had arranged that he would be taken hastily some miles from the actual battlefield, to avoid any possibility that he might be captured, wounded or, heaven forbid, killed.

The Lydian generals were all hanging their heads. Croesus, salivating with fury, at present looked more like a mad dog than a king.

'Will no-one... will none of you, tell me how to rid my kingdom of this Persian upstart?' Croesus demanded.

None of the generals said a word.

'Well?' Croesus shouted.

One general, the oldest and most senior of all, cleared his throat, then said:

'We outnumber them, your Majesty. We believe they have about forty thousand men; we have more than seventy thousand including our allies. Moreover, our soldiers are defending their homeland and so will fight fiercely.'

Croesus breathed deeply. He wiped his mouth with the back of the palm of his left hand. He nodded slowly, then stared at the other officers. 'Well, do any others of you have anything to say?'

There was a rather long silence, then another general said:

'Our archers are well prepared, your Majesty. Lydian archers are the best in the world. Our cavalry will lead our attack, of course, but our archers are so numerous and skilful they could win victory by themselves, even if they were not supported by cavalry and footsoldiers.'

There were a few not especially convinced nods. The generals all knew that the Persians had excellent shields, their own superb archers and...

The Immortals.

The generals all supposed their king knew about the Immortals and the fabled bells they wore that had so often rung the death-knells of their enemies, but none of the generals seemed to think this a good time to remind him of this.

Croesus clicked his fingers impatiently. 'Go!' he said. 'Prepare your men for war. Tell them they are fighting for Lydia. Bid them to be brave. Tell them none must die without taking at least one Persian with them.'

The generals promised that they would. Then they quickly hurried out of the royal tent and retreated to their own quarters.

Croesus stood in his tent and fumed.

He tried to console himself by eating large chunks of the delicious sweet jelly confection so popular in Lydia among those who could afford it. But for once Croesus found no consolation in eating. For, having great faith in the pronouncements of the oracle at the Temple of Sibanyi, south of Sardis, which he had consulted only the previous day regarding the likely result of the battle against the Persians, Croesus's mind was still filled with the halting words the chief magus of the oracle had spoken to him.

'Sire, I have consulted the oracle as you instructed. The word of the oracle is this, which I... I only relay as the mere humble magus of the oracle.'

'Get to the point,' Croesus had commanded him.

'Sire, the oracle says that... it says that your dynasty must... must be punished because it is founded on the appetite of Nyssia and the treachery of Gyges, the first ruler of the Mermnadae. Against the Persians... against them, sire, you shall win no victory, no peace, but the land of Lydia shall be invaded and ruled by a foreign power.'

That was the moment Croesus struck the chief magus of the oracle in the face with the open palm of his right hand.

The man fell to the ground, but Croesus had felt no satisfaction at seeing the magus prostrate there.

Instead, he had felt only fear. And one thought stayed firmly at the front of his pampered brain.

What will the Persians do to me if they capture me?

On the fifth day after crossing the border into Lydia, the Persians came within a day's march of the massed forces of the Lydians. Fresh emissaries on horseback had been sent, again with the message that Cyrus meant no harm to the Lydian nation but simply wished to include it within the great protective fold of the Persian Empire. But if the Lydians insisted on fighting, it would be bloody and terrible.

A day or so after the emissaries had been sent, they returned with a personal sealed message from King Croesus to Cyrus. At once, Cyrus tore off the tightly-wound wrapper from the tablet.

The tablet was itself inscribed in Persian cuneiform: Cyrus could only assume that some literate Persian had made his home in Lydia and for this purpose acted as his, Croesus's, translator:

Has not the king of Persia enough nations in his saddle-bag already? the tablet read. *Lydia shall never be subject to foreign rule. If you turn around now and return to your land, I give you my word that you and your soldiers shall receive a safe passage back to the borders of your own empire.*

Cyrus read these words calmly. This was the response he was expecting.

He turned to Asha and Harpagus, who were standing close by him.

'At first light we attack,' he said. 'Croesus is not being reasonable.'

The Persians marched on and made camp within sight of the Lydian encampments, illuminated by the light of a thousand camp fires.

Cyrus sat and meditated by a camp fire his servants had prepared. The servants cooked his food over the fire, but Cyrus sought no special rations compared to his soldiers. His food and drink – barley-porridge and goat's cheese, with diluted date wine – were just the same as that which his soldiers ate and drank.

Meanwhile, several miles away, Croesus was being served a splendid meal of sturgeon caught from a river in the fabled frozen land of the remote north-west. The fish had then been smoked so as to keep on the long journey back to Lydia. Croesus, who usually loved sturgeon, felt furious about many things, including the unfortunate fact that, at that moment, he felt too nervous to do more than pick at his supper.

'Perhaps Croesus will attack by night,' Harpagus said, thought-fully, as he, Asha and Cyrus ate their barley-porridge from bowls of brass.

'No, I do not believe he shall,' said Cyrus.

'Why not?' asked Asha.

Cyrus shrugged. 'I have heard that Croesus does not like to fight but prefers to watch battles from a safe vantage point a few miles away. That being so, he is not likely to launch an attack at night, is he, when he cannot fully enjoy the spectacle?'

'Then perhaps *we* should attack at night,' suggested Harpagus.

Cyrus tried to smile. He did not smile much nowadays. 'No,' he said. 'I think it would be unfair not to give Croesus a good view of the annihilation of his army.'

After Cyrus, Asha and Harpagus had eaten their frugal supper, Cyrus turned to Harpagus. 'Before the sun is up,' Cyrus instructed, 'order the camel-men to bring all the camels to the very front of our forces. The mounted camels will make our first charge, and I will charge with them.'

'You want a charge of *camels*?' Harpagus said.

'Yes,' said Cyrus.

'But why?' Harpagus asked.

Cyrus nodded slowly. 'Trust me. Just do as I say.'

'Of course,' said Harpagus.

For much of the rest of the night Cyrus lay half-awake, mourning Roshan.

He tried to chase away his despair and grief, but failed.

Cyrus was up well before sunrise, and put on his battle-armour.

Shortly afterwards, he led the charge of camels that heralded the onset of the vast Persian assault on the Lydian army.

No Lydian soldier who came within striking distance of his sword had the slightest chance.

36. Croesus Observes Events

King Croesus, viewing the battle from the safety of a hilltop about five hundred paces from the level plain where the two armies were clashing, had at that moment the sincerest of hopes that the sheer advantage in numbers his own forces had over the Persians would yield him victory.

When Croesus saw the Lydian cavalry charging, his spirits, very low until that moment, definitely began to improve. Croesus had won many battles with that charge: or rather his cavalry had.

Croesus's military technique was not sophisticated. His plan was to send his cavalry in to make the first assault on an enemy and to kill as many of the enemy as they could. In all the past battles Croesus could remember the first assault had been so destructive that the enemy would retreat, and could then be pursued by foot-soldiers. On the other hand, if the enemy managed itself to advance, it could be cut down by the Lydian archers wielding powerful bows made from wood strengthened by cow-horn.

But Croesus knew deep within himself that the forces that had opposed him in those days had been against much lesser opponents than the Persians.

Moreover, Croesus hadn't reckoned with the Persians' *camels.*

He had seen camels before, but he did not own any. There were few camels in Lydia: only some in the far east of the country and a few on display in circuses or in the spectacles staged by travelling players who spared no effort to entertain.

But while Croesus had seen camels before, the Lydian horses had not.

When the proud Lydian steeds set eyes on the strange, hump-backed, long-limbed beasts lumbering in their ungainly yet concerted way toward them, Croesus was appalled to see that the entire body of the Lydian cavalry drew to an almost instantaneous and loudly neighing standstill. The horses were terrified. Many threw their mounts.

Cyrus, himself on camel-back, was leading the charge. Persian swords and spears caused bloody havoc among the mounted Lydians or those who were in the desperate situation of having lost their mounts or were dizzy from having been hurled from their saddles to the hard ground. The carnage was indescribable, but even this was nothing compared with what happened next.

The ten thousand Immortals charged on magnificent black stallions, the bells in their long hair ringing like a myriad death-clarions.

Every Immortal was armed with a sword and spear, and in each Immortal's heart burned the creed of his devotion to the art of war. They were a terrible sight to see. They shrieked war-whoops as they launched themselves onto the remaining Lydian cavalry and the cowering Lydian footsoldiers. Croesus's generals gave the order to the archers to prepare to fire, just waiting for the moment when the Immortals would be within range.

But even as the Lydian archers awaited the word of command, the Persian archers fired at the Lydian archers from vantage positions around the side of the main charge.

The Lydian archers, so used to being the most powerful predators in the field of battle, became the prey. Their heads, eyes, faces, throats, chests and limbs were pierced by Persian arrows, whose fish-hook points made them impossible to pull out without tearing sinews, veins, arteries, muscles and nerves.

As the Immortals, now reaching the Lydian army, began to cause bloody ruin among the Lydian cavalry and footsoldiers, most of the Lydian archers were too much preoccupied with their own agony and dying to help them. Some Lydian archers did now manage to loose their arrows, and in that first wave of the battle perhaps four score Immortals, despite their hard leather body-armour and bronze helmets, paid the ultimate sacrifice for Cyrus and the Empire. But with the Lydian archers already close to being a spent force in the battle, the result was inevitable.

All this Croesus saw from his safe vantage point atop the hill. The richest king in the known world could not stop his jaw sagging as he watched the Persian bowmen inflict murderous chaos on his army and the Immortals riding through the Lydian ranks and delivering death to all who were so unwise as to get in their way.

Croesus tried to console himself with the knowledge that his legions of footsoldiers were still intact, and that despite the obvious great strength of the Immortals, the Persians were still heavily outnumbered. But what Croesus had overlooked was the fragility of the loyalty of the smaller neighbouring states whose own armies he had purchased and who accounted for about twenty thousand of the nominally Lydian soldiers in the field.

For, as Croesus watched with renewed horror, he saw the king of Phrygia, one of the neighbouring states he had bribed to help him, leading his soldiers off the field of battle.

Then to Croesus's even greater consternation, he saw the Cappadocian banner on the back of a galloping mounted soldier who was heading into the Persian lines, with the mounted Cappadocian soldiers following him and throwing away their weapons as they did so.

Croesus cursed loudly and violently.

The Cappadocians were deserting into the Persian lines.

Croesus looked on in despair while the Cilicians followed them.

Croesus had seen enough.

He had a small detachment of his bodyguards with him; as many as he could spare from the army.

Croesus drew a heavy breath. With awed fascination and even greater horror, he now saw that the main body of the Persian army had not yet even been engaged.

The Immortals had taken on the remnants of the Lydian cavalry and then the Lydian footsoldiers, and were triumphing. Tens of thousands of other mounted Persian soldiers and footsoldiers were still standing in disciplined ranks on the plain, waiting for the command to charge into battle.

Croesus was simply unable to believe that the Immortals could be so powerful and successful, but he had no choice but to believe it, for he could see the Immortals in action with his very own eyes.

In a daze of horror and disbelief, Croesus turned to his small band of bodyguards. He glanced at the two he regarded as the most reliable of all.

'Go into the field and make your way to the Persian king. Tell him from me that I wish to sue for peace. Your journey shall be hazardous. If you succeed, I shall make you each a personal gift of five gold bars from a secret treasury I have of my own, which the Persians cannot possibly know about. If either of you die, I shall give the same amount of gold to your widows. Either you or your widows will never want for money again. Now, go, and may fortune bless you in your quest to speak to the king of kings.'

The day was won.

By nightfall about fifteen thousand Lydian soldiers – bowmen, mounted soldiers and footsoldiers – lay dead or dying on the battlefield.

The bodies were already decomposing in the hot sun. Ravens and crows were pecking at the corpses' dead eyes, the insides of their noses, and any other soft tissue the hungry carrion-eaters could find.

The remnants of the Lydian army were building funeral pyres to incinerate some of the bodies, but none of the Lydians who had survived the carnage imagined there would be time or wood enough to burn every corpse; the vast majority would be left to decompose where they fell.

In the Persian camp, which now included the armies of Cappadocia and Cilicia, the mood was triumphant. Losses had been relatively small: altogether about six score Immortals and about ten score of Cyrus's archers and infantry had breathed their last breath.

Cyrus had lost count of the number of Lydians who had fallen to his sword. He had sustained a small wound to his right shoulder, and an arrow pierced his left hand. Cyrus had removed the arrow himself by slicing off its point and pulling the arrow back out of its entry hole.

Of his two wounds, the wound to his hand was the worst, but his medical man had assured him it was a clean wound and that fortunately no tendon had been damaged.

'Thank you,' Cyrus told the physician, who began at once to stitch and bind his hand to stem what was left of the bleeding. Two of Cyrus's servants now approached him; one with a pitcher of water and a cup of glazed and fired clay, the other with a large bunch of ripe yellow grapes and a plate of roasted goat's meat. Cyrus thanked the two servants but said he was not hungry.

'Please, offer the food to our guest,' Cyrus said.

The 'guest', King Croesus of Lydia, was sitting in the most comfortable chair in Cyrus's tent.

Croesus, who until that moment had been terrified that he might be executed at any time, was trying his best to look as humble and polite as he possibly could.

Croesus glanced at his mighty captor with awe and reverence as a servant brought the food over. Despite his fear, he was starving, and was also eager to show his gratitude, so he began eating the food at once. As he did, he allowed himself a tentative, hesitant sense of relief. He was far from being a stupid man, just a stubborn, conceited and selfish one. He knew perfectly well that captors do not usually feed prisoners they are about to execute.

Croesus felt great awe, too, that the king of the Persians could shrug off such a painful-looking wound.

Croesus's interpreter, an officer, was among those decomposing on the battlefield.

'You is... wise and great king,' Croesus stammered out to Cyrus, in the rudimentary Persian he had heard Persian merchants say to him when they visited the royal court at Sardis.

Croesus, watching Cyrus having his hand stitched up, could not understand how such a horrible operation could be performed on a man without him screaming with pain. He had not thought such bravery possible.

Cyrus, speaking to Croesus through one of the Persians' interpreters, nodded at the Lydian king. 'I wish you'd accepted my offer of an alliance, Croesus, of your excellent nation into our Empire. Thousands perished today who did not need to do so.'

Croesus hung his head in shame.

Harpagus now rounded on Croesus. Again speaking through the interpreter, Harpagus barked, 'You thought Astyages a good king? You thought I should have been executed for killing him? Did you not know that the king you said was so good commanded my thirteen-year-old son Artabaz to be roasted alive and his flesh served to me under the guise of it being roast boar?'

Croesus, very curious as to whether Harpagus had eaten any of it, knew that he ought definitely not to ask for clarity on that matter.

Indeed, Croesus decided it would be best not to make any response at all, but rather to look humble, embarrassed and mistaken.

Under the circumstances he found adopting that appearance easy enough.

37. A Royal Wedding

'Let this day be set in the immortal book of time as a day of the greatest joy for our sacred Empire and for our mighty king and his bride!' intoned Ashavan, the chief magus of the Persian Empire, one morning six months later. 'The heart of our Ahura-Mazda-beloved emperor, Cyrus the Great, king of kings, founder of the empire of the Persians, has been bestowed on a lady of infinite worth, who has a beauty as undeniable as his own greatness, and with every quality of thought and goodness that makes her most fit to be a consort to the most splendid monarch the world has ever known!'

Ashavan, to whom it was said Ahura-Mazda spoke directly every night as the magus slept (a rumour Ashavan did nothing to dispel), was wearing a splendid cream-coloured holy vestment edged with a rich thread of pure gold and interspersed with emeralds.

The magus raised his right hand and touched Cyrus gently on the forehead.

'May a thousand blessings from Ahura-Mazda guard your life forever, great king,' Ashavan intoned. 'May Ahura-Mazda bring your wedded union happiness, peace, and an heir for our glorious Empire!'

Cyrus bowed his head to Ahura-Mazda's own principal servant on earth, the only citizen of all the Persian Empire to whom it was fitting for the king to show obedience.

For a period of some months after his return from Lydia, Cyrus had gone about his daily business with his usual devotion and efficiency, and with the grief and despair that had become habitual to him, too.

Finally, Asha, whose Immortals had played such a decisive part in Lydia's conquest, spoke to him.

Again, Asha expressed his deep condolences over Roshan. But he had told Cyrus that it remained the case that the Persian Empire would need an heir, a successor, and that the mightier the Empire grew, the more vital the need for an heir and successor became.

Cyrus, meditating alone deep into the night, had thought equally deeply over what Asha had said.

The next day, Cyrus asked to see Cassadane and her father again.

Cyrus was struck even more, on that second meeting, by how extraordinarily beautiful Cassadane was.

He was also surprised to discover that he liked her even more than he had the first time they had met.

Cyrus knew he could never, would never, love Cassadane the way he had loved Roshan. But he was intensely lonely, for once his passionate times with Roshan had put an end to his years of chastity and asceticism, a river of affection had flowed in his heart, and Cyrus now knew that it could not be easily stemmed.

A few days later he had seen Cassadane and Farnaspes again. This time, at the end of the evening, Cyrus asked Cassadane whether she would do him the honour of becoming his wife. This question marked Cyrus out as a very special kind of Persian, as well as a very special king, for the usual form would have been for Cyrus, as a king, to have asked Farnaspes for Cassadane's hand.

Cassadane had burst into tears when Cyrus asked her to marry him. He apologized for having upset her, but she replied, with a frankness that delighted Cyrus, that her tears were those of joy.

As for Cyrus, he was as happy as he could have been, with the loss of Roshan still scorching his soul. Cassadane was beautiful, modest, intelligent and true of heart. He knew she would be a wonderful wife. He also knew that he would do his utmost to make her happy.

Cyrus was happy enough to marry Cassadane not even to mind that, in marrying her, he would be doing exactly what Raiva had wanted him to do.

The chief magus Ashavan fell silent. The great temple in Ecbatana, a splendid structure of white stone that towered over every other building in the capital of Media, had not seen a royal wedding in many decades. Cyrus had chosen to marry in Ecbatana rather than at Anshan. He wanted the people of Media to feel part of the joyous marriage between two Persians.

The interior of the temple, with its great high walls of solid stone, was fragrant with the burning of incense.

The guests at the wedding included everyone of significant status in the empire: Asha, Raiva (who seemed to Cyrus sleeker than ever), Queen Mandane, Cassadane's father Farnaspes, and Akinlana. As for Harpagus, he was seated at his own suggestion in a rear aisle some distance from Mandane.

Cyrus, conscious of the delicate scent of rose-water from Cassadane's veiled hair close by him, looked ahead at a model of the great golden orb of the sun suspended by almost invisible wires against the wall at the front of the temple's interior. The wall was painted sky-blue, Cyrus knew, by the extremely valuable pigment of powdered lapis lazuli, hand ground by craftsmen. Against the blue background the wall was decorated with golden stars that showed all the constellations: the work of Ahura-Mazda, creator of all things.

Cyrus, seeing those constellations, thought of how small by comparison the works of humankind were, and how short a human life was compared to the untold ages of the lives of the stars. But he forced himself to stop thinking about this, telling himself *I'm getting married, this isn't the day to be thinking about death.*

Cyrus glanced at the beautiful young woman by his side: the woman who was at that very moment pledging herself to be his wife. His eyes met hers, but he saw that she was too shy, at that splendid and solemn moment, to do anything other than briefly acknowledge him with a timid glance of recognition.

'Now, in the sight of Ahura-Mazda, I declare that you are husband and wife,' Ashavan said.

Cyrus bent his head down towards Cassadane and gently pulled away enough of the gossamer veil that covered her head for her lovely almond-shaped face to be clearly visible to him.

Cyrus kissed her, feeling her cool, exquisite lips against his own.

After he gently broke the kiss, Cyrus smiled at Cassadane. For a moment his emotion was so raw that he felt like crying. But he did not, for he knew that if he had wept, his tears would have been for Roshan, and he did not want his new wife to see him weeping such tears.

Cyrus turned to the golden orb that symbolized both the sun and Ahura-Mazda, the god of the world. He bent his head briefly toward the golden orb, to show his submission to Ahura-Mazda and worship of the god himself, who saw everything in the human world and by whose mercy everything lived, and who judged a man's or woman's life when they died.

Finally, Cyrus turned to Cassadane.

'I shall be forever loyal to you, my beloved queen,' he murmured.

The festivities of the afternoon and evening embraced the whole city of Ecbatana, now an infinitely more joyous and lively city than it had ever been under the dominion of the tyrant Astyages.

In the afternoon Cyrus and Cassadane hosted a great banquet for the people of Ecbatana. As it was not possible for everyone in the populous city to be invited, Cyrus had given instructions that the list of guests must not be restricted to the wealthy, but must also include many of the city's poor, who were chosen by ballot to attend. The evening saw splendid performances by dancers and musicians, theatrical pieces, and displays of swordsmanship by some of the Immortals who were most gifted in that art.

Cyrus knew that Cassadane was growing tired. He gave Asha the great privilege of being his representative for the remainder of the evening. Cyrus then bade farewell to his guests and retired with Cassadane to their bedchamber at the palace in Ecbatana.

The palace at Pasargadae would soon be ready to live in, but it had not yet attained that state of readiness.

Cyrus had not yet appointed a replacement for Roshan as principal gardener at Pasargadae. He knew that he would soon have little choice but to do so, but for the moment he did not have the heart.

Cyrus let Cassadane bathe and prepare herself for bed before he himself bathed and joined her in the bedroom.

He knew she would be nervous and shy, and she was. But when at last he joined her in bed, he was delighted to see that she had made herself naked for him.

He had learnt much about the body of a woman from his short but intense time with Roshan. She had taught him during their time by the red lake how to make love to a woman properly: that women could enjoy just as much pleasure as men could, and that to make a woman replete with pleasure was indeed a delight for a loving man.

Cyrus did not forget the lessons Roshan had taught him during his first night with his queen Cassadane, nor for many, many nights afterwards.

That first night Cyrus knew that Cassadane was a virgin, that virginity must always be respected, and that the taking of it is a privilege and responsibility even for the king of Persia.

Cyrus spent a long time kissing and caressing Cassadane until her body, like a luscious ripe warm young fruit in his arms, was glowing with love, and until she was completely out of breath and trembling with passion and desire, so much so that she actually began to beg him to enter her.

When he did so, Cassadane's hot breath was sweet and panting against his cheeks.

Cyrus was still in many respects inexperienced in the art of love, but he realized that Ahura-Mazda had created love in order to delight men and women equally.

And so Cyrus and Cassadane gave themselves to those delights, while in the background, beyond the thrilled murmurings of his beautiful young queen yet again losing herself in her ecstasy, Cyrus could make out the faint sounds of music, dancing, applause and laughter as the festivities to celebrate his wedding continued.

38. King and commander

'Do you love her?' Harpagus asked.

Six months had passed. The new palace at Pasargadae was almost finished. The gardens already were. Cyrus had ordered the most senior horticulturists in Lydia to go to Pasargadae and supervise their completion.

Cyrus himself had seen nothing of Pasargadae since the start of the Lydian campaign. Apart from returning to Ecbatana for a few days to be married, he had spent much of his time in the Lydian capital, Sardis, making the arrangements to bring Lydia completely within the fold of the Persian Empire.

Cyrus, who had by now mastered a good deal of the Lydian language, had at first, of course, been a stranger in Sardis. He was greatly helped in his task of becoming acquainted with Sardis and the Lydian people by King Croesus, who was almost embarrassingly helpful and eager to assist in every way he could.

Croesus ordered Lydians to make themselves available to Cyrus for any purpose he might have. Such was Croesus's deference to Cyrus nowadays, he had even asked his conqueror's permission to pay the promised five bars of gold to the body-guards who had embarked on the hazardous journey across the battlefield to tell Cyrus of Croesus's willingness to surrender. Cyrus granted this permission, feeling it would be unjust to the brave men to deny them the promised reward for their bravery. The bodyguards were now rich, though they remained loyal officers in the combined Persian and Lydian army.

Cyrus took pains to explain to Croesus and the Lydian noblemen that the watchwords of the Persian Empire were tolerance and understanding, at least as long as the vanquished peoples behaved themselves and did not attempt to rebel.

'You and the citizens of Lydia may worship any god you please,' Cyrus informed Croesus and the Lydian nobility in a meeting in the great hall of the palace of Sardis. 'Those of you who may choose to convert to the worship of Ahura-Mazda will honour me greatly. But throughout the empire, freedom of religion is our greatest gift to the nations who are conjoined to us. We Persians are a tolerant people, perhaps because we were once under the rule of a tyrant and so now we have no desire to be tyrants ourselves.'

The following morning, Croesus asked to speak to Cyrus privately. When they were alone, he informed Cyrus that he intended to abandon the religion of the Lydians and become a devotee of Ahura-Mazda.

Cyrus was, of course, aware of Croesus's motives, but gave no indication of this. He smiled at Croesus.

'I am flattered by your decision,' Cyrus told the former king.

After the combined nations of Persia and Media, Lydia was the largest country within the empire. This, and its remoteness from the Persian heartland, made Cyrus aware of the dangers of dissent. There had indeed already been one rebellion, in northern Lydia, but it had only involved a few towns and had easily been controlled. The ringleaders had been imprisoned and the prime instigator executed. Cyrus, conscious of the scope of the task of bringing such a large nation under his control, kept more than twenty thousand Persian soldiers stationed in Lydia at an encampment not far from the capital.

Cyrus himself lived temporarily in the royal palace at Sardis with Cassadane. Rather than occupying Croesus's former luxurious quarters, he chose a more humble set of rooms near the top of one of the palace's great towers. He told Cassadane that he had chosen the room in the tower for the view it gave over Sardis, and Lydia.

As for Cassadane, she adapted to life in a subjugated foreign power with great willingness. Cyrus knew that the accommodation in the tower was nothing like the comfort in which she had lived in her father's large house at Anshan, but the new queen never once complained.

'Do you love her?'

Harpagus had posed the question late one evening as he and Cyrus, alone in the library of the palace at Sardis, were poring over a map of Lydia.

The two men had worked hard for some time. Presently a servant had brought a wine-skin containing an amber-coloured Lydian wine made with resin. The wine was popular among the Persians stationed in Lydia. Harpagus, and for once Cyrus too, had drunk from it.

Cyrus looked thoughtfully at Harpagus.

Cyrus cleared his throat. 'Do I love whom?'

Harpagus smiled. 'We both know who I mean.'

Cyrus nodded slowly. 'Yes,' he murmured. 'Yes, I do love her. I always did. I should have told her sooner. And now... now it is too late.'

Harpagus looked astonished. 'Why do you say that? Surely she hasn't already succumbed to the attentions of some young Lydian stud, like Queen Nyssia did when she seduced and then married that whelp Gyges after he killed Candaules in this very palace? Is there perhaps something in the warm air here in Sardis that makes women's loins restless?'

'Harpagus,' said Cyrus, 'I think the wine is getting the better of you, which thankfully for me, is not the first time that has happened. I have no idea at all what you are talking about.'

Harpagus looked levelly at Cyrus. 'I asked you a question, that is all. I asked you whether you loved Queen Cassadane.'

'Oh, I see.'

'Who did you think I meant?'

Cyrus could not bring himself to reply.

'Did you think I meant Lady Roshan?' Harpagus murmured.

Cyrus said nothing.

'Do you still love *her*?' Harpagus asked, faintly.

'I don't know. But I do know that I miss her.'

'Then... why did you marry Cassadane?'

'You know the answer to that... or you can guess. Roshan is dead; I cannot marry a dead woman. I am very fond of Cassadane. She is good, brave, honest and loyal. And it is my duty to furnish my empire with an heir.'

'But... can you ever love Cassadane as you love even the memory of Roshan?'

Cyrus made no reply.

'I think Ahura-Mazda sometimes likes to jest with us,' Harpagus said, a few moments later. 'And while he jests, he breaks our hearts.'

Cyrus did not reply immediately. Finally he said, 'Perhaps that is so. But sometimes Ahura-Mazda restores our hearts and our souls, too. And sometimes he rewards us. Speaking of which, I have a job for you.'

'Cyrus, I already have a job. I am commander of your army.'

Cyrus smiled. 'Yes, and when we are ready to take Babylon...'

'You *mean this*? Babylon?'

'Yes. I know perfectly well that Babylon must be brought into the fold of our empire, or our empire can never be secure. The Babylonian king, Nabonidus, is scholarly, or likes to think he is, but he is a sombre, cold-hearted person and not even popular with his own subjects, mainly because most of them prefer to worship Marduk, the bull-calf of the sun, rather than the moon-god Sin, whom Nabonidus favours. I heard he was negotiating with Croesus to provide military aid to Lydia; had we delayed our invasion we would doubtless have had to confront units of the Babylonian army as well as the other hired armies Croesus purchased.'

'When do you plan to move on Babylon?'

'I haven't yet decided for certain. Perhaps in a year or two. When we have brought Lydia properly into our empire and given it the benefit of Persian organization and Persian ways, you shall have your old job back and command the army on its march to Babylon. But that lies in the future. Meanwhile, I intend to appoint you governor of Lydia.'

Harpagus clasped Cyrus's right hand with his own. 'It is a great honour, Cyrus. A great, great honour. I thank you with all my heart.'

'I think Ushtana will also enjoy this new career of yours.'

'Cyrus... Cyrus, she will love it. My wife has often spoken of Lydia, and how much she loved her girlhood here. She will be so, so happy.'

'I am glad to hear it. This new promotion, however, is no more than your loyalty deserves. You have done much wickedness, Harpagus, but... somehow, in truth I do not even now truly know how, I have managed to find it within myself to forgive you. Perhaps it is partly because the appalling wickedness you committed happened when you were young, and the vassal of the most evil king who has ever lived. Moreover, you have removed Astyages's vile presence from the world.'

There was a silence. The two men just stared at each other.

'Cyrus, in accepting the great honour you have bestowed on me I shall be all you wish me to be,' Harpagus murmured, finally breaking the silence.

'I do not doubt it. Then, help me turn Lydia into the jewel of our Empire.'

'I shall, with all the energy of my hands and all the power of my thought. And I know my wife shall do the same.'

'Good,' said Cyrus. 'Very good. And now I shall return to *my* wife.' He cleared his throat. 'My real, living wife. Not the wife I sometimes have in my dreams.'

Harpagus nodded slowly, but said nothing.

Cyrus turned and left the room.

39. The Empire Builder

But it was to be a full nine years before Cyrus considered Lydia and the rest of his empire secure enough for him to move against the Babylonians.

It was not that Cyrus feared the military strength of Babylon. He was far from contemptuous of their strength, but he knew that the Babylonians had been no real match for the Persian army even before the might of what remained of the Lydian army was added to the Persian forces. Cyrus was also aware that in the few weeks before the battle against the Lydians, Croesus had made impassioned appeals to the Babylonians for assistance. Now that Lydia was part of the Persian Empire, the Babylonians were bereft of an ally that might otherwise have sprung to their aid.

Cyrus was confident his army could overwhelm the Babylonians, given that the Persians could somehow acquire a knowledge of how exactly to penetrate the extremely well-fortified city.

In the meantime, he wanted his empire to be as impressive as the legendary, almost mystical, city of Babylon itself, before he would attempt to conquer that very city.

In particular, Cyrus wished the Persian Empire to be as famous for its prosperity and agriculture as it was for its conquests. He had not taken over Lydia in order to plunder it; in fact he urged the men to whom he delegated the economic management of the empire to learn from the Lydians the secrets of successful commerce and the most productive kind of agricultural activity.

He was aware that founding an empire which benefited only the wealthy and powerful would be easy. The real talent, Cyrus knew, would be to create an empire that benefited everyone who lived within it.

This was what Cyrus wanted to achieve, and he had already begun making it happen. But now he wanted to *continue* making it happen.

Which meant planning and achieving successes not on the field of battle but in the countryside, where there was much to be done to make people more prosperous in the less fertile regions of the empire, and in many of the towns and cities, where trade and prosperity had suffered for many decades because of local rivalries and disputes with neighbours.

Such rivalries and disputes now having ended, Cyrus was convinced he could make his people even richer.

Yet while making all of the empire prosperous was vitally important to him, it was not enough. He also wanted the great Persian Empire to be a moral inspiration to the world.

He particularly wished his empire to be renowned for the quality he prized most of all: its tolerance of the creeds and cultures of all who lived within it.

Nine years.

Nine years that saw Cassadane present Cyrus with a son they called Cambyses, after Cyrus's true father. Nine years that saw Cambyses grow until he was on the edge of young manhood.

Nine years that saw Cyrus bid an emotional farewell to Mandane, who died peacefully in her sleep two months before a visit Cyrus made to Harpagus at Sardis to tell him that the time had finally come to move against Babylon.

Nine years that saw Cyrus and his empire grow renowned throughout Asia, Europe, and even in India and the strange, exotic lands that lay yet farther east.

Nine years in which Cyrus never completely forgot Roshan, not for one moment of his waking life. She was rarely completely absent from his dreams.

As for Croesus, he died a few years after the conquest of Lydia. Cyrus, putting into practice, in how he treated the Lydian king and the former Lydian noblemen, his beliefs about extending tolerance and understanding to foreign people, had looked after

Croesus well. He had given the former king a country house on the outskirts of Sardis, and a generous pension, on the understanding that he stayed out of politics.

This Croesus was only too happy to do. Soon after Lydia had fallen, his queen deserted him for one of the two suddenly enriched bodyguards. She informed Croesus, with a Nyssia-like indifference to her husband's feelings, that she had been having an affair with the bodyguard for several months.

Croesus, who despite all his cowardice and weakness was an affectionate and uxurious fellow, was severely distressed by his wife's abandonment of him. Before long however, he found consolation in the arms of an extraordinary person called Zanda: a Moorish dancer who had come to Lydia to perform at a celebration held by Harpagus to mark his accession to the governorship.

Zanda was as tall as the tallest of men, though she had the face (a singularly beautiful face), tanned skin, long flowing black hair, ample breasts and slim waist of a gorgeous Moorish woman. However, she was also rumoured to possess the organ regarded as the most obvious indicator of the male sex.

Whatever the truth of the matter, Croesus saw Zanda performing at Harpagus's celebration and was instantly smitten.

Within a month, having hastily arranged to be divorced from his disloyal queen, Croesus married Zanda. It was said by many rumour-mongers in Sardis that Zanda had been careful to deny Croesus full relations until the wedding night, and that it was only then, in the privacy of their marital bed, that the former king discovered the truth about his bride.

If indeed this was so, Croesus did not abandon Zanda or annul the marriage. Quite the contrary; Croesus was said to look happier after his marriage to Zanda than he had ever been even when he was king of Lydia. He enjoyed two years of happy marriage to her, and one night died in his wife's arms during, it was said, a particularly strenuous bout of love-making. By the time the servants had come into the marital bedroom to offer assistance, Zanda was fully dressed, and so the mystery of her precise nature was not solved even then.

Cyrus was happy for Zanda to live on in Croesus's home. He regarded Croesus's widow as a friend, and usually paid her a visit when he was in Lydia and had time to see her. But he never discovered the truth of the rumours about Zanda, and while he imagined she would have been happy to have told him had he asked, he was too courteous to do so. While Cyrus was a perfectly competent and eager lover to his wife Cassadane, deep down he had never lost his shyness and reticence about matters relating to private life.

He was only too aware of this, for Cassadane had often teased him about it.

Cyrus had often wondered whether Roshan might have cured him of this shyness, if he had married her.

But he hadn't, and now it was too late.

40. A Hero

Asha, his hair cut so it only reached the top of his shoulders rather than falling six inches or so below them, and with the bells in his hair temporarily removed out of respect for Nabonidus, king of Babylon, looked levelly at that fabled monarch.

'And who exactly are you?' Nabonidus demanded, through his interpreter.

The Babylonian king was, Asha knew, about fifty years of age though he looked at least ten years older. Nabonidus had a lean, joyless, ascetic appearance. His face was gaunt and grey. Asha had no difficulty in believing what Cyrus had told him: that the king was an ardent worshipper of the

Babylonian moon-god, whose name in the Babylonian language was Sin.

The Babylonian king wore a robe as pale, Asha thought, as the moon itself. Nabonidus, Asha saw, had the cold look of a dedicated scholar who preferred studying the past to living in the present.

'I am an emissary from the Persian army, your Majesty,' Asha said, 'sent by the great emperor Cyrus to parley with you. Your own emissaries told the Persians you would permit one of us to return with them to speak with you. I am only a common soldier. I was one of many who volunteered to come to speak with you here in Babylon, and the emperor was gracious enough to select me.'

King Nabonidus looked hard at Asha. 'You hold no particular military or political rank in the Persian army?'

'No, your Majesty,' Asha lied. He hated lying. But he heartily despised Nabonidus, even though he had only just met him, and this made lying easier. Cyrus and Asha had agreed that the truth about Asha's true rank must be kept from Nabonidus, who would otherwise surely hold Asha in Babylon and seek to ransom him. Cyrus had, however, said he wanted Asha to be the emissary, and that he trusted Asha's ability to find a point of vulnerability in Babylon's defences.

'My emissaries,' Nabonidus said, 'tell me that a force of more than thirty thousand Persians, including the ten thousand soldiers known as the "Immortals", has made its camp about a day's march south of Babylon, by the banks of the our river. Is that correct?'

'Yes, your Majesty.'

He knew that was no lie. Cyrus and the army were indeed encamped south of Babylon by the Euphrates, which flowed north to south through Babylonia, and through the heart of the great city of Babylon itself before discharging itself into sea.

The evening before, Cyrus had spoken privately to Asha.

'I have gambled that by bringing the army this far, our proximity will frighten Nabonidus into yielding Babylon, and his throne, to our Empire,' Cyrus said. 'But if he does not, we shall have to find another way to take Babylon. The city's walls are tall and impregnable, and I do not intend to waste the lives of my men finding out what I know already: that the walls will be impossible to breach unless Ahura-Mazda were to blow them down. We must discover some point of vulnerability, or we shall have no choice but to lay siege to Babylon.'

'At least that's an option for us,' Asha said.

'Yes,' said Cyrus, 'but Nabonidus's stores within the city of grain and other food are known to be enormous. We might be obliged to lay the siege for a long time. And meanwhile, how can we feed our own army if we have a lengthy siege? If we take food from the Babylonians who live here in the surrounding countryside they will soon hate us, and how does it profit us to create hatred in the hearts of the people whom we want to bring into our Empire?'

Nabonidus was receiving Asha in the splendid royal palace, a massive structure of polished limestone in the heart of Babylon. Asha was aware that his brother Raiva had often made visits to Babylon, in his capacity as a merchant. Indeed, Cyrus – knowing this – had insisted that Raiva come along on the Babylonian expedition to advise Cyrus on the geography of Babylonia. Raiva, by now one of the richest men in Persia, had travelled in considerable style, in a splendid caravan and accompanied by a number of beautiful female servants.

Asha knew that the origins of Babylon were lost in the haze of the past when history did not exist. He also knew that the Babylonians, renowned for being the most cultured people in the region, had learned to write down their language in cuneiform long before the Persians mastered that skill.

Asha was also aware that the fertility of the Euphrates supported a large population used to living a prosperous and industrious life, cultivating the land and living quietly and contentedly on the fruits of that cultivation. He also knew that much of Babylonia was intersected with little canals and artificial tributaries of the river for conveying the water over their land for the purpose of irrigation. The Babylonians were an ingenious people.

Nabonidus's library was stuffed full of tablets and scrolls that lay on innumerable wooden shelves.

'So, Emissary, your master truly believes I shall simply relinquish Babylonia, does he?' Nabonidus said, again through his interpreter, who was as gaunt and grey-faced as Nabonidus was.

'No,' said Asha, 'he does not. He simply urges you to consider that it would be a reasonable thing to do.'

'Ah, yes,' said Nabonidus, 'that word "reasonable" is one of your master's favourites, is it not? The good King Astyages of Media was obviously not reasonable, for I hear he was murdered by his treacherous former general Harpagus, the commander of your army. My neighbour and ally Croesus was also evidently unreasonable, and now Lydia belongs to your master, too. Tell me, what exactly does your king wish me to do so as to be reasonable?'

Asha shrugged. 'Your Majesty, my emperor does not want war with Babylon. He simply asks that you grant him sovereignty over Babylonia and agree that your military forces will fight for the united army of the Persian Empire when called upon to do so. Cyrus does not wish to loot or ruin Babylon. Indeed,' Asha drew a breath, then said, 'last night, just before I set out on my mission here, my emperor personally told me, his humble emissary, that he has great admiration for Babylon, and the industriousness of your people and the quality of your horticulture.'

'Do not be impertinent,' Nabonidus retorted sharply. 'Our Hanging Gardens are a wonder of the world. You may call them by their name.'

'I am using the word my master used.'

Nabonidus just stared at Asha. Finally Nabonidus – his grey, cold-looking, ascetic lips invested with a contemptuous curl – said, 'I have no doubt that your master, the Persian emperor, has no true appreciation of the fruits of civilization such as our magnificent Hanging Gardens. How could he, when he was, I understand, born a lowly peasant, the son of an impoverished goat-herd?'

Asha said nothing. He knew he had to remain calm in the face of this grave insult to Cyrus.

Nabonidus nodded. 'Yes,' he added, 'your master was once a mere peasant, for all that he has gained much since then by military conquest.'

The king paused for a moment to clear his throat, then said:

'However, you may tell your master that Nabonidus, the king of Babylon, is prepared to make him an annual payment of one thousand gold bars, with one-half of the first instalment to be paid now and the remaining half in six months' time, and further instalments to be paid in full on each annual anniversary of the agreement. In return for the payment, Persia is to leave us alone.'

It occurred to Asha, not for the first time, that kings outside Persia could be more stupid than anybody would ever have believed possible.

'Your Majesty,' Asha said, 'my master does not seek tribute, gold, silver, or anything else from you. He merely asks for your friendship and loyalty.'

'He seeks my *friendship*?' the king echoed through his interpreter, 'when he is threatening to rob me of my kingdom?'

'He merely seeks sovereignty over your nation, and for your soldiers to fight for him,' Asha said.

'That is robbery under a different name,' the king hissed. 'My offer is a generous one. If you repudiate it, I shall assume you have been given instructions in advance to refuse such an offer.'

Asha said nothing. The king, exasperated, looked hard at him. Still, Asha made no reply.

'If, emissary, your master is so foolish as to try to invade Babylon he shall fail,' Nabonidus said. 'Our walls are made of stone many paces thick. You have already seen how high our walls are. They cannot be breached by any mortal army.'

Asha knew he shouldn't rise to this challenge, but he couldn't resist it. He cleared his throat, then said:

'I never went to school, your Majesty, for *I* was born a peasant too, in the same small town as where my emperor Cyrus was born. Oh, and my parents, who were hard-working, innocent farmers, were murdered by the soldiers of the man you call the good King Astyages. Since those days, I have tried to make up for my lack of education. I have, for example, heard about the Trojans, who when besieged by the Greeks, were confident their walls could not be breached. Yet breached they were.'

'Only because those cunning snakes the Greeks resorted to crude subterfuge!' Nabonidus retorted via his interpreter. 'A wooden horse, indeed! The Trojans were fools to admit it into their city. But I am not a fool.' Nabonidus's voice rose to an almost hysterical shout. *'Our walls shall never be breached!'*

Asha said nothing, but recalled the advice Cyrus had given him the previous evening. *Under no circumstances lose your temper. In negotiation, the most important skill is the need to keep calm. The first side to lose their temper normally loses the upper hand.*

That being so, Nabonidus seemed well intent on losing. He was breathing hard, and even some touches of ruddiness had leaked into the grey of his countenance. Nabonidus began pacing around his library like a mad man, breathing faster and faster, and occasionally snatching little glances at Asha.

Finally the king came to a standstill only a couple of feet from Asha, who saw at once the anger and seething resentment that he knew so often lurks close to the surface in the soul of the outwardly ascetic and repressed man.

'If your master, this former peasant Cyrus, whom some misguided fools call Cyrus the Great, will not have my gold,' said Nabonidus, 'he shall certainly not have my kingdom. I shall defend Babylonia to my dying breath, and so shall my army and my people. All my people love me, for I am their guardian. They know that I shall always...'

But as the interpreter was speaking these words in Persian, Asha suddenly cleared his throat rather loudly. The interpreter, startled by this, fell abruptly silent.

'Your Majesty,' said Asha, unable to resist interrupting, for his love for Cyrus was so great that he detested hearing him abused, 'not all your people love you.'

The interpreter, hearing these words, looked fearful. But Nabonidus barked an order at him, and instantly the interpreter translated Asha's words into Babylonian for the king's benefit.

'*What... what do you mean?*' the king demanded of Asha.

'I mean,' Asha returned, 'that most of your people worship the god Marduk, the patron deity of the city of Babylon. You do not heed their requests for more temples to be built devoted to Marduk, but you try to force the worship of your moon-god Sin upon them. You also oblige many of the people of Babylon to work as forced labourers. As for the Jews, you keep them here in a state of semi-slavery, when they wish to return to their homeland.'

'You slanderous villain!' Nabonidus cried. 'Your master Cyrus is a peasant... you are his mere mouthpiece and by your own admission a peasant too... I shall not have a peasant denouncing my beloved god Sin. As for the Jews, they are vermin and infidels and should consider themselves lucky I permit them to live in Babylon at all!'

Asha made no reply. He knew he had gone too far. But he realized now that it had been fortunate he had, as Nabonidus's fury meant that the Persian intelligence about the internal dissent to Nabonidus's rule was correct. This being so, Asha thought, Nabonidus's rule would probably not, after all, survive a long siege, nor perhaps even a short one.

That is a point of vulnerability, Asha thought. *Now all I have to do is to get home alive.*

Nabonidus stared in revulsion at Asha, then marched to the door of the library. He flung the door open, barked harsh words of command, retreated back into the library and looked with unabashed hatred at Asha. A moment later, twelve fully armed Babylonian palace guards burst into the library, their swords drawn.

Asha was unarmed. He knew that fighting the guards would be futile: even he, unarmed, could not overcome a detachment of a dozen armed guards. *Surely no man could, except perhaps Cyrus.* Asha hardly ever felt fear; he had trained himself not to feel such a restrictive emotion. His dominant feeling at that moment was surprise at just how foolish Nabonidus could be.

Asha soon discovered that Nabonidus was even more stupid than he'd proved himself to be so far, for a few moments later, Asha found himself grabbed by three of the guards and frogmarched outside the palace and into its grounds that backed onto the Euphrates. By the time they reached the western bank of the river, which flowed south, he was still held tightly by the guards.

Nabonidus arrived some minutes later; evidently he regarded it as undignified to walk at too fast a pace. His interpreter was with him.

At the riverbank, Nabonidus came over to Asha. Suddenly, to Asha's amazement, speaking fluent Persian, the king whispered in his ear.

'You think yourself very clever,' Nabonidus hissed. 'But I am cleverer than you. For you see, your brother Raiva is a close friend of mine. He sent a message to me via my people in the countryside. He told me you would be coming here as an emissary of your peasant-king, and denying who you really are. You are Raiva's foolish younger brother Asha, the leader of the Immortals. You shall never see Persia again.'

'You... you speak Persian,' Asha stammered.

'Yes, fool, I do,' Nabonidus whispered hoarsely. 'I have long benefited from the trade between our countries, and I have found it useful for my enrichment to learn your coarse peasant language.'

Asha, breathless with astonishment at hearing the full extent of his brother's treachery, was speechless. The next thing he knew was that the king shouted out an order. A moment later, the guards who were holding Asha tossed him into the Euphrates.

Asha, hitting the warm water and knowing what was likely to happen now, instantly used all his strength to dive as deep as he could.

He was not quick enough.

He saw a volley of Babylonian arrows racing toward him through the water like demon-fish. He dodged them as well as he could, but two struck him: one in the left forearm, the other in his right thigh.

The pain of the arrows was dulled by the water, but the two brutal piercings of his body were still agonizing.

Asha knew at once that his chances of survival were slim. He knew he had only one thing in his favour: that the flow of the river was southward and rapid, and the Persians lay in that direction. If he could somehow survive the journey, if he could avoid bleeding to death... he would see his wife and son again, and could denounce his evil brother to Cyrus.

Then, even through his pain, a terrible thought occurred to Asha: *If Raiva can betray me, what betrayal might he have wrought on Lady Roshan?*

His thoughts sped on. *I told Raiva I was being asked to take the tablet to Cyrus. Raiva came to see me at my home, and I left the tablet on a table when I went into the kitchen to speak to Farna-dukta.*

Whatever was in the tablet I took to Roshan, it must have made her want to end her life. Cyrus told me his tablet contained a marriage proposal. He said he believed Roshan killed herself because in a moment of madness she did not think he would ever think of her as his equal. But... what if that was not true? What if... Raiva somehow switched the tablets when I was not in the room, and replaced it with some other tablet of his own composition?

Asha knew that cuneiform tablets could easily be forged, because everyone wrote cuneiform in much the same way. That was why the cursive signature was so important.

But what if Raiva somehow found a way to imitate Roshan's signature...? He must have had several examples of it, in tablets from her to him declining his offer of marriage.

The idea that Raiva could do such a thing felt even more appalling to Asha than his arrow-wounds that were now bleeding freely, but now he knew that Raiva had betrayed him, his own brother, Asha realized that it was, in fact, perfectly possible Raiva could have stooped so low as to betray Cyrus, and Roshan.

After all, Asha thought, as the pain of the arrow-wounds bit even deeper, *Raiva, my brother, betrayed me.*

Asha knew he absolutely had to get back to the Persian lines and speak with Cyrus.

He knew he couldn't use his hands to stem the bleeding from the two arrow wounds, because he had to swim as fast as he could before surfacing. He also knew he couldn't hold his breath much longer.

The river's flow swept the brave, betrayed, suspicious, bleeding, already exhausted Asha beyond the grounds of the royal palace and through the centre of the great city with its tall buildings and busy streets. The Euphrates was wide here. Some fishermen and ferry-men in their boats called out to him, obviously unaware of what had happened. But Asha knew that to leave the river or ask anyone for their help would be equivalent to committing suicide.

After several agonising minutes, during which Asha was losing blood all the time, the river brought him within sight of the huge, massy city walls. Asha felt even more certain that he must surely die, for here the river surely went through small holes in the walls, and how could he pass through them?

But then, as he came to the walls, Asha, even in his pain and distress, and hearing as he did the beating of the wings of Ahura-Mazda's angels, saw, in a moment of stupendous revelation, how the Babylonians protected themselves from invasion by their river. As he saw that, he knew that if only he *could* make it to the Persian lines, the days of Babylon being an independent city would be numbered...

Some time later, Cyrus, puzzled as to how Asha's mission was progressing, received a sudden visit from one of Asha's servants.

'Your Majesty... we have just dragged my master, the leader of the Immortals, out of the water of the great river! He is gravely injured, and we all fear his soul shall soon be with Ahura-Mazda. He said he will speak to no-one but you.'

Cyrus just ran. Barely a minute later, he was with Asha. There was a crowd of Persian soldiers around the fallen warrior, but the crowd parted for the great king.

The face of the husband of Farna-dukta and father of Ariya was as pale as parchment. Asha was lying on the grass close by the river bank. A healer was attending to his wounds.

Cyrus saw an entire arrow sticking in Asha's left forearm; there was part of another sticking out from his right thigh.

Asha's head was being cradled by Tiridaad, a caption of the Immortals. At once, Cyrus took over the cradling. Someone called out for somebody to fetch 'his brother, the merchant.'

'Asha, Asha, speak to me,' Cyrus said, 'What happened?'

Asha coughed. Blood dribbled out of his mouth.

'Cyrus,' Asha murmured, 'Nabondidus... he ordered me to be thrown into the water. He... he told his men to shoot arrows after me.'

Cyrus glanced at the healer, avoiding Asha's gaze as he did so. The healer shook his head gravely.

'Cyrus... listen,' Asha murmured. 'Outside Babylon... there is a great iron portcullis where the river flows under the wall... to the south. They have narrowed the river there, also. Yet the portcullis does not reach to the bottom of the river, but stops about a man's height above the bottom.'

'Asha, how do you know this?' Cyrus asked.

'Because... to get out of Babylon, Cyrus, I had to swim deep, deep under the portcullis. Your army could easily...'

He fell silent.

'Yes, I see,' Cyrus murmured. 'And on the north side...'

'There will surely be one there, too,' Asha gasped.

Cyrus knew at once how Babylon could be won, remembered Roshan and her little garden in their village of Paritakna, and how he had tried to help her...

He cradled his beloved friend's uninjured arm. 'Asha, you shall get well. Just try to stay strong.'

'No, Cyrus, no... I've lost too much blood. Cyrus, *I can see Ahura-Mazda*. He is golden, shimmering, beautiful... His angels are coming for me... there are bells in their hair. But the angels are not warriors; they are singing to me.'

Asha drew a frantic, tortured breath. 'Cyrus, listen, my brother is...'

But he fell silent.

'What?' Cyrus asked. 'Your brother is what?'

'My brother is a...' said Asha, but he did not have the strength to say it. When, a few moments later, he spoke again, he murmured, so quietly that only Cyrus could hear him, 'Cyrus, listen, Lady Roshan... she may be...'

'She may be... what?'

But Asha coughed, then breathed like a rasp sharpening a sword.

Cyrus, appalled and astonished to hear Asha say Roshan's name, stared down at his friend in amazement. A sudden memory of all four of them – Roshan, Asha, Raiva and himself – playing together in the dusty village square of Paritakna sprang into Cyrus's mind.

'*What is it, Asha?* What are you trying to say?'

Asha's eyes stared blankly upward. He coughed again, then again. Finally, hoarsely, he murmured, 'Farna-dukta... Ariya... I love them.'

'I know it, Asha,' Cyrus said. He was in tears. 'I know you do. But what were you trying to tell me about Roshan?'

But Asha said no more. He gurgled.

Cyrus saw the light of life die in his friend's eyes as clearly as when the sun suddenly sets beneath the summit of a mountain.

The knowledge that Ahura-Mazda would take good care of Asha did not console Cyrus at all.

He wept uncontrollably.

As he did, the crowd parted and Raiva, well-fed, plump and sleek, appeared. He stared down at his dead brother.

'He should never have volunteered to go to Babylon,' said Raiva, calmly shaking his head.

Cyrus, breathless, his eyes full of tears, just glared at him.

BOOK THREE

UNDYING LOVE

41. The Conquest of Babylon

Cyrus never again thought Raiva trustworthy after that moment. He hadn't completely trusted him for years; the two men were now mutually respectful acquaintances rather than the friends they had once been; but at that instant when Cyrus saw how Raiva reacted to Asha's death, he realized there was a terrible new coldness about Raiva that extended even to how he felt when he saw that his brother had died.

Once Asha's body had been properly cared for and brought into a makeshift funeral tent, and after Cyrus had led the entire army in prayers to ask Ahura-Mazda to care for Asha in the eternal afterlife, Cyrus asked to see Raiva in private.

'What do you think Asha was trying to say to me?' Cyrus demanded.

'Cyrus,' Raiva said, 'the loss of blood... his mind was addled.'

'No,' said Cyrus, 'Asha told me with perfect clarity about the river defences of the Babylonians. He used what was left of his strength to tell me that. But that was not all. He was also trying to tell me something about you and Roshan.'

Raiva made no reply.

'What could he have been trying to tell me?' Cyrus demanded. 'Did you lie with her?'

Raiva shook his head. 'No, Cyrus, I did not. I swear that by Ahura-Mazda.' Cyrus felt relieved; he knew Raiva well enough to know that Raiva would have been proud to admit the truth had he in fact lain with Roshan.

Cyrus just stared at his dead friend's brother. 'Well? Then what else could he have been trying to tell me?'

'I don't know, Cyrus,' Raiva said.

Cyrus went on looking at him for some moments, before saying:

'Very well. But I warn you, Raiva, time reveals everything. If there is something you wish to tell me, you had better do so now.'

'Cyrus,' said Raiva. 'I have nothing to tell you because there *is* nothing to tell you.'

Cyrus looked hard at Raiva, then turned from him.

Some weeks later, King Nabonidus was in his library, perusing some tablets containing lengthy invocations to Sin, when there was a hasty knock on the door.

Nabonidus loathed being disturbed when lost in intellectual pleasures. In fact, he hated being disturbed at all. He was not really suited to being king; he much preferred perusing centuries-old tablets and scrolls to having to listen to the tedious demands and bickering of his people. In particular, even though Babylon's treasury contained vast sums, many of the houses were old and in a poor state of repair. But Nabonidus could not be bothered to expend funds from the treasury to improve the dwellings. Nabonidus would have preferred a life as a senior member of Babylon's scholastic community, but being king paid better. Besides, his father had been king, so Nabonidus felt he had no choice in the matter.

He called out to whoever was behind the door to go away and leave him in peace, but the frantic man, one of the palace guards, called back, as respectfully as he could, that he had 'truly urgent news.'

Nabonidus gave an impatient grunt, got up and headed to the heavy wooden door that was decorated with carvings of Nabonidus in discussions with Sin, a god who was represented as having wings and thoughtful human features superimposed on a moon-face. Nabonidus called out to the guard to open the door. The guard at once did so.

The guard saw the king and bowed low.

'Well, what is it?' Nabonidus demanded.

'It's... it's our river, your Majesty!'

'Well, what about it?'

'Your Majesty,' the guard replied, standing up again, 'our river... it is drying up!'

Nabonidus, convinced that the guard had drunk too much wine and had somehow found the courage to try to play a trick on him, the great king of Babylonia, slapped the guard across the face.

'You dare... you dare to practise your follies on me?'

'Your Majesty, it is *true*,' the guard pleaded, rubbing his sore face. 'Come... come and see for yourself.'

'I will throw you into a dungeon for your impertinence.'

'Come your Majesty, come and look. Our river is drying up!'

'Nonsense! The Euphrates has flowed since time began and shall flow for eternity.'

'Sire,' the guard begged, 'our river is now so shallow that children are plucking fish from it as if picking ripe vegetables from the fields!'

At this continued nonsense Nabonidus felt he had no choice but to strike his guard once more. The guard pleaded with Nabonidus to look for himself. Something about the conviction of the man, even with his nose bleeding, impressed the king, and he followed him. Nabonidus loudly cursed every drop of blood from the man's nose that fell onto the limestone paving-slabs.

And then the king, who had overtaken the guard during the quick walk, was outside his palace. He hurried down toward the river bank and reached a spot close to where he had given the order that that impertinent and lying fool, sent by the peasant who ruled Persia, should be thrown into the river and shot to death with arrows.

Dozens of Nabonidus's guards and courtiers were lining the bank of the Euphrates. Scores of people thronged the bank on the other side of the river, more than a hundred paces distant.

Once the guards and courtiers saw their king, they moved quickly out of the way and bowed to him, but some did not move rapidly enough and Nabonidus impatiently pushed them from his path.

When Nabonidus saw the river, he gasped.

His first thought, as a devoted worshipper of Sin, was that the moon-god had, after all, disapproved of the killing of the Persian, and that what was happening was Sin's revenge.

The level of the Euphrates was already scarcely deeper than the length of a woman's arm. Dozens of adults and many children had waded into the river and were picking up floundering fish, including large Euphrates perch, a renowned delicay in Babylon.

Nabonidus felt like swooning.

What can be happening?

The water level continued to drop, until there was not even any need for the impromptu fishermen to reach for the floundering fish in the shallow water. Now, the water was gone completely and the unfortunate denizens of the river were flapping their lives away on the dank, green, muddy river-bottom where they could be picked up as if on offer, free of charge, at Babylon's large fish-market. Nabonidus saw two small children struggling together to carry a perch that was almost as big as either of them.

Nabonidus rushed to the large temple he had built to Sin in the grounds of the royal palace. The king was fervently praying to the moon-god to make the river flow again.

Praying as he was, Nabonidus did not see what was happening in the city.

The Euphrates, 'our river', so vital for providing drinking-water, and for washing, bathing and for trade and commerce, was such an accepted, matter-of-fact part of daily life in Babylon that its sudden disappearance threw the city into total panic and chaos.

Hundreds of people earned their living from fishing, or ferrying people across the river from one bank to the other. In a single afternoon, the fishing and ferrying trades vanished. The abundant fish of Babylon could indeed be picked up by anyone; as for the ferrying services, these were no longer needed, as you could simply walk across the damp riverbed. A terrible sense swept the city that the traditional way of life was lost forever, for if the fishing and ferrying businesses were no more, what about those hundreds who earned *their* living from people who worked in those businesses?

But it was not only economic confidence that vanished in one afternoon. The populace of Babylon was a mix of several different religions, almost all of which were periodically oppressed by the king and his soldiers, for Nabonidus essentially regarded anyone who did not worship Sin as an infidel.

The Jews were in particular subject to regular bouts of oppression. They lived under laws that gave them the lowest status in the city. They had been exiled to Babylon earlier that same century by the Babylonian king Nebuchadnezzar, who had conquered the Jewish kingdom of Judah. Many Jews had worked hard and resourcefully, even in the unfavourable conditions they suffered in Babylon, and had won prosperity in exile, yet still yearned to return home. Judah, though, was a Babylonian possession, and as Nabonidus had refused their pleas to be allowed to return to their homeland, they had no choice but to remain in Babylon.

Yet no matter the religion to which a particular Babylonian adhered, when the waters of the Euphrates disappeared with such terrifying speed, all pious Babylonians felt that the magical vanishing of the water could only be a punishment for whatever wickedness they were most recently conscious of practising.

For the rest of the day, Babylon spiralled out of control. All day-to-day working life stopped, and people allowed themselves to sink into a frenzy of fear and guilt. Babylon had always been a crowded city. That everyone's friends, relatives, fellow workers, customers were equally distraught and frenzied only fanned the flames of the madness that engulfed the city. People stopped eating and drinking, besmirched themselves with charcoal, and tore their clothes, and generally behaved as if they had lost their minds.

Many Babylonians, even those who were not especially pious, believed the river's unaccountable disappearance meant that the end of the world must be nigh. With that prospect terrifying them, the social and religious inhibitions that had been so necessary for the smooth running of the busy, wealthy, crowded city went the way of the waters of the Euphrates.

Babylon descended into anarchy.

For the next nine days and nights, normal life in Babylon was suspended. King Nabonidus spent his entire time in the great temple of Sin, begging forgiveness from the moon-god, pleading with the inert and indifferent silver statue of Sin to restore the flow of the river. Meanwhile, all the other temples and places of worship of the city were full of the fearful who were convinced that the world would soon vanish just as the waters of the Euphrates had.

Other, more practically-minded, Babylonians continued sporting with whomever they had found to be their companion for what they assumed would be their last few days on earth.

Then, on the tenth day, even stranger things began to happen. A bizarre and on the face of it completely unbelievable rumour began to spread through the frantic, chaotic, half-starved city. The rumours said that the waters of the Euphrates had been replaced by an army of avenging angels with bells in their hair, who were coming toward Babylon along the dry bed of the mother river.

The chaos and panic had made the Babylonians so dis-organized that the Babylonian army was completely useless – and leaderless, for Nabonidus, who had made himself the leader of it, even though he was far too old to lead it properly, was doing nothing but abjectly praying to Sin. The soldiers were too panicked, and afraid to report for duty, even if any of their captains had summoned them to do so.

The army of avenging angels was in truth the Immortals, who led the march on Babylon along the now-dry riverbed, with Cyrus at their helm.

Downstream, a day's march away, the rest of Cyrus's army waited to hear whether they would be needed for the war against Babylon. This portion of the Persian army had, however, already played its part in the conquest of Babylon. The entire Persian army, some fourteen days ago, had – about five thousand paces north of Babylon – begun digging a short, but broad and deep, artificial drainage channel. This sent the Euphrates flowing into an old canal working that took the massive flow of the river past Babylon, to rejoin the Euphrates proper a few thousand paces south of the city.

Of course, this new, artificial diversion could easily be destroyed by collapsing the walls of the newly-built drainage canal, but for now it enabled Cyrus to breach the walls of Babylon from underneath, so that he and his men could walk into Babylon along the dry bed of the very river into which the treacherous and wicked Nabonidus had had Asha thrown, and then given the vile order that he be shot.

Sin the moon-god had not taken his revenge.

Cyrus had.

The remaining portion of the Persian army was not needed. Cyrus's own diagnosis of Nabonidus's rule had been accurate. Nabonidus had not been particularly popular even before the Persians invaded the city. The sight of the great Persian army under the command of Cyrus aided by a new general, Gobryas, and the appearance of the ten thousand Immortals under the leadership of Tiridaad – an Immortal elevated to leadership of that indomitable sect following the death of Asha – persuaded even those who retained some vestigial loyalty to Nabonidus that resisting Cyrus was futile. Babylon fell without a fight.

Within two days, Cyrus was declared king of Babylon, and Nabonidus had been tried by a Persian court for the murder of Asha. Cyrus was not one of the judges, but he attended the trial, and at the end of it, after Nabonidus had been found guilty, he pronounced sentence.

'You yourself, Nabonidus,' Cyrus told the fallen king, 'would have had no hesitation in ordering the execution of someone charged with the crime of which you have been convicted. In truth, execution is a just punishment for your wickedness. But if I command your death, those of your former subjects who still feel some small feelings of loyalty to you may have those feelings awoken. They may even begin to hate me and my people.'

Cyrus stared at Nabonidus for a few moments, as if expecting a response. But Nabonidus said nothing, only hung his grey head in shame.

'Moreover,' Cyrus went on, 'you have been such a bad king, Nabonidus, that I do not want the loyal Persian I would appoint as your executioner to have your death on his conscience. Therefore, instead of commanding your death, my sentence is that you shall be exiled immediately and irrevocably from the city of Babylon and the nation of Babylonia. You have until tomorrow morning to make preparations, then you must leave. If you are found in Babylonia after two days of your banishment, the soldier who kills you shall have my personal friendship. Now, begone, murderer, and live the rest of your life far from this beautiful city you pollute by your very presence.'

Nabonidus got down on his knees to beg forgiveness, wept profusely, and hailed Cyrus as the greatest leader on earth.

But Cyrus was unmoved. 'Be grateful for the mercy of the Persian people who are permitting you to escape with your life. I have nothing more to say.'

After Nabonidus had been bundled out of the courtroom, Cyrus was approached by an important Babylonian Jew, who like so many prominent Babylonians had been eager to observe the trial of King Nabonidus.

The instant Cyrus saw the Jew, Cyrus's face broke into an expression of the utmost delight.

It was Daniel, the man Cyrus remembered from his childhood in Paritakna, the man who had told him that King Astyages of Media deserved to die.

Daniel did not recognize Cyrus, for Cyrus had only been a boy of ten when they had last met. But Cyrus certainly recognized Daniel, who was silvery-haired now, which gave his presence even more nobility.

When Cyrus told Daniel who he was, the people in the courtroom were treated to the astonishing sight of the great, all-mighty emperor of the Persian Empire embracing an elderly Jew, and calling him friend.

'Truly, God moves in a mysterious way, that He makes a poor village boy the greatest leader of the known world!' Daniel exclaimed, once their clasp of friendship was finally broken.

'Indeed, the ways of Ahura-Mazda are mysterious,' said Cyrus.

'You call him Ahura-Mazda,' said Daniel, 'we call him Yahweh, but I think enigmatic wisdom is common to both our deities.'

Cyrus smiled. 'Very probably you are right. It is good to see you again, Daniel. I have heard you have a request for me.'

'Yes, sire, I do.'

'Then speak.'

'Most esteemed Majesty, we Jews are almost all industrious and hard-working people. We have brought much prosperity to Babylon and Babylonia, but we are captives here. We have long yearned to return home to our land of Judah, which – as you will know – is a Babylonian possession. May I wish you every happiness and success in your reign here, your Majesty, and ask that some day, perhaps in the next few months, you may be able to consider my request that my people and I be permitted to return to Judah?'

Cyrus smiled. He stood up, and looked not only at Daniel but also at the two dozen or so other Jews who had come with him to support him as he pleaded his case.

'Daniel,' said Cyrus, 'I know that your people have been oppressed here and that nonetheless you have all worked hard and rebuilt your fortunes. I say to you now, your people are free to return to Judah from this moment henceforth. I free all your people from your yoke, and I wish you success and happiness in your homeland. Moreover, on your return journey I shall send a large detachment of my soldiers to guard you all and ensure you a safe passage.'

Daniel, who looked unsteady on his feet, was obviously scarcely able to believe his ears.

'Can... can this be true?' he stammered.

'Yes,' Cyrus replied. 'It is true, and it shall be so.'

That evening, Jewish homes all around Babylon – and, in the next few days, throughout all Babylonia, for good news travels fast – said prayers for Cyrus, who has justly been called the deliverer of the Jews from their captivity in Babylon.

Later on the same afternoon, when Cyrus had given Daniel the tidings of the freeing of the Jews, Cyrus went to visit the fabled Hanging Gardens of Babylon.

He discovered that even though they were known as the Hanging Gardens they did not, in fact, hang down luxuriantly from high battlements or lofty terraces, as he had expected. Instead, the Hanging Gardens were a wonderfully varied and complex structure consisting of ingeniously-designed arches and walls. These supported a succession of broad terraces, rising one above another, with flights of stone steps for ascending to them. The magnificent gardens had been planted and nurtured on the terraces. By now Cyrus knew that the gardens had originally been made for a Median princess who had married the king of Babylon.

Cyrus, looking up in awe at the Hanging Gardens from a distance of two or three hundred paces, was astonished to see that the highest terrace or platform of all was several hundred feet from the ground and indeed so high that it had been necessary to build arches upon arches within the supporting structure in order to get the platform to the required height.

A week later, when the waters of the Euphrates had again started to flow following Cyrus's orders that the artificial drainage canal be demolished, Cyrus, Harpagus, and a number of Persian senior military men and engineers spent much of one afternoon walking round the gardens and climbing the steps that led up to them.

Cyrus was astonished to discover that the downward thrust of the arches that supported the highest terrace of all was itself counterbalanced by a prodigious wall of stone more than twenty paces in thickness. This wall surrounded the gardens on all sides. Upon this wall the entire weight of the terraces and the gardens themselves was placed.

Cyrus, seeing this, could not help thinking that the position of the wall in relation to the Hanging Gardens was very similar to his own position as leader of the entire Persian Empire.

Cyrus told Harpagus and the others who were with him that he would like some time to himself. Harpagus asked Cyrus whether he perchance felt bowed down by the responsibilities of now being master of Babylon now as well as of Lydia and of the rest of the empire. He told Cyrus that if he did, he should not worry as he had many friends and generals who would help him to bear this burden. Cyrus smiled and shook his head.

'No, Harpagus,' said Cyrus. 'I do not fear the new responsibility of Babylon added to my other responsibilities.'

Cyrus pointed to the great wall that supported the entire Hanging Gardens. 'Look how that wall supports the entire edifice of the Hanging Gardens. Now, think of me as merely one of the stone slabs of that wall. Because there are other slabs – by which I mean you, and my generals, and my friends and the people of Persia – my responsibilities are not a burden to me, but an honour, for I know that we shall triumph in all we set out to achieve.'

Cyrus paused briefly, then added:

'And after my death, if my deeds earn me the right to dwell in Ahura-Mazda's kingdom, the empire shall, I know, be carried triumphantly into its future by people who believe in it as much as I do.'

Harpagus and the others, all rendered thoughtful by these words of their great leader, wished their king a good evening and left him.

Cyrus walked alone around the Hanging Gardens until dusk fell. He had the entire gardens to himself; Harpagus had closed them to the public in order to ensure that the Persian delegation was undisturbed.

The profusion of plants, greenery and flowers of every conceivable hue and shade was intoxicating. Cyrus hardly felt he was on earth at all, but that he was already wandering in the heavenly kingdom promised by Ahura-Mazda to those who had lived a good and faithful life on earth.

Suddenly, as Cyrus wandered in ecstasy on the terraces of the Hanging Gardens of Babylon, he began to weep.

He felt utterly immersed in almost unimaginable beauty.

Yet he also knew he was weeping because he was thinking of Roshan, and how she had told him that she yearned to see the Hanging Gardens.

Thinking of her, he felt certain that Roshan's ghost, though invisible, would have loved to have been there with him now.

Cyrus consoled himself with the thought that perhaps she was.

42. Man and Wife

Cyrus's deliverance of the Jews soon made him a hero of Jewish history and culture. He was fated to become one of the few people, not of Jewish faith, spoken of with reverence and affection in what would one day be known as the Old Testament, where it is written:

Thus says the Lord to Cyrus His anointed, whom I have taken by the right hand, to subdue the nations before him, and to loose the loins of kings; to open doors before him so that gates will not be shut: I will go before you and make the rough places smooth; I will shatter the doors of bronze, and cut through their iron bars. And I will give you the treasures of darkness, and hidden riches of secret places, that you may know that I, the Lord, which call thee by thy name, am the God.

Another tribute to Cyrus was no less fervent. The people of Babylon themselves were grateful to him for freeing them from the dominion of Nabonidus, whose own god, Sin, was far less popular than the favoured Babylonian god, Marduk. Cyrus also at once released funds from the Babylonian treasury to pay for much-needed repairs to the houses in the city.

This other tribute was a cylinder of brown clay, inscribed by one of the best-known scribes in Babylon in cuneiform after the fall of Babylon to the Persians,

The scribe began with an attack on the character of Nabonidus; listing his crimes, among these the desecration of the temples of the gods and the imposition of forced labour upon many of the populace. Because of these offences, the writer declared, the Babylonian god Marduk withdrew his support from the Babylonian king and called a foreign king, Cyrus of the Persians, to enter Babylon and become its new ruler with the god's divine blessing.

The worship of Marduk, the king of the gods, the scribe continued, *Nabonidus changed into abomination. Daily he used to do evil against Babylon. And so the god Marduk looked through all the countries, searching for a righteous ruler willing to allow Marduk's effigy to be carried at the head of the annual procession. Then Marduk pronounced the name of Cyrus, king of Anshan, and declared him to become the ruler of all the world. For Cyrus is king of the world, great king, legitimate king, king of Babylon, king of Sumer and Akkad, king of the four quarters of the earth, son of Cambyses, great king, king of Anshan, of a family which always exercised kingship.*

The cylinder's scribe, warming to his theme, went on to describe the pious deeds Cyrus performed after his conquest. *For Cyrus restored peace to Babylon and the other cities sacred to Marduk, freed their inhabitants from their yoke and from the dilapidated housing in which many of them lived. Cyrus also repaired the ruined temples in the cities he conquered, restored their cults, and returned their sacred images as well as their former inhabitants which Nabonidus had commanded to be taken to Babylon.*

Once the cylinder had been inscribed and allowed to dry, it was buried with much reverence and ceremony (an event Cyrus himself attended) in the foundations of Esagilda, a recently-built grand temple in Babylon dedicated to Marduk. There the cylinder was laid to rest, for evermore... or until such time as Marduk, in his wisdom, saw fit to loose the foundations of the temple and for new human eyes to see the cylinder that was testimony to the goodness that had come to Babylon after the wicked infidel Nabonidus was deposed and sent by Cyrus into perpetual banishment.

With the conquest and liberation of Babylon, Cyrus finally laid claim to the title by which many already referred to him: *Cyrus the Great.*

He became the leader of the greatest empire the world had ever known.

Not only were Cyrus's days of being an obscure peasant now a distant memory, but so were his days of being solely the king merely of a union of two countries, Media and Persia. He was now Cyrus the Great, a king and emperor who governed an empire containing more than fifty million souls.

Many great leaders of history were later to compromise their youthful idealism when they attained supreme power. Cyrus did not. If anything, now that he had attained his greatness, he believed even more in his creed of tolerance, understanding, goodwill, and respect for everyone who lived in his empire, even the most humble who earned their living through back-breaking work on the land or by herding goats or sheep.

Cyrus always said it was the will of Ahura-Mazda that had made him emperor, and that in Ahura-Mazda's kingdom everyone was equal, for at the moment of death all material possessions and worldly success were instantly erased.

After the conquest of Babylon, Cyrus was as happy as it was possible for him to be, given that he still thought of Roshan every day and, every day, even now, mourned her.

Cyrus also often wondered what Asha had been trying to tell him about Roshan in the moments before he had slipped away into the shades of death. Cyrus, in his daily meditation and prayers to Ahura-Mazda, the creator of the universe, thought endlessly of this.

But he finally found himself forced to confront the likelihood that he would never know the truth, at least not until he saw Asha and Roshan again in Ahura-Mazda's kingdom.

It also occurred to Cyrus that had he been like Astyages, he would have had Raiva tortured to reveal what he knew, if indeed he knew anything.

But I am not like Astyages, Cyrus thought.

That was one of his most treasured articles of faith.

Aside from his continuing grief over Roshan, and his perplexity about what Asha had been trying to say, there was every reason why Cyrus should have been the happiest man on earth. Cassadane had always loved him, and still did, and she had never ceased to be anything other than an ardent lover and devoted wife.

Cyrus and Cassadane's son, Cambyses, now twelve years old, was being educated by the leading scholars of the empire. The boy's training in the art of warfare was no less vigorous than his academic studies. Akinlana, now quite an elderly man, gave Cambyses extensive training in meditation, a discipline from which Cyrus himself still gained so much.

Cyrus and Cassadane spent most of their time at Pasargadae, in Cyrus's new palace. The gardens surrounding it were miraculous in their beauty and in the profusion of flowers and plants they displayed. Some, who had been fortunate enough to see the Hanging Gardens of Babylon, said that the gardens of Pasargadae rivalled even them. The Lydian gardener whom Cyrus had appointed to carry on the work that Roshan started had based much of his work on Roshan's own ingenious designs, which she left behind her in Pasargadae. He had even successfully pursued Roshan's idea of creating channels from a nearby river to ensure a continual source of irrigation.

Cyrus indeed made his principal home at Pasargadae, but he and Cassadane (Cambyses tended to stay with his tutors and instructors) spent their year in different parts of the empire. The emperor and his queen usually passed the summer at Ecbatana and then moved to Pasargadae for the rest of the year, though Cyrus was often in the Lydian capital of Sardis and in Babylon too.

Yet Cyrus never lived in ostentation in his various homes but instead, with the exception of Pasargadae, preferred to dwell in homely comfort in an outlying wing of his palaces. Cyrus, having met kings such as Astyages, Croesus, and Nabonidus, could never feel comfortable living in the formerly sumptuous parts of their palaces designed for their indulgence.

Cyrus loved Cassadane very much, yet he knew, deep down, that while he did love her, he was always holding back some part of himself from his wife.

Some time after they were married, Cassadane asked him about Lady Roshan, and why he thought she had killed herself. Cyrus, for whom the reason why Roshan had done so was the greatest mystery of his life, shook his head slowly and, unable to conceal his sadness, said 'I do not know.'

'Were you once lovers, Cyrus?' Cassadane murmured. She had never asked him that before.

He had waited some time before he gave his answer, then finally murmured:

'Yes, we were.'

Cassadane was silent for some time before saying:

'Did she kill herself because you chose to marry me?'

Cyrus had been enormously relieved that she had asked him a question to which he could answer, with absolute sincerity and great emphasis:

'No.'

'How do you know that?' Cassadane asked.

'All I can say is that I am certain of it,' said Cyrus. He knew he could hardly tell Cassadane that what had triggered Roshan's strange wish to make an end of herself was a tablet he had sent to Roshan asking her to marry him. But he knew that he had answered his wife's question with complete honesty, for it was only some months after his solitary visit to the red lake, now a holy lake, and named after Roshan, that he had finally decided to marry Cassadane.

Cassadane had hardly ever mentioned Roshan's name to him again.

And so it came as a complete surprise to Cyrus one night in their bedroom at Pasargadae, when they had been married for a full twelve years and after they had made love in their gentle, mutually considerate way, that Cassadane, instead of going to sleep in his arms as she so liked to do, used a night-candle to light the oil lamp on the table by her side of the bed.

She sat up in bed, her beautiful breasts glowing with sweat. She turned her lovely face to him, smoothing her black hair from her eyes as she did so.

'You still think about her, don't you?' she said.

For a moment, exhausted and content from their love-making and looking forward to sleep, Cyrus was silent. Then he said:

'Lady Roshan, you mean?'

'Yes. I'm not suggesting you still love her, Cyrus. But I do believe you still think of her.'

Cyrus drew a breath and looked at his beautiful wife.

He had told the truth all his life, and he did so now.

'Yes,' he said. 'I do still think of her.'

'And... *do* you still love her?' Cassadane asked.

Cyrus looked into her beautiful eyes. 'You are my wife.'

'Yes,' replied Cassadane. 'I am your wife and the mother of your first-born son Cambyses, and of your second son and of your daughter. So tell me, what is the answer to my question?'

After a pause Cyrus said, 'I do think of Lady Roshan, yes. I sometimes miss her, even though I have not seen her for twelve years, and I know I can never see her again, outside Ahura-Mazda's kingdom. I love you, Cassadane, but if what I have just told you about Lady Roshan means that I still have some loving feelings toward... Lady Roshan's ghost, then perhaps I do.'

Cassadane, her eyes bright with affection and passion, did not reply at once. She reached out her right hand with its long, smooth fingers, and stroked his forehead gently.

'I suppose I don't know much about love,' Cassadane said, at last. 'You were my first man and if ever anything were to separate us I would never seek another. I love you with every fibre of my soul. You are a great man. You are our king. At a time when the world is full of tyranny and cruelty you have created an empire radiant with the light of goodness. Within our borders there is no slavery, there is tolerance, industriousness, sincerity and security. I have a wonderful husband. Yet... how can I say that I understand him completely?'

Cassadane did not say anything else for a few moments, then gave a gentle shrug. 'But perhaps no wife should ever expect to understand her husband completely, especially when she is married to one of the greatest men on earth.'

Cassadane fell silent again.

Cyrus did not know what to say.

'I know that some part of you still loves Roshan,' Cassadane murmured, 'and that this will always be so. I also know that she is dead. I'm not jealous, for who can be jealous of a memory? And after all, you have been wonderful to me. And you are indeed the greatest of men. You have rid the world of much of its wickedness, and you have even tamed deserts and turned them into gardens.'

Cyrus thought *Roshan began that work, not me.* But he said nothing.

Cassadane started stroking Cyrus's forehead again with her right hand. Cyrus gently took hold of Cassadane's free left hand, feeling her slender, warm, soft long fingers.

'You are my wife,' he said to her.

'Yes.'

They made love again, more tenderly than ever.

43. A New Life

'O Dionysus, god of fruitfulness, fertility and love, have mercy on my plight! Guide me in my fearful dilemma, when I love two women and do not know which one to choose as my wife! What a wretch am I! For if I give my troth to Helen I must entirely forsake Aphrodite. Yet to spend my days in delights with Aphrodite means eternally renouncing the radiant Helen! Was ever mortal man beset by such a quandary?'

The speaker, whose name was Thespis, was a Greek man in his sixties. Handsome, with a closely-shaved white beard and skin the colour and texture of beaten leather, he had a look of prosperity about him. Yet his eyes, blue and luminescent, did not have the cunning and avarice that had in recent years always been in Raiva's eyes. Instead, the eyes of Thespis expressed something completely different: the ardour and humility of one who yearns to achieve great heights in art, but is only too aware of his limitations.

Thespis had delivered his speech on the stage of an open-air theatre that his wealth had enabled him to have built to his command and design. The stage was constructed from carved blocks of white marble, shipped at considerable expense to the estate Thespis owned on the island of Aegina, half a morning's journey by trireme from the city of Athens.

The theatre was Thespis's private property. Its backdrop was the same Aegean Sea, loaded with romance and history, that King Agamemnon and his fleet had sailed more than seven centuries earlier, on their way to lay siege to Troy, one of whose princes had stolen a Grecian queen of peerless beauty.

The Aegean, with its abundant fish, squid and shellfish, burgeoning maritime trade and glorious vistas, had in every sense nourished the birth of a Grecian civilization that was already beginning to surpass its Egyptian counterpart on the southern side of the sea. The Greeks themselves called the Aegean 'our sea', just as the now content and once again industrious Babylonians, blessed by the rule of Cyrus, were as proud as ever to call the Euphrates, whose flow had once been briefly disrupted, 'our river.'

There were more than a hundred carved seats in the theatre auditorium. Thespis, a man as popular as he was wealthy, had a great number of friends. Many of them, even those who lived long distances away, travelled to attend the performances he gave at the theatre. After the performance Thespis would offer them accommodation in his large and beautiful home. He was rehearsing today for a performance that would be held in a few days' time.

With one exception, Thespis did not allow his friends to attend his rehearsals.

That exception was sitting in the midst of the otherwise empty rows of limestone seats.

Until a few years ago, Thespis had been a successful importer of silk, the mysterious, much desired and consequently extremely valuable fabric obtained from the remote, enigmatic land of China. Silk, light and close to translucent if given a loose weave, was much favoured by wealthy Greek merchants as the perfect fabric for the night attire of their wives and lovers.

Thespis, who owned several large dyeing and weaving houses in the city of Athens, had made his fortune from that favour. He also bought and traded raw silk thread from Lydian, Indian and Persian merchants.

The days when Thespis needed to work for his living were long gone. He was now the richest man in Aegina, and still highly regarded on the mainland as a man of business and much influence.

Yet ironically, despite having spent thirty years building up his wealth from silk, Thespis had never actually learned exactly what silk *was*.

The foreign merchants with whom he traded (he privately doubted they knew any more of the truth than he did) had assured him that in the distant land of China, silk was simply plucked from the leaves of a certain kind of tree and spun into thread. Thespis had frequently wondered, and sometimes still did, whether such a beautiful and hugely valuable substance could possibly be obtained in this way. He supposed that the Chinese themselves, doubtless canny people who wished to preserve the secret of their precious export, were not in the least inclined to reveal the truth about it. Moreover, Thespis had never been to China nor had ever met a Chinese silk-merchant.

Still, Thespis had not cared too much about the truth of silk even during his working days. His ignorance had not prevented him from building a very considerable fortune from that mysterious and beautiful substance. Now, in his retirement, the truth of the origins of silk seemed even less important to him, and certainly vastly less important than the immortal truths of the human heart.

Ever since his retirement he had applied himself to those truths. Thespis was now able to devote himself to his lifelong passion for the theatre. He even had the time to write his own verse, which consisted of poetry and soliloquies, in the rhetorical and impassioned style that was the current fashion. He also took great care to study the skills of acting. Thespis was eager to become an accomplished actor himself. Yet he always worried that he had started to devote himself to this fascinating art too late in his life, and that his aspirations would never be matched by his accomplishments.

The one member of his audience watched his rehearsal with careful concentration from her marble seat a few rows from the stage, Thespis continued his affected lament on stage about the dilemma of being in love with two women simultaneously.

His acting was, in truth, amateurish, but like many amateur actors before and since, what Thespis lacked in technique he gained in gusto and enthusiasm. The verses he wrote were, at least, a little more memorable than his acting, for he had some natural talent as a writer and his regular exercising of that talent was improving it.

Once he had finished his soliloquy he bowed to his audience. She applauded his words and the energy of his performance. Having done so, she rose from her seat that was softened by a silk cushion, stuffed with horsehair, that he had insisted she used – she did not need it, but she was always deferential to Thespis. She walked down a few steps, then clambered up onto the stage to join her friend.

He looked at her, his eyes keenly seeking out her response.

'*What did you think?*' he asked her, with an amateur's eagerness for praise.

She shrugged. 'I loved the words, Thespis, certainly. The acting was... well, a little excessively mannered, perhaps?'

He frowned. 'I know, *I know*. It is unfortunately in my nature to over-act. I wish I could cure myself of the habit.' Thespis paused for a moment. 'Or perhaps it is only because no man in his right mind would ever dream of being so foolish as to love someone else, having once set eyes on *you*, that you find the monologue impossible to credit?'

His friend smiled faintly. 'Oh, Thespis, a man of culture and taste such as you really should flatter a little less blatantly.'

'I assure you I do not flatter you, my dear. After all, we know each other well enough to be honest with each other.'

'Yes,' she said, 'we do.'

That was true. No-one else in the world knew the story of her life as thoroughly as Thespis did, not even her twelve-year-old son, Smerdis.

She was glad she had told Thespis the story, for it meant that, at night when she lay alone in her comfortable bed in his house (they were close friends, but not husband and wife, nor had they ever been lovers), she could better believe that a story such as hers, which seemed to her in many respects so dream-like, could have been possible.

44. Slavery

Born in a small, impoverished town in Media, she had when young eked out a living as a bandit-woman of the countryside, in league with three male friends she had known since childhood, one of whom she had always secretly loved, but that life had come to an end when the bandits were scattered by the king's army and their leader captured. Then, an extra-ordinary sequence of events led to Ahura-Mazda blessing the man she loved with the utmost favour. For he had been elevated to being a prince of Persia, and then the emperor of the Persian Empire.

Suddenly she was no longer an outcast, but instead an ennobled lady in the Persian capital of Anshan, waiting patiently for the moment when this man would ask for her hand in marriage. For she knew perfectly well that in secret, he loved her, just as she loved him.

Then, finally, when he had become the king not only of Persia but also of Media, and had blessed her with his love, the king had merely asked her to create beautiful gardens around his new palace at Pasargadae. At first she had been furious with him, thinking he had no feelings for her, but to her delight they had at last become lovers and she had begun the job of creating his garden with the same passion and love she gave to him.

And she had, indeed, been working happily in the gardens of the man she loved, confident that soon he would honour a pledge he had made, by the lake, to marry her, when one afternoon her life was rocked by an earthquake whose reverberations, were even now – she knew – still shaking her.

That afternoon, when she returned from a solitary expedition into the open countryside to gather cuttings for the gardens she was creating, she found another of her three friends from her childhood town, a man called Asha, waiting for her. He said he had been in Pasargadae for two days, waiting for her to arrive back from her expedition. Asha's brother Raiva had once asked to marry her himself, but she had told him she did not love him and would never marry him.

Asha gave her a sealed tablet from Cyrus. Asha told her he had no idea of the contents of the tablet.

She went to open the sealed tablet in her own room in Pasargadae, in complete privacy.

The tablet was indeed written by the king, the man she loved, the man she thought wanted her to become his wife.

But it was not a tablet to her. Instead, it was a tablet, a marriage proposal from the king to a young woman called Cassadane, whom she knew by sight (though she had never met Cassadane) as a virginal young woman of great beauty, whose father Farnaspes was one of the richest men in Persia.

After seeing the tablet, Roshan was so shocked she vomited.

Once she had emptied her stomach, and cleaned herself up, she went to see Asha and again asked him whether he had seen the contents of the tablet. He fervently denied he had, and she knew Asha well enough to be certain he was telling the truth. Asha, she knew, did not like lying and indeed she had never known him to lie.

She was, in any case, by now certain what must have happened.

Cyrus had, she supposed, written to her on some matter connected with her work at Pasargadae, and also written to Cassadane, proposing marriage.

Obviously, Cyrus had given the wrong tablet to Asha.

She told Asha she would at once set off with him for Anshan, to see Cyrus, and indeed she had, with guards accompanying them until they reached the town of Zarqan, whence they rode on by themselves. But when they were only a few miles from Anshan, riding thither in the slowly brightening dawn, she ordered Asha to stop. She told him that she had a tablet for the emperor, but that she wanted Asha to wait for the sun to move a hand's-length across the sky before delivering it. He promised her he would do this. Then she galloped off.

When she was far from Asha she was astonished to see a horse and rider chasing after her. For some minutes she thought, desperately hoped, it might be Cyrus, but it was not.

It was Raiva, who said he had just met his brother Asha, who had told him the direction in which she had gone. Raiva told her he came to her out of friendship, and with tidings that Cyrus was going to marry Cassadane.

She said she knew this already.

Raiva then told her that the previous evening the king had entertained Farnaspes and Cassadane in his private dining-room, and kissed Cassadane. Raiva said he could prove this with the testimony of a royal servant who had seen them.

But she had shaken her head and said she did not wish to hear; she already knew the worst. She confided in Raiva that to avenge herself on Cyrus she planned to make him believe she had taken her own life, and that Asha would shortly deliver a tablet that would tell Cyrus precisely that.

'Cyrus shall, no doubt, believe that I have done exactly what I say I intend to do in the tablet,' she said, 'for I shall arrange evidence that shall leave the wicked betrayer in no doubt. As for you, Raiva, you can tell Cyrus the truth of my deception if you wish. But if you do that you will be a fool, for I know you do not love Cyrus, and if I am allowed to pursue my scheme he will suffer for his disloyalty to the end of his days, for he shall believe I killed myself because of him.'

Raiva assured her he would not interfere. But he asked her what she planned to do, if she did not intend to take her own life.

She admitted she did not know. So Raiva kindly said he would arrange a new life for her in Greece.

She was shocked at how kind Raiva was being.

'Greece is a wonderful country,' Raiva told her. 'I have travelled there on business twice. The weather is usually hot but the breeze from the sea gives the maritime regions a splendid climate. The food and wine of Greece are delicious, the landscapes beautiful. You will be happy, and far from the intrigues and disappointments of Persia.'

'But what shall I live on there?' she asked.

Raiva shrugged. 'Your magnificent bracelet, obviously.'

But she told Raiva that she would not, after all, take the bracelet with her and sell it; that she did not want to think, after leaving Persia, that she was living on the generosity of the man who had betrayed her so abominably. So she left the bracelet by the lake, with her clothes, for Cyrus to find. Raiva had already told her that, for old times' sake, he would give her some silver with which she could start her new life.

So, that very day, after she had visited the shores of the red lake and left evidence there for Cyrus of her self-destruction, she set off westward in secret in Raiva's caravan with him. She had expected Raiva to make fresh advances to her, but he did not. He seemed to her much more engrossed in carrying forwards the scheme on which they had embarked. Raiva took her as far as the Lydian town of Cassar, where he introduced her to a friend of his, a Greek merchant called Odysseus. Raiva gave her the silver he had promised her, and left her in the safekeeping of Odysseus.

She had thanked Raiva, and embraced and kissed him.

'Goodbye,' Raiva said to her. 'I hope we may meet again.'

'We shall, if Ahura-Mazda wills it,' Roshan said.

Yes, she remembered all that. But there was much else she remembered.

'You are sorry to be leaving Persia?' Odysseus had asked her, as the carriage in which he and she were travelling, along with four of his male servants who took it in turns to ride at the front steering the horses, began to gather speed.

Roshan had shaken her head. 'There is nothing for me here.'

Odysseus nodded. 'I know from Raiva what has happened. I have pledged to him to help you to a new life in Greece, and I shall honour my pledge.'

The journey west was calm and uneventful at first. Odysseus did not even make the overtures to her she had assumed he would make. They travelled for more than ten days, stopping at night to sleep in tents Odysseus had brought along, and buying food from villages they passed.

The nightmare began on the night of the eleventh day, when the carriage was nearing the sea that separated the continent of Asia from that of Europe.

The first Roshan knew of the nightmare was when her tent was surrounded by unfamiliar voices: Lydians, judging from the sound of their language. Roshan reached for her sword even as her tent collapsed around her. She fought and fought, but the Lydians were armed and there were too many of them. She killed one of the marauders by stabbing him through the neck, but then the others were on her, and they managed to disarm her, then they bound her and took her away into a carriage of their own, in which were already about a dozen other bound slaves, both men and women. Roshan had had a sudden flashing memory of being a girl in Paritakna and seeing the chained slaves arriving in the town square.

She wondered what would become of her. She thought it likely she would be dragged out of the carriage at any moment and executed for killing one of the slave-traders.

But that did not happen. Instead, after hearing various shouts from outside (she thought they might have been made by Odysseus and his servants; perhaps they were killed, for she never saw any sign of them again), the carriage began to move, and she was taken, along with the other slaves, to a new life.

During the next few days, the Lydian slave-traders stole her silver, and made numerous attempts to ravish her, there in the carriage in full view of the other slaves, but she resisted so fiercely they knew that they would have to kill her in order to achieve their aim, and none of them appeared to want to kill such a valuable new property.

Roshan could never shake off the suspicion that Raiva was somehow behind her enslavement, and that Odysseus had connived with her capture and had perhaps even received a share of the silver Raiva might have received in payment for her.

Roshan thought she would be taken to the Lydian capital, Sardis, but the Lydian slave-caravan (which turned out to consist of more than a dozen slave-laden carriages) turned out not to be making for Lydia at all, but Greece. Roshan knew this for certain when, on one of the occasions she and the other bound slaves were let out of the carriage, under heavy guard, for exercise, fresh air, and bodily necessities (which had to be performed, humiliatingly, in full view of the guards). Roshan caught a glimpse of a great blue sun-drenched sea to the west, and knew this must be the fabled Aegean sea of the Greeks.

Taken to Greece under very different conditions to the ones she had been expecting, she was sold to a wealthy Greek merchant on the mainland. He set her to work washing the pots and dishes in his kitchens. Roshan's Greek was initially non-existent, but she soon learned enough of the language from the other workers in the kitchens to get by. Escape was impossible; she was always well guarded.

Inevitably, a few weeks after her arrival there, the night came when the merchant (whose wife had seemed to Roshan even more unpleasant then he was) stole into her tiny bedroom, intending to have his way with her. Preferring death to ravishment, Roshan punched the merchant unconscious. The guards soon arrived. They were about to kill her when the merchant's wife appeared on the scene. She shouted out at the guards to stop.

She looked hard at Roshan, whose fists were still clenched as the guards, their swords drawn, surrounded her. Then the merchant's wife began to speak to her.

Roshan knew enough Greek by now to understand what the merchant's wife was saying to her. The wife, after having never spoken a friendly word to Roshan, now seemed grateful that their most beautiful slave had not succumbed to her husband's advances. She told Roshan she would not be executed, but sent to toil on the family's olive-plantations instead.

Again, escape was impossible, for the plantations were also well guarded, but the work was comparatively humane, and soon the merchant's wife even began to appreciate the recommendations Roshan made for how new trees might be planted in more efficient rows than had been so before, and how the scant water that fell on the plantation after rain might be used more effectively. Roshan could not help thinking that she had made an accidentally wise choice in going to live among the Greeks, for ultimately they seemed a kinder people than any she had ever known. She attributed this to the excellent climate of the country.

Some months after she began to work on the olive-groves, she was delivered of a boy, whom she called Smerdis.

She knew he was Cyrus's son, and though she did not for one moment ever imagine Cyrus would ever see him, she could not help being proud that she would always have part of Cyrus with her as long as she had her son.

But she could never forgive Cyrus for how he had betrayed her. She heard that he had taken Lydia, for the Greeks were only too aware of how this Persian conquest brought the formerly remote Persian Empire to their own frontiers. But there was no news confirming that Cyrus had indeed married Cassadane.

After two years of service as a slave in the olive-groves, by which time the merchant had died, the merchant's wife (who had by now even become something of a friend to her, and who was widely rumoured by the servants to have poisoned her husband) approached her. Roshan spoke Greek fluently by now. The Greeks called her 'Roshana'.

'Tell me, Roshana, my dear,' the merchant's wife said. 'Would you like to work in one of our silk workshops? I have noticed you have nimble fingers, and perhaps you will take to silk-weaving.'

Roshan agreed. She was still a slave, with no property of her own, no rights, and no wages beyond the board and lodging she and Smerdis received, but the merchant's wife arranged medical help for Smerdis when he needed it, which endeared her to Roshan even more.

Roshan worked in the silk-weaving workshop for more than three years. During those years, having craved news about Cyrus for so long, she finally learned about Cyrus and Cassadane from Greek silk traders. The Persian king Cyrus the Great, the traders said, had married Cassadane, the youngest daughter of the Persian merchant Farnaspes, soon after Cyrus returned, victorious, from Lydia.

This terrible confirmation of all Roshan had feared, this dreadful realization that Cyrus had, in fact, married Cassadane within barely a few months of believing that she, Roshan, had killed herself for love, cast from her mind any remaining thoughts of tenderness toward the father of her son.

Instead, she began to form the plan that before she went to her grave she would have revenge on him.

Then one day, Roshan chanced to meet Thespis, who was one of the most important customers of the silk workshop where she worked.

Thespis was delighted to become acquainted with an intelligent woman who spoke Persian and who could help him in his dealings with Persian merchants whom he suspected (not incorrectly, as it turned out) of trying to cheat him. He paid the merchant's wife well for Roshan. To Roshan's amazement, Thespis seemed embarrassed about the whole idea of slavery, and insisted on giving her a wage from the moment she began working for him. Thespis was always good to her and Smerdis. Nor did Thespis have any intimate designs on her; he made it clear that he merely wished to be her friend.

Some months after she had started working for Thespis, he freed her.

And so even after she was free, Roshan continued to work for Thespis, who regularly increased her wages. When he retired from the silk trade, Roshan became his housekeeper, occasional cook, gardener, companion – and favourite audience member.

But she never lost her determination to revenge herself upon Cyrus, if ever such an opportunity were to arise.

When Roshan watched Thespis rehearsing, that beautiful day by the Aegean beneath the cloudless sky, almost twelve years had passed since she had left Persia.

Once the rehearsal was finished, the performer and his audience went to lunch.

They strolled from the theatre to the terrace where lunch would be served. They were an attractive pair: Thespis with his well-trimmed white beard contrasting with the leathery colour of his skin, and Roshan, almost as tall as he was, more beautiful now than ever.

Her hair was still tawny, her movements still strong yet also lithe. Roshan was forty years old now, but her youthful beauty, far from fading, had transformed into something more mature and even lovelier. Her facial features were sharply decisive, and there was as always something wild and free about her looks and manner.

The lunch Thespis and Roshan enjoyed that day began with olives marinated in herbs and spices, followed by a wonderful warm spicy stew made from goat's meat, herbs, pepper and chillies. Roshan had created this recipe from her knowledge of Persian cuisine and had shown Thespis's other cooks how to make it.

They ate on the terrace, looking out at the splendid sight of the sea that Homer, the blind poet, had described a few centuries ago as 'wine-dark'. That day, the sea seemed a deeper blue even than the splendid arch of the sky.

After their luncheon, Thespis and Roshan returned to the theatre. Thespis continued rehearsing his performance for the following evening. He listened to Roshan's advice and tried to act in a more realistic way. Then, suddenly, as Thespis began to launch into the monologue again, Roshan smiled, walked quickly onto the stage and listened to him as if she were one of the women of whom he was saying, in the character he was playing, that he loved.

For a moment Thespis was too shocked to speak. Another person on the stage, and, what was worse, a woman! He was stunned, but because the woman was Roshan, he seemed amused too.

'Roshana, my dear, what are you doing up here on the stage?'

'Stay in character, Thespis!' Roshan called out. 'Improvise. Talk to me as if I were Helen, or Aphrodite.'

'Roshana, such a conversation does not belong to Greek theatre!'

'Why not?' Roshan retorted. 'Do not such conversations happen in real life?'

Thespis, suddenly divining Roshan's meaning, gasped with the excitement of her extremely anarchic suggestion, then cleared his throat and fervently exclaimed:

'Helen... Helen, why do you... why do you torment me by telling me you love me? You know... you know I love Aphrodite.'

'You love me, too,' said Roshan, as if she were Helen.

'Yes... but how can I marry more than one woman?'

'You should... you should have married *me*,' Roshan as Helen exclaimed.

Thespis seemed to have run out of creative steam. He just stood there on the stage, evidently unable to think of what to say next.

'But... but you did not marry me,' Roshan went on, 'for you found someone younger and more beautiful. You had told me you loved me and wanted to marry me. But... at the very moment when, as your wife, I could have been happy all my life, you betrayed me. You forsook me for someone else, and in doing so confirmed everything I had always thought, that you never, *could* never, would never, regard me as your equal.'

Roshan drew a breath. 'Very well, we shall see whether a woman can be the equal of a man. Trust me.'

She fell silent.

Thespis just stared at Roshan in astonishment.

A moment later he realized that the stage of a Greek theatre could be used for characters to talk to one another just as they did in real life, and not only in mere soliloquies.

Though of course there could be no question of a woman taking part in any *acting*.

Thespis was a man of vision, but even he had his limitations.

45. Council of war

'The Massagetae must be taught a lesson,' Harpagus said.

It was a bright autumn morning, two years later, in the throne room at Pasargadae.

The throne room there was a little less spartan than the throne room at Anshan, but not greatly so. It had mosaics underfoot illustrating scenes from Cyrus's conquests, and large maps painted on the walls showing the growing Persian Empire. But there were no images of Cyrus fighting dragons or any similar images that Cyrus had seen in the throne rooms of kings whose nations he had conquered. He had no time for self-gratification.

He was in the room with Cassadane and Harpagus. Cassadane had for some time now played more and more of a role as Cyrus's advisor and confidante as well as his wife; yet she always deferred to Harpagus, the commander of the army, whose successful career in Cyrus's Persia continued to be permanent proof of Cyrus's willingness to pursue forgiveness and reconciliation.

Cyrus did not make Cassadane any special allowances: if he thought she was wrong he told her so, and he expected Harpagus to do the same.

'Harpagus, who exactly are the Massagetae and what have they done?' Cassadane asked.

Harpagus glanced at Cyrus, who gave a nod.

'They are hill-dwellers,' Harpagus said. 'They are the largest of the hill-tribes who gave us much trouble some years ago. They have always been belligerent, but until recently they've had the sense to respect our eastern border and not attack our border guards.'

'The Massagetae have plenty of land to the east, beyond our borders,' Cyrus said to his wife.

'Yes,' Harpagus agreed. 'Indeed, their own land stretches far into the mountains. We are not even sure where the eastern bounds of their land are.'

'What kind of terrain is it?' Cassadane asked. She knew all about geographical and military matters nowadays.

'My lady, being mostly high up,' Harpagus said, 'it is not especially fertile, which no doubt explains why they see no reason to respect our borders. Indeed, the Massagetae have always regarded our borders as an impertinence.'

'Is it possible,' said Cassadane, 'that the Massagetae have come to think that because we own such prizes as Lydia and Babylon we have become indifferent to our eastern boundaries and do not mind if our borders there are disrespected?'

'My lady, I believe that is a true assessment of how they think,' Harpagus said to Cassadane. 'I would also observe that there is little point having good relations with the Greeks in the west if we are seen as weak by wild peoples who are scarcely civilized. No empire perceived as weak can survive long, even if the people who perceive it as weak are fools.'

He looked hard at Cyrus. 'The Massagetae fight merely for the pleasure and thrill of battle. They love hand-to-hand combat above all, and those who seek to lead them must excel in it. Cyrus, the Massagetae are merely savages who must be confined to their hillside hell so they can get on with the life they live there.'

'That does not seem very charitable of you, Harpagus,' Cassadane said.

'My lady,' Harpagus replied, 'you are right. But equally there is nothing charitable about the Massagetae. As I say, I believe we must teach them a lesson.'

'Yes,' said Cyrus. 'We must and we shall.' He looked hard at a map on the table that showed what was known of the extent of the territory of the Massagetae. He glanced at Harpagus. 'What precise intelligence do we have about the Massagetae leadership?

'As always with the Massagetae,' said Harpagus, 'our information is only shadowy and vague. But I have heard reports from our men stationed in the east of our empire that the queen of the Massagetae, the one who was so unreasonable in past years, has grown old and handed power to her daughter. They say the old queen is a witch who uses sorcery, and that the new queen employs it to an even greater extent. Whether or not that is so, what is certain is that among the Massagetae the queens are often leaders. Some soldiers say they have heard that the daughter is devoted to making Persia squirm... I say we should make *her* squirm.'

He glanced at Cyrus. 'These people are animals,' Harpagus added. 'They even like to look like animals, for they wear masks made from the faces of creatures they have killed. Indeed, they love only slaughter, and I could not guarantee your safety if you were anywhere in the proximity of the Massagetae. They would love nothing more than to kill you.'

'No doubt that is true,' said Cyrus, 'but I shall personally command the force we send to the Massagetae. I shall take whatever steps necessary to prevent them being any further threat to the people of that region.'

While the army was preparing for the march eastward, Cyrus stayed himself at the palace in Anshan, further east than Pasargadae and also closer to the army's headquarters. One morning, only a few days before the date set for the army's departure, Cyrus had an unexpected visitor.

Raiva.

Cyrus and Raiva had met very few times since Asha's death, and then only when others were present. Raiva, now, was sleeker than ever, and plumper. It was rumoured that his wealth nowadays exceeded even that of Cyrus's father-in-law Farnaspes.

'Raiva,' Cyrus said, not shaking his hand, 'when my servant announced you I thought of asking him to tell you that I was too busy to see you, but that would have been discourteous. However, I *am* busy, and have little time to spare for you.'

'Cyrus, you do not need to hate me. We are, after all, old friends.'

'Raiva, I do not seek to hate anyone in the world, and especially none of the subjects of our empire. If I did choose to hate someone it would be Harpagus, but as you know I have found it in myself to forgive even him, and today he and I work better together than ever. Nor do I hate you, Raiva.'

'Then why do you never come to see me?'

'Because,' said Cyrus, 'I am afraid to say I no longer feel warmth towards you. I saw your face at the instant when *you* saw Asha's dead body. I saw a coldness in your expression that I cannot forget... or forgive.'

'Cyrus, I have given a considerable amount of money to Farna-dukta.'

'I know you have, and I should hope you did. But silver is merely silver, Raiva, it is not the god you have come to think it is. Besides, Asha was trying to tell me something about Roshan... and about you... just before he died. I do not know what he was trying to say to me, and when I asked you, you denied having any idea of that, just as you did when I asked you about it subsequently.'

'Cyrus... as I have told you, I have no idea what my brother might have been trying to say. I can only think, now, that as he felt life slipping from him, he thought of the old days, when he, you, Roshan and I were all friends together.'

'You have had an abundance of time to think of that explanation, Raiva. However, this is, as I say, a busy time for me. Why have you come to see me?'

'Cyrus, I have heard you are planning an expedition to the land of the Massagetae. I wish to accompany your army.'

Cyrus, astonished, just stared at him. 'Are you serious?'

'Yes, I am.'

'*Why* do you want to come?'

'Cyrus, when we were younger we would ride together. Let us ride together again.'

'You are older now, Raiva. You are plumper, too. And, though I scarcely need to tell you this, you are much richer. You do not need to risk your life in dangerous military ventures.'

'Yes, Cyrus, I have grown rich in Persia. I have a good life. I think often of how hard you, my king, have worked to create this great empire. I know there will be dangers on the journey, for the Indian merchants I know who must pass through Massagetae territory to bring their goods to Persia greatly fear the Massagetae, even though the merchants pay them generous tribute for allowing them to pass. I want to come with you, Cyrus... I want to show you I am still brave, still a loyal son of Media and that I can face danger.'

Cyrus looked hard at him. 'Can you still fight?'

'I'm sure I can.'

'Well, you may need to, so I suggest you go on an immediate diet and undertake intense weapons practice.'

'I am already doing both those things.'

'I see.' Cyrus looked levelly at Raiva.

'I am serious in my request, Cyrus,' Raiva said.

Cyrus himself now lapsed into silence for some time. At last he said:

'Very well, Raiva, you may come. But I cannot assign any of our warriors to your protection. You must fend for yourself. If you cannot do that, then you must stay at home with your gold, silver, and your other possessions and comforts.'

'I will look after myself,' said Raiva.

'Oh, I do not doubt it,' Cyrus said. 'After, all, you always have.'

46. The March to the East

The hills, then mountains, that heralded the onset of Massagetae territory grew higher and more rugged as the Persian army penetrated more and more deeply into them.

Cyrus, with Harpagus by his side, led his army of the ten thousand Immortals, assisted by five thousand infantry, into this alien world.

Cyrus was wearing the dark blue cloak.

Its hood was down, though it could readily be raised to protect the head in the event of a sand-storm.

Throughout the journey, Raiva had seemed to Cyrus, at least on the occasions when Cyrus spoke to him, to be deeply immersed in thought: *thoughts about silver*, Cyrus assumed.

Cyrus had not permitted Raiva to ride at the front, but Raiva was riding somewhere in the middle of the army; Cyrus did not exactly know where. Privately, Cyrus was impressed at how well Raiva had been keeping up.

So far, there had been no sight of the Massagetae. Cyrus did not find this surprising, though. *They'll know we're heading to their territory. They'll want to draw us deep into the heart of the Massagetae nation before sending emissaries to parley, or – more likely – launch an attack.*

As the day began to wane, the Persians searched for somewhere to make camp. They had not yet quite left the part of the Massagetae territory that had been mapped by the Persian Empire; it was known that a short way ahead there lay a valley, overlooked by three hills, and apparently accessible only by a few narrow mountain passes. Beyond the valley, the maps the Persians had of the hills were blank.

'We shall set up camp when we reach the valley beyond,' Cyrus said to Harpagus.

'Yes,' Harpagus said. 'I think the soldiers will prefer to make camp on our map rather than off it.'

Once the Persians had entered the valley and ensured that the mountain passes were heavily guarded by teams of Immortals who would sleep in shifts, the thousands of soldiers set their tents on the floor of the valley and began to cook their food.

Cyrus, looking at his army at rest, smiled to himself as he reflected that the scene, to an outsider, would have seemed peaceful, but Cyrus knew that his men were experts at converting themselves from peaceful visitors to avenging warriors in less time than it takes to draw a sword.

If the Massagetae are foolish enough to attempt to attack us through the mountain passes during the night they will sorely regret it, Cyrus thought, as, after finalizing with Harpagus the plans for the following day's campaigning, he retired to his tent for the night.

It was typical of Cyrus that when campaigning with his men he ate the same food they did, and slept in a simple field tent identical to that used by his men.

The Massagetae were not so rash as to attack the Persians during the night. The early morning sun, its warmth welcome on the cold floor of the mountain valley, rose on a scene that might have seemed a purely peaceful one until a perceptive eye had spotted the great numbers of soldiers who rubbed the sleep from their eyes as they sharpened their swords, spears and arrows...

At that moment, close to a summit of one of the three hills that overlooked the valley, a pair of eyes as acute as those of an eagle extraordinarily keen in the bright morning sun, was surveying the vast Persian encampment.

The owner of the eyes smiled.

Some distance away, and hiding in a great shallow cleft of a hillside, were close to seven thousand Massagetae warriors.

Men who know these hillsides better than they know their own wives, the new queen of the Massagetae thought, as she stared down at the Persians.

She crept backwards some way from the hillside, returned to her horse and put on her helmet. With one exception, the Massagetae warriors all wore helmets fashioned from the heads of animals they had slain.

The one exception was the queen herself, who had been given her helmet by the former queen, who had passed to her, along with the helmet, all the power and authority of the Massagetae. It was a splendidly decorated helmet, based around the face of a snow-leopard, with precious stones and a plume of feathers of the Golden Eagle which the Massagetae regarded as the king of all the birds of the air.

The new Massagetae queen returned to her ranks, where her bodyguards were waiting for her. There were a dozen altogether; hand-picked by her from the ranks of the army. They were charged with defending her life, whatever the cost to them.

'Your highness should not put herself at such risk,' said Ledor, the strongest and fiercest of all her bodyguards.

'I needed to see for myself the lay-out of the battlefield, rather than rely on advance scouts,' the queen said, in the complex, guttural tongue of the Massagetae.

She looked around at all her bodyguards. None of their faces were visible. Each was wearing a helmet fashioned from the head of an animal, including foxes, lynxes and bears, and with the skin of the animal's face stretched taut over a leather mask that had eyeholes and an opening at the mouth. The rest of the mask was made from the skin and fur of the same animal. The effect of the stretched facial skin over the leather mask was, the queen knew, terrifying to enemies, though she had herself grown used to it by now.

'We shall attack shortly before sundown,' she said. 'By sundown the valley floor shall be strewn with the bodies of Persians... and their king.'

Throughout the day Cyrus went round his army and spoke to them, encouraged them and cracked jokes with them. He knew that the success of this mission depended on the morale of his men.

Advance scouts had been sent deeper into Massagetae territory to find vantage points and gather intelligence. By mid-afternoon, Cyrus was awaiting their return with considerable impatience.

One thing puzzled him.

So far he had seen no sign of Raiva. Nor, it appeared, had anyone else. Not that this meant Raiva was not there, among them, but Cyrus was surprised Raiva did not show his face, or pay a visit to his own tent to boast about how well he had managed to keep up with the army on its hard journey into Massagetae territory.

By late afternoon the Persian scouts had still not returned.

'They have either been captured or killed,' Harpagus said, as he and Cyrus sat in Cyrus's tent.

'I hope not,' Cyrus said.

'They must have been. Which means the Massagetae are near, for the scouts could not have travelled far this afternoon in these hills.'

'Yes,' Cyrus agreed.

He opened a flap of the tent, went outside and sniffed the hillside breeze, as if he thought he could smell the Massagetae.

After a few moments he came back into the tent.

He smiled. 'I do not think the queen of the Massagetae is much like our late friend Croesus of Lydia.'

'What do you mean, Cyrus?' Harpagus asked.

'I mean,' said Cyrus, 'that I have somehow become convinced that the Massagetae will attack shortly before sundown. Ready our men.'

As the afternoon wore on, the queen of the Massagetae waited, her bodyguards silent around her and her army all behind her, for the moment when she would launch their attack.

As she waited, she remembered how she had first won the confidence and trust of the Massagetae, that morning almost two years ago, when she had arrived in their territory with her son. There, before the queen's court, she had agreed to the old queen's suggestion that she challenge a male Massagetae warrior in hand-to-hand combat without weapons.

The queen, the oldest of all the Massagetae, was so old that none of the Massagetae could remember how she had become queen. Yet there was a rumour that, long ago – when, it was said, women had fought alongside men in the ranks of the Massagetae – the woman who became the old queen had fought against a male contender for the rule of the Massagetae and had killed him with her bare hands.

For centuries, there had been a tradition that a ruler of the tribe had to kill a rival in combat without weapons.

Yet, as the years had advanced since the days when the old queen had become ruler, the role of women among the Massagetae had softened. It had become accepted that when the old queen knew that her time to die was approaching, she would nominate a male warrior from the tribe as her successor.

But she had not done so. Instead, she had nominated another woman, the beautiful stranger from the land of the Aegeans, who had arrived amongst the Massagetae accompanied by a boy of twelve. The beautiful stranger and her son had only been living amongst the Massagetae for a few weeks, and yet the stranger had already managed to learn much of the Massagetae language.

'I wish you to be queen after my death,' the old queen had told her.

There was, however, one condition. The beautiful stranger was obliged to fight a Massagetae warrior – a man – in unarmed combat.

'If you are the fighter you claim to be, stranger,' the old queen had told her, 'you will prevail. If not, you will die. And if you die, your son shall be killed too.'

The strong young warrior whom the old queen had selected to fight this beautiful and bold stranger had begun the one-to-one combat with a scornful laugh, and his friends had laughed too, at the idea of him having an easy win against a mere *woman* from that soft far-off land of the Aegeans.

That warrior had protested to the old queen at the indignity of being pitted in bare-handed combat against the beautiful stranger.

'Your majesty, please spare me this ignominy. She is made to make a man's bed a place of delight, not to fight him.'

But the old queen commanded the combat to take place in the blazing midday sun on a hilltop where the Massagetae carried out their executions, as there was ample surrounding space for onlookers to stand. The male warrior wore only a grey loin-cloth, while the beautiful stranger wore a similar loin-cloth and coarse tunic of uncured goat's-skin.

In short order the warrior was surprised by the beautiful foreign woman, whose strength and determination astonished him. After the most furious and breathless of struggles, in which she had used her speed and agility to their best advantage, she finally closed in on him and grabbed him round the neck. The warrior, exhausted, panting, bathed in sweat, and his soul now scorched by fear of her and terrified that his life was about to end here, now, at this place of death and in front of the entire tribe, struggled to fight her off, but his strength was gone.

He could smell her own sweat as she grappled with him, and in one terrible moment he caught a glimpse of the determination in her eyes, and in that instant he saw her beauty and the sweat glistening on her forehead, and was perplexed at how a creature so beautiful could be so deadly. Her tunic had grown ragged and windowed in their struggle, and her breasts were bare. He was almost out of his mind with fear, but he tried his best to resist her, knowing that if he stayed on his feet he might have a chance of survival. But she gave his legs a sudden vicious kick and they fell from under him as she wrenched him to the ground, her left forearm squeezing his throat and her left shoulder pressing ferociously against the back of his head to crush his windpipe in a relentless vice. The sweat on her arm served to make her grip on his neck slip even closer. Feeling the agony of her grasp, his mind flooded with despair and terror, and he tried desperately to slip even a finger between her forearm and his neck, but she was too strong. He started to choke and what little strength he had left drained from his arms.

Indifferent to the warrior's desperate gurgles for mercy, she proceeded to choke the life out of him in front of hundreds of Massagetae men and women, who had regarded him until that moment as one of their very best fighters.

Finally, she let the warrior's dead body fall away onto the ground and stood up amid gasps of amazement from the battle-hardened Massagetae. There had at first been only some scattered, astonished applause, but soon it had risen into a great swell of sound that echoed among the surrounding hills.

The old queen had died a few days later, as if now happy to go to eternal rest, knowing that her land was in safe hands.

The new queen smiled as she remembered her victory over the male Massagetae warrior. *Truly, I showed him that day that a woman was more than the equal of a man.*

She raised her right hand.

A moment later she gave the command to attack.

Wearing the mask of a female snow-leopard, she charged on horseback at the head of her army, down a hillside that, in a flashing moment of recollection, she realized reminded her of when she had charged down many a lesser hillside with *him*, the king of the Persians, before he had been king, when he was merely the leader of a band of desperate desert raiders of King Astyages's caravans.

She charged down this greater hill, thought of the Persian king, and wondered what, truly, her real motives *were*.

Did she want to kill the Persian king as she had killed the warrior she had fought in unarmed combat? Did she want to capture and humiliate Cyrus the Great? Or did she merely wish to capture him, and never allow him to return to Persia and to the rich man's daughter he had married but to stay with *her*, here in the hills, for evermore, to be her sport and pleasure?

47. Memories

As Roshan galloped down toward the valley, the speed of her charge somehow seemed in her imagination to slow down into a single instant of stillness. In that moment, all her memories of Cyrus flowed through her mind at a curiously leisurely pace, as if she was living her life again in the fullness of that instant.

What did she see?

Everything...

She saw herself playing with Cyrus in the dust on a sunny day in the town square of Paritakna. She saw him helping her build her little garden, she saw him trying to dam the stream in Paritakna to create a flow of water for her garden.

She saw herself older, a girl, and he a boy, and she recalled with terrible anguish the day when the soldiers came and killed her parents and also the people he thought were his parents. She saw her own parents dead in front of her eyes, and Paritakna, the town they loved, burned all around them, along with so many of the townspeople.

She saw herself as a bandit, fighting for a living alongside the man she loved so fiercely, though she would rather have died than revealed her true feelings. She saw the day they went into a village that had seem to be deserted, and found themselves in an ambush, where he was captured, and taken to Ecbatana, to what she was certain would be his execution.

She remembered how much she had wept that day, so much so she thought she might die from weeping. She had never told him about that, nor about the sleepless nights she'd endured after he had been taken, nor how she had tried so hard to persuade the remnants of his band of outlaws to come with her to Ecbatana to try to rescue him. They had all said, those men, that it would be an impossible undertaking, and that they would all die if they attempted it.

And so, in secret, so that there was no chance of any of them finding out and betraying her (for she was sure that one of them had betrayed them into the hands of Astyages's men), she went to Ecbatana alone, on horseback, and reached the city even before he did, for the caravan was far slower than her horse, even with the rests it took and the feeding, watering and sleeping.

When she reached Ecbatana, using some of her scant silver to buy herself the cheapest of lodgings, she had done all she could to find out what was happening to him.

She had expected to hear that he had been executed, but then... the most astonishing news she could ever imagine reached her ears.

He had been revealed, in the king's presence, to be the long-lost son of Princess Mandane, who was the king's daughter and the queen of Persia!

The news had seemed so extraordinary to Roshan that she had sought confirmation from gossip-mongers, but they had only confirmed the revelation.

The rumours were true. Her Cyrus, the man she loved, had been elevated by destiny and Ahura-Mazda to almost the greatest height possible to imagine.

Roshan heard more, too. The following day she was told that Cyrus and his mother were heading back to Anshan in the company of guards. Roshan knew enough about Astyages to know that the man she loved should not be trusting him. She would very willingly have escorted Cyrus home to Anshan from Ecbatana, but she knew that would be impossible, and most likely fatally dangerous for both of them.

And so, instead, she returned to her band, ahead of the caravan that she knew would be taking Cyrus and his mother to Anshan along the only road from the capital of Media to the capital of Persia. Roshan knew of a mountain pass along that route, from where she and the others could watch the caravan passing...

She had made Raiva, Asha and the others swear, on their lives, that they would never tell Cyrus she had risked hers to go to Ecbatana to find out what was happening to him. *He*, fool that he was, had thought she and the others were waiting for the caravan at the mountain pass by a merely happy stroke of fate, and he had never asked any of them what the truth was. But of course, she had often reflected, he was no doubt intoxicated with his own sense of destiny!

She remembered everything else: how she had saved his life when the treacherous soldiers who were escorting him would have killed him. She remembered that fateful meeting with the murderer Harpagus, and the role Cyrus and she had played in uniting the armies of Persia and Media. She remembered the death of Cambyses that led to Cyrus becoming king of Persia, the long-overdue killing of Astyages, the growth of the Persian empire and Cyrus's doctrine of tolerance, and... finally, their admission, at last, of their feelings for each other... and then... the love they had found.

Until he betrayed her...

Until he betrayed her, and married a younger woman instead, that perfumed rich man's daughter Cassadane.

He never truly believed I was his equal, Roshan thought. *Today he shall discover that I am.*

And then the memories fled, and she was back there, on the hillside, leading her army of warriors into the heart of the

Persian forces. Surely, soon, she would find him, and at last have her revenge?

48. Destiny

'*Death to the Persians!*' Roshan shouted.

The voice of a twelve-year-old boy at once joined in, '*Death to King Cyrus of Persia!*'

The boy galloped beside her like lightning, just as she was.

He was her son, Smerdis.

She was infinitely proud of him. She had made him strong, brave, fearless; she had made him into everything she would have wanted to be herself, had she been born a man. She had loved him and nurtured him, she had inspired him with a great sense of everything he could be; she had made him a boy who, already, in his thoughts and courageousness and deeds, was a man.

He was an intelligent boy. He had learnt Persian from her, and Greek from his play-fellows and from the people all around them. And now, he spoke the strange guttural language of the Massagetae, too.

She had never told him that the king of Persia was his father. That was her secret, her infinitely precious secret, that she had kept to her breast.

For she did not want her son to know that the king of Persia had once briefly loved her, and then had spurned her and married some pampered, scented, foolish, idle, spoilt daughter of a rich merchant.

And so she had told Smerdis nothing other than that his father was a wonderful man, a kind man, a good man, a Persian, but that soon after she had met him and they had fallen in love, he had died.

Of course, Smerdis knew that the leader of the Persians was a wicked king called Cyrus. How could he not, when his mother had so often spoken of the Persian king, whose subjects foolishly called him Cyrus the Great; the king who conquered nations and sought to rule the world? That was all Smerdis had ever heard from his mother about Cyrus. And so Smerdis, ever since he could remember, had known the Persian king to be a wicked tyrant.

'If I can ever get near him, mother, when I am older, I shall kill him,' Smerdis, when still small enough to spend time on his mother's lap, had assured her. He had assured her of that then, and he had made the same promise to her many times since.

That promise, to kill the king of Persia, was the boy Smerdis's creed. That was his belief, that was his purpose, that was his world.

Now, as mother and son rode together, she in her queen's mask, he in his mask fashioned from the face of a wildcat, her pride in her brave and fearless son was boundless, the son she had borne into the world, had suckled and nurtured, and whom she had made into a fearless and beautiful boy who, she felt certain, must have some remarkable destiny of his own.

She glanced at Smerdis and flushed with pride inside her mask.

Then she looked straight ahead again, and thought of the Persian king, the deceitful and wicked traitor to her love, the man who had spurned her, who had cast her aside as if she had been a mere plaything for his sport whose novelty had worn off after a mere three days.

And yet... even though for all the thirteen years of her exile, she had been filled with relentless hate of him and a piercing jealousy of the woman he had married, as she charged to battle against him, her son charging at her side, a terrible and entirely unexpected thought filled her mind.

Do I hate him or love him?

She was appalled to find herself thinking this.

She could not explain where the thought came from, but nor could she make it vanish.

And now she saw the Persian ranks come into sight, she still wondered what the truth of her feelings really was...

Except that now she knew one thing, one thing for certain.

If I am to die, I shall at least do all I can to survive until I have spoken with him.

And then she saw him.

She saw him, in the dark blue hooded cloak, the hood down.

It was the cloak she remembered so well from the time she had spent at the lake with him.

Her eyes were at once so full of tears that she had to blink them away.

Why is he still wearing it? she wondered. *Why?*

The flashing thought struck her that he might have somehow discovered who the new queen of the Massagetae really was, and that he might have chosen to wear the cloak to taunt her.

But she knew it was surely impossible he could have known about who the new queen was, and besides... even if had known that, why would he have kept the dark blue hooded cloak all this time?

As she was still furiously blinking away her tears, she saw the Immortals heading towards them.

The Immortals, Roshan thought. *The invincible Immortals. The most feared mounted army in the world.*

In a moment of sudden panic for the life of her son, she barked at him a command to wheel to the left and leave the charge.

'No, mother! I want to fight with you!'

'You are only a boy! Obey me! I am your mother and your queen!'

Only now Smerdis abruptly obeyed her, and wheeled to the left. At once, the charging horses of the Massagetae passed him and Roshan caught a mere glimpse of her son as she hurtled furiously onwards, towards the enemy.

And then she saw Cyrus.

There he was, in all his glory. There he was, Cyrus the Great, the man she had loved, the man – she realized now, now as she set eyes on him for the first time in thirteen years – she had never ceased loving. There he was, at the head of the Immortals.

She saw no sign of Asha; she wondered where he was.

Roshan made her horse gallop even faster, so that now she edged out in front of even her very fastest mounted soldiers. *Women not the equal of men?* she thought. *We shall see.*

And now she knew, for certain, beyond all doubt, that he had seen *her*. And though she knew he could not possibly have any idea who she really was, she could tell he was fascinated by the sight of her in her mask.

Oh, she knew he would know she was a woman, for he would have been told that the Massagetae had a new queen, but he would have no idea what manner of woman he was facing, or that it was *her*: the woman he had once claimed to love.

And then the two mounted armies met in a thunderous clash of iron and bronze, a haze of sweat and horseflesh, and in a din of cries of anger, agony and vengeance...

She had fought for her life many times, but never as fiercely as *this*.

It seemed to Roshan, fighting with a sword in her right hand and a Massagetae axe in her left, that all the demons and vile spirits of the wicked world beyond the goodness of

Ahura-Mazda's kingdom had fled the hell where they lived, and had come here to join in the fray and incite the armies to greater violence and slaughter.

She had charged directly at Cyrus right away, and very nearly managed to unseat him with her mount, but he wheeled and drew his great sword, and she was infinitely dismayed to find herself thinking, *the man I have loved all my life is going to kill me*, but she was fast too, and faster, and she turned her horse around like a whirlwind and, ducking the first blow Cyrus aimed at her, swung her axe in his direction, but more to frighten him than to hurt him, for at that moment she found the strength in her arm fail, and she knew, in a moment of total revelation and truth, that she could never kill him, that she loved him too much, and as she realized this, strength drained from her left arm, and the axe fell to the ground.

At once she drew her sword, but several Immortals were heading for her now. They came at her so fast they were upon her in a moment. She supposed them eager to protect him, their royal master, from the sorcery (she had spread that rumour deliberately, to frighten him) of the Massagetae queen. But even as the Immortals raced towards her, she heard him, Cyrus, Cyrus the Great Betrayer, cry out to them, 'No! She is mine!'

And the moment she heard this, for all that she knew his meaning must be different to what she hoped, she felt the deepest thrill in her heart and in her loins that she had ever felt, for the sound of his voice, which she had not heard for thirteen years, was, she was suddenly instantly and completely appalled to realize, for her the sweetest sound in all the world.

He wheeled again, there in the dark blue cloak as he was. She thought now it *could not* be the cloak they had lain upon, for why would he be wearing it? He wheeled again, and looked hard at her, and she knew for certain that he meant to kill her, the new queen of the Massagetae, for how could he have known, in her mask as she was, who she really was?

Roshan was vaguely aware of the Immortals around her standing back, while vicious fighting went on in all directions beyond them. She was puzzled at seeing no sign of Asha. Her bodyguards were close by too. She swiftly looked at them all through her mask, and she was sure they knew what her look meant. *This is the combat of kings... or queens*, and they stood back, obviously not intending to interfere.

Or at least all her bodyguards stood back, except one, who wore a helmet with the skin of the face of a desert fox stretched across it. Roshan was speechless as, to her complete disbelief, he now suddenly fired an arrow from his drawn bow *at her.*

... at me, she thought, even as it was much, much too late for her to have the slightest chance to dodge the speeding dart.

The arrow struck her in her right side, between her bronze breast-plate and back-plate. She felt its iron tip pierce her skin, and then she felt a terrible pain within her, and a jolt of agony that shot through her whole body. An instant later, she was surprised, as she fell off her horse and landed, hard, on the hard ground, that the fall made her feel so little fresh pain.

Somehow, she knew she must already be dying. She wondered, with a hazy abstraction as if she were wondering on someone else's behalf, how long her dying would take.

Cyrus, red-faced and almost out of his mind with fury at the extraordinary sight of one of the Massagetae queen's own bodyguards shooting her and depriving him of the opportunity to force the Massagetae queen to parlay, turned his horse to face the treacherous bodyguard.

The other Massagetae bodyguards had also turned toward the traitor. Cyrus could see they were only moments from wreaking a bloody revenge on the wretch, but Cyrus raised his right hand at the Immortals standing by and they intervened and forced the Massagetae bodyguards to retreat.

The bodyguard who had fired the arrow suddenly whipped off his helmet.

'Cyrus!' the soldier exclaimed, in Persian. 'I give you, as a gift, the life of the Massagetae queen!'

It was Raiva.

'*Raiva!*' Cyrus exclaimed, his voice hoarse. 'You!'

'Cyrus,' Raiva said, breathlessly. 'I was afraid this wicked witch would use sorcery upon you. I feared that the fight would never have been fair. I risked my life to enter the Massagetae lands and kill one of the witch's bodyguards. I took his place. And now,' he looked down at fallen form of the queen, 'I give you *her* life.'

Cyrus just stared at Raiva, whose own life the Immortals were doing all they could to spare from the fury of the other Massagetae bodyguards.

Harpagus, his sword well bloodied, came to stand beside Cyrus. As he did so, Cyrus heard the sound of the fighting around them start to diminish. He could guess what had happened: the Massagetae soldiers had already begun to hear that their queen was injured, probably mortally; and they had no more stomach for the fight.

Cyrus quickly dismounted and hurried over to unmask the Massagetae queen of her strange, sinister mask.

He found leather clips at the back of her head, quickly untied them and removed her helmet.

Then he saw her face.

'*Roshan!*' he gasped.

For a moment he was overwhelmed with the feeling that the battle had somehow ceased to exist and there were now only he and she there on the floor of the valley. Cyrus took a step back in horror, bewilderment, utter astonishment... and love.

His shock was succeeded a moments later by an appalled realization of what had happened to her.

He knelt down by her, lifted her head gently and cradled it on his lap.

His cheeks felt suddenly wet. He wondered why. Then he understood. His own eyes had sent forth tears of their own accord.

As he felt the tears running down his cheeks, he also felt the quietness of the silenced warriors and the quenched battle all around him even before he turned to see it for himself.

Only Harpagus stood close by him.

Glancing at her, Cyrus gently stroked her hair.

'Roshan,' he murmured. 'Roshan...'

She smiled faintly at him. 'Now do you believe women are the equal of men?' she replied, so softly that none but Cyrus and Harpagus could hear her.

'Roshan,' Cyrus said. 'I always believed it.' He looked into her eyes and it was as if she and he were back at the red lake where they had made love so many moons ago, but yet it seemed like only yesterday.

'You are alive,' he whispered, 'you were alive all the time. But how can you be here? How can you be... *her?*'

She did not bother to answer his question. Instead, with a strange painful sadness, she murmured, '... why did you not marry me?'

'Why do you think? Because... because I believed you were dead.'

'I saw the tablet, the tablet you sent me,' she said, her breath coming fast and thick. 'I saw the tablet in which you proposed marriage to Cassadane. I saw it, and I met Raiva on my way back to Anshan, and he told me that the previous evening you had asked Cassadane to marry you, and had kissed her.'

'*What... what tablet are you talking about?* I sent you a tablet asking you to be my wife!'

She just stared at him. 'You did? But that... that was not the tablet I received!'

Cyrus was about to speak, but he faltered, for at once he had understood everything.

The realization of what must have happened stabbed his mind like a flung spear.

He glanced at Raiva, whose normally plump and self-satisfied face was now struck with guilt.

Cyrus hardly even needed to ask him to deny what was obviously the truth.

'I... gave the tablet to Asha,' Cyrus gasped. 'You must... somehow have switched it... Asha would not even have known about the exchange... I know Asha would never betray me. But when he lay dying by the Euphrates he must have suspected you.'

For a moment Cyrus fell silent, then, in front of the great mass of assembled Persian and Massagetae soldiers, he said to Raiva:

'Did you betray your brother's true identity to King Nabonidus of Babylon, too? Is that why Asha was shot by Nabonidus's guards?'

Raiva made no reply.

'Cyrus,' Roshan murmured faintly. 'Had I received a tablet from you, proposing marriage, I... I would have said yes.'

Cyrus glanced down at her.

'Raiva knows many merchants,' she said, 'they most likely found out about my journey to the Massagetae. Raiva must have known he had to silence me, for if I remained alive you might have found out the truth from me...'

Cyrus looked up at Raiva. 'This is true, isn't it?'

'Cyrus,' said Raiva, 'she is dying. Her mind is addled. I had no idea it was her. How could I? I believed Lady Roshan was dead. My only desire was to kill the Massagetae queen.'

Cyrus nodded slowly. '"Her mind is addled". I have heard that expression before. Yes, indeed. I once knew a man who said much the same thing about his dying brother. What did you say then? Something about the loss of blood having affected his mind?'

Raiva made no reply.

Cyrus shook his head, appalled at the fearsome extent of Raiva's treachery that somehow Cyrus was seeing in his own imagination like a great black venomous snake, its vile body entwined around all the evil in the world. 'How could you do this, Raiva? Were your riches not enough for you? Was your success in the empire I created not enough for you? Did I wrong you in some other life, that you can betray me so monstrously?'

Raiva did not reply for a moment, but just stared hard at Cyrus.

'You think you are the only man who loved her,' Raiva said, sullenly. '*You are not.* I loved her too. I loved her all my life. But she would never have me. *Never, never, never.*'

Cyrus nodded with sudden breathless understanding. He suddenly felt supremely foolish for not having already guessed at the simplicity of Raiva's motive. Cyrus was suddenly aware of having devoted so much of his life to fulfilling his own sense of destiny, to concentrating his thoughts on higher purposes, that he had allowed himself to forget that the ignoble, the treacherous and the vile can believe *they* are pursuing a sense of destiny, too.

Cyrus looked down with the profoundest affection at Roshan.

'Cyrus,' she murmured, 'suddenly I feel better. Perhaps I shall recover.'

'Yes,' said Cyrus. 'Yes, I think you will.'

But there was a lump in his throat as he said this, and he felt his tears hot in his eyes. He knew, from seeing so many deaths in battle, that the imminence of death numbs pain, as the soul prepares to leave the body and make its journey to Ahura-Mazda, in the hope that Ahura-Mazda may receive it.

Cyrus looked into Roshan's eyes. 'Don't leave me.'

'Never,' she whispered.

They looked into each other's eyes. Cyrus knew her strength was fading fast. She smiled, but this time more faintly '*Cyrus,*' she whispered, again too quietly for anyone but him and Harpagus to hear, '*you have a son, I called him Smerdis. Look!*'

Cyrus turned in the direction of her gaze, and saw a handsome, fresh-faced boy of about twelve or thirteen striding fast towards them. The boy was in full Massagetae battle-dress.

'Cyrus!' Roshan whispered. 'He has your eyes! Do you not see the fire in them?'

Cyrus smiled. 'Yes. Yes, I do.' And Cyrus now saw the boy start to rush towards him. Instantly the Immortals stepped into the boy's path. But Cyrus immediately called out, 'No! Let him come through!'

The boy came running towards them. Cyrus smiled, and lifted his right arm to greet him. '*Smerdis... my son!*'

But the boy was not listening. He bent down, reached with his right hand for his dagger, found it, and stabbed Cyrus in the chest with a blow whose strength and accuracy was that of a young warrior in the prime of life, the son of a man who was among the greatest warriors who ever lived.

Smerdis glanced at Roshan.

'*I have avenged you, mother!*'

'No!' Roshan cried. 'No! *He is your father!*'

Smerdis stepped back. The dagger was still deep in Cyrus's chest.

'*My father!*' Smerdis gasped.

'Yes!' Roshan cried.

Cyrus, the agony of the injury already rendering him only half conscious, caught a glimpse of Harpagus, a look of utter horror and dismay on his face, drawing his massive sword, and obviously meaning to strike off Smerdis's head with one blow.

'*Harpagus, no, he is my son!*' cried Cyrus, with all that was left of his strength, for Smerdis's dagger had cut his heart almost in two, and already his brain was starting to be starved of fresh blood.

Harpagus glanced at Cyrus.

'Spare him...' Cyrus murmured, only audibly enough for Harpagus to hear. 'Now is your time to redeem yourself!'

Those were almost the last words Cyrus spoke. A terrible weakness had come over him. He managed to turn, just once, to the woman of his soul, 'Roshan...I love you,' he said, and then his heart ceased to beat.

'I love you,' Roshan said. They were the last words Cyrus heard as he slumped to one side. The dreadful agony in his breast began to ease. And then the pain ebbed away and all he could see was himself and Roshan, back at the lake, the lake where they had spent their happiest moments. The dark blue cloak was on the ground nearby, and the sun was rising.

Roshan saw Harpagus back away from Smerdis, she saw him sheathe his mighty sword, and now she looked at her boy.

'Smerdis,' she murmured, herself now so weak she could hardly speak, 'you have killed... your father.'

'Mother, I did not know! You always said he was the enemy!'

Roshan shook her head. 'I... I was wrong. He loved me all the time... and I loved him.'

Smerdis knelt down and embraced her.

'My son,' she whispered. 'Promise me that you will find your love ... no matter how long it takes... and that when you find it you will embrace it with your soul... and never let it go.'

Smerdis gasped, 'Mother, I shall. I shall do what you ask.' And perhaps Roshan heard him, or perhaps not. No-one would know. Her blood-drenched body sank into Cyrus's lap, their blood mingled, and her soul, in truth so close by his during all the past years, joined his in Ahura-Mazda's kingdom.

Cyrus and Roshan lay dead. Smerdis knelt down next to them. The Immortals, seeing the passing of their great leader, swiftly unknotted bells from their hair and rang them. The clean mountain air was filled with the ringing of thousands of bells, clarion-calls summoning Cyrus's soul to join the illustrious band of the great departed who dwell with Ahura-Mazda forever in his kingdom.

Harpagus, as if he was only now liberated from his sins, as if only now he was reborn to do nothing but good upon this earth, took three great steps towards Raiva, drawing his sword again as he strode towards the traitor. A moment later, with a single *swish* of his mighty sword, he cut off Raiva's head.

The head flew through the air with sudden strange energy, as if momentarily propelled not only by the force of the sword's stroke but also by the departing soul of a demon. The head landed bloodily on the ground, falling face-forwards.

Weak with grief, and still armed with his mighty sword, Harpagus now turned towards Smerdis.

'No-one who seeks to avenge his mother's death can be blamed for doing so' said Harpagus, 'for all would seek to avenge such a death rather than show forgiveness, except' his voice hoarse in his great grief, 'one whose soul is almost the equal of Ahura-Mazda himself.'

Yet Smerdis still stared in terror at the giant warrior, as if he expected that at any moment Harpagus would change his mind and kill him.

But again Harpagus sheathed his sword. 'Hear me, boy. Tomorrow, at the first light of day, you and I, and our generals, shall meet. We shall discuss how the Massagetae and the Persians might live in peace. Come, boy, lay your hands on your mother's and father's heads, and bid them farewell.'

Smerdis did so, weeping now; yet with nobility, like a prince, laid his hands on Roshan's and Cyrus's dead foreheads.

The myriad bells of the Immortals rang again.

Harpagus glanced up, once, at the vault of the great arch of the heavens Ahura-Mazda had created.

49. Afterwards

The Massagetae, by universal consent, chose the boy Smerdis as their king. In doing so, for the first time in their known history they chose a ruler who did not have to prove himself or herself in deadly combat.

Smerdis, the boy-king wearing his father's blue hooded cloak, forged an agreement of alliance with the Persian Empire. This alliance gave the Massagetae extensive farming land west of the Persian border in exchange for providing warriors to the Persian army and guaranteeing the safe passage of trading missions over the hills and mountains controlled by the Massagetae.

Smerdis did not rest and searched lands near and far to find his true love.

After Cyrus's death, Cambyses succeeded him as king of the Persian Empire. Like the leaders of that empire who followed him, Cambyses always sought negotiation with other nations and was as passionately opposed to slavery as Cyrus had been. Cambyses followed the precepts of tolerance and understanding, and frequently consulted his friend Smerdis on vital matters relating to the empire.

The Immortals, having continued their tradition of bell-wearing after Asha's death in his memory, decided after Cyrus's death to end this tradition. As earnest of this, their new leader, Tiridaad, on the day Cyrus was laid to rest in a rock vault on Mount Alvand, carefully with his own hands dug a small hole in the ground close by Cyrus's body, laid a bell in it and covered the bell with earth.

The Persian Empire, which continued to expand after Cyrus's death, lasted for more than a further two centuries. In the centuries beyond that, many Roman emperors dreamed of invading and conquering Persia, but none ever attempted to do so, very likely dissuaded by the story of Cyrus and of the indomitable will of the Persians.

Cassadane never remarried. She heard from Harpagus the whole story of Raiva's betrayal, and of her husband's love for Roshan, but she forgave Cyrus, and praised Ahura-Mazda for the many joyous years that she, Cyrus's only wife, had spent with the great king.

History no longer recalls Roshan's name, though a legend of a wildly beautiful Persian woman, who loved Cyrus the Great and became the queen of the Massagetae, endured for many years in Persian folklore.

As for Roshan's friend Thespis, he is still remembered as the founder of the great dramatic tradition of Greece.

Which is curious, for Thespis himself always said that it was never his own idea for two or more characters to perform and engage with one another on the stage. He says that this was, rather, the idea of a friend of his, a beautiful Persian woman he rescued from slavery, but who once vanished with her son leaving nothing behind save a note that said *thank you for being my friend when I most needed one.*

'I have always wondered what became of her,' Thespis would say.

For the rest of his life, every year on the evening of the anniversary of Roshan's disappearance, Thespis would light a candle in her memory on the terrace at his home on Aegina. He would watch the flame flickering in the sea-breeze, and he would sit there, looking out to sea and thinking of Roshan, as the candle slowly burnt itself out.

And he would imagine that, at any moment, Roshana, as beautiful and self-assured as ever, might stroll onto the terrace, and that they could again talk together of theatre, of art, of life, and of the majesty of the human heart.

50. The Girl

The wind was tapping at the door of the emporium. Its tapping mingled with the sound of the ringing bell.

Now, the stranger in the dark blue hooded cloak used his right forefinger to stop the bell ringing.

There was a strange, uneasy silence.

'My friend looks thoughtful,' the master of the emporium murmured.

The stranger, his face still obscured, laid the bell back down on the black lacquered tray.

'You wish to buy it?' the proprietor asked him.

'No,' the stranger said, speaking for the first time. 'I do not want to buy the bell. Tomorrow, I may return and buy something else, or perhaps I shall not return.'

The man spoke the local language fluently, but with an accent that sounded unfamiliar to the keeper of the emporium.

'I think there may be a sandstorm approaching,' the shop-keeper said.

'Yes' said the stranger, 'I have know that for many hours.'

'Sir, I have a room upstairs for guests! It is quiet and comfortable, and the cost is modest. You will be happy there, even if Allah in his wisdom has chosen to prepare the worst sandstorm in the world.'

The stranger plunged into thought, as if balancing the convenience of not having to look elsewhere for a lodging with the prospect of being obliged to listen to more of the shopkeeper's nonsense.

While he was locked thus in thought, the shop door opened and a girl walked in. She was about twenty, or perhaps a year or two older. She was holding a black lacquered tray, on which reposed a large piece of folded and well-stuffed pitta bread on a plate.

'Father, I have brought a snack for you from the food-seller next door,' she said, with a glance at the master of the emporium.

Now, for the first time since his return, the stranger brought down the hood of his blue hooded cloak, revealing a darkly handsome man, who had the appearance of a man in his twenties, with well-trimmed beard and deep, intelligent brown eyes.

It was indeed a fierce storm, and the stranger was grateful for the room. The shopkeeper, who said the sound of the hurtling sand always gave him a headache, retired to bed early, leaving his daughter and the man talking, with all proper courtesy and respect, until late into the night. As they talked, they were oblivious to the swirling storm outside.

By morning the sandstorm had blown itself out.

There was little bought and sold in the marketplace that day, for sand covered almost everything, and stall-holders spent most of their time clearing the flurries from around their stalls.

The girl worked for much of the day helping the owner of the bazaar where she worked clear sand away. In the evening, she was permitted by her father to go for an evening stroll with the stranger, of whom the master of the emporium had already formed the highest opinion.

The market was silent.

Somewhere in the distance, a few braziers burned.

The tourists had sought their expensive beds, and the snake-charmers, magicians, musicians and beggars who made a living – or an approximation of one – from the tourists, were all asleep in their humble homes, or behind the counters of closed stalls.

The stranger and the girl walked across the silent marketplace side-by-side.

'I never asked you what your name was,' she asked him, shyly.

'Smerdis,' he replied.

'It is a beautiful name. It is an ancient name of our beloved land.'

'Yes,' he murmured.

'Are you a traveller?' she asked.

'Yes.'

'Have you been travelling long?'

He smiled. 'For a very long time indeed.'

They continued walking silently together across the wide expanse of the almost deserted marketplace.

A moment came when their hands reached out, touched and found each other.

He turned and looked at her. She gazed at him in the same instant.

He smiled, and she returned the smile.

The wind picked up.

He gently wrapped his dark blue cloak around her shoulders.

Now, they walked on as one.